Critical Mass

ALSO BY DANIEL SUAREZ

Daemon
Freedom™
Kill Decision
Influx
Change Agent
Delta-v

Critical Mass

A NOVEL

DANIEL SUAREZ

DUTTON

DUTTON

An imprint of Penguin Random House LLC
penguinrandomhouse.com

LIBRARY OF CONGRESS CATALOGING-IN-PUBLICATION DATA

Names: Suarez, Daniel, 1964- author.
Title: Critical mass : a novel / Daniel Suarez.
Description: [New York] : Dutton, [2023]
Identifiers: LCCN 2022017530 (print) | LCCN 2022017531 (ebook) |
ISBN 9780593183632 (hardcover) | ISBN 9780593183649 (ebook) |
Subjects: LCGFT: Science fiction. | Novels.
Classification: LCC PS3619.U327 Cr 2023 (print) | LCC PS3619.U327 (ebook) |
DDC 813/.6—dc23
LC record available at https://lccn.loc.gov/2022017530
LC ebook record available at https://lccn.loc.gov/2022017531

Printed in the United States of America
1st Printing

For Michelle Sites, my guiding star

Give me but a place on which to stand, and I will move the world.

—Archimedes of Syracuse

Critical Mass

Prologue

Adedayo Adisa stared at a holographic model of Earth floating translucent before him. With a hand gesture he altered a red line that skimmed the virtual planet's atmosphere, causing the line to plunge downward and terminate on the model's surface. Another adjustment and the line once more rebounded back into space. Gesture after gesture resulted in more of the same—either burning up on reentry or skipping back off into space. No iteration resulted in a stable planetary orbit.

Footsteps sounded on the decking behind him and then the wheel of the habitat's pressure door rotated, creaking open.

He turned to see Isabel Abarca step into the compartment and unclip her long black hair. She rubbed her scalp as she sighed in exhaustion. Her faded blue flight suit was patched with white Kapton tape in several places.

She resealed the pressure door behind her, then looked up. "The number two oxygen generator needs maintenance. We'll have to cannibalize parts from Hab 2." She noticed the holographic model. "How are they doing?"

Adisa's Nigerian accent was thicker than usual, betraying his stress. "Their spacecraft is on course to encounter Earth in twenty-six days."

She smiled. "Then you did it, Ade." Abarca came up to look over his shoulder. "So they'll make it back to Earth."

"Yes—but only momentarily." He tried another failed trajectory.

Abarca's smile faded and she sank into a seat next to him at the galley table. She stared at the holographic model, too.

Adisa remained uneasy. "Because of their delayed departure, high velocity was necessary to encounter Earth—which means they will have difficulty slowing on arrival. On their current trajectory our crewmates will skim Earth's atmosphere at over 100,000 kilometers per hour. At that speed orbital capture through aerobraking is difficult. They are likely to either plunge too deeply into the atmosphere—burn up and die—or sail straight through and back into deep space. Lost forever."

"*How* likely?"

It was several moments before he answered. "Atmospheric variability makes it impossible to know for certain, but their autopilot software will not even calculate an aerobrake solution at that velocity. The required deceleration might kill them. Which means they will have to pilot the craft manually through unknowable variables—all while under 10 or more g's. A feat that I have been unable to model."

Abarca studied the hologram silently as the virtual ship burned up yet again.

"I fear that by guiding them onto this trajectory I have not saved our crewmates—but killed them."

"There was no other choice, Ade." She put a hand on his shoulder. "We were out of time, and that piecemeal propulsion system was imprecise. Without your course corrections they would have missed the Earth entirely."

He gazed at the hologram. "That was only necessary because I took too long integrating systems. If I had finished on schedule, we would have made the transfer window to Earth and all returned home safely. The fault is mine."

"It was no one's fault. Rushing that work could have caused ten other failures. Again: missing the Earth entirely."

"It hardly matters now." He lowered his head. "Do I contact them? Do I let them know?"

"No. They'll realize their situation soon enough. Allow them their hope."

He sat for several moments in silence. "I compelled them to go."

"*We* compelled them." She leaned down into his view. "If they stayed, we'd all starve."

He turned to her. "So we get to survive while our friends die?"

She gave him a woeful look. "Oh, Ade. The *Konstantin* is breaking down; even if we had the parts, two people can't maintain this ship." She turned to the hologram. "That was the last chance for any of us to get back."

"I had to stay behind, but *you* did not."

"We discussed this. A captain doesn't leave people behind. And as it turns out, it made no difference."

Adisa nodded.

"If anyone deserves blame, it's me. I'm the one who recruited you all."

"Then you should blame Nathan Joyce—he recruited you."

She laughed grimly. "I guess there's blame enough to go round."

"We all knew the risks, but I had hoped I would at least get Priya, James, and Han back home safely. Instead, the entire expedition has failed."

"I disagree." Abarca gestured toward the curving aluminum wall of the habitat's core, upon which scores of "firsts" were scrawled like graffiti in permanent marker ink. "Look at the history we've made out here. We've gone farther and longer in deep space than anyone. We perfected asteroid mining. We sent back thousands of tons of refined materials toward lunar orbit—enough to get humanity started in the cosmos. I'd say that's a success."

Adisa studied the achievements on the wall—many written by crewmates now deceased. "Do you really think it will make a difference, what we did out here?"

Abarca was about to respond when Klaxons sounded an alarm. A synthetic female voice said, *"Critical alert: new radar contact. Repeat: new radar contact."* Strobe lights flashed on the ceiling.

Adisa gazed up and sighed. "More debris . . ." With a wave of his hand, he swept aside the hologram of Earth and brought up another virtual window, this one showing the ship's radar console. A blip glowed a hundred kilometers out from their position alongside the asteroid Ryugu. "Wait . . . this is something else."

Abarca pondered the screen. "Is it the *Argo*?"

She was referring to a robotic mothership sent to Ryugu three years earlier by a billionaire competitor of their boss, Nathan Joyce. Several such billionaire "Space Titans" were vying to mine off-world resources, and kilometer-wide Ryugu was the most promising asteroid in the inner solar system. However, unlike the *Konstantin*, the *Argo* was autonomous and had lain dormant ever since its dozen mining crafts broke down—defeated by the asteroid's highly abrasive regolith.

Though not before killing a member of the *Konstantin*'s crew.

"No. The *Argo* has not moved." Adisa pointed at a different blip well over a hundred kilometers out and off to the side. "This is something new." He checked the telemetry. "And it is adjusting course to match Ryugu's orbit."

Abarca opened up another virtual window—this one a feed to an optics array. She aimed a camera at the incoming bogey, and in a moment they had a visual. The virtual screen revealed an ungainly spacecraft against a background of stars. "I'll be damned . . ."

The mystery vessel consisted of a propulsion unit docked to a series of other modules—the lead one an old Soyuz capsule. The ship's rocket engine was oriented away from them, burning silently to circularize its orbit.

Adisa zoomed in the image. "No visible markings. Perhaps a robotic resupply craft?"

She pointed. "Those look to be life support modules. A small centrifuge segment."

"Perhaps it is a rescue vessel meant for us."

"It's too late for a return trajectory to Earth, and mission control would have told us."

Adisa nodded glumly, then checked comms. "If someone is aboard, they are not hailing us."

She stopped short. "Maybe because they believe the crew of the *Konstantin* is dead."

Adisa looked at her. "So you think this was sent by the new owners?"

"Don't grant them that much legitimacy. They're Nathan's creditors, nothing more."

"But why would they send a ship?"

"This could be a replacement crew."

Adisa was taken aback. "You think they would actually send *people* out here?"

"It's starting to make sense. Their refusal to honor our contracts with Nathan, even though we mined all these resources—and then remotely shutting down our life support. If you hadn't found a work-around we'd all be dead. The plan might always have been to get rid of us and recrew the ship with their own people during Ryugu's next close approach to Earth."

Adisa looked aghast. "If it is a replacement crew, what happens when they discover us still alive?"

She studied the screen. "I don't know."

The incoming vessel continued its circularization burn, edging closer by the minute.

Abarca spoke without taking her eyes off the screen. "How many mules are still operational?"

"Just one. At the upper airlock."

"Move it into the supply yard."

"Surely you are not thinking of ramming them?"

"No, but I'm keeping our options open."

Adisa instantiated a virtual command console in his biphasic crystal work glasses. Suddenly an augmented-reality 3D model of the *Konstantin* rotated before him. The *Konstantin* looked more like a collection of construction cranes than a spaceship. Its spine was a 250-meter-long box truss of carbon fiber girders—only the bow of which protruded above the horizon of the asteroid and into sunlight. The mast there was studded with solar panels, communications antennas, and a laser transmitter.

The main body of the *Konstantin* sheltered in permanent shadow behind the asteroid—on station, 3 kilometers above Ryugu's darkened surface. The ship's upper airlock stood well aft of the solar mast with four docking ports arrayed at compass points—two of which were occupied by well-worn mule spacecraft. Only one of which was still operational.

Adisa remotely activated this mule, undocked it, and telepiloted the craft beyond the sweep of the *Konstantin's* three rotating radial arms. These arms each extended a hundred meters from a central habitat at the ship's waist and consisted of a box truss through which a narrow tunnel ran to inflated habitat modules at the end. The radial arms rotated three times a minute to simulate gravity; Isabel and Adisa sat in one of these: Hab 1.

He remotely piloted the mule down the length of the *Konstantin*, and the craft glided past empty construction scaffolding, past the *Konstantin's* chemical refinery, lower airlock, and engine room—which was empty. The rocket engines had been unstepped to power robotic tugs returning refined resources toward an orbit around Earth's moon.

The lack of main engines meant the *Konstantin* was now a permanent fixture at Ryugu.

Pivoting the mule, Adisa could see a series of small robotic spacecraft orbiting along the asteroid's terminator line. These used parabolic mirrors to concentrate the Sun's light for "optical mining" of bagged boulders, which had been teased away from the asteroid's surface in its minuscule gravity. The delicate flight control dance of the mining robots was managed by systems the crew had perfected over the past four years, and operations were now largely automated. The system was producing thousands of tons of refined resources per month and would continue to do so into the foreseeable future. Still, with a total mass of 450 million tons, it would take centuries to consume Ryugu at this rate.

Abarca clicked through virtual UIs. "We need to notify mission control. Would that alert this new ship to our presence?"

"No. The long-range laser comms are secure."

Abarca opened the laser comm channel and checked her HUD display. "We're at just over three light-minutes from Earth—which means more than six minutes before we get a reply." She keyed the transmit button. "*Konstantin* to mission control. *Konstantin* to mission control. Mayday. Mayday. We have an unidentified, potentially hostile spacecraft inbound and maneuvering to match our trajectory for possible docking. This is an emergency. Please advise. Out."

Adisa, meanwhile, nestled the remotely piloted mule among bladder tanks of refined ammonia, water ice, and cylinders of silica in the nearby supply yard. By then the interloper's spacecraft had arrived. Its rocket engine cut out a few hundred meters away. Silent puffs of thruster gas issued from various nozzles as it maneuvered precisely toward the upper airlock of the *Konstantin*.

Abarca watched the monitor. "That thing must mass at least 30 tons."

This was a small percentage of the *Konstantin*'s mass, but in a collision it could still destroy the radial arms of the *Konstantin*'s hab units as they swept past in rotation. Fortunately, the mystery spacecraft seemed to be expertly piloted.

Abarca switched to an exterior camera focused on the docking ports. "That's not being remotely controlled. Not at this distance from Earth."

"It could be autonomous."

"I wouldn't count on it."

She brought up additional holographic user interfaces. "The *Konstantin* won't respond to their remote commands, correct?"

"Correct, my bypass will prevent it, but anyone on that vessel will soon become suspicious."

"They could think it's a malfunction. Our exterior is scarred with micro-meteor damage."

He tapped virtual controls. "Yes, but that will not stop them from manu-ally docking and working the airlock."

"Can you disable the docking port or the hatches?"

"No. The *Konstantin* was not designed to keep people out."

She grimaced. "And they'll outnumber us."

"Eight people, if it is a standard crew. I see no way to prevent their tak-ing physical control of the *Konstantin*." He turned to her. "Should we also message James, Priya, and Han—to tell them we might be boarded?"

Abarca considered this. "Would that reveal our presence?"

"Quite possibly. The radio transmitter is not secure."

"Then no. Besides, all it would do is worry them."

Abarca and Adisa watched the monitor as the unknown vessel docked. It was distant enough that they felt no shudder or clunk of metal.

"Whoever it is, they have skill."

Abarca switched to a camera inside the *Konstantin*'s upper airlock, a hun-dred meters away along the ship's lightweight box truss superstructure. After several moments, she pointed. "There . . ."

The surveillance camera showed the hatch open, and then four individu-als in ungainly, light gray space suits floated in one by one through the dock-ing port in microgravity. They were soon followed by four more. What should have been a joyous sight—the arrival of a crew from Earth after four long years—was instead disquieting.

"Obsolete EVA suits. Orlan-Ms." Adisa poked at the communications console.

"Cutting costs. That sounds like Joyce's creditors all right."

"I cannot intercept their comms. They appear to be using encrypted radio. Might they be military?"

The intruders were clearly communicating with one another, but their faces were concealed behind reflective visors; their radio chatter blasts of static. The new arrivals were visibly agitated by their inability to control anything on the *Konstantin*. They repeatedly tried to tap virtual controls that were linked to a ship that did not exist. After a few frustrated moments, most of them continued deeper into the *Konstantin*, entering the 2-meter-diameter microgravity tunnel that ran its length.

Meanwhile, two of the intruders opened one of the unoccupied docking hatches and emerged from the *Konstantin* to begin a space walk. They clipped tethers onto an exterior rail and moved forward, hand over hand, along the *Konstantin*'s solar mast—clearly knowing where they were going.

Adisa switched to an exterior view from the mule's distant cameras— zooming in on the two space walkers. "They are headed to the comm array— to restore their long-range communications. They will find my bypass."

Abarca keyed the laser comm channel. "*Konstantin* to mission control, we have been boarded by eight unidentified individuals—possibly a hostile replacement crew. They are moving now to cut our communications. I will keep this channel open as long as possible. Repeat . . ."

As Abarca continued to transmit, the two space walkers reached the comm tower and discovered Adisa's modifications, including the cables running to his bypass enclosure. In a few moments they yanked its cables.

"That is it." He turned to her. "We have lost our connection with mission control."

They both stared in horror as the space walkers worked to restore the original wiring to the laser transmitter—relinking to hostile management back on Earth.

Adisa's mind raced, and he brought up a virtual shell console. "I can cripple their transmitter—at the ship's OS level. They would be unlikely to find the cause."

She nodded. "Do it. Buy us some time."

Adisa swiftly wrote a shell script that locked out all the transmitter ports. He then inserted the script into several core services that launched during the ship's OS startup. In a few minutes he was finished. "I have disabled their transmitter."

"Good." She was focused on the surveillance monitors. The intruders inside the ship were now moving into the Central Hab—the junction to all three radial arms and the habs at their ends.

Abarca switched cameras to monitor their progress. "We could physically bar the hatch to this hab. It'll take them at least five minutes to winch down the hab tunnel, and we still have sysadmin control of the *Konstantin*."

"But they now have physical control of the ship's computer core, Isabel. They could reinstall the entire ship's OS and then detect us on surveillance cameras."

She nodded. "And purge our atmosphere. Like last time. We are in a tight spot here, Ade."

"Do you think they will kill us?"

"Their employers already tried to, and that's who sent these people."

Adisa pointed at a surveillance monitor. "Look. They found the Far Star..."

On-screen, one of the intruders lifted a glittering kiwi-fruit-sized diamond from its perch on the wall of the Central Hab. They held it up for the others to see and appeared to celebrate. The stone was a 250-carat diamond James Tighe had discovered during mining operations. Nicole Clarke, the *Konstantin*'s original captain and resident geologist, had cut it into a flawless, brilliant pear diamond they named the Far Star—before she died of cancer. The stone was worth several hundred million back on Earth and no doubt was on a manifest of objects for the new crew to secure.

"They knew right where to look for it." She turned to him. "And next they'll probably start searching for our bodies. Here in the habs."

Two of the intruders opened the pressure door to access the *Konstantin*'s computer core, while the other two pairs went "down" into the spin-gravity wells of the habitat modules, leaving the third module—the Fab Hab workshop—for last.

Intruders were headed their way.

"What do we do, Isabel?"

"I'm thinking." She studied the surveillance cameras as two of the intruders clipped in to the winch and slowly descended the hundred-meter airless tunnel toward their hab unit.

"There are only two of them coming toward us. We have the element of surprise." Adisa got up and rushed into the living quarters. After a few moments he emerged with an ice ax.

"What do you plan to do with that?"

"We must be prepared to defend ourselves."

She grabbed it from him. "You're not killing anyone with my climbing ax."

"Then what are we doing? Are we accepting our fate?"

They stood staring at each other. Adisa's thoughts raced as the moments ticked by, but no solution to their predicament came to mind.

All too soon the *clunk* of boots sounded on the ceiling of the hab unit directly above them. They both looked upward.

He whispered, "They are here."

Abarca entered the hab core and stared up at the airlock hatch in the ceiling. Adisa moved alongside her. The airlock was already cycling.

She placed the ice ax out of sight, leaning it against the wall next to her. "No matter what happens, it has been an honor crewing with you, Adedayo Adisa."

He nodded. "And with you, Isabel Abarca."

They hugged and looked back up at the ceiling as the rattling air pump stopped.

The hatch lever slid aside, then the lid lurched open with a loud squeak, demonstrating the wear of years. In a few moments, a gray booted foot appeared, probing for the top ladder rung. Then another boot followed, and the intruder started descending shakily into the full spin-gravity of the living quarters. A bulky space suit with a life support pack became visible. A second set of boots followed close behind.

Abarca and Adisa silently stood their ground.

Reaching the base of the ladder, the first intruder planted their feet on the deck, and unsteadily turned around in the bulky space suit. In a moment the reflective visor finally came into view.

The intruder suddenly snapped alert—startled at the first sight of Abarca and Adisa.

And now they could clearly see the flag of North Korea sewn onto the suit's chest plate.

PART ONE

Earthbound

CHAPTER 1

Reckoning

JULY 14, 2038

Erika Lisowski sat in a deserted waiting area on sublevel 2B of the FBI's gleaming new headquarters in Washington, DC. Before long, a dour woman at a built-in reception desk motioned to her, and Lisowski stood to approach.

The woman pointed to a grid of numbered cubbyhole shelves installed in the wall. "Place all electronic devices on your person in any open box and note the number."

Lisowski realized she was about to enter a SCIF—a sensitive compartmented information facility. No electronics permitted, and that meant the place would be shielded against radio signals as well. Such facilities were common enough in DC, but not in Lisowski's work as a NASA economist. It confirmed that whatever was about to be discussed was not meant to be seen or heard beyond these walls. That was telling.

Lisowski powered down her phone and stowed it in one of the cubbyholes, taking a chit for the box number. She then followed the receptionist's pointed finger to a suited man standing next to a closed door. He held up a scanning wand. "Arms out at your sides, please."

She did as instructed, and he waved the device across her body. Then he scanned and inspected her purse.

Finished, he opened the door and said, "They're waiting inside for you."

She entered, and the door closed immediately behind her. There was a modest-sized conference room with an American flag draped on a pole in the corner. In the center was a long table occupied on one side by a dozen solemn men and women in suits and one or two in military uniform. They resembled a row of judges. None of them wore identification, and there were no name tags on the table in front of them. Two female agents stood to either side of Lisowski, and one pulled out the lone chair opposite the officials.

It appeared she would be on her own—a situation to which she'd grown accustomed. Lisowski placed her purse on the floor and sat down.

Directly across from her, a prim and pinched-faced man in a freshly pressed charcoal gray suit flipped through a thick file. He looked up and stared intensely into her eyes. "Dr. Lisowski, do you know why you've been called here today?"

She spoke calmly. "I do not."

"This is a classified disciplinary hearing, convened to assess whether your conduct warrants immediate termination from NASA."

She processed this news. "I see. Then why are we at FBI headquarters and not at NASA?"

"Because if this panel concludes termination is warranted, you will be arrested and charged with espionage under Title 18 of the federal criminal code."

So that was the game plan. *Intimidation.* A poor choice. One that suggested desperation.

"What's extraordinary is that you thought your activities would not be discovered."

"What 'activities'?" She scanned the faces of the other officials. Who among them was the real person in charge here? She suspected *not* the one talking to her.

He continued. "We have irrefutable evidence of your involvement in numerous breaches of NASA's code of ethical conduct, not to mention federal law. You face not only dismissal from NASA and forfeiture of your pension, but also decades in federal prison. Do you understand the gravity of your situation?"

"I understand." Lisowski let a beat pass. "But then, if your plan was to arrest me, you would have. So why don't we cut the bullshit and get to the real discussion?"

Her interlocutor was taken aback and took to rearranging his papers.

One of the men in uniform chuckled slightly to himself.

A woman on the panel spoke up. "Okay, Erika—let's all cut the bullshit.

Three months ago a small asteroid burned up above Europe, illuminating the night sky over millions of people. You may have seen videos of it on the Internet."

Lisowski said nothing.

"Well, it wasn't an asteroid, and it didn't burn up. It was an unidentified spacecraft inbound from beyond the Moon at over 65,000 miles per hour, performing a controlled aerobraking maneuver—no easy feat. Two days later that same spacecraft came around again and circularized into low Earth orbit—before issuing a mayday call. Its crew said they were a lifeboat from the Luxembourg-flagged asteroid mining ship *Konstantin*. Have you ever heard of such a spacecraft—the *Konstantin*?"

Lisowski contemplated the question. "I know that Nathan Joyce—"

"The tech billionaire."

"Yes. Joyce planned to build an asteroid mining vessel, but the news said it was all a scam. Just a Ponzi scheme to dig himself out of debt."

The woman stared hard at Lisowski. "And conveniently Mr. Joyce committed suicide before he could be arrested for embezzlement and tax evasion."

"I don't expect it was convenient for Mr. Joyce."

"And yet, you know that's not the entire truth."

Lisowski remained silent.

The woman continued. "The Chinese rescued the lifeboat's crew in low Earth orbit. One of the three occupants was a former taikonaut—son of one of the richest men in China—an industrialist who is also a high-ranking Communist Party member. The CCP confiscated the spacecraft in LEO, claiming right of salvage. Imagery and spectral analysis suggest the ship's aerodynamic skin was crafted from a seamless piece of cobalt steel—estimated to be more than 50 tons in mass. That's some lifeboat. And there's no record of any such craft launching from Earth."

A man on the panel said, "We have reason to believe that the Chinese are behind this crewed deep space mission—and that it is somehow linked to you and the late Nathan Joyce."

Lisowski laughed bitterly. "This is so predictable."

"You find this amusing?"

"No. I find it pathetic. That lifeboat was not built by China—which is no doubt why they seized it. In fact, it wasn't built on Earth at all. It was built in deep space by the crew that flew it."

"Then you admit you were aware of the existence of this spacecraft?"

"Yes."

"And what do you know about the asteroid mining ship *Konstantin?*"

Lisowski took a deep breath. She had carried this secret for so long now—years—but secrecy was no longer possible. *Here goes.* "I advised Nathan Joyce to build the *Konstantin*—a 346-ton spin-gravity asteroid mining vessel—in lunar orbit back in 2032. Very much as his publicly released blueprint depicted it."

Several of the panelists eagerly began taking notes.

"But it wasn't a *proposed* spacecraft; he actually built it. In pieces. Secretly. The *Konstantin* departed lunar orbit on an unsanctioned asteroid mining mission on December 13, 2033, with a commercial crew of eight—and to this day remains in the vicinity of the near-Earth asteroid Ryugu. More importantly, its crew has already returned thousands of tons of refined water ice, iron, nickel, cobalt, ammonia, nitrogen, and silica toward cislunar space—resources, in fact, equal in mass to more than half of *everything* humanity has ever launched into orbit. But then, I suspect these resources are the real reason I was called here today." She studied the panelists' faces for any tells.

"Why did you not alert your superiors to the existence of Joyce's illicit spacecraft?"

Lisowski remained stone-faced. "Nathan himself announced it publicly everywhere he went. His videos are all over the Internet."

"What I *mean* is: Why did you not alert your superiors that Joyce was *actually* building the spacecraft—and with funding from questionable sources?"

"Because if I had, then it wouldn't have happened."

"Who else within NASA or the US government was aware of the *Konstantin's* construction in lunar orbit?"

Lisowski shrugged. "I have no idea. I can only speak for myself."

Her interviewer did not seem satisfied with this answer. "You had no other help or accomplices?"

Another man on the panel said, "You've already confessed to criminal conspiracy."

Lisowski recalled her grandfather gazing at the stars in his backyard—his dreams for humanity thwarted decades ago. She resolved not to back down. "It's 2038, and we're only just now establishing a permanent presence on the Moon. Meanwhile, climate change is tearing apart civilization—it won't wait for us to get our shit together. Humanity is half a century behind where we should be."

A couple members of the panel nodded in agreement. She took mental note of them.

One of the other panelists said, "Your little space mission resulted in the deaths of at least three—and possibly five—of the crew, not to mention the embezzlement of *twenty-four billion dollars*."

Lisowski turned on the panelist. "Our 'little space mission' accomplished a thousand firsts and has greatly accelerated human progress in space. As for the funding, I wasn't consulted by Nathan on how he raised the money. But over half of it was embezzled from dictators, criminal organizations, and corporate tax evaders, and to my mind put to more productive use."

"You say these miners accomplished firsts. Where is the hard data returned from this mission?"

Lisowski was pleased by this shift in the conversation. So they wanted things from her. She still had leverage. "I have in my possession all the scientific, telemetry, and physiological data from the expedition. Daily medical records from the ship's flight surgeon—a treasure trove of data on human survival in deep space, particularly regarding GCRs, radiation shielding, and spin-gravity research. Obviously, this data must be shared with the scientific community."

Several of the panelists scribbled this down, too.

Her first interviewer was not appeased. "These were unethical and unlawful human experiments."

"The crew of the *Konstantin* was well aware of the risks they were taking. We don't prevent climbers from risking their necks on mountains here on Earth. So why are we preventing them from climbing mountains out in space? No taxpayer money was lost on this expedition. These were private individuals from several nations—so it hardly constitutes a geostrategic threat."

"You don't get to decide that."

The pinched-faced man slid a piece of paper across the table to her. "Dr. Lisowski, the Justice Department is prepared to offer immunity from prosecution—providing you cooperate with investigators and reveal every-thing you know about the *Konstantin* spacecraft, its crew, how it was fi-nanced, and the people who built it—as well as detailed information on the resources returned to lunar orbit. Providing that you hold back *nothing* from us, you can still avoid prison."

Lisowski raised an eyebrow. "Immunity from prosecution. How very gen-erous of you." She pulled the piece of paper toward her and studied it. "And here I am without an attorney."

"This isn't a negotiation."

The woman said, "You will, of course, be demoted—down from GS-15 Step 5 to GS-14 Step 1—from an executive to a program manager, and be-cause you abused your authority, you will report to the new program executive for emerging space. Likewise, the existence of the resources returned by the asteroid miners as well as the existence of the *Konstantin* itself has been clas-sified on national security grounds—a secrecy you will maintain or be in breach of this agreement."

Lisowski perused the document. "So the government is building yet another *cylinder of excellence* and locking this up."

The woman added, "Sign that document, Erika, and you can put your legal and professional troubles behind you. Start to rebuild your career."

Lisowski looked up. "Why not ask for my resignation?"

"There are many within NASA who respect your family's Apollo lineage. No one wants to tarnish your family's or the agency's good name."

"Then I'll give you the answer my grandfather would have . . ." She slid the paper back. "Go to hell. I will never sign this."

There was a tense silence.

An older man at the end of the table, who had yet to speak, said, "You will accept the demotion and keep your knowledge of the *Konstantin* secret or face dismissal, arrest, and prosecution. In case you hadn't noticed, we are in a geopolitical and astropolitical struggle against a rival power."

Lisowski turned to him. She didn't recognize the man—but neither did she recognize anyone else here. Defense? Intelligence? Executive branch? It was impossible to know. But he was clearly the one in charge. "You brought me here because you don't want 5,000 tons of strategic resources in deep space to fall into the hands of the Chinese."

The man shot back, "We brought you here, Dr. Lisowski, because your extracurricular activities have gone far enough—and we both know it's *11,000* tons that the *Konstantin* has returned, not 5,000."

She tried not to blink.

"We don't need your cooperation or the cooperation of your asteroid miners to obtain those resources. The United States has had full situational awareness in cislunar space for over a decade. The orbital elements of those robotic tugs is already known to us, and regardless of what you do, or do not do, they will be secured for the United States before the Chinese government can seize them. The only question is whether you want to go to prison."

She continued to stare. "You think confiscating those resources helps you?"

"The professed doctrine of the CCP is to surpass the United States as the dominant space power by 2045—and they're well on their way to doing just that. These resources in lunar orbit change the equation."

Lisowski resolved to press the issue. "So the US takes possession of the resources—then what?"

One of the men in military uniform answered. "They'll be used to establish a strategic propellant and minerals reserve for multi-orbit logistics—to counter potential Chinese aggression in deep space."

Lisowski didn't relent. "A *reserve*? Keeping those resources out of the hands of the CCP isn't the goal. *Using* them is the goal. Those resources need to be employed as a stepping-stone to obtain *more* resources—for all humanity. And damned soon. They should be used to unify the people of Earth in building a complete cislunar industrial infrastructure. To provide global leadership to combat climate change. For access to limitless, sustainable clean energy. They shouldn't be hoarded for some what-if scenario that ultimately leads to doom. *Dying last* isn't a vision for the future."

"Dr. Lisowski—"

"What the world needs is a *frontier*—one capable of absorbing the creative ambitions of this next generation. Capable of delivering new resources and energy without increasing conflict or environmental damage. Capable of delivering prosperity to the entire globe. Space *is* that frontier, and if you want a space culture that is friendly to democracy, commerce, and international rule of law, then you must establish it yourself—and you must establish it first."

The panelists exchanged looks.

The older man leaned forward. "And you feel better qualified than us to accomplish that?"

"No, not me. Let the asteroid miners take charge of those resources in lunar orbit."

He scowled. "You want us to turn over a critical strategic asset to a handful of reckless adventurers—only one of whom is American?"

"Those 'reckless adventurers' are responsible for obtaining the resources in the first place. And their backgrounds are a benefit, not a drawback. It helps deflect worldwide opposition to a purely American or Chinese push into deep space."

"For what purpose?"

"Bootstrapping an entire off-world economy."

They again exchanged looks.

"Those thousands of tons of asteroid resources at the top of Earth's gravity well can provide the seed from which a Second Age of Exploration can grow. With it we can establish the first international commodities exchange in space, giving the democracies of the world major-league soft power we don't want held over us. It could lead to the establishment of a space bond market—and liquidity for massive space infrastructural projects. Which is exactly what's needed to save civilization here on Earth. And saving human civilization is how we remain indispensable. We cannot *bomb* our way to security in the twenty-first century. Instead, we must build—and in new domains."

"The CCP will not just sit idly by while all this happens."

"That's fine. Free people have a natural advantage on frontiers. Authoritarian subjects wait for permission, but free people take action and innovate. They can rapidly expand human presence in cislunar space—before totalitarian powers seize the L-points and hold them against us."

The older man seemed unmoved. "You exaggerate the power of free markets in space, Doctor. Our billionaire Space Titans haven't been able to make the economics work. Jack Macy's and George Burkette's reusable rockets wouldn't even be profitable without billions in government subsidies, and I don't see Macy colonizing Mars yet, despite all his talk."

Lisowski countered. "Reusable rockets were never going to lift millions of tons into orbit—not without doing massive damage to the environment. Think about what it's going to take to truly establish ourselves in deep space …" She counted off on her fingers. "In-space manufacturing, viable long-term habitats, in situ resource extraction and energy collection, reliable radiation shielding, debris mitigation. Individually, each of these technologies has only a limited commercial payoff, but by going for the *whole enchilada* at once, Nathan Joyce made a massive leap possible. All we need is the courage to capitalize on the opportunity he gave us."

The entire panel looked to the older man.

He glowered at her.

She waded into the silence. "Chaos is expanding here on Earth. There are renewed calls for border walls to hold back millions of climate refugees. There are budget shortfalls. Unstable markets. Social division. Serious poverty is growing here in the US. You will not be able to secure the political will here in Washington to do what must be done in space. It will seem too remote and disconnected from politicians' constituencies. These asteroid miners *do* have the will. They're the ones who mined these resources in deep space. Let them take action."

The older man at the end of the table said, "And if these asteroid miners of yours fail, we will have lost a critical strategic advantage."

She remained focused. "I will do everything in my power to make sure they do not fail."

One of the other panelists observed, "She's done pretty well so far, sir."

Another added, "At no cost to the taxpayers."

The older man pondered this. "Let's not forget that one of these surviving asteroid miners is a Chinese national. In fact, he's linked directly to CCP leadership."

One of the panelists opened a file. "Captain Jin Hua Han, former fighter pilot and taikonaut, age forty-two. Son of multibillionaire industrialist Jin Longwei. He was dismissed from the CNSA as psychologically unfit—deemed 'disrespectful of authority and prone to excessive risk-taking.'"

One of the military officers said, "He flew the hell out of that return vehicle, sir."

The older man said, "What about his father? The man's a senior party member."

"They're estranged, with no known financial ties."

"And the other two asteroid miners?"

The panelist flipped to another page. "James Tighe—American, also forty-two. He was an itinerant cave diver prior to the *Konstantin* expedition. No college. Juvenile criminal record. No employment history to speak of. A video of him went viral on the Internet some years back—some sort of cave rescue. But that's about it."

"Hmph. And the woman?"

"Priya Chindarkar—Indian national, age forty. Roboticist. Formally disowned by her family back in Mumbai."

"What for?"

"Refusing an arranged marriage. Got herself a full scholarship to the University of Colorado. Then a doctorate in robotics from the Indian Institute of Technology. Worked for the Indian Space Research Organisation designing planetary rovers before joining the *Konstantin* expedition."

"And what have these three been doing since they returned to Earth? Where are they now?"

"In the EU, sir—Luxembourg City. We have them under surveillance. The Chinese and Russians are surveilling them as well, most likely in hopes of obtaining the orbital elements of those asteroid resources. With the help of their attorney, the miners have rebooted Nathan Joyce's old company, Catalyst Corporation, and they're trying to raise private capital to return to orbit."

"Then let's buy them out—before the Chinese do."

"The miners are only selling a small stake—for liquidity to return to orbit and, we suspect, to attempt rescue of two crewmates they left behind at Ryugu."

"How does rescuing their friends accomplish any of the things you described, Dr. Lisowski?"

She answered immediately. "Because those refined asteroid resources were placed at the very edge of Earth's gravity well—in a lunar distant retrograde orbit. That means the miners will need to build their rescue ship out there, and in order to do that, they'll need to establish industrial infrastructure in deep space—human habitats, power generation, machinery. And they'll need to do it fast because Ryugu's next close approach to Earth occurs in just four years' time."

The older man stared. "These crewmates they left behind—do we know if they're still alive?"

The military officer said, "No, sir. All communications with the *Konstantin* have been lost."

"What nationality were they?"

The panelist again flipped through the file. "Isabel Abarca, the flight surgeon, is a well-known Argentinian mountain climber, by now age forty-four. She's famous for climbing all the highest mountains in the world, Alpine style."

"What's that mean?"

"It means without fixed ropes or supplementary oxygen."

"Presumably she's relaxed her oxygen prohibition out in space."

Slight chuckles among the panel.

"The other crew member, Adedayo Adisa, is a twenty-something satellite hacker from Nigeria. Part of an orbital ransomware gang based in the slums of Lagos."

"An adrenaline junkie and a satellite thief—these are the sort of people our miners want to rescue, and yet you expect us to rely on them, Doctor?" The older man turned back to the panelist. "And who are the miners raising capital from? Burkette? Macy?"

"Not from the Space Titans, no. Mostly eco-venture funds. Tech investors. No ties to criminal organizations or sovereign capital."

"And these investors are aware of the asteroid resources in lunar orbit?"

"Yes. Word of the *Konstantin* expedition has gotten out to certain aerospace circles. That's how they're raising capital."

The woman who first interviewed Lisowski asked, "Who else knows what these miners have accomplished in space? Anyone in media?"

"There are rumors circulating. It won't be long before the knowledge goes public—whether or not Dr. Lisowski here maintains secrecy."

The older man at the end of the table shook his head. "That won't do. We can't have these asteroid miners becoming heroes. Heroes are too difficult to control."

"Video will eventually get out. We'll never contain the secret."

"We don't have to." One of the officials who had yet to speak, a man in his thirties, leaned forward. "Excuse me, sir, but Nathan Joyce deliberately projected a P. T. Barnum–like persona to deflect serious scrutiny. In short: no one really believed he was capable of this, and the public still believes he was a con artist. We can work with that. The asteroid miners' past association with Joyce should make it easy to convince the public that they're just grifters trying to defraud investors. We can mount a psyops campaign to discredit them so the general public believes they never went to Ryugu. Even if they have video evidence, that proves nothing nowadays."

Lisowski was appalled. "But these miners have made history. Why would you do that?"

The old man turned to her. "So they must rely on *us* to return to orbit." He glanced toward the other man. "Do it. I want there to be no doubt in the public's mind that these asteroid miners are con artists. We can't have them becoming heroes. Not until we're certain they're *our* heroes."

Lisowski felt rage building, but she tamped down her anger. Too much was at stake to allow personal feelings to intrude. Especially since she was so very close to success.

The old man scanned the panelists. "We need to have a sit-down with these three surviving miners—to make certain they know what's expected of them, and under what terms we'll permit them to return to space." He looked at Lisowski. "You're in contact with their attorney, Doctor—this Lukas Rochat fellow?"

Lisowski replied, "Yes, he was Nathan Joyce's protégé. He's now CEO of the new Catalyst Corporation."

"Have him arrange a meeting."

"I can schedule a videoconference with the asteroid miners."

"No. I want nothing recorded or transmitted." He tapped the table for emphasis. "An in-person meeting only. Here in the US. In a SCIF."

Lisowski frowned. "I can't promise they'll go for that. Jin Han is former PLA air force. He won't be able to enter the US easily. Not in the current political climate."

The older man was undeterred. "We'll grant a special-purpose visa, and we won't stamp his passport." He regarded Lisowski for a moment. "Do you think you can arrange such an in-person meeting with our asteroid miners, Doctor?"

Lisowski nodded. "I can try."

"If you want to stay out of prison, you'll do more than try."

Lisowski picked up the plea agreement from the table. "For that, I'll require my old position and authority to operate as I did before." She met his gaze.

After a moment, the old man sighed. "Very well. Just get it done."

With that, she crumpled the plea agreement into a ball and tossed it toward the man in the charcoal suit. Lisowski then grabbed her things, and turned for the door.

CHAPTER 2

Prognosis

J ames Tighe sat in a medical examination room, drumming his fingers impatiently. Ever since he had returned from space, he felt as though the entire solar system was one big ticking clock and he was behind schedule.

Looking around, he suddenly had a memory of Isabel Abarca's medical bay on the asteroid mining ship *Konstantin*. That was so much more compact than this examination room. So dense with equipment. He recalled the distinctive smell and sounds of the *Konstantin* and powerful emotions returned.

She and Adedayo Adisa were now stranded, alone, tens of millions of kilometers—soon to be *hundreds* of millions of kilometers—from Earth until the asteroid Ryugu orbited around again. No matter what anyone did, their rescue could not occur sooner, and yet, innumerable obstacles would have to be overcome well before then if there was to be any chance of rendezvousing with the asteroid. Would they even be alive by the time Tighe and his partners could reach them? Were they alive even now?

That question was more than he could grapple with at the moment. So instead he stood and looked out the window at the skyline of Luxembourg City, where Lukas Rochat had set up their company. The entire commercial space industry seemed to have offices here in Luxembourg for legal reasons. Or political reasons. Or tax reasons. Tighe couldn't recall which. Maybe all of them. Catalyst support staff had leased him a sterile corporate apartment a few blocks from their headquarters, and for the first time in his life he suddenly had a real mailing address. Tighe had spent so many years on caving expeditions and later in deep space that he hardly knew how to exist like a normal person. Instead, he was restless to reequip and get back into space. How to achieve that was the question.

A gentle knock came at the door, and a doctor in a lab coat entered—a bespectacled, clean-cut Caucasian man. He clutched a folder under his arm and nodded in greeting. "Good afternoon, Mr. Teeg." He spoke English with a slight French accent.

"It's pronounced 'Tie.'"

"Apologies." The doctor jotted a note in the folder.

Tighe took a seat once more.

The doctor sat down on a high stool. "I asked for you to come in so that we could review your test results in person. Have you driven here today?"

Tighe shook his head. "No. Why, are we doing another biopsy?"

"No, no." The doctor placed a hand on the folder. "I must tell you the lab results came back positive. The mass in your liver is a malignant neoplasm—a very serious cancer."

On hearing this news, Tighe's prevailing emotion was simply disappointment. Apparently his cumulative radiation exposure in deep space had finally caught up with him. He recalled a conversation years ago with one of Joyce's recruiters back on Ascension Island about why they preferred asteroid mining candidates in their thirties and forties: *Most of you will die of old age before developing serious cancers.*

Wrong again.

"We don't yet know if it has spread, and determining this will require additional tests. However, it is important that you know this type of cancer—caught at this stage—is not necessarily terminal." The oncologist looked Tighe in the eye. "With a rigorous schedule of chemo and radiation therapy, there is likelihood of containment. Possibly of full remission."

Tighe nodded. He was feeling strangely detached, almost as if he was watching this on television.

"Do you understand what I am telling you, Mr. Tighe?"

"Yes. You're telling me I need to undergo chemotherapy."

"Correct. What we call *neoadjuvant* therapy, to prepare you for follow-up radiation treatment. The idea is that we want to shrink the tumor first."

"How long would the chemo last?"

The doctor started writing in his folder. "I want to start you on a monthly cycle of two biweekly chemo sessions and depending on the results, tentatively aim to commence radiation treatments within two months."

Tighe winced. "I don't know where I'll be in two months."

"I suggest you clear your schedule."

"And what are the side effects of the chemo?"

"The more common side effects include fatigue, vomiting, hair loss, bruising, loss of appetite. However, sometimes the side effects can be more debilitating—in which case we would change your medications. Certainly you should consider reducing your work schedule, or if possible taking a leave of absence."

Tighe was already shaking his head. "I can't. I need to travel for work."

"Travel is a very bad idea. Chemotherapy suppresses your immune system, making you susceptible to viruses and infections."

"But I need to work."

"Mr. Tighe, getting better should be all that you are focused on. Is your job more important than your life?"

Tighe contemplated Jin Han and Priya Chindarkar trying to finance and organize a deep space rescue mission within the next four years without him—in time to be ready for Ryugu's next close encounter with Earth. He owed his life to Adisa and Abarca. How many times had they both saved his? The next few months would be crucial. Was his work more important than his life? "In a way, yes. It is."

The doctor looked confounded. "It may feel that way, but I doubt that is actually the case."

"I can't be incapacitated right now."

"With an aggressive program of chemotherapy, we can reduce the size of your tumor and provide a reasonable chance of remission through radiation treatment."

"And I'd be out of action for how long?"

"Six months. Perhaps a year. However, you would likely survive."

"But no guarantee."

"There is never a guarantee. All cancers are different. Your treatment might not succeed, but this approach gives you the best probability."

"What if I reduced my chemo meds—to avoid side effects?"

The doctor frowned. "It could make radiation treatment impractical. This type of cancer is aggressive, and it would likely spread. Your illness could then become terminal."

"But how long from now? Are we talking years?"

"Without chemo? Perhaps a year."

"Could I push that date back a bit with a reduced chemo schedule? But stay on my feet for most of that time?"

Now the doctor looked alarmed. "That is a very unwise approach."

"I understand, but is it possible?"

"I . . . Do you have a family, Mr. Tighe?"

"No. No wife or children."

"Brothers? Sisters? Parents?"

He stared. "None who are close."

"What is your occupation?"

"I work in the space industry."

"And is your work physically strenuous?"

"You could say that."

"Then this is not sensible. You need chemotherapy and bed rest, not travel and exertion."

"The work I do means life or death for *other* people. Do you understand? I need to travel, and I need to function."

"Your coworkers would not be able to count on you."

"Not in space, no. But before then. That's all I need."

The doctor apparently saw the resolve in Tighe's eyes. He tapped his pen on the folder and sighed. "You do realize this makes it likely your cancer will progress?"

"I'll take all the meds I can handle—until the side effects start making it too difficult to work."

The doctor jotted down notes in the folder. "I strongly advise you against this approach."

"Yes, I know you do, and I appreciate it. I really do."

"Are you certain you won't reconsider, Mr. Tighe?"

"Yes, I'm certain. Thank you, Doctor."

———

Despite the oppressive heat, Tighe didn't take the tram back to the office. Instead, lost in thought, he strolled along Boulevard Franklin Delano Roosevelt. Strange that several of Luxembourg City's streets were named after US presidents. Was it because of World War II? The Cold War? No doubt historic figures had left their mark on this city, but like all things, the details eventually faded into the background of everyday life—simply becoming someone's street address. He imagined the momentous events he himself had lived through—the first crewed voyage beyond Earth's orbit; the longest journey into deep space; the first off-world mining at industrial scale. Perhaps Tighe's name would one day become a history test answer for bored teenagers.

It was another scorching day in Luxembourg—over a hundred degrees. He suspected that at some point climate change would make this the new normal for summer in Europe, but the punishing conditions matched his mood.

Tighe walked for a while without a destination. He didn't want to speak with anyone—not until he'd come to terms with his diagnosis. He thought back to how Nicole Clarke, the first captain of the *Konstantin*, had died—or more specifically how he'd euthanized her at her own request. In deep space. Before her cancer got nastier. Perhaps he'd do the same to himself when the time came. She'd gone peacefully. Rather than sulk about it, he should probably accept the fact that dying of old age was never in the cards for him. In truth, half of the people he cared about were no longer among the living. A gallery of remembered faces brought a pang of loss all over again.

But what to tell Chindarkar and Jin about his medical situation? They would no doubt insist on a full course of chemo. And radiation treatment. He'd be out of action for most of the next year. Perhaps even become a burden to them.

Not if they don't know about my cancer.

Still, what if his illness made him unreliable and that put others at risk? Well, that wasn't likely to happen until they launched to space, and there were a thousand hurdles to clear before that would even be possible. So there was time yet before he had to come clean to them.

Pondering this, he wandered the Chemin de la Corniche and then down a winding cobblestone lane that descended along the cliffs to the Alzette River—where he meandered through the quaint streets of the Grund, largely deserted owing to the heat. This medieval quarter seemed centuries removed from the private space industry, whose investors and astropreneurs had brought an economic boom to the rest of the city.

It was strangely comforting to contemplate a medieval world where technology wasn't constantly hurtling forward, humanity clinging on for dear life, but that was nonsense, of course. The world back then was imagined to be full of demons and witches. Climate change or no, the twenty-first century still had its advantages.

Chemo being one of them.

Tighe passed by shops and flats and saw people inside enmeshed in their rooted lives. All the things he never chose. How many times had he orbited over this city at 17,000 miles per hour? Too high to see these human moments.

What *was* certain was that his time in deep space had done more than damage his DNA—it had also altered his outlook on life. Before the *Konstantin* expedition, Tighe did not recall having a purpose, but after the expedition, his sense of purpose was all he could think about. This, at least, was something he could hold on to.

Tighe's phone sounded. Very few people had his number, so despite his reluctance, he wiped the sweat off his hands and pulled the device from his jacket pocket. He wasn't surprised by the caller and picked up. "Yes, Lukas."

"*Where are you?*"

"Down in the Grund."

"*The Grund? We have an investor meet and greet right now. Here in the office. It's on your schedule. We need you here.*"

Time must have slipped away from him. The very last thing Tighe felt like doing at the moment was pumping up the Catalyst Corporation "brand story" with investors. But they needed the liquidity to get back into space—at least twenty-five million dollars per person for a seat on a rocket from either Macy's or Burkette's company. Where and how they'd manage in orbit after that was still an open question, and one that would require Earthly investors to answer.

Tighe nodded. "Right. I'm on my way."

"*Hurry. And be ready to discuss your experiences in space. Investors love that.*"

Tighe took the Luxtram back toward the eastern edge of the city, and exited near Avenue John F. Kennedy, where he gazed up at the modern building where Catalyst Corporation leased space. True to form, Rochat had selected one of the toniest addresses in town, but as Tighe passed through security and the ground-floor atrium, it was impossible to deny the energy of the place. Sharp young people clustered in the common areas. He felt like a senior citizen as he moved anonymously through the throngs of youthful engineers.

Rochat insisted Catalyst remain low-profile—despite their high-profile address. So they had no listing in the building directory and no signage on their door. Instead, they were meant to be an insider-only secret. Nathan Joyce had made the Catalyst name infamous for fraud, and yet there was something about reusing the name that appealed to Tighe's innate stubborness. Joyce had been many things—a liar, a megalomaniac, and a user of people—but he was not, in the final analysis, wrong about the mission of Catalyst Corporation.

Tighe exited the elevator and buzzed through the heavy double doors of their unmarked class A corporate suite. Inside, the place looked more like a law firm than an asteroid mining company. The fashion-model-handsome receptionist looked up and spoke into his headset as Tighe entered. "Mr. Tighe is here, Mr. Rochat."

Tighe noticed a throng of guests in the glass-walled conference room beyond.

A Russian-accented voice nearby said, "Not like you to be late, J.T."

Tighe turned to see former cosmonaut Sevastian "Yak" Yakovlev coming down the hall toward him. A fellow asteroid mining trainee and veteran of multiple Roscosmos missions, Yak had nearly gone on the *Konstantin* expedition—having been an alternate. He'd also been instrumental in getting Tighe, Jin, and Chindarkar back to Earth alive after Joyce's bankruptcy and suicide. For this reason, Yak was now a board member of the new Catalyst and today actually looked the part with a sport coat, slacks, and collared shirt. His thick beard was carefully groomed.

He studied Tighe. "Where have you been?"

"Just went for a walk. Guess I lost track of time."

Yak said, deadpan, "Perhaps it was heatstroke."

Tighe gazed toward the crowded conference room. It was precisely where he did not want to be. "You headed in?"

Yak clapped Tighe on the shoulder. "*Nyet.* It is you, Han, and Priya who investors wish to speak with."

"You did two stints on the ISS."

"But I did not crew on *Konstantin.* If we get money from these people, I will go to space with you this time."

Beyond Yak, some ways down the hall, Tighe spotted Jin Han, his crewmate on the *Konstantin* expedition and one of the three who made it back alive. Jin was escorting a Caucasian woman and two Black girls in their mid-teens.

In answer to Tighe's quizzical expression, Yak said, "David's ex-wife and twin daughters. They are shareholders now. As we promised him."

Tighe nodded. He now recognized David Morra's ex-wife from the photograph Morra had kept in his quarters back on the *Konstantin.* Her auburn hair remained unchanged, and though they were much older now, Tighe recalled the girls from the same photo. That photo, Tighe realized, was now interred with Morra's remains in a cairn orbiting the asteroid Ryugu, many millions of miles in deep space.

"You should introduce yourself."

Seeing Morra's widow for the first time in person, Tighe felt a sudden dryness in his throat. He had been present at Morra's death. In fact, Morra had saved him and Jin—and possibly the entire crew of the *Konstantin*—by sacrificing his own life to disable a competitor's malfunctioning machine.

Morra had also been Tighe's closest friend.

He realized he could not face Morra's widow and children. Not yet. Perhaps it was Tighe's recent diagnosis, but the memory of Morra's death—and of all the things Tighe could have or should have done—was too much at the moment. He shook his head. "I can't. Not right now."

A voice behind Tighe said, "I agree. You need to freshen up first."

He turned to see Lukas Rochat, the thirty-something CEO of Catalyst, dressed as usual in a bespoke suit with a colorful pocket square and standing with someone Tighe didn't know, a short Latino man in his late twenties.

Rochat frowned. "Why are you all sweaty, J.T.?"

Yak answered for him. "He went for a walk."

Rochat tugged Tighe in the opposite direction from Jin and Morra's family. "You'll have time to meet them before we head off to Ascension Island. Right now I need you to chat up potential investors." He gestured to the Latino man. "This is Ramón Marín, our new director of systems architecture. He'll bring you up to speed on—"

Tighe held up his hand. "Let's just get past today's meet and greet first." He turned. "No offense, Ramón, but I'm still reacclimating."

Marín nodded. "Of course. It's an honor to meet you, Mr. Tighe, and I'm available whenever you have time."

Tighe turned back to Rochat. "So we're returning to Ascension?"

"Next week. For meetings with mission control and to train on new systems. Please make a point of speaking with Ramón before then, since he's entering orbital certification training there."

Yak raised his eyebrows and looked to Marín. "Then you will be accompanying us to orbit?"

Marín looked surprised to be asked anything. "Not initially, but once you've established a base of operations in orbit, yes."

Tighe spoke to Rochat. "Just send me the flight details for Ascension."

"Not necessary. One of our investors is providing his personal aircraft for our use."

Tighe was relieved—much less hassle for such a long flight to the South Atlantic. "Good."

"We'll be stopping off in Lagos on the way." He looked Tighe in the eye. "We located Adedayo's family."

Tighe brightened and glanced toward Yak. "That is *great* news." Adisa had grown up in one of the worst slums in Lagos, Nigeria; locating his family no doubt required more than an Internet search.

"We're setting up his mother and siblings with a nice home on Victoria Island."

"Outstanding."

"But right now we have guests to meet." Rochat nudged Tighe down the hall. "Use the bathroom in my office to freshen up."

Marín added, "Again, it is an honor to meet you."

Tighe headed to the private restroom in Rochat's corner office and splashed some water on his face. He then stared into the mirror and tried to see himself as anything other than a dead man walking. After a few moments of deep breathing to psych himself up, he headed out to make an appearance.

Entering the conference room, he moved among the guests. Priya Chindarkar spotted him and nodded greeting while she chatted with two Japanese businessmen.

It seemed surreal—the dense knot of accredited investors, all under NDA, from Europe, Asia, the US, sipping wine and nibbling appetizers plucked from wandering wheeled robots. No human catering staff allowed. That would have undermined secrecy. The event had the triumphal air of a Skull and Bones Society meeting. You had to be *this* in the know to be here at all.

On a good day Tighe had little patience for self-promotion, but having just been diagnosed with cancer made it almost unbearable. However, Rochat was right about one thing: they needed these people's money if they were to have any chance to get back into space—and save Abarca and Adisa. This was where he needed to be.

Rochat raised his voice to get everyone's attention and then gave a speech about the Catalyst mission—during which Tighe's mind wandered—followed by a toast to the trio of returned asteroid miners. A Catalyst staffer handed Tighe a glass of champagne.

Rochat followed up with a photo presentation of the *Konstantin* expedition—video of the crew conducting mining operations at the asteroid Ryugu. All eyes were riveted to the virtual screen—scenes never before shown. The asteroid mining ship *Konstantin*. The excitement in the room was palpable. This was *happening*, and they were in on it early.

Tighe, on the other hand, felt it was far too late. They needed to get back into space *yesterday*.

Finally Chindarkar, dressed in a blazer and slacks, gave a compelling technical presentation on the optical mining and mule robots they'd employed on the expedition, along with the telepresence system. Tighe mostly tuned out, and was roused only by the applause when it concluded.

Almost instantly men and women were in front of him, being introduced by Rochat. Money people in their thirties and forties. Self-described risk-takers, though they seemed to confuse themselves with their money. Nathan

Joyce would have eaten this lot alive. Tighe nodded at intervals as they talked, until ultimately asking a variation of the same question: *What was it like out there?* He told them what he'd felt and seen and that seemed to enthrall them. Mercifully Rochat had confiscated all phones from attendees—so no selfies.

Chindarkar came up to him and as an aside asked, "You okay, J.T.? You don't seem your usual charming self."

"You're hilarious." He met her gaze. It would be especially hard to conceal his illness from her. Their relationship had reverted to professional terms since their return to Earth. Perhaps they both understood that the stresses of deep space were what had sparked their romance. Yet, their bond—and the bond they both shared with Jin—went much deeper than sex. He trusted them both with his life, and for that very reason he couldn't tell her about his diagnosis—because she would do anything to save him, just as he would do for her. She'd tell him to take a leave of absence—from which he might never return.

She studied the room. "You know, there were years in deep space when I would have given anything to be in a crowd like this." She looked out the window. "To know that this view was real and not a light field projection. Now here we are, and I just want to go and hide."

He nodded. They really did understand each other.

A well-groomed Caucasian man in his fifties stepped up to them. "Dr. Chindarkar, I enjoyed our conversation, and I was glad to speak with Mr. Jin. This must be the elusive Mr. Tighe."

Tighe detected a slight Scandinavian accent. It reminded him of someone he greatly missed. The kind face of his former lover, Eike Dahl, flashed in his mind, and her death stung anew. He pushed the memory away and extended his hand. "Yes. It's a pleasure."

"I'm Marius Hanssen. It's good to meet you." They shook hands.

Chindarkar gestured. "James, Marius here is our anchor investor. He's the founder of the largest wind turbine and solar energy fund in Norway. He is fully committed to getting humanity to net-zero carbon emissions."

"To *negative* carbon emissions. We need to do more than stop emitting CO_2; we must repair the damage."

"Yes. Marius, this is James Tighe, the cave explorer."

"Your reputation precedes you—in this room at least."

Rochat leaned in and whispered something to Chindarkar. She looked up. "James, I'm needed to answer technical questions."

He nodded to her.

As she departed, Hanssen pointed past Tighe's shoulder. "Now *that* is historic."

Tighe turned around to notice for the first time that a large framed photograph had recently been installed in a lighted display between shelving units in the boardroom. It was a photo he hadn't seen in five years—one taken by the *Konstantin*'s construction manager, Julian Kerner, the day before the *Konstantin* departed lunar orbit. It was a picture of the crew of the first commercial asteroid mining vessel in history, smiling, arm in arm, as they floated in microgravity in the ship's large Central Hab.

The people in this photo had become his family.

This print was much larger than the original. Below each of their images, they had signed their names—eight in all. Captain Nicole Clarke, Adedayo Adisa, Amy Tsukada, David Morra, Isabel Abarca, Tighe himself, Jin Han, and Priya Chindarkar. Tighe unconsciously touched his fingers against the glass.

Those smiling faces. He tried to recall what they had felt that day—what he had felt. Clarke, Morra, and Tsukada were now dead, interred in a makeshift cairn orbiting Ryugu. Their remains would most likely be preserved for hundreds of millions of years. Looking just as they had on the day they died.

Abarca and Adisa, on the other hand, were stranded back at Ryugu, possibly alive. But possibly not. All communication lost. Word had reached them that the new owners of the *Konstantin* (Joyce's creditors) had sent a crew to retake control of the ship, but communication with them had apparently been lost as well.

What had happened?

Hanssen stood alongside. "I look forward to the day when everyone knows what you and your colleagues have accomplished in space."

Tighe nodded grimly. "It's hard nowadays to get people to believe things. At least good things."

"Yes, our sense-making apparatus appears to be broken." He looked intensely at Tighe. "How do you rate our chances, Mr. Tighe?"

"Of what?"

"Of not extincting ourselves."

"Honestly? Not great if we need everyone's cooperation."

"I hope you're not suggesting draconian measures."

"No, and I don't think that would work either."

"Hmm. Our species does seem to have reached an inflection point. To those who believe that humanity cannot go extinct—that we will persist despite climatic upheaval . . . Well, I have a fossil record to show them." Hanssen grimaced. "In some ways I envy my predecessors. The rich of a few centuries ago did not have to contend with the end of civilization. They could just enjoy their money. However, I have to try and buy my grandchildren a future, and I suspect it won't come cheap."

"If our conversation is going to be this bleak, Marius, we should drink something stronger."

Hanssen laughed. "I wouldn't be here if I didn't think there was hope. I was actually very much inspired by Nathan Joyce."

Tighe's expression must have let slip his feelings, because Hanssen said, "You were not a fan?"

Tighe chose his words carefully. "Let's put it this way: Nathan was a man who believed what he was saying when he was saying it. I'd be the first to admit he had vision, but he was also a world-class bastard."

"No doubt. Yet, changing the world is bound to require someone with such traits. Still, I'm glad I'm investing in *your* iteration of Catalyst Corporation and not his."

"I'll toast to that." Tighe took a sip of champagne.

"You know, I've spent my life growing businesses that pull investment away from fossil fuels and carbon-intensive industry. I've funded the construction of millions of square meters of solar arrays on three continents. Thousands of wind turbines. Geothermal and thermophotovoltaic energy plants. Most of it profitable. But may I confess a secret?"

"Go ahead."

"It won't be enough to save us. Even the *ruins* left behind by bankrupt fossil fuel companies continue to pollute. There are twenty-nine million abandoned, uncapped oil and gas wells around the world—each one of them spewing the emissions of fifteen hundred automobiles. Sealing them would require trillions and take decades."

Tighe was taken aback at this news.

"However, even if today we reduced carbon emissions to zero—and we're far from that—the amount of CO_2 already in the atmosphere will cause the Earth to keep warming for a century or more. It's already 'baked in,' as you Americans say. And now the wildfires in Siberia and the US West and Canada are billowing billions more tons of carbon into the atmosphere. Droughts are devastating agriculture. Tropical diseases like dengue fever are spreading in the British Isles. And all of this has caused the more reactionary elements of society to finally acknowledge that anthropogenic climate change is real."

"Better late than never."

Hanssen gave Tighe a look. "That was always the prevailing view, but I fear that it may instead become a rationalization for genocide. We already see nations around the world determined to defend their share of what is now a clearly shrinking pie."

Tighe considered this.

"So I've come to realize that arguments of 'no-growth' or of living Spartan lives will not win over people. Nearly 3.5 billion people already live lives of bare subsistence. Can we ethically say to them that they must remain in dire circumstances—that they cannot develop their own economies and hope for a better future for their children?

"No, what you and your colleagues are doing out in space is humanity's best hope for a livable future, Mr. Tighe. It's the only way we're going to obtain the resources and energy necessary to rescue civilization in time. That's why I'm investing in you, and it is why you *must* succeed."

Tighe could see the sincere conviction in Hanssen's eyes and suddenly felt ashamed of his own concerns. He had cancer, yes, and two of his closest friends were stranded in deep space, admittedly due to their own tendencies toward risk-taking—but all of that was scarcely an atom of suffering compared to what the future might hold for humanity.

So Tighe decided he would press on as long as he drew breath. It was the best way he could think of to honor those who had already died in his place.

CHAPTER 3

Liftoff

AUGUST 18, 2038

Priya Chindarkar stood on the sidewalk in front of Catalyst's offices in the predawn. Traffic on Avenue John F. Kennedy was minimal at this hour, allowing her to appreciate the wide-open sky in relative tranquility. She was not yet fully reacclimated to Earth, and so the atmosphere overhead still seemed magical—and comforting. Eons of ancestors had evolved her for this environment, and she closed her eyes to take a deep breath of cool morning air, fragrant with life. The planet Earth was home.

At that moment, the idea of returning to the void of deep space brought on a sense of dread—one she immediately tamped down. Her time out in space was not yet done.

Thus resolved, Chindarkar opened her eyes to see a compact electric car roll to a stop at the curb. Inside, Sevastian Yakovlev leaned over from the passenger seat and exchanged a passionate kiss with the young woman behind the wheel.

Jin Han stepped up alongside Chindarkar. "He already has a Luxembourg girlfriend, I see."

"It's what he does."

Jin had a rucksack slung over his shoulder and wore an orderly business casual outfit, as usual. He checked his smart watch with performative impatience.

After a few moments, Yak exited the vehicle and waved as the woman drove away, before approaching Jin and Chindarkar, who stood next to a black SUV. He smiled broadly. "Good morning."

Jin spoke. "You are late."

He checked the time. "Barely five minutes." Yak looked around. "And I do not see J.T. So it makes no difference."

Chindarkar glanced at her own watch. "He's got a point, Han."

Jin turned to her. "Did J.T. respond to your text?"

She shook her head.

They waited another ten minutes, Jin pacing.

Then Yak pointed toward a bus coming down the boulevard. They watched it approach.

As it glided to a stop, James Tighe exited, carrying a small duffel bag, and jaywalked across the street toward them. "Sorry I'm late."

Jin frowned. "We said five a.m."

Tighe said, "Sorry. I couldn't sleep, so I took a sleeping pill."

Priya studied him. "You feeling okay, J.T.?"

"Yeah, still trying to get adjusted to Earth." He handed his duffel bag to the driver, who had come out to meet them.

Jin opened the door of the SUV. "J.T., we will need to keep to a tight schedule to have any hope of rendezvousing with Ryugu."

"I realize that, and I'll get it together."

Chindarkar said, "He's working on it, Han."

They all got into the SUV and rode in uncomfortable silence for a minute or so. Chindarkar noticed that Tighe still seemed bleary-eyed. She touched the back of her hand to his forehead. "Maybe you caught something since you've been back. It's been a while since we've been exposed to planet-side germs."

He turned to her. "I'm fine. I just need a good night's sleep."

After a drive of only a few miles in light traffic, the SUV passed through a gate and onto a fenced lawn less than a mile from the Luxembourg airport. To Chindarkar's surprise, the vehicle rolled across grass toward a looming silhouette.

Tighe muttered, "What in the . . . ?"

They all leaned forward to peer out the windshield.

Instead of the private jet they were expecting, there was an *airship*, tied down not on a tarmac but on a broad stretch of lawn. It towered over the SUV. The massive craft was decidedly sleeker and more modern than the airships

Chindarkar recalled seeing in historic news reels. Instead, this one had a lifting-body shape. The name "Eos" was painted in stylized letters on the stern rudder. Solar panels gleamed along its top and sides in the dawn light. Several electrically powered props within computer-controlled nacelles whirred as they adjusted themselves to keep the airship stable just a meter or so above the ground. A dozen tether lines traced down from points on the hull to elaborate spikes in the turf.

As the SUV came to a stop, they got out and stared up at the craft.

Yak smiled to himself. "Interesting. I have traveled in most flying machines, but not yet dirigible."

Jin scanned its length. "Dirigibles lack a superstructure—which this definitely has." He pointed. "This is an airship."

An open ramp led up to a long cupola grafted beneath the gas envelope. The cupola was easily 40 meters long with dozens of windows.

Uniformed porters approached in a golf cart, rolling to a stop alongside the SUV. "Good morning. May we stow your luggage?"

The driver popped the SUV's trunk and the porters got busy. One of them glanced up. "Please proceed to the gangway. We'll place the bags in your cabins."

Chindarkar fell in alongside Tighe as they crossed the lawn toward the behemoth. "Our *cabins*, he says. And here I thought we were going to be in a cramped private jet."

Behind them Jin said, "It will take us *days* to cross Africa in this thing."

Tighe glanced back to him. "So much for the schedule."

Chindarkar was first up the gangway, where a smiling steward in a jacket and tie met them with a tray of pastries on white linen. "*God morgen*, and welcome aboard the *Eos*."

"Thank you . . ." Chindarkar took a croissant. "What does *Eos* mean?"

"Eos was the Greek goddess of the dawn—sister of Helios, god of the Sun, and Selene, goddess of the Moon."

"How poetic." She gazed along the length of the massive vessel. "Frankly, I'm surprised that an eco-entrepreneur like Mr. Hanssen would own such an enormous personal aircraft."

The steward was unfazed. "Marius believes that living well, responsibly, is the most compelling case for environmentalism. Unlike a jet aircraft, this is a zero-carbon-emission vehicle, with interior amenities constructed from repurposed materials. Due to its onboard solar array, it can also recharge while still airborne." He stepped aside to allow Chindarkar to enter. "I think you will find her very comfortable."

The team moved inside to behold an astonishing foyer and sitting area—with broad windows arrayed beyond railings to maximize viewing angles, outward and downward. A peaked ceiling with soft, diffuse chandelier lights, and half a dozen sofas with coffee tables in tasteful woods and muted whites and earth tones. A fully stocked bar with several stools stood just beyond. It looked like the salon of a super yacht—but one that sailed the sky.

"Wow . . ."

Tighe gestured behind them.

The others turned sternward to see a narrow hallway lined with doors and the glass wall of a conference room at the far end.

It was from this direction that Lukas Rochat approached, dressed as usual in a tailored suit. A young Latino man in a collared shirt and jacket trailed behind him. "Did you remember your passports?"

Jin glowered at Rochat. "We are not children, Lukas."

"Years in deep space may have made you forget that borders still matter down here."

Chindarkar leaned around Rochat to lock eyes with the Latino man—who was small in stature and seemed introverted. She extended her hand. "Hi. I'm Priya."

Rochat stepped aside. "Sorry. I thought you'd already met. This is Ramón Marín, our new director of systems architecture."

Tighe said, "We *have* met."

Chindarkar and Jin shook his hand. "Good to meet you, Ramón."

"He's coming with us to Ascension—to enter the orbital certification program, since we'll eventually need his skill set in orbit. If all goes well."

"It's a great honor to meet you all." Marín spoke English with a pronounced Spanish accent.

She asked, "Where are you from?"

"Venezuela. Originally."

"And what is it you do?"

Rochat answered for him. "He designs and maintains data systems and communications. Among other things . . ." He turned to Marín. "If you'll excuse us, Ramón."

"Of course. Again, I look forward to working with you all." He nodded to them and moved off, entering one of the doors along the hallway.

Chindarkar looked after him. "He seems nice—although, you should let him do his own talking, Lukas."

"Perhaps later."

Chindarkar sat down on a sofa and looked around. "This is really nice." She took a bite of the croissant.

Tighe and Yak moved forward, past the bar area.

Just then a man in a black flight uniform and peaked hat approached from the pilothouse at the bow. He extended his hand to Tighe. "Welcome aboard. I'm Captain Bernsen." He shook hands, first with Tighe, then Yak. "We will be departing in a few minutes. The forecast calls for light winds and clear skies down through France. So it should be lovely sailing today."

Jin asked, "How long will the flight to Lagos take?"

"Depending on winds, our journey should take approximately a day and a half. We'll be departing France near Marseilles, out over the Mediterranean to Algeria, then Niger, and finally western Nigeria. Estimated arrival in Lagos on Saturday afternoon."

Jin turned to Rochat. "Depending on winds . . ."

Rochat said, "I realize you may find this mode of transport archaic, Han, but climate change has made casual jet travel problematic. Private jets have their tail numbers read at almost every airport—the fliers shamed in social media. And our host—and main investor—Marius Hanssen takes carbon sequestration very seriously."

Yak pointed out the window. "Look at that . . ."

They all turned to see one of the airship's rope lines anchored in the grass suddenly rise as the spike at its end took flight. It was apparently a lawnmower-sized octocopter drone with an auger at its base that it used to burrow into the ground. It—and several other drones like it—were reversing their augers and lifting off, coiling their rope lines in as they went, preparing to dock back onto the hull of the mothership.

Yak observed this with interest. "Tether lines handled by drones. Clever." He accepted a steaming coffee in a porcelain cup and saucer from the steward. A silver urn was placed on the table before him. "Slow or not, I could get used to this type of travel."

After a few more minutes of preparation, the electric motors of the airship revved outside, and the vessel moved forward, lifting up and away from the ground smoothly, gently.

Tighe took note of the silver coffeepot standing on the table in front of him as they ascended gradually. It barely quivered. The storybook medieval streets of Luxembourg City came into view in the downward-angled windows nearby.

The team busied themselves sightseeing for the next twenty minutes or so as the airship cruised southward in the dawn light over a patchwork of fields, forests, and villages. The countryside below was serene and picturesque. The flight was smooth, and the sky dotted with just a few puffs of white clouds, whose ceiling they gradually approached.

Rochat spoke to the nearby steward. "Can you please serve breakfast in the conference room in approximately one hour?"

"Of course, Mr. Rochat."

He turned to the others. "Since we have this travel time, let's use it for confidential business. There's a great deal we need to discuss." Rochat motioned for them to follow.

The team moved aft along a hallway of numbered cabin doors and toward the glass-walled conference room.

CHAPTER 4

Master Plan

As they entered the airship's conference room, Priya Chindarkar walked around a long table ringed by a dozen chairs, with windows to either side providing breathtaking aerial views. She gazed at the ground far below. "This is really something."

Lukas Rochat tapped a button near the door to lower translucent shades. "And more secure against eavesdropping than our corporate offices. Let's get started."

They all took their seats, with Rochat claiming the head of the table.

Rochat opened his dispatch case and placed a Rubik's Cube–sized electronic device on the table beside him. He spoke to it. "Commence stenographer mode. Inaugural board meeting, Catalyst Corporation 2.0. Quorum requirements met. In attendance are board members . . ." He pointed, apparently for the benefit of the system's integral camera. ". . . Priya Chindarkar, Jin Han, James Tighe, Sevastian Yakovlev, and myself. Proxy votes—Isabel Abarca by Jin Han. Adedayo Adisa by Priya Chindarkar. Documentation on file."

Rochat glanced around the table. "Those here in attendance collectively represent 63.64 percent of voting shares in Catalyst Corporation. As the chief executive officer, I hereby open this meeting of the board of directors."

Rochat passed out folders. "The first item on the agenda is our plan for getting you all back into space to secure our resources in lunar orbit. Toward that end, I move that we accept an invitation to meet with representatives of the United States government at Cape Canaveral Space Force Station in Florida."

Jin frowned. *"Space Force?"*

"Space Force Station is merely the location, Han. We'll be meeting with numerous officials."

"But why meet with the US government at all? We should buy seats on one of Macy's or Burkette's commercial rockets. They routinely launch crews into low Earth orbit."

Rochat replied, "And both of them launch out of the Cape—meaning you'd still need FAA clearance."

"Then launch us out of Kourou, French Guiana, like I did back in 2032. We have the money to pay our way."

"*Nathan Joyce* had the money to pay your way to orbit in '32, but right now our funding is contingent on Catalyst establishing legal title to those asteroid resources in lunar orbit." Rochat looked around the table. "And that legal title has yet to be established here on Earth."

Tighe said, "I thought that was what the *Konstantin*'s Luxembourg registry was for—to give us rights to what we mined in space."

"Yes, but the *Konstantin* expedition was not, strictly speaking, legal. Meaning the provenance of those resources is still in question. Even in Luxembourg."

"We mined those resources. We refined them and brought them back to lunar orbit. Three of our friends *died* doing it. Those resources wouldn't exist without us."

"All true, J.T., but those resources are also a major strategic objective in the current space race between the US and China. Both of their mining operations at the lunar south pole, in Shackleton Crater, have so far produced only a tiny fraction of material compared to what you brought back from Ryugu. So at the moment our 5,000 tons of propellant and refined metals in lunar orbit are *the* prize in this astropolitical competition for control of cislunar space. They can greatly expand orbital operations of whichever country gains control of them. So expect considerable political pressure for us to pick a side, and know that we will make enemies of whomever we reject. Either way, we are going to have to negotiate with a spacefaring nation for your return to space."

Jin frowned. "You already seem to have chosen the United States."

Tighe gave him the side-eye. "Would you prefer we choose the CCP?"

"That is not the point. I want to avoid entanglement with either superpower."

"Han, the Space Coast in Florida is the cheapest, most reliable *crewed* mission launch site there is, and without US government approval, you are not getting back into orbit from any spaceport in the Western world. The EU will not defy Washington on this."

"Can we not gain orbit as we did last time?"

"You mean through deceit?"

"I mean through plausible cover—taking an orbital training program. Satellite servicing or—"

Rochat shook his head. "There's far too much attention on all of you this time around. It's no secret why you want to regain orbit." He paused. "And there's an additional reason for us to go to Cape Canaveral—a contact of mine within NASA has reached out to personally request a meeting there."

Tighe asked, "What contact?"

"NASA's liaison to the private space industry—a program executive named Erika Lisowski. She worked secretly with Nathan for years—and was aware of the *Konstantin* expedition from the very start."

Yak seemed suddenly intrigued.

Chindarkar cast a wary look toward Rochat. "The fact that she worked with Nathan is a strike *against* her as far as I'm concerned."

Tighe nodded. "Priya's right. Why would we trust her?"

Yak answered before Rochat could. "Because she saved your lives."

They all turned to him in surprise.

Yak continued. "After Nathan's embezzlement was discovered—and after he flew stunt plane into tarmac—she gave us critical information. Without her, after Nathan's death, we would not have been able to return you to Earth."

Chindarkar recalled Yak's capcom role back on Earth while they were at Ryugu. He was privy to things the *Konstantin* crew was not.

Rochat added, "Yak is right. She broke laws to save you all."

Tighe considered this. "And this Lisowski person wants to meet?"

"She asked for us to meet with the US government, yes."

Chindarkar asked, "Would they be willing to give us access to the Lunar Gateway as a base of operations?"

Jin shook his head. "The Lunar Gateway is off-limits to Chinese nationals."

Chindarkar said, "And China's *Chang'e* lunar station is off-limits to Americans."

Yak shrugged. "It does not matter. Neither has spin-gravity, so neither are suitable long-term habitats from which we can work."

"For the sake of argument, let's say we find somewhere to operate in space—what are we building up there?" Chindarkar looked around the table.

Tighe said, "A rescue ship."

"What kind of ship? How big? Where do we get the design? It's got to be at least as capable as the *Konstantin* was—which means spin-gravity. Able to bring us how many millions of kilometers out and back?"

Jin replied, "Ryugu's next swing by Earth occurs in July 2042, but it only comes within 60 million kilometers this time."

Tighe whistled. "That's ten times the distance we traveled outbound in the *Konstantin*."

Chindarkar did the math. "And 10 million kilometers farther than our return trip—we burned through a thousand tons of fuel to get that tiny spacecraft up to the velocity we did."

Yak said, "Propellant we have."

Jin pondered this. "Nathan's team at Lunargistics took many years to design the *Konstantin*, but the actual construction in lunar orbit required only two years. Perhaps we could reuse their existing design to save time."

Yak said, "What is minimum acceleration outbound to encounter Ryugu in 2042?"

Jin answered immediately. "A delta-v of about 4.9 kilometers per second, but there's another 2 kilometers per second to rendezvous with the asteroid. We should aim for twice that total to reduce transit time. Otherwise, we'll be facing too much radiation exposure."

Chindarkar looked skeptical. "For a vessel the size of the *Konstantin*? That'll take huge amounts of propellant."

Rochat cleared his throat. "You're forgetting something. Setting aside the fact that our current investors would not be keen on your plundering the resources of this company to launch a rescue—"

Tighe interrupted. "Don't even start with that, Lukas."

Jin piped in. "We are rescuing Isabel and Ade."

Chindarkar leaned forward. "Guys, let's hear him."

Rochat held up his hands. "Be that as it may. You have a more prosaic obstacle to contend with . . ." He activated a software-defined light projector on the table before them. A holographic screen materialized, displaying a manifest of the resources the team had returned from Ryugu via robotic tugs. Each of the tugs was named after one of their fallen colleagues and consisted of a bundle of spherical polymer tanks containing various refined materials.

First shipment	Metric tons	Second shipment	Metric tons
water	720	water	3,000
ammonia	120	ammonia	500
nitrogen	140	nitrogen	550
iron	40	iron	200
nickel	36	nickel	180
cobalt	26	cobalt	100
Total tonnage	**1,082**	**Total tonnage**	**4,530**

He pointed. "Our two robot tugs currently accessible in lunar orbit total about 5,600 tons of payload, plus silica and polymer superstructures of about 500 tons more. But over half the total payload is water ice—3,700 tons; about a million US gallons. Another 600 and 700 tons are ammonia and nitrogen, respectively." He highlighted the next lines with a pointer. "And just a thousand tons of materials you can build with, a bit over half of that in metals. The rest is silica and polymers."

Chindarkar said, "So? That's a thousand tons—a couple times the mass of the *Konstantin*."

"Yes, but the *Konstantin* was constructed of ultralight composites launched up from Earth, not the iron, nickel, and cobalt you currently have in orbit. Look at the mass of the small return craft you built out of cobalt steel—60 tons. Yet, we've got less than 600 tons of metal to work with. Not enough mass to build a ship comparable to the *Konstantin*. Not out of iron and nickel. And polymer won't be strong enough for spin-gravity."

Jin pondered this, then said, "We have a third shipment en route. Thirteen hundred tons more of metal carbonyls."

"Not yet, you don't. The *Amy Tsukada* is still parked out near Ryugu. Its rocket engines aren't set to fire until March 17, 2039—the next low-delta-v return window. And one or more of its engines could fail to ignite."

Jin nodded in agreement. "Of course, Lukas is right. We cannot rely upon its arrival."

Rochat continued. "Even if the rockets fire perfectly, it won't arrive in cislunar space until December 2041—just six months before your rescue mission must depart for Ryugu. And remember: Where in cislunar orbit are you going to be based to build this new rescue ship? Don't suggest the Hotel LEO or any of the other commercial space stations in low Earth orbit, because we all know that bringing thousands of tons of resources that close to Earth would risk their being seized by a sovereign power—and whatever you built in LEO would have to be propelled back out of Earth's gravity well all over again."

Rochat studied the faces around the table. "You don't have enough building material to rescue Isabel and Ade, but even if you did, you wouldn't have anything at all left over to establish a cislunar economy—which was the whole point of the expedition and the cause for which Nicole, David, and Amy sacrificed their lives."

The group sat in sober silence, while the airship's electric motors droned outside.

Rochat concluded, "No, if you are going to have any hope of rescuing Isabel and Ade, you're going to need more resources in orbit than you currently have. Much more."

Jin leveled a serious gaze. "What are you proposing, Lukas?"

"Here's what we need to do . . ." Rochat gestured and a holographic 3D model materialized beside him. It depicted a diagram of the Earth and the Moon, with the Moon's orbit and Lagrange points highlighted—in short, Earth's celestial neighborhood.

He clicked a remote and a dot appeared somewhat beyond the Moon. "You're all familiar with Lagrange points—the five points of gravitational equilibrium that occur within any two-body—"

Chindarkar interrupted. "Lukas, please. You hardly need to explain Lagrange points to us."

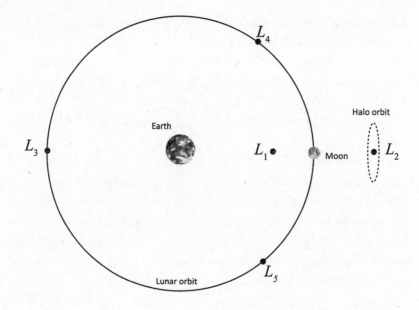

Rochat nodded. "Yes . . . Well, what I propose is that we utilize the resources you've returned from Ryugu to first build—not a rescue ship—but a spin-gravity *station* at the L2 point." The 3D model zoomed in to the L2 point beyond the Moon to reveal a wheel-like rotating space station that seemed to dwarf the *Konstantin*.

Tighe exclaimed, "Wait a minute. If we don't have the mass to build a rescue ship, how do we have the mass to build a whole space station? And why would we?"

"I will explain how—"

Jin interjected, "Where did this design come from?"

Rochat turned. "The same German team that designed the *Konstantin*."

"Lunargistics? Under whose direction? And with what money?"

Yak piped in. "Han is right. I thought new Catalyst Corporation only recently acquired funds."

Rochat sighed. "Can you at least let me finish outlining my plan?"

"*Your* plan?" Jin gestured to the model. "No offense, Lukas, but I am an aerospace engineer. Yak is an astronautical engineer. You are an *attorney*."

Rochat cast a look his way. "A *space* attorney—astro esquire."

Chindarkar replied, "What you are is our legal representative here on Earth. You're not a mission planner."

"I worked closely with Nathan Joyce for several years, and I learned a great many things from him."

"So this is *Nathan's* plan?"

Rochat paused, then held up his hands. "Now, wait. Hear me out."

The entire team groaned.

Jin shoved his folder away. "You are proposing we use a plan conceived by the pathological liar who sent us out into space without enough fuel to get back?"

Tighe added, "And who financed the expedition by embezzling from dictators and criminal syndicates—people who later tried to kill us?"

Rochat nodded. "I acknowledge that under Nathan Joyce's leadership Catalyst Corporation was less than transparent. However—"

The group groaned again in response.

Chindarkar said, "Were you really expecting to pass Nathan's plan off as your own, Lukas? And did you think that we would accept it?"

Rochat put the remote down. "What I was expecting is that you would immediately reject any plan if I told you it was Nathan's."

"Then you expected right."

"Well, if you're so convinced this plan is foolish, then I guess you don't want to see Nathan's video presentation."

They were all taken aback.

Tighe scowled. "*Video presentation?* What video presentation?"

Rochat searched through his device's UI. "Your expedition to Ryugu was merely *phase one* of Catalyst Corporation's master plan. Nathan also prepared a phase two—which he detailed in an investor video. A video I found among the files he left behind. I believe it was intended to attract a second round of funding in the event phase one was successful."

The team exchanged looks.

Chindarkar raised her eyebrows. "Well, we returned resources to lunar orbit. So phase one *did* succeed."

Jin bristled. "Except for the minor detail of our crewmates dying."

Tighe added, "Phase two might just finish us off."

The group sat in silence for several moments.

But then Yak said, "Frankly, now I am curious. Should we not at least watch this video?"

Jin turned toward him, appalled. "Are you joking? Nathan sent us into deep space with no way to return."

"And yet return you did. One might say Nathan had faith in you."

"Easy to say—since you did not go, Yak."

"Only because I did not make final cut. I would have gone. You know this."

Jin eventually nodded. In fact, as an ex-cosmonaut maxed out on radiation exposure, Yak seemed more at home in space than any of them.

Chindarkar looked to Jin. "Han, we refined the propellant to make it back. No doubt that's what Nathan was counting on."

"But what if we couldn't have? Do not try to defend Nathan."

Yak said, "No one here would—but there could be useful designs in this 'phase two' of Nathan's plan. He clearly had engineers working on more than just *Konstantin*. The spin-gravity space station Lukas showed us looks promising. Perhaps years of design work. Years we do not have to spare."

After a moment Rochat waded into the silence. "Look, I'll just press play, and you can tell me when to stop . . ." He clicked a button on his remote.

A virtual video screen projected into thin air at the end of the boardroom table. Text appeared on a white background in plain Arial typeface, as if a rough edit:

Catalyst Corporation Master Plan

Phase Two

06/20/2034

ver 0.391

Chindarkar observed, "Seven months after we left . . ."

Suddenly the handsome face of the late, thirty-something billionaire Nathan Joyce replaced the info card. He sat on the edge of his desk in his bookshelf-lined study back on Baliceaux Island, viewed in medium close-up. It was like seeing a ghost—a ghost who had changed the course of all their lives.

Joyce nodded toward the camera. *"What I'm going to share with you today*

*will make your other investments seem quaint by comparison—both in scope
and in potential reward. We stand at the threshold of a new era. An energy
and resource expansion greater than that experienced during the first Age
of Exploration between 1400 and 1650 AD."*

Joyce stood and walked up to a mounted model of the spaceship
Konstantin—a ship that in real life this particular audience had ridden to
the far side of the Sun.

*"With the proven success of Catalyst Corporation's historic mining opera-
tion at the asteroid Ryugu, thousands of tons of highly valuable commodities
are now available for use in the vicinity of our Moon—many billions of dollars'
worth and hundreds of rocket launches if they were sent up from Earth. And
there are 450 million tons more where that came from.*

*"Asteroid mining is now TRL-8-proven technology. In addition to the re-
sources we've returned, Catalyst also owns scores of now highly valuable
patents and enjoys unparalleled experience in crewed operations, spin-
gravity, and radiation shielding in deep space. And yet, we are just getting
started. In fact, we are now ready to execute the next phase of Catalyst Corporation's master plan."*

A placeholder card appeared, reading: STOCK VIDEO OF NATURAL DI-
SASTERS.

*"Make no mistake, Earth markets are growth-constrained, grappling with
the disruption of climate change and all its attendant calamities—drought,
storms, floods, pandemics, supply-chain and political chaos, uncontrolled
migrations, rising ocean levels, resource conflicts—over both water and arable land. Meanwhile, out in space, we have no such limitations. Instead, we
will be creating entire new domains and industries that can help Earth restore
its natural climate and its general prosperity—as well as initiating a rapid
industrial expansion that could persist for many thousands of years. For us,
the sky is just the beginning."*

The video cut back to Joyce, who held up a cautionary finger. *"But how do
we execute on this celestial expansion? Precisely how will Catalyst Corporation utilize the asteroid resources we have in lunar orbit to make this new era
of Earth prosperity a reality?"* He paused for effect. *"Let me show you . . ."*

A view of space filled the virtual screen, and a familiar robot tug passed
into view—a spacecraft the team in this room had built in reality and

christened the *Nicole Clarke*. The image panned to reveal the spacecraft was headed toward Earth's moon.

"*At present, we alone possess resources in a trajectory and in the refined physical form necessary to commence game-changing, large-scale construction in cislunar space. And by moving first, we will have immense standards-making power—in deep space communications, transport infrastructure, logistics, cislunar finance, market-making, energy systems, life support systems, and much more.*

"*That's why Catalyst Corporation—the unrivaled pioneer in asteroid mining—will counterintuitively utilize the first resources we've returned from an asteroid to accelerate the mining of Earth's moon. In fact, near-Earth asteroid mining was a prerequisite of our lunar mining plan...*"

The image zoomed down to the lunar south pole, focusing on Shackleton Crater and terrain features labeled "Peaks of Eternal Light."

"*China and the US are currently engaged in intense competition over the water ice and carbon dioxide traps within the strategic, permanently shadowed craters at the lunar south pole.*"

The image showed the lights of two lunar bases at the rim of the crater in proximity to each other.

Joyce continued. "*These efforts are occurring in an operating environment just 21 kilometers across and are fraught with political and military peril. Yes, millions of tons of water ice exist in Shackleton Crater and in the surrounding craters; however, there is some degree of water chemically bound in all lunar regolith, and the logistical complications of mining Shackleton ice—both in dealing with off-planar, lunar polar orbits, as well as the astropolitical tensions in this confined, strategic location—make it a region that Catalyst intends to avoid. Instead, we have more ambitious plans made possible by the asteroid resources now at our disposal...*"

The image zoomed back out and centered on the lunar equator, marked by a blue line girding the Moon.

"*It is our contention that, except for scientific and commercial outposts, the Moon should not be colonized by humanity. Lunar surface operations should be, wherever possible, unmanned and automated, with the goal to cost-effectively launch vast amounts of material from the lunar surface up into orbit, where it can be used to build and operate at scale in open space.*

Humanity should, in short, avoid gravity wells wherever possible until we establish a formidable industrial, energy, and transportation infrastructure out in our solar system. To achieve this, we're going to need mass. Not just tens of thousands of tons—but millions and billions of tons.

"*The nature of the contest for cislunar space—whether Earth powers realize it or not—is that the entity with the most mass on-orbit first, wins. Ryugu provided us crucial seed material at low delta-v costs, which we can now use to gain rapid, cost-effective access to the vast resources of our Moon. We do that by building the first substantial, permanent, human habitat from which to operate long-term in deep space. And we build it in a halo orbit around L2, 60,000 kilometers past the Moon.*"

With that, the scene changed to a 3D model of cislunar space, with a dot on the far side of the Moon labeled "L2." The image zoomed in to reveal the dot as the robot tug spacecraft.

"*Using the resources we now have in lunar orbit, we will construct the first portion of what will eventually become a much larger spin-gravity space station, but which for the moment will remain only partially completed.*"

The robot tug transformed into the same ring-like space station Rochat had shown earlier—although naked beams and girders encompassed most of its circumference. Nonetheless it began rotating.

"*Orbiting L2 at this distance still gives us line of sight to both Earth and the Moon's far side, but also provides low delta-v transitions from cislunar to deep space, helping to facilitate continued flow of both asteroid and lunar resources. When finished, this EM-L2 station will be able to host not just our operations, but those of dozens of astropreneur startups, executing their own business plans with the resources and energy we will make available to them—in exchange for pre-IPO stock in their firms.*"

The station model expanded to include a central axis upon which enclosures and inscrutable machinery appeared. Antenna masts sprouted from one end.

"*This station will also serve as a base for teleoperations from which we'll construct a reliable and abundant energy source in the form of a 200-ton, 50-megawatt solar power satellite—or SPS—capable of transmitting electrical power over great distances using microwaves.*"

The image zoomed out as an animation showed the construction of a gossamer-like structure made of faceted mirrors that was nearly as large as the space station itself.

"This SPS is not meant to power the space station. Instead..."

A small spacecraft docked with the solar power satellite and towed it around to the other side of the Moon, facing Earth.

"... we will relocate this satellite to a halo orbit around L1, setting the stage for lunar surface operations."

The spacecraft detached from the solar power satellite and then descended toward the lunar surface.

"Unlike competing mining efforts centered at the lunar poles, Catalyst Corporation intends to engage in undifferentiated regolith collection on the lunar equator at roughly 33.1 degrees longitude—close by Cape Bruce and Maskelyne-A Crater, roughly 3,000 kilometers from the nearest crewed lunar base—and far away from astropolitical competition. Here there exist vast mares of powdered surface regolith more than 2 meters deep, rich in iron, oxygen, silicon, and aluminum, but also containing a low percentage of water in the form of hydrates, as well as titanium, calcium, magnesium, sodium, potassium, and also trace amounts of phosphorus, thorium, uranium, and rare Earth metals.

"We will not be refining this material on the Moon's surface. Instead, we will harvest it, and transport it directly into orbit. But more on that later..."

As the lunar lander descended, a vast gray plain with hills in the distance filled the screen. The animation depicted the robotic lander touching down, a scouring cloud of dust radiating away from it until the rocket cut out. Cranes on the lander lowered wheeled robots that ventured forth to erect a large net-like grid on poles.

"After deploying a rectenna to receive microwave energy from the satellite in a Lissajous orbit overhead, our lunar base will have access to uninterrupted power, even during the two-week-long lunar night."

The animation then showed wheeled robots with bulldozer blades extending a road away from the base.

"Construction equipment directly teleoperated by personnel on the L2 station will build a permanent landing pad along with a surrounding berm to receive future lunar landers."

The animation showed new lunar landers arriving with additional equipment and materials, which the robots then unloaded.

"Setting the stage for the main project: construction of a lunar electromagnetic launch—or LEML—system, a 1.4-kilometer-long 'mass-driver' track running eastward along the lunar equator. In the near perfect vacuum of the Moon—and with access to 50 megawatts of on-demand power from our lunar-stationary satellite overhead—this mass-driver will enable us to accelerate bricks of lunar regolith past the Moon's escape velocity up to 2.53 kilometers per second without the need for chemical propellant, hurling them into orbit on an achromatic trajectory . . ."

The animation zoomed out as a glowing-hot slug launched along a track to arc over the hemisphere of the Moon, reaching tens of thousands of kilometers back to L2, where it slowed and cooled, its energy expended, and floated within the gravitational equilibrium of the Lagrange point.

". . . all the way back toward L2 and the vicinity of our space station."

The image zoomed back in to the ring-shaped space station, where a spinning, cone-shaped spacecraft scooped up the bricks of lunar regolith.

"Once completed, our lunar mass-driver will be capable of hurling a 10-kilogram brick into orbit every two seconds—totaling 157,000 tons of resource-rich material per year—where it will be collected and refined at our L2 space station."

The image cut back to Joyce in his office. He strolled again toward his desk. *"With this extraordinary wealth of new lunar material available to us in cislunar space, Catalyst will be able to vastly expand our capabilities—including building additional mass-drivers and solar power satellites to further expand our raw materials and propellant supply chain, and also in building new asteroid mining spacecraft to exploit still more near-Earth asteroids."*

Joyce walked past his desk and stood next to a model of an elongated tether with a gondola on one end and a counterweight on the other.

"But Catalyst will also be in a position to build a comprehensive cislunar transportation infrastructure, enabling cost-effective and sustainable launches from Earth as well as travel to and from LEO, GEO, and lunar orbits. We will achieve this through a series of 3,000-ton, 500-kilometer-long

rotating skyhooks in low Earth orbit, as well as rotating tether assemblies in higher orbits to transfer their momentum into customer payloads, sending them to desired cislunar destinations—either higher or lower in orbit."

Here an animation showed a long, thin structure rotating like a lawn mower blade as it orbited Earth. It had an off-center axis of rotation, with a cupola at the end of the longer span, which dipped down into the Earth's atmosphere briefly as the structure orbited past it—causing its tip, labeled "skyhook," to momentarily pause before rotating back up into orbit again. At the apex of its trajectory, the skyhook appeared to fling a dot of payload onto a higher trajectory, where it was soon intercepted by a synchronized rotating tether in upper orbit.

Joyce narrated. *"The technologies and materials to build these tethers are well understood—Spectra and Zylon polyethylene fibers woven with aluminum wire can handle the forces involved. All that is required to deploy them is the mass, production capacity, and propellant in orbit—all of which we will have."*

The animation zoomed in to a sleek aircraft taking off from an airport and accelerating through the Earth's atmosphere. *"Through the use of current scramjet aircraft intercepting a skyhook at 100 kilometers altitude, we can lift 14 tons of cargo from Earth to anywhere in cislunar space at a fraction of the cost of a reusable rocket. Later generations of skyhooks and scramjets will be able to lift still more. This will allow us to launch people and specialty equipment not yet producible in space up into orbit, and to do so more cheaply, safely, and with much less damage to the environment than traditional rockets. However, we have more urgent markets to address here on Earth . . ."*

The image cut back to Joyce as he walked up to a model of a solar power satellite identical to the one in his Moon mining animation.

". . . namely in energy. As we build out the cislunar transport network, Catalyst will also use our growing inventory of resources in orbit to build truly massive solar power satellites—each capable of transmitting to the Earth's surface not just 50 megawatts, but 2 or more gigawatts of electricity."

The image zoomed in to depict the construction of a chandelier-like solar power satellite similar to the one that powered the lunar mass-driver; however, this one dwarfed the equipment and people constructing it.

"*These 7,500-ton behemoths—3 kilometers wide by 5 kilometers tall with microwave transmitters over a kilometer in diameter—can be placed in geostationary orbit, beaming clean, sustainable energy 24 hours a day down to 7-kilometer-wide rectennas on the Earth's surface. The beam can also be split to supply different cities without the need to run high-voltage power lines over land. Likewise, the beam can be redirected in milliseconds to serve cities in need, allowing grid operators near-instant load balancing.*"

The animation showed the huge satellite being maneuvered to geostationary orbit, 36,000 kilometers above Earth.

"*At present, global civilization requires approximately 22 terawatts of constant energy to function, but the UN estimates at least 55 terawatts will be needed by 2100 AD. The only way to satisfy that demand in an increasingly chaotic world is by beaming energy down from space.*"

The image zoomed out to show more solar power satellites populating geostationary orbit.

"*Fortunately, 332 terawatts can be drawn from the geosynchronous belt, safely populated with solar power satellites.*"

Joyce once more stood next to his solar power satellite model.

"*By constructing a mass-driver on the Moon's surface and establishing the infrastructure for cislunar industry, Catalyst Corporation is poised to deliver on cost-effective, sustainable space transportation and unlimited space-based energy, and in the process to also become the largest transport and energy firm in human history.*

"*But it doesn't end there. Atmospheric CO_2 is already approaching four hundred and fifty parts per million, a level that last occurred six million years ago, on an almost alien Earth wholly unsuited to Homo sapiens and the animals and crop plants we depend upon for our survival. The most optimistic studies predict that climate change will shave an estimated 20 percent off global GDP by 2100 AD—an economic loss of two thousand trillion dollars. If we want to return our economy and climate to normalcy by restoring Earth to preindustrial levels of CO_2, then we must actually pull CO_2 out of the atmosphere—and that will require even more energy. Vast amounts of it.*"

The screen showed renderings of an Earth-based power substation with arrays of fan housings pulling in ambient air.

"*Here, too, Catalyst is ready to leverage its spaceborne power solutions,* *beaming terawatts of energy down to surface CO_2-removal plants, essentially reversing combustion—and in the process creating flexible, efficient, carbon-neutral liquid fuels as a by-product, even as we reduce overall CO_2 concentrations in the atmosphere. Why is this important?"*

The screen depicted scenes of environmental devastation and pollution juxtaposed with high-tech electrical manufacturing.

"Because increased mining to obtain the lithium, cobalt, and rare Earth minerals used in electric vehicle production is devastating ecosystems worldwide, and also releasing vast amounts of carbon as forests are leveled and water sources polluted with heavy metals. Likewise, wind turbines, solar panels, batteries, and electric motors all require those same ecologically devastating rare Earth metals for their manufacture. It turns out that 'green energy' is not so green. At least, that is, unless Earth markets purchase our off-world-sourced cobalt and rare Earth minerals, which Catalyst's lunar mining operations will be able to supply."

The screen displayed the Earth ringed by a belt of solar power satellites in geosynchronous orbit, beaming invisible energy to Earth, while below, a massive tether rotated in low Earth orbit.

"Ready access to and from space and more clean energy than we can use on Earth—plus limitless energy and resources available for industry in space. That is the opportunity. Every expansionist stage in human history was sparked by either new modes of transport, vast increases in energy, or vast increases in resources. Our move into cislunar space will entail all three, and to a degree that will enable a multi-thousand-year continual economic expansion. That, or we continue on the path we are on. Ever-increasing chaos. Shortages. Conflict. And eventual extinction."

The image instead panned out into cislunar space, where a glittering celestial civilization was already taking shape.

"Yes, space will challenge us, have no doubt, but this is the very challenge humanity needs to cure us of our propensity for bullshit—because space is where bullshit goes to die. Out there only facts and competence keep you alive. Superstition, uneducated guesses, and comforting lies are what must go extinct. Not us."

The screen returned to a view of Joyce, standing next to his solar power satellite model. He walked back to sit on the edge of his desk.

"I wish there was a cataclysmic asteroid hurtling toward Earth, to spur us to this necessary task. Instead, we face risks of our own making, and our ability to reach space could disappear as we get consumed by Earthly crises. To reach this next stage of civilization—and to create unimaginable wealth for ourselves and for others—we must make this leap. And we must do it now, while the orbital window remains open to us. We may not get another chance." Joyce paused before he said, *"Join us . . ."*

With that, the screen went black, and the Catalyst Corporation logo slowly resolved from the void.

Rochat turned the screen off. He looked up.

The team sat in stunned silence.

Pointedly, no one had asked Rochat to stop the video.

Hours later, Chindarkar sat alone in a wraparound sofa upholstered in what she'd been told was "mushroom-derived leather." She gazed through a broad window in the floor of the airship—pondering the alpine city of Grenoble, France, passing by three thousand meters below. The view was breathtaking, with a fortress overlooking the city and a river winding along the foot of mountain cliffs. The ice-capped Alps loomed to the east and north.

Earth was so beautiful. Chindarkar felt gratitude to everyone and everything on it, and she'd felt this way ever since returning from space. Astronauts called this the *overview effect*. After years in deep space, she intimately understood just how rare and fragile the jewel of Earth was—the only place in the universe known to harbor life. In the entire vastness of space, all we had was each other. If only everyone in the world realized that.

Chindarkar thought about her family back in Mumbai. Her conservative, Kshatriya-caste parents had disowned her, their eldest daughter—had refused to accept her independent spirit. Since returning to Earth she had looked up her brothers and sisters on social media—peeked into their seemingly happy lives through photos of family gatherings. Her father's stern face in several of them. They had moved on without her as if she had died, and yet, here she was. Chindarkar knew that Tighe's situation was not unlike her own. Or Jin's, for that matter. Most of the *Konstantin* crew members were unlikely to be missed.

Yet, even though Chindarkar had been cast out of her own family, she was still part of the human family—and the family of all living things. Joyce's investor video had outlined a plan to rescue civilization from climate change, while also putting it on a path for centuries of prosperity. If what Joyce said was true and the fate of Earth's biosphere hung in the balance, then as a board member of Catalyst Corporation, she was in a position to act. In fact, she bore a responsibility to do so. This master plan was so much more than a rescue mission for Abarca and Adedayo.

Just then she noticed Jin approaching from the stern. He joined Chindarkar, sliding onto the curving sofa.

"Where are the others?" Chindarkar asked.

"J.T. went to his cabin—to catch up on sleep. But Yak and I have been going through the designs Nathan left behind. There is a lot. His people did years of work on phase two—the L2 station has electrical, life support, thermal management, waste, integrated SCADA systems, software—all of it already designed."

"There will still be problems. Glitches. You and I both know it."

"Yes, but that would be true for anything we design as well, and regardless of my personal opinion of Nathan, the *Konstantin* kept us alive in deep space for over four years."

She leaned forward, fists balled under her chin, gazing down at the terrain slowly passing by below. "I ran the numbers. Lukas is right; we don't have the resources in orbit to build a capable rescue ship. An unfinished lunar station and a mass-driver on the Moon's surface is arguably our best bet for obtaining what we need." She looked up. "Plus, it also lays the foundation for an entire off-world economy."

Jin thought for a moment. "No wonder Nathan pushed us for every ton we could put on those first shipments."

"L2 is a good location. From there we get low delta-v access to deep space, the Moon, and the Earth."

"Yes, but will China, Russia, and the US allow us to build this station?"

"Even if they do, how long would it take us?"

"To build the space station . . . the solar power satellite . . . and the mass-driver on the lunar surface. I figure several years at least."

"And we'd still have to build a rescue ship. Ryugu comes around again in just four years."

"It will be tight."

Chindarkar looked to him hopefully. "Others can help us. There's room for dozens of people on that space station—even in the partially completed initial portion."

Jin appeared to be reconciling himself to the plan. "We do need a spin-gravity station in deep space if we mean to stay in orbit for long. And no one else has one."

Chindarkar found herself nodding along with his thinking. Microgravity was not optional for months or years in space. "But where do we stay while we build the station?"

Jin said, "Earth. Lunargistics has a plan to use telepresence construction robots for most of the work—like they did with the *Konstantin*."

"So then we need permission from an Earth nation to launch telepresence construction robots."

They looked at each other.

Jin asked, "Why do you suppose Nathan did not build this mass-driver on the Moon to begin with, rather than go through with our *Konstantin* asteroid mission? Would it not have been easier?"

Chindarkar shook her head. "To launch all the mass we now have in orbit up from Earth? That would have cost more than twenty-four billion. Much more."

Jin added, "And they wouldn't have let him build it. Maybe they will stop us, too."

They sat considering this for several minutes as the beautiful landscape of Earth passed beneath them.

CHAPTER 5

Ajegunle

James Tighe awoke in his cabin in the early evening—unsure of what day it was. A wave of nausea came over him, and he raced to his en suite bathroom to vomit. The droning of the airship motors helped conceal his retching, but he ran the faucet just in case. When he finished, he cleaned up and went back to sit on the edge of the bed.

A little over a week and the chemo meds were already kicking his ass.

Tighe stared through the wide, downward-angled window. The sprawling city of Lagos, Nigeria, shimmered below in the twilight. It was unmistakably huge—thirty million people, and according to Lukas Rochat, the fastest-growing city in the world. Tighe knew that Adedayo Adisa had grown up somewhere down in that cauldron of ruthless competition, and Adisa's siblings and mother were there still, living in abject poverty. Helping Adisa's family was the very least the team could do.

If Tighe skipped his meds, perhaps he'd have the energy to go along when they landed tomorrow morning. He *needed* to go.

Tighe lay back down and sleep soon enveloped him once more.

The next morning, Tighe, Jin Han, Priya Chindarkar, Sevastian Yakovlev, and Rochat descended the airship gangway and emerged into harsh sunlight and withering humidity. The scent of smoke and trash immediately swept over them. It was an odor Tighe recalled from his many years in the less developed precincts of the world.

The *Eos* had landed in an unfinished business park built on a several-hundred-acre landfill jutting out into the Atlantic. The sandy peninsula was spiked by half-finished high-rise office buildings that already appeared to be decaying. The abortive waterfront development was lapped by ocean waves in places and crisscrossed by a semi-submerged grid of streets-to-nowhere, replete with sidewalks. The actual city skyline was visible a couple kilometers to the north.

Three black Range Rovers and a police van were parked near the airship, with a dozen or so armed men standing around. Meanwhile, two uniformed Nigerian customs officials spoke with Captain Bernsen as they examined the airship's documentation and the passengers' passports. These they stamped and returned after a cursory examination.

Tighe's energy levels were low, but he hoped that skipping his meds would see him through the day. He looked out at their security detail—a lean, sharp-looking crew of West Africans dressed in khakis and pastel polo shirts, most of whom carried black polymer submachine guns on single-point slings. But instead of looking toward Tighe, their eyes were cast outward, scanning for threats. They each wore radio earpieces. Clearly not a low-rent group. Probably a corporate security team.

Leave it to Rochat to overreact. The man was Swiss, after all. Nigeria probably seemed like a *Mad Max* film to him.

Rochat, himself, was dressed more casually than Tighe had ever seen him, and was busy stowing his passport in a zipper pocket before motioning to his companions. "Captain Bernsen will handle the rest. Let's get moving."

Tighe nodded toward the motorcade. "We're taking all of this?"

"Yes. Lagos is one of the most dangerous cities in Africa, and Ajegunle—Adisa's neighborhood—is its most dangerous district. Security is not optional."

Rochat advanced toward the head of the security team and extended his hand. "Mr. Tinubu, you come highly recommended."

Tinubu was a bald-headed, imposing man who extended his beefy hands for a two-handed shake. The cadence of his accent reminded Tighe of Adisa. "Mr. Rochat. It is a pleasure. The area boys will be no problem for you today. I assure you."

Tighe noticed that Yak was still on the gangway. "You coming?"

Yak shook his head. "I remain here in case of trouble."

"Capcom again?"

"For now, yes."

Tinubu opened the rear passenger door of a Range Rover and rapped his knuckles on the extra-thick doorframe. He looked to Rochat. "As you can see, your vehicle is armored. You will all be perfectly safe."

Visibly pleased, Rochat got inside. Tighe, Jin, and Chindarkar joined him.

Tighe leaned toward Rochat. "Couldn't find a tank?"

"I'd rather be prepared."

"In my experience the best defense is to fit in."

Tinubu got into the front passenger seat and spoke to Rochat. "We will bring you to the residence of Mrs. Adisa in Ajegunle. It is only a few klicks, but will take some time due to traffic."

With that, the motorcade accelerated rapidly. The roar of old internal combustion engines brought back memories from Tighe's childhood. Before long they reached the business park's front gates, and armed guards there waved them through. The motorcade then raced out onto the streets of Victoria Island and drove aggressively through moderate traffic, the lead vehicle making way by flashing their headlights and honking.

Chindarkar spoke to Tinubu. "Do we need to drive this fast?"

Tinubu craned his neck. "It is no problem, miss."

Tighe watched the waterfront roll past. As ramshackle as Lagos appeared, it was bustling; people moved about everywhere, most of them young, pushing hand wagons, driving electric scooters, or hawking wares. It was a hive of activity—none of it hyperefficient. But then, there were plenty of people to do it.

After ascending onto a brand-new elevated expressway, they crossed several harbor bridges at speed. In the distance stood sprawling factories whose buildings bore Chinese-character logos. Mandarin-language video billboards along the highway presented a fast-moving montage of products, showcasing the manufacturing expertise of various contract factories—everything from electronic components to textiles to plastics.

Rochat spoke to Tinubu. "I had no idea Nigeria had so much industry."

"Chinese-owned." He waved his hand. "All of this."

After a few kilometers their motorcade had crossed over water and exited the expressway to descend into a warren of dilapidated low-rise structures that stretched clear to the horizon. The reek of trash and shit enfolded them like a curtain. It was a stench so dense it made Tighe wince.

Tinubu pointed at a nearby brown waterway choked with trash. "It is the canal. City services are unfortunately lacking in this precinct."

It was the sort of understatement that made a mockery of the reality just beyond the window. The haze of smoke made it difficult to see far along the canal. Soon their vehicles got bogged down in surface street traffic as they headed deeper into the neighborhoods. Towering cranes indicated a container port close by. People walked and rode motorbikes around their SUV—but no one peered too closely into its tinted windows as it inched along in traffic.

Tighe noticed extremely thin video screens peppering wall surfaces in clusters here and there—silently playing advertisements on endless short loops. They were placed haphazardly, with pieces torn off here and there. "What's with the video screens everywhere?" A nearby ad scrolled Chinese letters.

Tinubu groaned. "Video stickers. They are a pestilence!"

Tighe tried to understand. "So . . . they're *stickers?*"

Rochat interjected. "Technology has moved on while you were away. Cheap, thin-film video screens that absorb wireless energy. Ad companies use them now. They're banned in the EU."

Jin made a face. "I can see why. They are awful."

Soon their motorcade inched down narrow lanes lined by apartment blocks—dingy, four-story buildings whose balcony railings and windowsills were festooned with clothes hanging out to dry and studded with small satellite dishes. Faded political posters and banners featuring the faces of local party bosses filled the gaps in between. The ground floors were populated with mobile phone stalls, bodegas with cases of bottled water piled high, and shops crowded with mannequin torsos featuring colorful garments. Tighe glanced up to see a large, soot-stained Christian cross, mounted on a railing. On the wall nearby someone had stenciled in bold white paint the English words: *This building not for sale. Beware of 419.*

He was about to ask Tinubu about it, when the lead Range Rover halted, sending their SUV to a jolting stop as well. Leaning forward, Tighe could see that a battered white police pickup truck blocked the road ahead. Uniformed officers stood around it with long guns.

Tinubu cursed under his breath and motioned to the driver. "Back up, and go around." But glancing backward, his face turned grim.

Tighe looked behind the SUV to see more policemen blocking the road, accompanied by men in street clothes carrying assault rifles. The men flanked a washed and waxed champagne-colored Bentley SUV, out of which stepped a Nigerian man in a blue silk shirt, slacks, and designer glasses. A gold chronograph glinted on his wrist.

Meanwhile, the street all around their motorcade rapidly emptied of pedestrians—who suddenly ducked into alleys and doorways. Shopkeepers pulled in merchandise and closed security shutters.

Rochat looked around nervously. "I thought we arranged for protection, Mr. Tinubu."

Tinubu waved off Rochat's comment. "There is nothing for it, Mr. Rochat. These are police. Clearly you have not been honest with me about your purpose here. I think this man will speak with you."

"What man?"

Looking through the rear window, Tighe studied the calm indifference of the man, who was now leaning against the Bentley's hood. Tighe had traveled enough in the world to recognize the situation they were in. He opened the door and stuck one foot out. "Everyone, stay in the car."

Rochat looked up. "You're going out there?"

Chindarkar said, "Lukas is right. We should stay together."

Tighe got out and peered back into the vehicle. "We're not leaving here until they let us. I'm going to see what they want." He closed the Range Rover door and started down the empty stretch of littered street toward the Bentley. Then he noticed that Jin was alongside him.

Jin spoke without taking his eyes off the armed men. "We never EVA alone, J.T. You know that."

Tighe cracked a slight smile and nodded. Of course Jin was right—and he was glad to have him. They closed the distance together. As they approached the Bentley, armed men to either side slid their fingers onto triggers.

The man leaning on the Bentley's hood suddenly spread his arms and smiled with perfect white teeth. "Mr. Jin. Mr. Tighe. I am so glad you came all the way from Luxembourg to visit Adedayo's mother. Your concern for her welfare is touching." His British-accented English was impeccable. His clothing immaculate.

Tighe said, "Let me guess: you must be Adedayo's *oga*."

The man raised his eyebrows. "I am impressed. Your familiarity with Lagosian culture saves us time."

Jin asked, "What do you want?"

"Merely what is mine, Mr. Jin."

Adisa had taught Tighe that the word *oga* defined a sort of boss figure in Lagos—a patron to whom one owed tribute. Adisa was just a skinny, self-taught, but supremely gifted hacker who'd been forced to join a cybercrime gang that ransomed satellites. This was how he had come to Nathan Joyce's attention, hijacking one of Catalyst's comsats on behalf of this gang. The same gang that later sold Adisa's name to Joyce. The gang presumably headed by the man now standing before them.

The oga continued. "Please appreciate that in Lagos no man is an island. I made Adedayo the man he is. He would be nothing without me."

Tighe concealed his rising anger.

"Adedayo's absence has cost me dearly, and Mr. Joyce's premature death left me without the compensation I was promised, and now I learn that Adedayo is not dead—but alive and in space. Earning good money. Thanks to me."

Jin said, "How do you know all this?"

"Because your communications are not secure. Not from us. You came in here thinking an armored car would protect you, but even now your phones broadcast your secrets."

Tighe said, "Everything Adedayo accomplished was due to his own intelligence and courage."

"I am certain Nigeria's National Space Research and Development Agency will be very proud of their Yoruba son. However, whatever Adedayo has earned in space rightfully belongs not to him, but to me."

Jin scowled. "By what right?"

"Adedayo and I have a legally binding contract." The oga extended his hand and a nearby man placed a clear tablet device in it. With a couple of gestures, the oga brought up a vibrant hologram that withstood even the light of day. It showed a Luxembourg government website. "I see here that Adedayo is listed as your company CTO. My people tell me that he also owns shares in this enterprise of yours—this 'Catalyst Corporation.'"

Jin surged forward to get in the oga's face. "Do not dare to—!"

Men to either side raised their weapons, and Tighe pulled Jin back. "Easy! Easy."

The oga remained calm. "You Chinese. You come to Africa, like the Europeans and Americans before you, and act as though you own our land and our people." Suddenly his expression softened, and he raised his hands. "But that is the way of the world, is it not? To live is to struggle. Your father is a great *oba*, Mr. Jin. So out of respect I will be forthright with you and claim only what is due me." He turned off the hologram. "Adedayo's shares in Catalyst Corporation must be transferred to a corporate entity that I control."

Tighe frowned. "Why would we *ever* do that?"

Jin added, "Or *how?* Those shares belong to Adedayo, not to us."

"They *belonged* to Adedayo; one of my companies is his sole heir."

"Heir? Ade is not dead."

"Adedayo has been missing for five years—and is now officially dead. My friends in the Nigerian National Population Commission made it so."

Tighe and Jin exchanged horrified looks.

"And I—not his family—inherit his holdings. In short: you and I are now business partners, gentlemen."

"We'll never agree to that," Tighe shot back.

The oga raised his eyebrows. "No?" He manipulated the tablet again and projected a holographic photo of a house. "Your attorney—hiding in that 'tank' over there—purchased this Victoria Island home, as a gift to Ms. Adisa and her children—Adedayo's brothers and sisters." He lowered the tablet. "Keep your house. Adedayo's family will have no need for it." He looked around at the ramshackle apartment buildings. "They are very comfortable here in AJ City, and as long as you make good on what you owe me, they will remain safe. Though I would not rate their chances if you defy me. Ajegunle can be a dangerous place without protection."

Tighe now realized the extent of their miscalculation. Far from safeguarding Adisa's family, by coming here, they had put them in mortal danger.

The oga again tapped at his device. "And now I know just how important our business is . . ." The holographic image changed to show a map of satellite orbits—hundreds of them—moving around the Earth. The oga zoomed in to highlight the details of one satellite in particular. "A US spy satellite has been retasked to place it directly overhead for your visit here today. Likewise, a Chinese drone circles us even now from several thousand feet. The Chinese and the Americans are tracking your every move. Following your airship.

Whatever you and Adedayo are doing has the attention of superpowers. Which means it is valuable indeed."

Tighe and Jin leaned forward to examine the hologram. It was difficult to say if the man was telling the truth, but it immediately seemed plausible that their team was being followed by the US and China—and now they knew how.

The oga smiled—then turned his back to them as he passed the tablet to his aide. "Give me my due, gentlemen, or I will deal harshly with Adedayo's family. My people will be in touch with Mr. Rochat—since he is too frightened to meet with me directly." He laughed as he made a circling motion with his hand, and the men around him—police included—moved to their vehicles. One of the men opened the Bentley's door and the oga got inside. In a few moments, the entire group was on the move, reversing, then accelerating down a side street, police lights flashing and sirens whooping.

Soon Tighe and Jin stood in the street alone.

Tighe shouted, "We arrived in a goddamn *airship*, Lukas! Blimps are literally used as advertisements. Then we drove an armored convoy into Ade's neighborhood. *Of course* his oga got wind of it, and now look at the position we're in. We've put Ade's entire family in danger. We should have been more discreet."

Rochat kept shaking his head. "The airship and our security detail made no difference. Mr. Tinubu tells me that Chinese agents have already contacted the Adisa family and shown them Adedayo's death certificate. They claim we were trying to cheat them out of his shares in Catalyst by buying them off with just a house."

"Why didn't you think this through? Handling our affairs here on Earth is your one and only job!" Tighe turned to look out the airship's glass wall at the expanse of ocean far below. He then turned to Chindarkar and Yak at the other end of the conference table. "So what do we do about this oga? We're not actually considering handing Ade's share of the company over to him, are we?"

Jin stared ahead. "We should pay off the oga from our own shares. Ade is not responsible for our carelessness."

Yak piped in. "If you think this Lagos gang will be satisfied by Adedayo's share, you are mistaken."

Chindarkar threw up her hands. "Yak, if we don't give this oga what he wants he could start killing Ade's brothers and sisters."

"Would they really do this?"

"Do we want to find out?"

Rochat said, "This just makes it all the more imperative that we get the protection of a major nation."

Tighe turned. "Would you please stop with that?"

Chindarkar shook her head sadly. "We haven't even left Earth and we're already losing control."

Tighe asked Rochat, "How long until we reach Ascension Island?"

Rochat answered blankly, "We'll be in the South Atlantic by tomorrow morning."

"Just get us there."

CHAPTER 6

Wide-Awake

AUGUST 21, 2038

Nearly a thousand kilometers south of the equator and smack in the middle of the Atlantic Ocean, the windswept terrain of Ascension Island was just as Tighe remembered it—though he, himself, felt like a different person. Years ago Ascension had seemed exotic. Now it just seemed small.

From the minibus window the South Atlantic stretched unbroken to the horizon in all directions, while the highest point on the island, Green Mountain, lay wreathed in cloud cover and lush with trees. Closer at hand the soil was reddish grit that barely supported plant life.

The minibus labored upslope, weaving in and out of ravines, and soon a familiar sight came into view: Devil's Ashpit Camp, the training facility where Tighe and his teammates had undergone candidate selection five years earlier. It was a collection of white corrugated-metal buildings surrounding an older concrete administration building dating back to the Cold War, when NASA ran the site as a tracking station during the Apollo program. On the far side of the camp stood two giant white satellite dishes aimed straight up. The entire facility was ringed by a security fence, but the gates opened automatically as their vehicle approached.

Tighe spotted his old barracks and noticed dozens of trainees jogging past in groups. "You have a new class of asteroid mining candidates?"

Lukas Rochat replied from the seat across the aisle, "They're not asteroid mining candidates, and instead of us paying them, they're paying *us*—or at least their companies are."

"What companies?"

"Venture-backed space startups. Most of these trainees are astropreneurs with a business plan for space—satellite servicing, orbital debris cleanup, on-orbit manufacturing, that sort of thing. Our spaceflight certification program is much in demand."

Tighe looked out at the trainees. "Interesting. I guess the world *has* moved on since we've been away."

Priya Chindarkar surveyed the grounds from the seat in front of him. "Lukas, I thought this whole camp was seized by the authorities after Nathan's death."

"It did go through a bankruptcy, but we now lease this facility and the equipment from the British government—in exchange for providing island jobs. There's not much else they could do with the site."

The minibus soon rolled to a stop in front of the camp's central administration building. Standing on the front steps was a familiar face: Gabriel Lacroix—mission control manager for the *Konstantin* expedition. He looked older than his fifty years, perhaps due to all the worry they'd put him through. This was the first time they'd seen him since their return to Earth, and he had been instrumental in making that happen.

Lacroix rarely smiled, but he was beaming as they exited the minibus.

"Gabriel!" Chindarkar raced toward him, arms extended.

"Comme tu es belle!" Lacroix hugged her, then shifted to accented English. "It has been so long."

Jin Han and Tighe came up alongside, carrying duffel bags.

Lacroix then hugged them both as well, kissing them on each cheek. To Tighe's surprise, Jin did not object to the familiarity. "So many times I feared we had lost you. And yet here you are." Lacroix grew momentarily somber. "At least some of you, eh?" Then he brightened again. "What feats you have accomplished."

"With your help." Chindarkar hugged him again.

By now Rochat, Sevastian Yakovlev, and Ramón Marín had exited the minibus—Rochat the only one without luggage. Marín stood respectfully apart from their reunion.

Lacroix shook hands with Rochat and then Yak, slapping his back. "Sevastian, we must show them what we have been up to while they were away, yes?"

Rochat checked his watch. "Well, now that I've delivered them to you, Gabriel, I will leave you to it."

Tighe cast a look his way. "Where are *you* going?"

"Florida. Before we meet with US officials I must get the terms of your visit in writing. The *Konstantin* expedition technically violated US law, and I don't want you arrested when we arrive."

"Well, handle that better than you did the Lagos visit."

"And keep us updated regarding Adedayo's oga," Jin chimed in.

"I told you I will handle it."

Lacroix looked at them quizzically.

Tighe said to him, "We had a situation back in Lagos." He turned back to Rochat. "But Lukas is working on a solution. Correct?"

"As I said, obtaining the patronage of a major superpower is our best bet when it comes to protecting Adedayo's family. Which makes Florida even more important to us."

Jin looked unconvinced.

"In any event, I will keep you all informed." Rochat shook Tighe's hand, then the others' in turn. "You have a full schedule here, but unless you hear otherwise, the *Eos* will return to bring you to Cape Canaveral sometime next week." He nodded to Marín. "Meanwhile, Gabriel, be sure to introduce Ramón here to the mission control team and get him settled in the training program. Provide any assistance he requires."

Lacroix replied, *"Oui, bien sûr."*

With that, Rochat entered the minibus. The group watched as the vehicle drove off toward the airfield. Lacroix said to Marín, "Proceed to barracks four. I will send someone for you presently." He then turned to the others. "As for the rest of you, there is something you need to hear . . ."

Sitting in the otherwise deserted mission control room alongside Lacroix, the group watched as he brought up a comm screen. "We received this message approximately two weeks after your departure from Ryugu . . ."

Suddenly Isabel Abarca's familiar voice came in over the control room speakers, echoing in the large space. It rooted Tighe to the spot.

"Konstantin *to mission control.* Konstantin *to mission control. Mayday. Mayday. We have an unidentified, potentially hostile spacecraft inbound and maneuvering to match our trajectory for possible docking. This is an emergency. Please advise. Out.*"

Lacroix said, "The next message was sent before we could reply to the first."

Abarca's voice filled the room once more. "*Konstantin to mission control, we have been boarded by eight unidentified individuals—possibly a hostile replacement crew. They are moving now to cut our communications. I will keep this channel open as long as possible . . .*"

"Moments later we lost comm laser lock. That was the last message received from the *Konstantin*."

Actually hearing Abarca's voice visibly affected the team. It made their rescue mission that much more urgent. And yet, as Tighe sat there, it also made him realize that the unthinkable might already have happened. He pushed the thought away.

Jin gritted his teeth and said, "It is frustrating that we cannot mount a rescue immediately."

A familiar voice from the door said, "Then we will use this time to prepare for one."

They all turned.

Standing in the control room doorway was Julian Kerner, the forty-something construction manager who had led the team that built the *Konstantin* in lunar orbit. He was also the last person to disembark from the ship prior to its departure for the asteroid Ryugu. The last friendly face the crew had seen in space.

A slight grin formed on Jin's face. "Herr Kerner . . ."

They all moved in and hugged, slapping Kerner on the back.

Afterward Kerner regarded them. "We have two crew members still to return to Earth—a problem I am already working to resolve. I am told you are here for the next week or so. Which means we have a great deal of training to complete and very little time." He gestured toward the door. "So it is best we get started."

Tighe, Yak, Chindarkar, and Jin stood in a large room containing half a dozen tables covered with an array of space suits, helmets, and other components.

Kerner paced between tables while the running songs of distant recruits came to them through the open windows.

Tighe grabbed a helmet off a table and examined it. Unlike the large ruggedized mining helmet integrated into the EVA suits back on the *Konstantin*, the helmet in Tighe's hands was detached and also lighter, with a clear faceplate visor instead of an opaque shell studded with arrays of tiny plenoptic cameras.

Tighe looked up. "Julian, why not keep the virtual visor helmets we had on the Ryugu expedition? Those were tough as hell, and the augmented reality system gave us near perfect visibility."

Jin studied an identical helmet at his own table. "I agree with J.T. This faceplate might shatter if struck by debris. Our old extravehicular mobility units were better."

Kerner stopped pacing and picked up one of the helmets. He then rooted around a nearby workbench until he came up with a pointed rock hammer. He placed the helmet facing visor-up on the table, then without warning proceeded to pound on the clear visor with all his strength, causing the contents of the tabletop to bounce with each hit. After half a dozen blows he picked up the helmet, wiped the visor with his hand, and showed it to them.

The faceplate looked barely scuffed.

"Transparent aluminum. As tough as the helmet itself. Integrated crystal display, much lighter weight, better battery life, and all of the features of the old EMU headgear."

Tighe looked back down at the helmet in his hands. "Get out of town . . ."

Yak nodded. "Extravehicular activity tech has advanced since you have been away."

Jin ran his finger along the helmet's coupling ring. "But this is not integral to the spacesuit like the EMU." He dropped the helmet and picked up a white undersuit spread out on the table. "So this cannot be an EVA work helmet." He looked up. "And it is overkill for a flight suit."

Chindarkar nodded. "Han's right. Aboard ship, a detached helmet is just something you have to search for in an emergency. I prefer the attached, zippered hoods on our old flight suits."

Tighe examined the fabric of the white undersuit on his table. It was thicker and coarser than he was used to. It had sections of denser fabric that looked like Kevlar reinforcement. "And for flight suits, these are too heavy."

Kerner regarded them. "They are not flight suits."

Tighe and the others exchanged puzzled looks.

Yak laughed. "Is EVA suit."

Tighe picked the suit up off the table to study it closely. *"This?"*

It was more substantial than a typical flight suit—which would only be worn inside a spacecraft to guard against sudden pressure loss—but nowhere near the weight of a traditional spacesuit. The industrial EMU spacesuits they had used on the *Konstantin* massed 150 kilos without life support packs and never came inside the ship; instead they docked to the ship's exterior like a small spacecraft. They didn't so much put them on as "enter them" through a hatch in the back.

Kerner nodded. "The helmet and suit you are holding is a fully capable EVA suit that masses just 41 kilograms."

"Forty-one?" Chindarkar whistled and held the suit up in front of her. "It looks formfitting. How do you slip into this while wearing an LCVG?"

She was referring to the long-johns-like liquid cooling and ventilation gar-ment that they wore beneath their space suits to distribute heat.

Kerner was poker-faced. "The LCVG is integral."

"This *includes* the LCVG?" She appeared skeptical.

Tighe looked up. "What about internal pressure?"

"That's why it's so light." Kerner lifted up a nearby suit. "This is called an *MCP*—or mechanical counterpressure—suit. Instead of atmospheric pressure against the vacuum of space, the formfitting material of the suit presses in on your body. Which means you don't need a pure oxygen environment in your suit to maintain mobility and breathability. It also means you can use normal air in your helmet—so no need for a pure oxygen prebreathe prior to an EVA."

"No two-hour prebreathe before suiting up?" Tighe was impressed. He took another look at the garment in his hands. "We just put on the suit and go straight out of the airlock?"

"That's correct."

Jin raised his eyebrows. *"That* is a game changer."

Chindarkar studied the fabric. "It means we could EVA in emergencies."

Jin said, "But there was a reason the suits remained outside the spacecraft at Ryugu. Positively charged regolith particles get into everything. They're an inhalation hazard. Hazardous to electronics. We can't wear these suits in and out of an airlock."

"They have a charge dissipation system for that, but they aren't meant for surface work. They're meant primarily for open space. You'll see next what we'll be using for lunar surface EVAs."

Jin looked closely at the fabric. "What about micrometeor and debris protection, or radiation shielding?"

"The laminate includes layers of boron-10—which has four orders of magnitude-greater cosmic ray stopping power than hydrogen. Plus, boron and carbon nanotubes for puncture resistance, and aerogels for temperature insulation. It'll stop a micrometeor as well as the EMU, but has better rad protection. All wrapped in a polyethylene skin. There are also outersuits you can pull on for additional protection under more extreme conditions. And these you can actually slip into and out of even while on EVA."

Chindarkar laid the suit back on the table. "Well, whoever came up with this tech really outdid themselves."

Jin looked up. "What does it cost?"

Yak answered instead of Kerner. "Per unit price of three million US dollars—helmet not included."

Chindarkar winced.

Kerner pointed. "Those are samples. We'll need an updated full-body scan from each of you today for a perfect fitting. The manufacturer will require several months to produce your suits. We intend to purchase two copies each."

Tighe placed the suit back on the table. "Twenty-four million for the four of us. That's some wardrobe budget."

Kerner checked the time. "And worth it. Come . . ." He gestured. "Let's get those body scans done and move on."

After disrobing, they each stood in a 3D scanning booth for several minutes to endure a detailed body scan. After years in deep space together, modesty was not a factor among them. Afterward, the team dressed and rejoined Kerner in front of the building, where he waited at the wheel of a golf cart. He immediately set off as they boarded, driving down lanes between the buildings.

Kerner spoke without taking his eyes off the road. "As usual, you won't be going on EVAs often. Let me show you what you'll be using for work on the lunar surface."

Tighe and his colleagues walked through an echoing concrete robotics lab among half a dozen humanoid robots wrapped in ruggedized polymer carapaces that resembled medieval armor. Each robot was of average human height, numbered, and painted in various neon colors—red, green, blue, orange, and yellow—with the word "TALOS" stenciled across their chest plates. The machines stood in charger units, and each one had twin whiplike antennas rising half a meter from their shoulder blades. Tighe pounded his fist on the chest of one of them.

It didn't budge.

"These things are tanks compared to the old Valkyrie telepresence robots we had on the Ryugu expedition."

Kerner came up behind him. "Ryugu had one-sixty-thousandth of Earth's gravity. The Moon has one-sixth Earth gravity. So you'll need a more powerful humanoid telepresence robot to get useful work done on the lunar surface. These weigh just over 150 kilos with a standard loadout."

Chindarkar studied one up close. "Can we try them out?"

"That's why we're here." Kerner gestured to a row of chairs and accessories nearby.

She approached and grabbed a crystal headset and pulled on haptic feedback gloves from a nearby table. "So they're operated like the Valkyries, then?"

Kerner nodded. "VR user interface. Log on and the system will activate your crystal—you'll need to remain seated during operation."

"Then how do we make it walk?"

"Slide one foot forward to walk—both to run. The software will handle foot movement and navigation over obstacles. You need only handle upper-body movements."

"Fancy." She sat in a nearby operator chair.

Tighe, Jin, and Yak all donned their own gear and sat in operator seats.

Kerner approached. "Select any robot with a full charge."

Tighe could see that Chindarkar was already jacked in, and her crystal headset had turned opaque, indicating she was in VR mode. She moved her arms as she interacted with an unseen user interface. "Got it . . . Linking to unit four . . ."

In a moment, the green Talos robot marked "4" seemed to come alive, its servo motors whining as it stepped clear of its charger and looked around the room.

Chindarkar said, "Wow. These feel like military-grade motors. What's the response time?"

Kerner answered, "Sub-millisecond. At 60,000 kilometers from the lunar surface, you're talking a transmission lag of about a fifth of a second. Human response time to direct stimuli is about the same. So the near-instant servo response is important to keep telepresence as close as possible to being there in person."

Her robot stroked its own shoulder antennas. "And bandwidth?"

"Five hundred megabit main channel, with a hundred megabit secondary."

Tighe interacted with his own crystal display to put it into VR mode. Once it went opaque, he navigated to a UI listing of available Talos robots, selecting red unit six. In a moment he was suddenly gazing through the stereoscopic vision of the robot's eyes to see his own human form sitting in a chair across the room. The vertigo he felt made him briefly nauseous—which he immediately noticed from the robot's POV. "This is freakier than usual."

Jin spoke on Tighe's right. "We are normally not in the same room as our avatar."

Tighe could see Jin had powered up the blue robot marked "2," while Yak powered up yellow "3." As Tighe turned, he also experienced the response time. "Man, Priya's not kidding. These motors are incredible." Tighe looked down to examine his robot hand as he opened and closed its fist. He turned his robot head, and it responded as fast as his neck muscles could in real life.

Tighe slid one foot forward, and his robot walked toward Jin's robot. He didn't need to literally walk; instead, his Talos took this foot gesture as the command to move. The farther forward he slid his foot, the faster it moved. When he drew back one foot or the other, the robot turned. When he slid both feet back, it stopped—or moved backward if he shifted them far enough. "Wow. Our old Valkyries were like invalids compared to this."

Chindarkar's and Yak's robots joined them so that they were now standing as a quartet, examining each other up close—poking robotic hands into each other's components.

Chindarkar's green "4" robot grabbed Tighe's robotic head and "stared" into his eyes. "What about optics?"

Kerner answered, "Stereoscopic 4K displays. Infrared and ultraviolet modes. Lidar scanners."

Tighe brushed her hands off. "Inappropriate touching, Priya. Didn't you get the memo from HR?"

She laughed and shoved him back, but his robot immediately recovered its footing. "Nice recovery."

"Woah. That wasn't me."

Kerner pushed Tighe's robot. Again it staggered backward, but recovered automatically without falling. Kerner said, "Unlike V-2's, Talos units automatically handle all balance, standing, and recovery from slips or falls. It's built into the software. You just aim where you want to go, and it will navigate the terrain while remaining upright. Lets you focus on upper-body tasks, not lower-body movement."

Jin's robot was examining its open hands. "Are these pressure pads I feel on the fingers and palms?"

"Tactile feedback sensors—you'll feel pressure when you hold things."

His robot grabbed at a handrail. "Impressive. That will be useful for situational awareness." Jin's robot then opened the service panel on the back of a unit still in its charger. "What sort of battery life? More than the Mark II Valkyries, I hope."

Kerner looked up from his tablet. "Less, actually—but it's also less of an issue because these robots can be continuously charged via a microwave beam." He pointed to the antennas.

Tighe said, "Wait, so we can operate continuously?"

"As long as you're line of sight to a transmitter—which you can transport with the robot itself. The transmitter is on a hardwired cable to a power source."

Chindarkar's robot walked in front of Kerner. "But it does have an onboard battery?"

"Yes. Two, in fact." He opened the front plate of another nearby robot in its charger, revealing two battery packs. "They have a front-facing dual battery configuration. So you can swap out one of your own batteries for a freshly charged one, even while remaining operational."

Tighe looked down at his own robotic chest, pressed a marked latch, and opened the chest plate to reveal the battery bay. "Man, we could have used these on Ryugu." He closed his own chest back up.

The telepresence robots now circled each other like suspicious inmates in an exercise yard.

Tighe called out, "Han! High five!" He held up an outstretched robotic hand.

Jin's robot turned to him, raised his hand, and they clacked the palms together with sufficient force to send them both momentarily backpedaling.

They all laughed uproariously.

"Couldn't do that with V-2's."

Kerner moved back. "Please don't break them."

Chindarkar asked, "How much per unit?"

Kerner answered, deadpan, "Less than the cost of dying on the Moon. But only barely. These are prototypes on loan from the manufacturer—who is eager to have a customer field-test them on the lunar surface. Which is why they'll be paying to transport them there. However, longer term, we'll need to build all but the most advanced components of such robots—the chips and optics—in situ, to save on launch costs from Earth."

"So these units are free to us?"

"For testing purposes. And with some strings attached."

"What sort of strings?"

"Testimonials. Promotional endorsements. This sort of thing."

Yak's robot was performing what looked like tai chi, making slow, graceful motions. "These machines will behave differently under Moon gravity."

"They have a useful feature for that." Kerner started tapping at a computer tablet. "The control software allows us to dampen or amplify your movements to compensate for variable gravity environments. On the Moon, for example, we can dial down the force of your movements to one-sixth actual. That way you won't suffer physics disorientation after a long telepresence work shift." He tapped a button.

Suddenly Tighe's robot felt like it was wading through molasses.

"That's you on a setting for Moon gravity, but of course, you're experiencing it under full Earth gravity."

Tighe's robot trudged along the floor, as did the others.

Chindarkar laughed. "Ugh. I hate it! Put it back, Julian."

"As you wish." Kerner poked at his tablet.

Tighe's robot was once again agile. "Much better." He shadowboxed with a nearby robot.

Kerner said, "I suggest you give them a field test, but before you go outside, please put on a jumper . . ." He pointed to a row of white garments hanging on racks on the far wall. Above each hung clear-plastic bubble helmets.

"A jumper?" Tighe guided his robot there, grabbing at the sleeve of one of the garments. They resembled nothing so much as footed, vinyl pajamas. "Why does a robot need pajamas?"

Chindarkar's robot came up alongside. "Or a helmet?" She tapped at one of the clear-plastic bubbles.

Kerner replied, "You do remember your asteroid training, yes? Lunar regolith is even finer than Ryugu's—finer than talcum powder—and as abrasive as diamond dust. On the Moon you'll need to prevent the regolith from destroying your robot's joints and optics. These garments are made of aramid fiber."

Jin's robot joined them, examining a jumper as well.

Kerner continued. "You dispose of them when they are worn. You will notice a menu item labeled 'Suit Up' in your HUD display. Each jumper and helmet has a unique radio frequency identification—or RFID—chip. Select the 'Suit Up' command and your robot will automatically detect and pull on the nearest jumper and helmet. There is another command to disrobe."

Tighe activated the command and suddenly his robot behaved as one possessed—the label "Auto-Operation" flashing in his HUD display. With the VR headset the experience was nauseating. "Well, this is unpleasant."

Kerner sighed. "Then close your eyes. I assure you, it is infinitely easier than trying to put the jumper on manually."

Jin commented, "It does seem to be doing the job."

Tighe risked a peek and could see that his robot had already put both feet into the legs and was putting its arms into the sleeves. Very shortly it sealed up the garment and pushed the clear-plastic bubble helmet over its head. Moments later he regained control of his robot. "Huh. It worked."

He turned to see Chindarkar's and Jin's robots were already donning their own jumpers. Moments later all three of them resembled retro spacemen/robots.

Chindarkar laughed hysterically, her robot staggering as it slapped its leg and clutched its belly. "You should see yourself, J.T. You look like an invader from Mars."

Tighe raised his arms and spoke robotically to Kerner, "Take us to your leader, human."

Kerner nodded patiently. "Yes, very amusing. Please, we have a busy schedule." He pointed out the open garage door. "Proceed to our next appointment in telepresence, and I'll follow shortly with the van."

The robots looked about.

"Where's our next appointment?"

Kerner poked at the tablet. "I put a waypoint on your HUD screen. Head to it, and I will meet you there."

"One kilometer? How's our connectivity with these things?"

"There's signal coverage on this half of the island."

Tighe clapped his robot hands. "Okay, let's do it." He slid his real-world feet forward and jogged his robot out the open roll-top door and onto the road between camp buildings. He glanced back to see Jin's blue-2, Chindarkar's green-4, and Yak's yellow-3 rushing up from behind—and gaining fast.

Chindarkar shouted, "Race you!"

"Hey!" Tighe slid his feet farther forward, causing his robot to sprint.

Soon the four robots were dashing down the road on rubber-soled feet. Tighe heard Kerner's voice close by, in the room where his own real body was.

"Please remember you are piloting robots! Be careful not to collide with anyone."

"Okay, okay."

The four robots remained neck and neck as they came up to the edge of the camp's physical training field.

"These things kick ass!"

Jin said, "But I am already at only 90 percent charge."

Chindarkar's robot pointed. "Look! Our old obstacle course."

Tighe turned his robot head to see the new class of candidates running the course, much as he had years ago, instructors barking at them. "Oh, hell yes..."

They veered toward it, and Chindarkar's green-4 was the first to fall in alongside the human recruits. "Make way, please!"

The candidates stepped back, some of them too exhausted to look much surprised at the appearance of "sentient" robots on their training course.

Tighe navigated his robot over a log spanning muddy water, and the machine maintained its balance masterfully. "This is really impressive, Julian. You seeing this?"

Kerner's voice said, "Of course I am. We have cameras everywhere."

Tighe approached a climbing wall. Two bewildered candidates—one a South Asian man, the other a Caucasian woman—stood aside as the robots gathered. Tighe's robot grabbed the thick rope hanging down. He "felt" the pressure of it in his hands and glanced over at Chindarkar's robot. "This is outstanding. Priya, feel the rope?"

"It's almost like being here." She started climbing.

Tighe noticed the nearby trainees staring. He called to them, "Don't feel bad. I was human the first time I ran this course, too." Then he started climbing the wall.

It was tricky at first, but he soon got the hang of it. Navigating the summit was tougher, and as he climbed over, his robot fell more than jumped down—but the machine automatically righted itself like a cat, absorbing the impact on coiled legs.

"I feel like I'm using cheat codes."

Kerner's voice said, "I assure you that actual operations on the moon will be sufficiently difficult."

Tighe was already running again, pushing to catch up to Chindarkar.

Jin's robot started passing Tighe's.

Yak's robot examined its wrist. "I have under 50 percent charge from our little race."

Kerner's voice said, "I told you that battery life would be a constraint, but most of the time you will be on wireless power. Now please proceed to your appointment without any more detours."

Chindarkar's robot grabbed Tighe's robot's hand. "C'mon, let's get moving."

———

They started jogging down the camp road again at a more sedate pace. The four robots navigated roughly a kilometer toward Kerner's GPS waypoint over hillsides of volcanic grit, buffeted by gusting winds. Given that he was still recovering from the chemo meds, Tighe was relieved to have the robot do all the actual running for him.

On a stretch of level ground up ahead they spotted a structure of wire netting suspended over poles, pulled taut by cables staked into the ground. Beneath the netting was a collection of Pelican cases, solar panels, and other gear, along with a lone figure gazing into a computer monitor.

"Over there . . ."

The quartet of humanoid robots in plastic suits and bubble helmets drew near a Japanese man in his thirties, who turned as he heard them—only to look gobsmacked as he noticed they weren't human. They came to a stop around him beneath the wire netting, their lensed eyes whirring to focus on his face. The man stood, confused.

Jin's robot said, "Julian Kerner sent us here."

The man was taken aback. "Ah . . . Yes, of course."

Chindarkar said, "Sorry about the robot avatars, but we were doing a test nearby. Do you mind?"

He shook his head and laughed. "No. It's no problem."

The real Tighe leaned his robot forward to extend its hand. "Good to meet you. I'm James Tighe."

The Japanese man tried to shake the robot's hand—but suddenly winced. "A bit tight."

"Oh god! Sorry. I hope I didn't hurt you."

Chindarkar said, "We're trying to get up to speed on these new telepresence units. There's an infirmary back at camp, if—"

The man rubbed his hand. "No, I'm fine. Thanks."

Tighe gestured to his companions. "Well, that's Priya Chindarkar. He's Jin Han. And that's Sevastian Yakovlev. Or at least their robots."

Instead of shaking hands, they nodded their bubble-shrouded heads in greeting.

The man bowed in return and smiled. He spoke English with almost no accent. "Akimitsu Hayashi, founder of Heliosat, at your service. Mr. Kerner told me to expect you."

Jin's robot glanced at its wrist. "I should warn you before we begin, Mr. Hayashi, that my battery is already down to a quarter charge, and I am uncertain how long I will be operational."

Yak's robot nodded. "I am down to 30 percent."

Hayashi held up his hands. "No, that is good. This is clearly why Mr. Kerner sent you." He started moving cases of equipment. "We develop commercial solar power satellite systems. I've done work for Nathan Joyce in the past." He looked up. "Mr. Joyce will be missed, but I was glad when your new CEO, Mr. Rochat, contacted me to say that you plan on building a solar power satellite in lunar orbit."

The robots exchanged looks.

"I gather you'll be using telepresence robots like these on the lunar surface?"

"That's the plan."

"Then let me give you a demonstration of our power system." He motioned for them to look up.

Wire netting was suspended roughly 5 meters overhead atop aluminum poles, with a mesh of about 10 centimeters. Taut stay cables moored to the ground provided enough tension to withstand the strong wind. Small copper plates appeared at the vertices of each square in the net, but the sky was still clearly visible.

"Above us you see a solid-state rectifying antenna—or 'rectenna' for short. It's a receiver for microwave energy."

Tighe's robot turned in place, staring upward. "It looks like a trapeze net."

"Because of the wavelengths we're dealing with, it does not need to be dense. Microwave energy is in the 12-centimeter range—roughly 5 inches. We could place the rectenna at ground level, but since 90 percent of visible light passes through, we can use the ground beneath for other things if we mount it high enough." He gestured to planter boxes arrayed on the ground around them. "One could raise crops, graze animals, or even place solar panels beneath it."

Chindarkar's robot looked up at the sky. "So this rectenna is for receiving microwaves transmitted from orbit."

"Yes . . ." Hayashi glanced at his watch. "In a few minutes I'll be able to show you our system in action." He brought them to a ruggedized laptop with twin holographic displays set up on a large component case. Cables ran from it to what appeared to be a transformer, as well as to various places on the rectenna grid. A hologram floating above the device showed the curvature of the Earth and the trajectory of a satellite marked "SPS-MINI." "We have a small-scale, solar power satellite in low Earth orbit, generating 50 kilowatts of electricity, and we've retasked it to pass overhead in time for this meeting. Once it enters the transmission cone it will beam energy with its microwave transmitter toward a reference signal on the rectenna just above us."

The robots gathered around him to look at the holographic display.

"Again, this is a small testbed satellite in low Earth orbit—beaming only enough energy to power a good-sized home. A production unit would be much larger and in geosynchronous orbit, where it would remain constantly overhead to beam down energy twenty-four/seven." He brought up an image of the satellite onto the screen. It resembled a tulip in shape, but constructed from hexagonal mirrored facets facing toward the Sun, with a flat transmitter on the Earthward side. "Your CEO says you plan on building a 50-megawatt lunar sat—which would be a thousand times more powerful and a thousand times larger than ours." He looked up from his screen and smiled. "Which would be awesome."

Suddenly the hologram turned green as a connection was established. It depicted a satellite well above the curve of the Earth.

"Look, the satellite is now 30 degrees above our horizon—sufficient to commence transmission." He pointed to another holographic display. "And there you see the kilowatts of electricity now being absorbed by the rectenna above us."

The display read "23 kilowatts." Then a few moments later, "23.5 kilowatts." There was no sound whatsoever emanating from the wire grid above them.

"We're now receiving electricity from orbit. You'll notice the energy transmitted is increasing as the satellite moves more directly overhead. But already we have more than enough energy to charge batteries or for immediate use." He looked at them. "And judging by those antennas on your robots, I should be able to help you out . . ."

Hayashi rooted around in his equipment cases, then uncoiled a cable, at the end of which was a copper-coated transmitter with a folding stand. He placed it on the ground and aimed it at the robots. "There. Are you getting a charge?"

Chindarkar's robot nodded. "I am. The display says I'm now charging."

Yak's and Jin's robots nodded as well.

Tighe glanced at his own display. Nothing. He then walked into the path of the transmitter and a charge indicator lit up in his display. "Incredible. So we could work without worrying about charge levels."

Hayashi answered, "Yes. Exactly."

"And this electricity is coming directly from orbit."

"It is."

Jin's robot looked up. "What about the microwave beam? We are robots, but is it dangerous to you, standing there?"

Hayashi shook his head. "Oh, no. The microwaves do not make it past the rectenna. Regardless, I could stand in the path of the beam. It meets the OSHA safety limit of 100 watts per square meter. Even higher than that wouldn't be immediately harmful—just not recommended. We're seeking legal clearance to increase the beam intensity to 230 watts per square meter—which was the old global safety standard."

Just then the crunching of tires on gravel came in on the wind. They all looked up to see Julian Kerner at the wheel of an electric van, which rolled to a stop not far off, at the edge of the rectenna netting.

The robots all waved.

Chindarkar turned to Mr. Hayashi. "It looks like our ride is here. Thank you for the demonstration. Very impressive. I'm sure Lukas will follow up."

"It was my pleasure."

The four robots headed toward Kerner's waiting van.

Tighe checked his charge display and called to Kerner as the engineer stepped out of the van. "What took you so long? We were almost out of juice."

"Should we stay here and charge a while?" Chindarkar asked.

Kerner shook his head and opened the van's sliding door. "I will drive you back to the lab, where we will resume with your real bodies. Again, there is much to cover, and very little time."

CHAPTER 7

Waterline

AUGUST 23, 2038

Route A1A ran flat and straight past a series of strip malls, budget hotels, and condo towers in Cocoa Beach, Florida. Midsummer—over a hundred degrees in the shade and as humid as vapor therapy. The joke went that the state bird was the mosquito.

Rochat wondered, *Who would willingly live here?*

The answer, of course, was engineers. The Space Coast was booming. Rising ocean levels were a concern, of course—if not for launch complexes, then for coastal cities—but Cocoa Beach was a short commute to Burkette's Starion Launch Systems, Macy's Zenith Corporation, and several other private space launch companies operating out of the Cape. However, judging by the Realtor signs on every block, sea-level, single-family homes were not in demand.

By contrast, across the street, Rochat's SUV passed by a new condo tower whose video signage boasted: "Category Five–proof" and "Storm-surge-rated." Never mind a pool—these condos advertised built-in, Internet-enabled storm shutters.

Makar Yegorov, Catalyst Corporation's hulking chief security officer, spoke from the front passenger seat. "We are close, Mr. Rochat."

Rochat nodded.

Their driver turned onto a residential street lined with mid-twentieth-century single-story, pastel-colored houses on quarter-acre lots. Every second home had hurricane damage and a "For Sale" sign in front of it—the nearest with an insert reading "Reduced!"

The SUV came to a stop.

"This is it." Yegorov stared at the driveway of a generic little house. He pulled out a radio frequency detector. "Let me go in first to scan for devices."

"That won't be necessary, Makar."

"I should check at least to see is safe."

"No. Wait here. And . . ." Rochat removed his phone from his jacket pocket and passed it to Yegorov. ". . . take this."

Yegorov held it up. "If there is problem, how will you contact me?"

"If there's a problem, it won't be one you can help me with."

Yegorov grumbled.

Rochat exited the SUV and Florida's climate immediately assaulted him. He might as well have stepped out onto the surface of Venus, or so it felt in his suit jacket and tie. He walked swiftly up the driveway and across a mildewed concrete porch. After he punched in a code on the front door's smart lock, it opened with a *click*, and he reentered the mercifully air-conditioned space.

Closing the door behind him, he surveyed an empty sitting room with louvered swing doors on the far side. The whole place smelled musty. His footsteps echoed as he crossed the parquet floor and pushed through the doors, into the kitchen.

There, he found Erika Lisowski sitting at a dinette table, sipping an iced tea. Her physical appearance always surprised him. He consistently remembered her as more imposing than she actually was. She was older than him by a decade at least—mid-forties—and in person she resembled nothing so much as a bland, mid-level DC bureaucrat. Unremarkable in clothing and appearance. However, he knew several billionaires and senators who had made the mistake of underestimating her.

She nodded to him calmly. "Lukas."

"Erika." He looked at the surrounding time capsule of mid-century Americana. "Interesting choice of venue."

"My late grandfather's house. He bought it back in '68."

Rochat sat down across from her. "During the Apollo program, then."

"That's right." She gazed around the room wistfully. "I spent a lot of time here as a little girl. It'll probably get plowed under along with the entire neighborhood to make way for another bunkerminium."

Rochat waited a beat out of respect for her lost childhood, then said, "I gather Sunday's meeting is still on at the Cape."

"It is. I wasn't invited. However, the fifth floor of the C-Ring will attend."

"I assume that's bureaucratese for something important. Do you have our provisional immunity from prosecution?"

She reached down to her bag on the floor and pulled out a folder—which she slid across the table to him. "This won't save you from them, Lukas."

Rochat flipped open the folder to see the seal of the US Justice Department, along with the signature of the attorney general. He looked up. "Erika, right now it is only a matter of time until either the US or China locates those robot tugs in lunar orbit, and when they do, Catalyst will no longer have any leverage. I need to make a deal before that happens."

"The US already knows the trajectories of your robot tugs."

Rochat's eyes widened.

"By now the Chinese might know, too. At this point it's likely just a race to see who gets to them first."

Rochat looked down at the documents. "Then what power do I have for this meeting?"

"You're not asking the right question, Lukas. You need more than control of those robot tugs to have any power."

"How do you figure that?"

"Because the financial system here on Earth can be used to exert control over you and your team. All your Earthly assets can be frozen at any time."

Rochat stared. "But I thought they wanted to arrange a deal."

"They do—for political cover. But they will still call all the shots in space."

"Okay, then I make what deal I can."

She shook her head. "That will only continue to expand the Cold War into space, and there isn't time for that. Not if we hope to save civilization and our biosphere."

"That's a fine sentiment, Erika, but not helpful for my meeting."

"That meeting isn't why I called you here." She paused. "Did you do as I asked with Ramón Marín?"

He nodded. "Yes. I delivered him for orbital certification training on Ascension Island a few days ago."

"Good. We need him ready."

"Ready for *what?*"

"That will become clear in time. Now, did you read the documentation on the Cislunar Commodity Exchange?"

Rochat gave her the side-eye. "I need your advice on my upcoming meeting, Erika."

"Did you review the CCE documentation?"

"Yes. It reads like a doctoral dissertation on crypto-economics. You're the economist, not me."

"It's vital you understand it. In order to avoid prolonged astropolitical conflict, this new cislunar economy needs to be compartmentalized from Earth's economy—from all its centuries of corruption and debt. And only by creating an economy from scratch in the vacuum of space can it be insulated from the climate-related upheavals of Earthly finance."

"Great. But what good is having virtual money out in space if we can't use it here on Earth? How will we purchase critical supplies or—?"

"You need only three things to establish an economy: a currency, a minting authority, and a record of ownership. The CCE provides all three."

"But you've already said the US knows where our asteroid resources are. They can just take them away while we're stuck down here. So we won't even get a chance to build this 'Cislunar Commodity Exchange' you're proposing."

"It's not just a proposal. Do you recall Nathan Joyce's other assets in lunar orbit—the comsats he launched to support lunar mining operations?"

"Yes, but that lunar mining market didn't materialize. Nathan took a massive loss."

"That's where you're wrong. There *is* lunar mining going on—just not the kind of mining people expected."

Rochat narrowed his eyes.

"The half dozen satellites Nathan placed in polar lunar orbits seven years ago were ostensibly comsat relays for lunar communications—and they can do that. But that's not the reason they were put there. Instead, they are ready and capable of forming a basic off-world transaction and settlement network. They're widely dispersed in deep space to make them difficult to eradicate. They were the first things Nathan had Adedayo Adisa secure against a cyberattack."

"Adedayo?" Rochat considered this news. "So you're telling me those satellites were launched to support this 'lūna' cryptocurrency described in your CCE white paper? Again, what good is virtual money in space if it can't be repatriated to Earth?"

"You won't be sending money to Earth. Money will be coming *from* Earth. Specifically: investment."

"Earth authorities will never allow that. They will demand regulatory control."

"They can't stop you from accepting existing cryptocurrencies in exchange for credits in your new off-world economy. They're just blockchain transactions—a tiny broadcast of text. No government can prevent that transfer, either to or from. And your servers are in deep space—not easily confiscated. Laser comms—not easily disrupted or eavesdropped upon. Especially if they're actively defended."

Rochat pondered this. "So... I establish an off-world blockchain economy with this Cislunar Commodity Exchange ... and accept cryptocurrency investments from Earth, exchanging this as-yet-worthless lūna coin for valuable Earth cryptocurrencies." He shook his head. "Why would investors do that?"

"Because the CCE's lūna coin will be backed by off-world resources and energy—both of which have intrinsic value, especially in lunar orbit. I expect the existing crypto-mining platforms in low Earth orbit will be enthusiastic allies to you."

"But ... the public has no reason to believe we really have resources in space. The media is already labeling us con men, and frankly, if the Americans or the Chinese grab our robot tugs, they'll make that true."

"Don't worry about that now. The important thing is that the network is already established in space. For an off-world economy to work, it must be clear that *everyone* on Earth will benefit. Space cannot just be for billionaires and superpowers. Otherwise cislunar industry will meet with nothing but opposition—from environmentalists, from anti-poverty activists, from rival governments. To prevent that, this push into space needs to benefit the broadest cross section of human beings possible ... worldwide—the rich and the poor. Big nations and small ones. Because rapid industrial expansion into space will be necessary if we're to have any hope of reversing climate change in time. Those are the stakes, Lukas."

He felt overwhelmed. "I don't know how to do any of that."

"You don't need to know. You just need to protect those who do."

"How?"

"By helping establish new legal precedents for deep space commerce. Do you think you can do that?"

"I can try."

"Good." She leaned back. "Speaking of legal issues: Were you able to make contact with Adedayo's people in Lagos?"

"Yes. The oga revealed himself. He is dangerous and demands we turn over Ade's shares in Catalyst Corporation."

She nodded. "Well, thanks to Nathan Joyce this isn't the first criminal organization you've had to deal with."

"It is the first *cyber gang* I've dealt with. We've already had network intrusions. I don't know that we're going to be able to protect our systems from them."

She leaned forward and stared into his eyes. "That's precisely what will make them so valuable to us."

CHAPTER 8

The Cape

AUGUST 29, 2038

Priya Chindarkar, James Tighe, Jin Han, Sevastian Yakovlev, and Lukas Rochat rode in an unmarked shuttle van as it swept through gentle rain on Cape Canaveral's empty roads, the wipers *swupping* rhythmically. Outside, the flat straight road was hemmed in by Florida scrubland, and they passed distant, inscrutable, bunker-like buildings bristling with antennas and piping, centered in isolated clearings.

The front seats of the van were occupied by two US servicemen, neither of them talkative.

Chindarkar noticed the absence of other vehicles on the roadways—whether because it was Sunday or because it was raining . . . or because they were being purposely secluded, she didn't know.

The shuttle van turned onto a road marked "W. Skid Strip."

"Check that out . . ." Tighe pointed ahead.

The others followed his gaze.

In the distance stood a line of tall gantry towers—rocket launchpads—stretching up the coast, faintly visible through the mist and rain.

"I have never seen them in person." Jin stared into the distance.

Chindarkar realized that, as a Chinese national, Jin hadn't been permitted to launch from the Cape. Instead, back in 2033 he had lifted off from Korou in French Guiana. Still, like any spacefarer, Jin seemed to hold a reverence for the launch site of the Apollo missions.

After a few more turns on isolated, arrow-straight roads, their van approached a structure that was a cross between a bunker and an office building—built to survive rocket debris raining down from on high. It sported an expanse of tinted glass at the front, but no windows whatsoever on its other walls. Neither was there any signage indicating its purpose.

The van came to a stop before a portico that capped a short sidewalk winding between decorative palm trees. Here, several uniformed security guards waited with umbrellas. They opened the van doors, and silently escorted Chindarkar and her colleagues up the building's front walk.

As they passed through security and into a narrow lobby, a dozen men and women—some in blue jumpsuits and others wearing neckties with white hard hats—stood to either side. This reception committee seemed to be a surprise to their security escort, who attempted to move the crowd back.

"Sirs! Ladies! Please. This building is closed today."

The nearest in the group—a trim man in his fifties, sporting a buzz cut—reached out to grip Chindarkar's hand. "Goddamn, you made some history. It's an honor to meet you, Dr. Chindarkar. Don't let the suits push you around."

She was taken aback. "Thanks."

"No. Thank *you*."

The security escort moved in to separate them. "Please, Colonel. Sir—"

The man shrugged off the guard as he turned to Tighe.

By then, another astronaut, a woman, gripped Chindarkar's hand—smiling as she did so. "You're an inspiration to us all."

She nodded. "I . . . Thanks."

As Chindarkar moved through the gauntlet of technicians and astronauts, the guards kept pushing them back—to little avail. The line of smiling faces pressed in. Word seemed to have gotten out to a certain breed of top secret test pilot, astronaut, and aerospace engineer, and they weren't about to miss their chance to meet the crew that had gone farther and achieved more in space than anyone in history.

By now the colonel who had shaken her and Tighe's hands stood alongside Jin, who watched in mute surprise as the man saluted him.

"Captain Jin. I'm told you flew that aerobrake maneuver. You, sir, are one hell of a pilot."

Jin paused, straightened, and saluted back—one pilot to another.

They then warmly shook hands. Other American astronauts reached to vigorously shake Jin's hand. Others patted him on the back. The respect of his American peers clearly surprised Jin, and he was consumed for several moments shaking hands and exchanging salutes.

Finally, more guards entered and cleared away the crowd. Chindarkar and her colleagues were whisked through a thick blast door, which led into a windowless conference room.

The door boomed shut behind them as they were led to open seats at a large conference table—around which waited a mix of civilian and military officials.

Chindarkar sat and looked toward Jin, who was visibly uneasy in a room populated by so many US government personnel. Beyond him sat Rochat, Tighe, and Yak.

At the head of the table stood an older, stern-faced man with a full head of carefully groomed white hair and an immaculate dark suit replete with an American flag lapel pin. He radiated cool confidence. "Dr. Chindarkar. Mr. Tighe. Captain Jin. Cosmonaut-scientist Yakovlev. Mr. Rochat. Thank you for agreeing to join us here today. We realize you have a busy travel schedule, so we'll get right to the point: the United States government is aware that three of you took part in an unlawful asteroid mining mission in deep space between 2033 and—"

"Excuse me." Rochat raised a tentative finger. "We take exception to the characterization of the Ryugu expedition as 'unlawful.' It was beyond the bounds of settled space law, but—"

"Relax, Counselor. You already have your immunity agreements." The elder man turned to address Chindarkar, Tighe, and Jin directly. "Besides, you have more serious concerns. In launching your expedition, Nathan Joyce defrauded some very dangerous people out of billions of dollars—money launderers working for despots and criminal syndicates. And those people are convinced they own this asteroid mining ship, *Konstantin*—as well as the asteroid resources you three returned to lunar orbit." He turned to Rochat. "In fact, Mr. Rochat, I'd venture to say that these dictators and criminals have a more legitimate claim to them than you."

Rochat cleared his throat. "Nathan Joyce's creditors have yet to establish in a court of competent jurisdiction either the existence of the *Konstantin* or the resources it is purported to have produced."

"Spare us your legal tap dance. The existence of the *Konstantin* and those resources is not in question, and this isn't just a legal game you're playing. Nathan Joyce didn't kill himself out of *shame*. He knew what awaited him, and I hope you do, too, if the accounts are not settled with these people. *Someone* owes them fourteen billion dollars, and do you really think the trajectory of your asteroid resources will long remain secret if some dictator or underworld figure grabs you and your friends in the middle of the night and tortures the orbital elements out of you?"

Chindarkar and the others turned to face Rochat. What suddenly seemed obvious to her had been obfuscated for some time by Rochat's investor cocktail receptions and visits with astropreneurs. *Why didn't I realize this? How could I have been so foolish?*

She thought of Adisa's family. And of Morra's family. Their identities would, of course, be known by now—especially with Adisa's oga involved. This was so far from what Chindarkar had wanted. How long had Rochat known about this?

Rochat didn't look bothered by this news—or even alarmed. Instead, he took a sip from a bottled water in front of him, then addressed the officials. "It is my understanding that the Chinese government made Mr. Joyce's offshore investors whole—and that the CCP now claims full ownership of the *Konstantin.*"

The older man raised an eyebrow. "And you think that improves your situation?" He gestured to Rochat, but spoke to Chindarkar, Jin, and Tighe. "It makes me wonder if Catalyst Corporation owns anything at all."

Chindarkar cursed under her breath.

Jin leaned toward Rochat. "*China* now claims ownership of the *Konstantin?* Why did you not tell us this news before today?"

Rochat hissed between clenched teeth. "Why do you think we're here, Han?"

The older man continued. "Fortunately for you, fourteen billion is not the full cost of the *Konstantin*; Joyce himself also staked ten billion—an investment the United States now claims in payment for back taxes and criminal penalties. So America, too, has a stake in the *Konstantin* and those resources."

He swiped at a computer tablet screen. "And yet, the Chinese did more than just purchase an interest in the *Konstantin.* They also provided technical and operational assistance to the replacement crew that arrived there not long after you three left."

Chindarkar sat up at attention. "You have information on the replacement crew?" She felt her heart race.

A satellite photograph of a launch facility suddenly appeared on a large screen behind the officials. "Our intel shows the new crew launched from North Korea's Tongch'ang complex—presumably to give plausible deniability to the CCP. The replacement crew arrived at the *Konstantin* on March 5."

Tighe said, "The day we lost contact."

"This new crew consisted of North Korean military . . ." Photos of individual North Korean officers appeared, one after another. ". . . zealots for 'Dear Leader,' fully committed to the 'glorious revolution.' Intercepted communications show they were chosen specifically to correct the main defect of Joyce's expedition: 'disobedient crew.'"

Chindarkar leaned forward. "Do you have any information on what happened to Isabel and Adedayo?"

The man looked up from his tablet. "I do . . ." Suddenly the screen played grainy video footage of a new spacecraft arriving at the *Konstantin*, whose three radial arms capped by habitats pirouetted silently. The arriving craft was fronted by an old Soyuz module and consisted of a hodgepodge of other modules.

Chindarkar called out, "This is actual footage of the North Koreans arriving?"

"How do you have this?" Jin asked.

Yak nodded to himself. "Celestial Robotics."

The older man confirmed. "Yes. Alan Goff's mining mother ship, *Argo*, 125 kilometers away. His mining robots might be down, but the mother ship is still operational, and Mr. Goff has been kind enough to provide us with ongoing surveillance imagery of the *Konstantin* and daily operations at Ryugu."

Chindarkar felt elated to see the *Konstantin* and Ryugu again. But then there was the North Korean spacecraft in the image. "Can you tell us if Isabel and Adedayo are still alive?"

The older man remained poker-faced. "We followed their daily movements prior to the arrival of the North Koreans. However, I am sorry to say, your colleagues have not been seen since." The screen cut to imagery of space walkers in old Russian-style EVA suits, who were now up close to the *Argo's* observation camera. Moments later the screen filled with static.

"Due to communications lag, the North Korean crew was able to seize control of Celestial Robotics' mother ship, the *Argo*, before Goff's techs could react. It was a violation of international law—a charge both China and North Korea deny. Officially, they deny even the existence of the *Konstantin* or any operations at Ryugu."

The screen went dark.

"And so we no longer have eyes on Ryugu or news of your colleagues."

The asteroid miners all sat in horrified silence.

The elder statesman's expression softened. "We all admire what you and your colleagues have achieved. In fact, you may be the greatest explorers who have ever lived. The world should know your names—and the names of those who were lost. We can make sure that happens, but you must work with us."

Tighe said, "We don't know yet that Isabel and Adedayo are dead. Help us get back into space. Help us send a rescue craft back to Ryugu."

Chindarkar added, "If NASA would provide technical and operational support to return us to the *Konstantin*, we could—"

"A ruthless dictatorship has taken physical possession of your old ship, Dr. Chindarkar. The *Konstantin* is lost." He paused. "But your resources in lunar orbit are not lost. We propose to purchase those resources from you—for five billion dollars in cash."

Jin shot back, "They are not for sale. We need them."

"Captain Jin, the US position is that we own them already—through seizure of Joyce's portion of the *Konstantin* expedition."

Rochat asked, "Then why would you *purchase* them from us?"

"In order to establish public provenance and lawful ownership. You mined them. We purchased them. And so rule of law prevails in space. We will pay the current market value of your company and, of course, acknowledge you as the legitimate owners of those resources—once we are able to physically secure them."

Tighe stared. "You expect us to simply abandon Isabel and Ade?"

Rochat answered instead. "J.T., we would have five billion dollars for their rescue."

The others glared at Rochat.

Jin said, "Of what use is a few billion to us?"

The man replied, "With it you can buy launch services to return to space—which we will license you to do."

Chindarkar countered. "Five billion wouldn't begin to cover the costs of building a crewed spin-gravity ship in cislunar orbit capable of reaching Ryugu four years from now. And we'll need more than money. We'll need your technical and logistical support."

The elder statesman held up his hand. "Let's be clear: your colleagues have accomplished an incredible feat, and the world is grateful, but we need to discuss the enormous potential of thousands of tons of resources in cislunar space—and the danger posed by authoritarian regimes off Earth."

Jin turned to glare at Rochat. "Why did you bring us here, Lukas?"

Rochat said, "Because if you wish to return to space, we have no choice, Han."

"It sounds to me like we should be talking with China—since they have control of the *Konstantin.*"

The elder statesman said, "And do you think the CCP will look favorably on you, Captain—given your disobedience and disloyalty? They already have the *Konstantin.* Surely you don't expect the CCP will let you keep those resources in lunar orbit. Why would they? Just so you can transform them into a new spacecraft to send right back toward Ryugu? Where those resources came from in the first place? That hardly advances your home country's strategic position. China might tell you what you want to hear, but they will not help you rescue your friends."

Jin seemed at a loss for words.

"Take the money and work with us, and get FAA clearance to return to space. Become the internationally celebrated figures you—and your fallen colleagues—deserve to be."

This time Jin replied immediately. "So instead of helping China dominate cislunar space, you expect us to help the US dominate it instead."

The man raised his eyebrows. "We don't expect you to help, Captain, or you, Comrade Yakovlev. But then, it isn't really up to you, is it? I believe your corporate charter requires a more democratic process." He turned to the others, this time encompassing Rochat in his gaze. "Will a majority of Catalyst shareholders vote to accept our offer and work with us in space? Or have Captain Jin and Comrade Yakovlev put themselves in charge?"

Jin pushed the chair back. "I will not sit here and listen to this." He turned to leave.

Yak laughed, shaking his head as though he wasn't surprised. "Things never change down here on Earth."

Tighe grabbed for Jin's sleeve. "Han, wait a second."

Chindarkar stood as well. "Han, we *must* get back into space, if we are to have any chance of rescuing Isabel and Ade."

He pulled away from Tighe. "Rescue them with what?"

Rochat scanned the table. "We still have quorum."

"In that case . . . excuse me." Yak stood up and headed to the exit.

Tighe and Chindarkar went after them.

Now alone, Rochat turned to the officials. "Please, just give us some time to deliberate."

Jin burst through the lobby door, emerging into the open air and the gentle Florida rain. Tighe and Chindarkar were close on his heels. He walked across the lawn and away from the soldiers waiting near the shuttle van.

Chindarkar grabbed his arm. "Stop acting like we're all against you."

"Are you not? You want us to help the US government spread their domination into space."

Tighe held up his hand. "No one here is saying that."

Jin gestured to the building. "You heard them. They want to take charge of the resources, or they will not help us. If we accept their deal, we cannot hope to return to Ryugu."

Chindarkar said, "If we negotiate rock-solid commitments—"

"What good are their commitments?"

Tighe said, "What good are China's commitments?"

Yak exited the building with more composure than the others. "Is as expected. This is what governments do, yes?"

Rochat emerged from the building as well. "You are being unreasonable, Han."

Jin walked toward him and stabbed a finger into Rochat's face. "You set us up! All this time and all you wanted was money."

"Five billion can purchase a lot of help. And you're forgetting you can't even get into orbit without cooperation from a major power. I told you: no private launch provider will risk angering the US government. And then there's the threat to Adedayo's family in Lagos—which we need help to resolve."

"Then we must talk to China."

Yak shrugged. "Or Russia."

Jin waved him off. "Russia cannot negotiate safety guarantees for Isabel and Ade. China controls the *Konstantin*."

Tighe stepped between them. "And why would we trust China? You heard the man: Have we heard anything from Isabel and Ade?"

Jin turned to him. "We could ask for proof that they're alive."

Chindarkar shook her head. "Even if they allowed us to communicate with Isabel and Ade, deepfakes are easy. They have thousands of hours of surveillance video from the *Konstantin* to draw from. We'll have no way of knowing whether Isabel and Ade are really still alive, Han. Not without going to Ryugu ourselves."

Jin stood in the rain. "Then we must keep those resources."

Rochat interjected. "There is still the money. And FAA clearance to access orbit."

"A few billion is nowhere near enough to mount a rescue."

Chindarkar added, "Or to carry out the phase two plan."

Rochat raised a finger. "You're forgetting that government approval can also bring investment guarantees. Low-interest loans. Introductions to new capital partners."

"More strings attached. Damn you, Lukas."

Rochat gestured to the building. "I will continue to negotiate. Perhaps I can secure at least a portion of the asteroid resources in addition to cash. Perhaps we can find partners to help us build the mass-driver—and obtain the resources we need."

The other four didn't look hopeful.

"In the meantime, I suggest you proceed as if we are going to implement phase two of the master plan. Which means you will have to continue evaluating the equipment you'll need in lunar orbit. That means taking meetings with potential tech partners while you're still here in the US."

The group exchanged grim looks.

"And I don't need to remind you that time is still of the essence."

CHAPTER 9

Smoke Screen

Jin Han and James Tighe stood at the edge of a yawning pit mine in the mountain desert of central Nevada. The landscape around them was both sun and dynamite-blasted, with monstrous 320-ton autonomous dump trucks rumbling past behind them. Below, at the bottom of the mine and the center of a coiling road, autonomous shovel loaders filled more trucks with ore.

Aside from a half dozen engineers in hard hats, there were no other humans in sight. A lead engineer stood between Jin and Tighe and was manipulating twin joysticks on a ruggedized controller. Before them, a collection of golf-cart-sized, six-wheeled robots zipped about, equipped with various tools: bulldozer blades, robotic arms, and augers. The words "Badger-100" were painted in bold letters on their steel housings.

The lead engineer spoke without turning toward them. "Your CEO claims you're planning lunar surface operations."

Jin adjusted his hard hat and nodded. "That is correct."

"What's your timeline?"

"We are seeking immediate delivery, but are not yet convinced your machines meet our needs."

The engineer gave him a look. "No offense, but we're not convinced of your bona fides. You guys are linked with Nathan Joyce—and his multibillion-dollar fraud gave the entire private space industry a black eye."

Jin sighed. "The media is publishing untruths about us."

"Yeah, well, we'll need payment in full, up-front for any orders, and as for our equipment . . ." He gestured toward another gigantic, autonomous dump truck roaring by. "We've been making mining robots for twenty years. We know how to ruggedize these machines for serious uptime—which is exactly what you'll need on the Moon." He turned back to the smaller robots. "But the advantage of our Badger line isn't autonomy, it's their neural learning. We call it 'shepherding.' You teleoperate one unit to 'show' the other ones what you want done, and they learn by observing. Then they improve on the efficiency of what you taught them. And it's easy to pull them away and teach them something else—all without writing a single line of code. That'll be handy up on the Moon."

He lowered the remote control, and they watched as the other robots started imitating what his robot was doing—moving bucketfuls of gravel from one pile to create another pile some distance away.

"Two-hundred-kilogram chassis, just one meter by half a meter in size, 100-kilowatt power unit, and an excavation rate of 1,600 kilograms per hour. Solar panel rechargeable, it's highly modular and reconfigurable—with a dozen attachments—and it can operate across a wide range of temperatures, atmospheres, and gravities. It can survive a lunar night cycle, though it will need power for its internal heating unit. And you can fit a dozen Badgers in a typical launch faring."

Jin and Tighe looked at each other. Tighe shrugged.

Jin said, "I wish our roboticist was here to help me evaluate."

"Yes. You mentioned that."

"What if we want to launch only the computer boards, optics, and advanced components—and depose the heavier metallic components in situ?"

"Aside from requiring deposition equipment and manufacturing facilities on the Moon, you'd also need a licensing deal with us—which is a much more serious financial commitment on your part. Again, up-front."

Jin and Tighe watched the robots going about their task efficiently without supervision.

Jin considered this, then nodded. "We will consult with our CEO and get back to you."

"You do that, and we'll see if you guys are truly serious."

The next morning Jin stood alongside a compact electric rental car in a motel parking lot and stared at the southern horizon. Towering smoke clouds extended into the stratosphere—clouds so colossal they were motionless, like some gigantic oil painting—fueled by wildfires raging across Arizona, Nevada, and Utah. It was a vast atmospheric wall.

Tighe's voice suddenly spoke behind him. "That looks ominous."

Jin turned to see Tighe approach, duffel bag over his shoulder—and his head newly bald. "You shaved your head?"

"Easier to deal with on the road."

"It took you three weeks to decide that?"

"You don't like it."

"Just an unusual decision. For you." Over the years they'd spent in deep space, at no point had Tighe shaved his head, and out there it might have actually made sense. It was beginning to concern Jin just how little he seemed to understand him.

Tighe rapped on the trunk.

Jin searched for the button on the key fob and popped the lid.

After stowing his bag, Tighe came up alongside and studied the smoke-filled horizon. "You were right about not flying through that."

"But travel by car has put us behind schedule. Our rescue spacecraft must be completed in lunar orbit forty-six months from now, and we have accomplished very little in these meetings."

Tighe grimaced. "You heard that mining engineer yesterday—our negative press is becoming a real problem . . ." Tighe produced his phone and tapped at its screen. "I tried to pay back some money I owed my brother-in-law—and he refused it. Sent me this instead . . ." Tighe handed over his phone.

Jin read aloud a text message from the screen: "'Keep your dirty money. When will you stop embarrassing this family?'" He clicked through to the linked news article—which included a recent photo of Jin, Tighe, and Priya Chindarkar somewhere in Luxembourg City beneath a headline that read "NewSpace Grifters Pan for Earth Gold."

"It says we're running a scam to sell nonexistent 'resources in space.'" Tighe gestured. "That's a major news site. Do a search for Catalyst Corporation, and this article comes up first."

Jin handed back the phone. "We must tell Lukas to sue them."

"Yeah, add that to the long list of things we need to do. Standing here on Earth, it's hard to prove to doubters that the *Konstantin* expedition ever actually happened." Tighe put away his phone. "Any word from Lukas yet about our government negotiations?"

Jin shook his head. "Nothing. And no word about the Lagos gang either. Or Adedayo's family."

"Lukas hasn't replied to my messages." Tighe leaned against the car. "We're wasting our time out here, Han. Without government support it's pointless to look for equipment partners." He suddenly fell to coughing.

"Someone must vet this robotic mining equipment, or we cannot conduct operations on the Moon."

"But how do we do that without Priya? She's the robot expert, not you or me."

"We cannot wait for her to return from India." Jin paused. "But I agree. She should not have left."

Tighe coughed again for several moments before replying. "Let's be happy for her. She's got a chance to finally reunite with some of her family."

"But it is bad timing."

Tighe nodded. "And it's the least of our problems. Look, you and I should head back to Luxembourg and demand some answers from Lukas—" Another coughing fit suddenly gripped him.

"You have been sick since Lagos."

Tighe leaned aside to spit onto the asphalt, then regained his composure. "I'm here, aren't I?"

"If we return to Luxembourg, I am concerned I will not regain entry to the US. But perhaps you are right—we may be on a fool's errand here." Jin looked south at the distant smoke clouds. "We should head to Las Vegas and catch a flight to the EU from there. Let's get going before they close the highway."

Hours later, Jin piloted the rental car south on Interstate 15 in Utah. Sagebrush desert stretched to the horizon in all directions, and by now the sky overhead was black. The air reeked of woodsmoke. Tighe was sleeping in the passenger seat, as he often did these days, so Jin listened to the news—a litany of natural disasters, economic chaos, political division, and overseas conflict. Most of it was linked to worsening climate. The world had indeed changed since they'd been away.

Soon the car's low-battery warning illuminated, and Jin took the next exit for a service center, passing by a large video billboard proclaiming "Jesus Is Lord," animated with a rippling American flag.

Though it was almost noon, the sky was preternaturally dark, and the service station's overhead lights had come on. Motorists here were charging EVs or refueling older internal combustion engine vehicles. Others headed to the fast-food outlets. Most people wore face masks against the smoke, and a few of these masks were novelty or fashion designs, a sign of the recurring crises being euphemistically termed "the Long Emergency" in American media. A bumper sticker on a nearby SUV proclaimed "The Rapture Is Nigh."

Jin parked in an open charging bay and plugged in. The display indicated it would take three hours for a full charge, so he left the air conditioning on for Tighe, who was still sleeping, and went to find a restroom.

Afterward, he bought a flavorless and colorless "green" tea for several dollars from a vending machine, then sat at a concrete picnic table across from the rental car and pulled out his phone to check messages.

No word from Rochat. Or from Chindarkar.

A group of men suddenly coalesced from passing motorists and surrounded Jin—some standing and others sitting down at his picnic table, as if they were with him, while still others sat on a bench behind his. Jin looked around in alarm and pocketed his phone. "It is not American custom to sit at a stranger's table uninvited."

One of the men—well-groomed, neatly dressed, and of Han Chinese descent—smiled as he replied in Mandarin, "But you and I are not Americans, Captain Jin. What a surprise to find you in this wasteland."

Jin studied the faces of the men around him. Some were Caucasian, and one a Latino, but most of them were Chinese. Jin turned back to the one who had spoken. "I have nothing to say to you."

The man reached into a shoulder bag and produced a computer tablet. After a few taps he turned the screen toward Jin. It displayed what appeared to be a surveillance photo of Jin saluting an American officer—an astronaut in a blue jumpsuit. It must have been taken at Cape Canaveral.

"Have you forgotten your loyalty oath, Captain?"

Jin sat in momentary shock. How had this photo been taken? Cape Canaveral was a secure US military base. He looked up from the screen.

"Nothing to say?"

"That salute was a professional courtesy, nothing more."

"But why were you there?" The man stowed the tablet. "I want to help you, Captain, but I cannot do that if you betray China. Are you making a deal with the Americans for those asteroid resources in lunar orbit? You may be unaware, but China has lawfully purchased the *Konstantin* and its payload."

Jin bristled. "Lawfully? There is nothing lawful about what happened out at—"

The man held up his hand. "You were right to be angry with Mr. Joyce's creditors, but they have been punished for what they did to you and your crewmates. In fact, those responsible for dismissing you from the CNSA space program have also been sacked. Beijing is proud of you, Captain. Great things await you back home. We want you to lead China's push into deep space."

"Did my father send you?"

The man shook his head. "No, your father is under house arrest."

Jin frowned. "Arrest? Why would he be under arrest?"

The man ignored the question. "You will be the most famous explorer since Zheng He. Schoolchildren will learn of your exploits for centuries to come. You will be admired for your accomplishments." The man gestured toward the rental car with Tighe still asleep in the passenger seat. "Leave this *guilo*. Come with us. Return to China. Become the hero you were meant to be."

Jin asked, "Are Isabel Abarca and Adedayo Adisa still alive?"

The man put a hand on Jin's shoulder. "I know only what they tell me, but come with us. You can ask the leadership yourself." The man's eyes looked past Jin.

Jin turned to see a local police car slowly drive by in the parking lot.

After a pause the man continued. "Do you really believe that Priya Chindarkar went to visit her brother and sister in India? And so urgently?"

Jin stared.

"Her family lives in Mumbai, but she flew in to Chennai—a thousand kilometers southeast. Do you know what *is* right next to Chennai? Satish Dhawan Space Centre."

Jin felt the shock course through him. *Why would Priya go to the Indian space agency?* He was afraid he knew why. But could he really believe that?

"Do you think that is a coincidence? She is passing the coordinates for your robot tugs to her government." He pressed a finger to his temple. "Think, Captain. These foreigners are deceiving you. Why did you wind up at Cape Canaveral? Why are you out here, wasting your time? They are trying to keep China down."

The man pointed again to the rental car. "James Tighe has been meeting with his American handlers your entire journey. How many times has he disappeared while you wondered where he was?"

Several more police cars suddenly entered the parking lot, along with a couple of unmarked vehicles.

The man noticed these, then calmly stood. "You know the way home, Captain."

"What of my father?"

"If you return to China, then I'm sure he will be fine." With that, the men all dispersed, walking in different directions just as the police cars pulled to a stop alongside.

Jin watched officers get out and accost several of the men, asking for ID. Yet none of the police bothered Jin. Instead he could see an unmarked black sedan parked across from him, a Caucasian woman and a Black man, both conservatively dressed, sitting inside—and looking directly at him.

He was being watched by both governments. Of course. There was a great deal at stake.

After a moment the black sedan rolled forward. The man in the passenger seat nodded to Jin, before the car departed the parking lot.

Jin turned to look at Tighe, still asleep in the rental car. Then he thought of Chindarkar supposedly visiting family in India.

Could he really afford to trust either of them, now that they had returned to Earth?

CHAPTER 10

Oga

Lukas Rochat watched his seven-year-old son contemplate the chessboard between them. "Your turn, Nigel."

His son chewed his lip whenever he concentrated, and Rochat wondered with some concern if that was going to become a habit. Still, he couldn't help but marvel that he'd had anything whatever to do with creating the boy—who seemed wholly wonderful. That Rochat would *ever* teach his son chess—particularly after his own father had terrorized him with the game as a child—was a testament to how much the past few years had revised Rochat's priorities. He now recognized the broad utility in learning at a young age to think three moves ahead of an opponent.

Nigel widened his eyes in realization and smiled. "I know!" He moved his bishop, then sat back, beaming.

The move wasn't terrible. "You're improving."

His son laughed. "You should give up now."

"Don't get ahead of yourself."

"Dad, what's the shortest time to lose a chess game?"

Just then the disembodied voice of an AI assistant spoke from the ceiling. "*Mr. Rochat, you have a call on the secure video line. Will you accept?*"

Rochat looked up.

Nigel groaned in exaggerated frustration. "But I'm winning."

"And you'll still be winning when I return." Rochat spoke to the ceiling, "Emily, what country is the call from?"

"*The call originates from Lyon, France; however, the IP address belongs to a known VPN. The caller's face and voice do not match any of your contacts.*"

Rochat nodded to himself. "Tell the caller I will be there momentarily."

"*I will ask them to hold.*"

His son whined, "Dad, let's finish."

Rochat stood. "Some things cannot wait, Nigel."

"You promised no calls today."

Rochat walked around the board and straightened his son's shirt. "You're right. I did promise, and I will try harder to keep my promises. But this call could make your future a lot brighter."

"That's what you always say."

"And I always mean it." Rochat turned to go. "I won't be long." He spoke to the ceiling. "Emily, add an hour to Nigel's video game allowance."

His son brightened considerably. "Make it two."

Rochat let a slight smirk escape. *That's my boy.* He turned to the ceiling. "Deal. Emily, make that two hours." Rochat then walked into the hall and up the main staircase.

It still amazed him that he could afford such a fine home—a 150-year-old stone mansion in the Kirchberg neighborhood of Luxembourg City, with high ceilings and tall windows—all newly restored. Just six years ago he was broke—his fledgling space law firm a failure. He'd been preparing to return in defeat to his partner and infant son in Switzerland when he uncovered Nathan Joyce's secret project. Since then he'd done everything possible to make himself indispensable to the billionaire. And it had worked. His partner finally joined him here from her law practice in Vevey, bringing Nigel. They were a family once more.

It was an acknowledgment of Rochat's success, but then, he no longer craved the trappings of material success as he once did. Instead, he desired actual power—in pursuit of a goal that Nathan Joyce had gifted him. A goal that would matter to his son's generation more than his own.

Rochat stopped in front of his home office and in a moment the facial recognition software identified him. The door clicked open, and he moved inside, pausing to be sure it locked behind him. He crossed the room—lined with books and architectural models of spacecraft and robots—toward a walk-in closet that had been retrofitted as his own secure communication facility.

Inside he confirmed the scanning system was already powered up. A glance at a monitor showed the caller was still waiting. Rochat closed and locked the door, checked a sensor to confirm no eavesdropping devices were present, then sat in a lone office chair, the focal point of an array of soft LED lights. Rochat checked his appearance in a reference monitor. Satisfied, he then spoke to the AI. "Emily, stop listening in this room."

"I will no longer listen here. Good-bye."

With that, Rochat dimmed the room at the edges, leaving himself in an island of soft light, surrounded by darkness. Then he connected the comm line. In a moment, a ghostly apparition resolved—a translucent hologram of a face he recognized from old World War II newsreels.

Before him sat a black-and-white projection of British prime minister Winston Churchill scowling. In a fairly convincing imitation of Churchill's voice, the deepfake said sternly, *"Do you think my time worthless?"*

Rochat hesitated. "How can I be certain this is you, if you won't show me your true face?"

"My own voice and face could be just as easily faked—especially were I to expose them on such frivolous transmissions as this. You know full well who I am and why I call."

The software did not entirely erase the cadence and accent of the speaker. There was a Nigerian voice still. "Mr. Oyekan."

The deepfake glared. *"You presume to speak names."*

"This channel is quantum encrypted. Any interception will immediately sever the line."

"Your sudden knowledge of QKD schemes interests me—particularly since you were so reckless back in Ajegunle." The Churchill avatar studied Rochat. *"May Joyce rot in hell. I too easily forget that you were his right hand. Did he teach you his mastery of acting the fool?"*

Rochat remained stone-faced. "Nathan taught me many things. One being that too many people read Sun Tzu and Machiavelli when instead they should read Robert Graves."

Churchill's silent appraisal continued for a beat. *"More likely Joyce bequeathed you his dossier on me."*

Oh, yes, Rochat thought. Nathan Joyce's files on businessmen, politicians, and underworld figures alike had proven highly useful. "I know you are a twin—or were a twin."

"*Hardly a revelation. The Yoruba have the highest rate of dizygotic twinning in the world.*"

"You are Taiwo Oyekan, oga of Ẹgbẹ Ọdẹ—the satellite hunters."

The deepfake of Churchill contemplated Rochat for several moments. "*My staff tells me you refuse to transfer ownership of Adedayo's shares to us. Must I demonstrate the earnestness of my wishes?*"

"I wanted to speak with you first."

"*Then you should have done so in person—as a man does—back when you were in Lagos. Instead of hiding in your armored car like a woman.*"

Rochat felt calm. Prepared. "I needed you to reveal yourself to me first—publicly—which you would only have done if you believed me a fool."

"*Do not trifle with me or Adedayo's family will suffer.*"

A musical note played, and Rochat saw that Oyekan had sent a file to him.

"*This is a death certificate for Adedayo Adisa—as well as his last will and testament listing one of my enterprises as his heir. I expect the formal transfer of ownership to be executed today in the presence of our notary in Luxembourg City.*"

Rochat didn't bother opening the document. "I have a newer version of Adedayo's will."

Churchill now looked genuinely angry. "*If you tell me his family inherits, then they will not be long for this world. You will dispose of any subsequent wills and do as I instruct. I warn you: diluting your company stock will be interpreted as theft. And I detest thieves.*"

Rochat replied coolly, "The situation has changed, Mr. Oyekan."

"*Do not take me for a fool. I know what it is that Joyce has done in space—this Konstantin vessel—and where Adedayo has been these past five years. Out at the asteroid Ryugu. Your network security is sloppy. You have no secrets from me, Mr. Rochat.*"

Rochat looked Churchill in the eye, just as Joyce had taught him to do when slipping in the metaphorical knife. "Was I sloppy, or did we let you in? The United States and Chinese governments are the ones you need to worry about—especially since you are now on their radar."

"*Is this your attempt to frighten me? To get me to walk away from what is rightfully mine?*"

"Not at all. I'm merely observing a fact: if you try to claim Adedayo Adisa's shares, they will be taken from you by your own patrons within the Nigerian government—who will sell them to either the Chinese or the Americans. You might get some cash, but that is all. These asteroid resources in lunar orbit are too strategically important to the superpowers to remain with you."

The deepfake avatar stared.

"You may believe you can conceal this transaction from your own patron, your *oba* in the Ministry of Defense. However, both China and the United States are well acquainted with the patronage network in Nigeria's ministries. They know who you work for. They will note the stock transfer and follow the trail of shell corporations—especially after they witnessed our public encounter in Lagos."

"This insolence will be punished."

"Your superiors will soon tell you to back off, and your side hustle with me will be brought to a swift end. The only thing that will change is that America or China will own part of Catalyst, instead of Adedayo."

"And I will have made money."

"Maybe. Maybe not. Either way, threatening me is pointless. The superpowers—and thus your *oba*—will not allow you to harm me."

Oyekan continued to stare, apparently trying to ascertain the truth of what he'd just heard. *"Then why do I have the feeling our meeting is not at an end?"*

Rochat leaned forward. "Because I wish to partner with you, Taiwo—with the Ẹgbẹ́ Ọdẹ—secretly and separate of Catalyst Corporation. I do not want the US or China, or your own patrons, to believe that you and I are anything but bitter enemies."

"We are enemies, of this I can assure you."

"Partner with me. I want you to secure our deep space communications satellites against cyberattack from Earth."

The avatar of Churchill laughed. *"Why would I betray my patrons and anger the Chinese and the Americans to partner with you?"*

"For shares that no one on Earth will know about. Shares that could one day be worth hundreds of billions—perhaps trillions."

"One day." Oyekan's deepfake sat for several moments in silence before he finally said, *"Like Nathan Joyce, you are a fool who will wind up dead."*

"Perhaps. But tell me, Mr. Oyekan, did your brother, Kehinde, provoke the powerful?"

Oyekan's avatar looked positively menacing now. *"Do not ever speak of my brother."*

"No. Your brother did not provoke the powerful. Instead, Kehinde was dutiful and loyal, and was nonetheless sacrificed as a pawn in a dispute between factions that no one even remembers. That is what it is to be powerless."

"You will find out that I am far from powerless."

"I often wonder why it is that Africa is still in thrall to the industrialized world. It is 2038, after all. Are Africans simply incapable of competing on the world stage, Mr. Oyekan?"

The deepfake pounded the arm of his chair angrily, shouting, *"What do you know of it? Colonialism did not end! Do you think the borders of the nations of Africa were drawn by Africans? They were set by colonizers in the Berlin Conference of 1885—running roughshod over our cultural boundaries. The Françafrique controlled the currencies, interest rates, and 70 percent of the foreign reserves of west and central Africa for decades! Their multinationals still have veto power over resource deals. American, British, and Chinese money is all around us, paying to divide us, one against the other. For centuries. No one in Africa rises except with the permission of the great powers. Patronage is what runs Africa. And whether you admit it or not, patronage runs the West as well, Mr. Rochat. You would do well to remember this."*

Rochat nodded. "Yes, there are always those who are willing to sell their own people's sovereignty to outsiders in exchange for wealth and power—to defeat their local rivals. There's nothing on Earth that can change that."

"Precisely."

"Nothing on Earth." He pointed up. "But that changes when we think in more dimensions."

Oyekan regarded Rochat warily.

"As long as the nations of Africa are not in control of their economic destiny, they will live in thrall to outside powers. Because those outside powers will always be able to reach in and pay off whatever political leaders, or generals, or warlords they need to get their way. But if Africa can generate its own wealth—beyond the Earthly interests that infest and divide it; wealth from a new frontier where no power at present holds command—then you would finally have a chance to break the cycle. To liberate your continent."

Oyekan studied Rochat. *"You believe me to be an idealist? I have seen what happens to idealists. That, too, is the history of Africa."*

"I'm not looking for an idealist. I want a partner with ambition and a desire to become very wealthy and very powerful. The great powers were not always great. No, they *took* what they have. 'Power concedes nothing without demand—'"

Oyekan finished the quote. *"'It never did, and it never will.'"* He stared at Rochat for several moments. *"You are more dangerous than I thought for a Swiss—dangerous to both of us. Do not forget that Joyce got himself killed. Do you intend to follow in his footsteps? I have no wish to."*

"Nathan was like Icarus. He flew too high, but I learned from his trajectory. I want Ẹgbẹ Ọdẹ to act as a shadow cybersecurity partner for something new—a decentralized autonomous organization, a DAO—in deep space formed with crypto assets that are not readily visible to outsiders. We have blockchain-driven smart contracts through which we are financing operations. That is where the real growth will occur in cislunar markets. I wanted you to discover the proof of those asteroid resources in lunar orbit because I am suggesting you step up and stake your own claim on this new frontier, Mr. Oyekan. After all, frontiers are not settled by saints."

"The superpowers will destroy you."

"What we're doing will ultimately benefit even them—though they can't yet see that. I want you to accept shares in our off-world commodity exchange for helping to secure its networks and communications against Earthly interference—which will be massive when we begin operations."

"Why would I ever trust you?"

"You won't have to. I know that crypto assets are the preferred medium of exchange in Lagos. So you are already familiar with the concept of 'trustless' exchange. Our Cislunar Commodity Exchange will be governed by smart contracts and trustless exchange. You will earn DAO tokens that give you participation in its governance."

"But what is the business? You have resources in orbit; how will you translate that into value—and influence—here on Earth?"

"By increasing the resources and energy of all humanity by several orders of magnitude in the next few decades—creating so much wealth that even the Earthly powers will benefit and not long be our enemies. We hope to create an international wave of development in space, in which all of humanity will be invested. You will be able to bring terawatts of clean energy to Africans, and provide enough economic might for them to throw off the shackles of neocolonialism once and for all. You may even become a historic African leader, equal to any who has come before."

Oyekan stared hard at Rochat once more. *"You think I am so weak-minded that I would believe this children's tale?"*

"You know the truth of what my colleagues have accomplished. Their courage and daring—Adedayo's courage right alongside them. They brought thousands of tons of strategic resources into lunar orbit. Resources that the superpowers of Earth are desperate to control. *Eight people in space did that, Taiwo.* Imagine what a few hundred more could do. Especially if someone helps them keep their systems secure from Earth interference while they work."

Rochat watched Oyekan figuring the odds—the seeming impossibility of something ending well, given his life experience. Finally he said, *"If I were to consider it, I would never submit to work for you."*

"There's no need. We would be partners, independently supporting the same DAO. What I bring to the organization is expertise in space law. The laws of Earth can be very useful when they are employed properly. But by pivoting to claim a stake in this new frontier in space, you can simply *buy* back Africa's sovereignty on the open market—not request it as a supplicant or demand it as something stolen from your ancestors. Outwitting your oppressors will command the respect of the world. Beat them at their own game—by creating a bigger one. A better one."

Oyekan stared in silence for several moments, then finally made a decision. *"Yes, you are indeed Nathan Joyce's protégé ..."*

CHAPTER 11

Through the Looking Glass

SEPTEMBER 15, 2038

J in Han and James Tighe trudged down the corridor of a drab Las Vegas suites hotel near the airport. They hadn't spoken much in the car, and Tighe was acting increasingly strange.

Jin studied him as they walked. The Chinese agent was right. There was something off.

Tighe stopped in front of his room, swiped his key card, then barely glanced over his shoulder. "When's the flight?"

Jin stopped at his room across the hall. "Tomorrow evening was the earliest available."

"Good. I could use a break."

"Read up on the specifications of the—"

"Yeah, I got it." With that Tighe entered his room, and the door slammed behind him.

Jin stared after Tighe for several moments—then entered his own room. It was the typical American corporate efficiency suite, with a small kitchen and sitting area. Chilled to near-freezing. As he headed toward the bedroom he noticed a pair of sturdy eyeglasses sitting in the center of the desk. A power-charging cord ran from the glasses to an outlet at the base of a nearby lamp. A small card stock note was tented next to it.

Jin dropped his bag on a kitchen barstool and approached the glasses. Something forgotten by the room's prior occupant?

To his alarm, the note was in Hanzi characters and said in neat black handwriting: *Open your eyes.* He glanced around warily then picked up the glasses, causing the too-short charging cord to pop out. He examined them more closely.

A blue LED light on one of the bows indicated they were powered on. He tentatively peered through the lenses, then slipped them on.

A voice behind him spoke in Mandarin, *"I am over here, Han."*

Startled, Jin spun around.

His father, Jin Longwei—or at least an augmented-reality apparition of him—sat on an illusory chair halfway to the kitchen. Looking older than his seventy years, he held up his hand. *"Please. Do not disconnect. It has been very difficult to contact you unnoticed, and I have been waiting here hours."*

Incredulous, Jin answered in Mandarin. "So I am expected to believe you are my father?"

The apparition looked pained. *"I tried to see you in person. You refused me."*

"And I will not see you now, whether you are real or not . . ." Jin reached to remove the glasses.

"Wait! Please. I am here to warn you. Do not believe Beijing's entreaties."

"You could be a deepfake controlled by the Americans. This conversation is pointless."

"Then ask me a question only I could answer."

"I barely know you. And you barely know me."

"There must be something we've shared. Over the years."

Jin considered the question, then said, "If you are my father, what did you say the day you sent me away—after BISS? Answer quickly."

His father concentrated, but then looked down. *"I don't recall. What is BISS?"*

Jin nodded to himself. "Oh, you are definitely my father." Jin stared. "BISS was my preparatory school. You said I was a bad investment. I was eleven, and I did not see you again for six years."

"I know I was hard on you, but the demands of our businesses were vast."

Suddenly Jin's phone warbled to indicate an incoming call. He glanced at it. *Rochat.*

"I see your own business makes demands of you, too."

Jin silenced his phone and slipped it into his pocket. "What is it you wanted to tell me . . . *Father?*" He spat the last word like a profanity.

The apparition looked dismayed by the emphasis. *"I wanted to warn you to not let Beijing use me as a bargaining chip."*

"Don't worry. I won't. Is that all?"

"You are angry at me still."

"You interceded on behalf of people who tried to *kill* me and my crewmates."

His father held up his hands. *"You must believe that I did not know. They told me you had joined a mutiny on their spacecraft and asked me to talk sense into you. I never dreamed they would try to harm you if I failed."*

Jin continued. "But what we achieved out in deep space was *nothing* to you. What *I* achieved was nothing to you."

"And you treated my hopes for you—my only son—as though they were nothing."

They stared at each other for several moments.

His father finally sighed and said, *"Your grandfather—my father—he was hard on me, too."*

"Did grandfather try to *kill* you?"

"I did not try to kill you, Han. I was lied to. They told me you had illegally gone to space and were defrauding business interests vital to China's future."

"And you believed them, instead of me—your own son. And you ignored the history my crewmates and I were making out there."

"I was concerned you were being led around like a dog by foreigners."

Jin sighed in disgust. "We are finished."

"Wait!" His father held out his hand. *"I realize now how much like your grandfather you are. I think he would have understood you. Because he never understood me."*

"Grandfather commanded an army division. I chafe against every rule. I am the opposite of Geming."

"Ah, that's where you're wrong." His father seemed to see some distant memory. *"Back in the '80s, China was poor. Your grandfather pushed Deng Xiaoping's reforms to their limit. He risked being purged dozens of times to pursue what were then illegal business ventures. He didn't follow rules. He made new ones. He took insane risks. And he succeeded, pulling China up in the process."*

Jin's father came out of his reverie. *"But it fell to me to grow the business. To make it respectable. To cooperate with authorities—not antagonize them. To do what was necessary for China to take its rightful place in the world."*

"You want me to congratulate you, Father? You already have people for that."

"Why must you be so cold to me? Understand: they will take everything our family has built if you don't do what they want."

"And you expect me to obey."

His father shook his head. *"No. I realize that now."*

Jin regarded his father with suspicion.

"I admit your lack of interest in the family business always angered me. I wanted you to have many children and bring our enterprises to new heights, but you saw things differently. Like my father did."

"I have to go."

"Wait." Jin's father tapped at his wrist. *"Let me show you something..."*

Another virtual screen appeared, hovering in midair. It looked to be a surveillance monitor, focused on a large wrought iron gate that Jin recognized. It was the main gate of his father's estate—the Jin residence in Beijing. The camera zoomed in slightly to focus on a young, clean-cut man waiting at the curb across the road. Several more young men stood nearby.

"At first I thought they were MSS agents monitoring me, but day by day there were more..."

The image fast-forwarded, past nights and days, then slowed to real-time again, showing now half a dozen well-dressed young men waiting patiently, eagerly at the gate, craning their necks whenever a vehicle approached or the gates opened.

"We ran facial recognition on them. Background checks. These are scientists. Test pilots. Entrepreneurs. Some of the best young minds in China. Waiting outside our gate each day." His father turned toward Jin. *"They come in hope of seeing you, Han."*

Jin looked curiously at the screen. The image fast-forwarded again, and now there were a dozen young men and a few young women as well.

"They know what you've done. I don't know how, but they know. You inspire them. They want to go where you are leading."

Jin studied the image—the expectant faces. He turned to his father.

Despite the pixelated projection, the intense anguish in his father's eyes was still visible. *"I was wrong, Han. Don't try to save me. But please . . . forgive me."*

Tighe's phone sounded somewhere in the semidarkness of his room. Unnaturally exhausted by his disease and the chemo meds, he struggled to awaken. "Aaah, what?" He fumbled for his phone on the nightstand. A glance at the screen. *Rochat.*

Tighe answered it. "I've been trying to reach you for days, Lukas."

Rochat's voice was high-pitched and tense. *"Is Han with you?"*

"What? No. He's in his own room. If you want to talk to Han, call Han."

"I did. Three times."

"What do you want?"

"Our robot tugs in lunar orbit—they have disappeared."

Tighe sat up straight and adjusted the phone to his ear. "Hold it. What?"

"I said that the asteroid resources you returned from Ryugu have disappeared from lunar orbit. The Nicole Clarke *and the* David Morra . . . *are gone."*

"How the hell could they be gone? Aren't you monitoring them?"

"Yes. The tugs orbited behind the Moon . . . but did not reappear. Their orbits were somehow altered. Beyond our sight."

"Where did they go?"

"We don't know. They could have been moved anywhere in cislunar space."

"By who?"

"Either the US, China, or Russia."

Tighe realized that the lives of his friends—sacrificed to secure those resources—might have been lost for nothing. He jumped up and punched a hole in the drywall, sending a shooting pain through his arm—followed immediately by exhaustion.

He mustered the energy to shout into the phone. "They lied to us! They were planning on taking the resources all along!"

"J.T., where is Han?"

"What?"

"The US government is accusing us of cutting a deal with China. They've frozen our company accounts. The Defense Department is livid. We might face sanctions."

Tighe scowled. "But we're the ones who got robbed."

"It doesn't matter. Without those resources, J.T., we are not only broke— with no leverage to regain orbit and mount a rescue mission—but our investors will sue us as well. This destroys us."

Tighe felt his rage building. "You told us the Chinese and the Russians wouldn't be able to locate those tugs in DRO."

"You forget: Sevastian and Han both know the orbital elements of those tugs."

"Fuck off. I don't believe Yak or Han would—"

"J.T., where is Han? Why is he not answering his phone?"

Jin stared at the spectral AR image of his father—and for the first time felt a connection that went beyond obligation, beyond what was expected of him as an only son. For the first time he saw respect in his father's eyes. "If what you say is true, and you have not taken the government's side against me . . ." He took a deep breath. "Then I could forgive you."

His father's face showed relief and then he nodded—but then suddenly he flicked out of existence.

The disappearance of the AR illusion momentarily disoriented Jin, just as several Chinese men pushed through his hotel room door in real life.

The first of these, a swarthy man with a fierce expression, aimed an index finger at Jin and shouted in Mandarin, "You are coming with us, Captain Jin. Stand up. Now!"

Jin removed the AR glasses, tossing them aside as he stood. "You have no right to be in here. Get out!"

More men surged into the room while their leader approached, keeping his finger aimed at Jin's face. "It is you who has no right. You violated your oath. You have betrayed—"

"I have betrayed nothing. Get out!"

"Where are those resources in lunar orbit, Captain?"

Jin pushed the man away. "That is my business, not yours."

The man grabbed Jin roughly. "It is the Party's business!" He stared hard. "Where have the tugs been moved?"

Jin was momentarily confused. "Moved? Who says they were moved?"

"Your American friends think we are blind, but we have eyes in space." He grabbed for Jin's hand, attempting a basic Qing Di Quan move that Jin recognized—and evaded. It was simple "Capture the Enemy Boxing," standard training in the PLA. Frustrated, the man shouted louder. "Tell us where they were moved!"

"Why do you keep saying they were moved?"

"You are corrupt—like your father. Did you sell out to Burkette? Macy? The Pentagon? The Americans lie to you. They aim to prevent China's rise, and they will never allow *any* of you into orbit again. Unless you honor your oath, we will not either."

Jin felt confusion and then outrage building. Memories of his tightly controlled childhood filled him with a rage that surprised even himself. He evaded the man's grip. "You think I am a stooge of the Americans? Yet you act as though the CCP owns me."

"We all owe our lives to the Party."

"Chinese history dates back three thousand years. The Party is not China. The Chinese *people* are China, and they will exist long after the CCP is gone."

"That is treason!"

Jin surveyed the room. The other men had edged around behind him—one of them preparing flex-cuffs. He turned back to face the lead man, who was grabbing Jin's shirt.

"Take him!"

Jin made his move, not evading the leader but pulling him close in—ramming a shoulder into the man's jaw and using the momentum to pull past and propel forward, driving a knee into the groin of the man beyond. Sweeping aside a punch coming from his left—knocking the wind out of the man with a body slam to his exposed ribs.

As the son of a multibillionaire, it had been drilled into Jin's head since childhood that kidnapping was an ever-present threat. However, traditional martial arts conditioning was impractical given Jin's educational commitments—which was why he had been instructed from an early age in Baji Quan—the art of eight extremities. With it, one did not strike primarily with fists or kicks, but with one's entire body as the weapon—shoulder and elbow strikes that focused explosive power in close-up fighting to incapacitate and move past an opponent. It was not a subtle form, but one whose core tenet was *advance, advance, advance.* In Jin's case, to escape from would-be kidnappers. His instructors had schooled him a thousand times in evading abduction.

Jin knew his only chance was to escape while his attackers were momentarily stunned.

But just then the hotel room door kicked in.

The whole room turned in surprise to see James Tighe standing in the doorway. He shouted in English, "What the hell is going on in here, Han?"

One of the men turned to him. *"Yáng lā jī!"*

The entire room erupted in shouts and rushing bodies. Jin glimpsed two men attack Tighe—punching and kicking him with devastating blows that sent Tighe staggering back through the open doorway and into the hotel corridor.

Someone in the hallway screamed, and another voice called in English, "Get the police!"

Jin continued advancing toward the open door—toward escape. A man behind Jin grabbed his wrist, while another tried to place flex-cuffs. Jin crouched low and rammed his body into the chest of the man with the flex-cuffs, then thrust his hip into the ribs of the other man, entwining a leg, unbalancing him, then shoving him to the ground.

More English voices shouted in the hall: "Call the police!"

A voice in Mandarin shouted, *"Tuōlí! Tuōlí!"* Disengage!

As Jin moved on to the next target, he found the men retreating. Two cornered intruders exited through the balcony door, then lowered themselves over the second-story railing.

"Tuōlí!" The leader staggered through the front door, blood flowing from his nose and mouth.

Jin gave chase and discovered Tighe on the floor in the corridor. The assailants fled in opposite directions down the hallway, past a group of dazed

Americans clutching their carry-on luggage close. Jin shouted toward them, "Did you phone the police?"

A man in a T-shirt and shorts was on his phone. "Yeah. They're on the way."

"Good. Thank you." Jin knelt next to Tighe, whose face was bruised and bloodied. "J.T., you are hurt."

Tighe coughed, but shook his head.

"Fighting is not your forte."

"No shit." Tighe tried to sit up. "Jesus Christ . . . Who the hell were those guys?"

"Wait for the police."

"Just get me to my room."

Jin lifted him to his feet, threw his arm around him, and helped Tighe to his door. Jin noticed an enormous and ugly bruise on Tighe's inner arm. "You are injured."

Once inside, Tighe sat on his sofa and took several deep breaths. "Tell me who those guys were, Han."

Jin retrieved ice from the fridge. "They were Chinese agents. Here to kidnap me. They claimed the asteroid resources had been moved and that I must have sold out to the Americans." He locked eyes with Tighe. "Why would they say that?"

"Because the robot tugs disappeared." Tighe lay down on the sofa, seemingly exhausted.

Jin stared. "*Disappeared?* Who told you this?"

Tighe struggled to get his T-shirt off. "Lukas phoned me. After he tried calling you. He said the robot tugs orbited to the far side of the Moon but never reappeared. They're gone. No one knows where."

Jin wrapped ice in a dish towel and placed it against Tighe's bruised eye.

"The US government knows, too. They think we cut a deal with the Chinese." Tighe gestured. "And then I find you in your room with a bunch of Chinese agents, and I get attacked."

Jin glared. "You are not suggesting that I betrayed you?"

"I'm not saying that. Maybe China promised you they'd rescue Isabel and Ade."

"How can you insult me like this! How do I know you have not betrayed *me* to the Americans? Or that Priya has not betrayed us both?" Jin pointed back toward his room and shouted, "Why would the CCP try to *kidnap* me, J.T.? Why did they demand to know the location of the tugs if China took them?" Jin suddenly noticed the constellation of mottled yellow, blue, and purple bruises all over Tighe's body now that he'd removed his shirt.

Tighe was itching his skin furiously and winced in pain. "All I know is that everything we worked for is *gone*. Everything David, Nicole, and Amy gave their lives for." Tears appeared in Tighe's eyes. "Now we can do *nothing* for Isabel and Ade. It's all gone to shit."

Jin was likewise horrified by this realization—but more immediately by the state of Tighe's body. And then it all became clear. Tighe's unnatural, permanent fatigue. It brought back memories of someone else. "James. Tell me what is going on. What is wrong with you? Those bruises are not new."

Tighe just shook his head. "It doesn't matter anymore."

Jin strode into Tighe's bathroom, where he noticed a collection of prescription medications on the counter. He searched through them, examining their labels.

In a moment he returned and sat on the arm of a chair across from Tighe. "Why did you not tell us?"

Tighe stared at the floor, his breathing ragged. "Because we both know I can't take a year off. We need to reach space. We need to be building in orbit."

"What is your diagnosis? How bad is it?"

"It's spread, I think."

"Who is your doctor? What is your treatment regimen?"

"It doesn't matter, Han."

Jin struggled for patience. He spoke softly. "I have put my life in your hands more times than I can remember, and you have never let me down. Yet, when it comes to your own life, James, you are one of the most irresponsible and reckless people I know. Why would you do this?" Jin felt a spasm of emotion he was not expecting. "Do you think that I do not care about you?"

Tighe shook his head. "This isn't about me." He searched for words. "So many people have died in my place already. I made myself a promise that I would either rescue Isabel and Ade or I would die trying—and it's a promise I intend to keep."

A siren was now audible in the distance.

"You're giving up. That is not the J.T. I know."

Tighe looked down. "It's over for me."

Jin studied him. "Do you remember what you said when we touched down in Karagandy? After our first sight of blue sky in four and a half years? Our first breath of fresh air?"

Tighe nodded weakly.

"You told Priya and me that we were the most important people on Earth to you."

Tighe wept and struggled for words. "I'm sorry. I just—"

Jin approached and gently held Tighe's head with both hands. "I consider you my *brother*, James. I have never had a brother, and I do not intend to lose you."

"You need to help Isabel and Ade."

Jin looked into his eyes. "*We* will help them."

TWO MONTHS LATER

CHAPTER 12

Adrift

L ying in bed, James Tighe stared up at a soffited ceiling in varying shades of white. The walls around him were surfaced in luxurious fabrics, burled wood, and metallic finishes, interspersed with modern art and tropical flower arrangements. The décor was even more opulent than the rooms on billionaire Nathan Joyce's private island, Baliceaux.

As he lay there, Tighe tried to ignore the IV drip he knew was hanging behind his right shoulder. If he let his mind wander, he could almost forget the needle taped into the back of his hand, too.

The gentle rolling motion of the room soothed him to sleep. In the background he felt as much as heard the bass rumble of distant engines. These were reassuring. Unwavering. And had been for many, many days.

Behind it all was the calming realization that he was slowly, steadily getting better.

A sharp knock roused him, and the door opened as two Chinese women in lab coats entered.

Tighe sat up in bed. "Doctor."

A perfectly coiffed woman in her sixties, Dr. Li smiled briefly. "How are we this morning, Mr. Tighe?" She examined readings from a translucent tablet, while the nurse checked his pulse and the IV drip line.

"Good. I think."

"Yes . . ." She tapped at the device while she talked. "The injections are taking effect. Your tumors are slowly dissolving, and your platelet count is almost within normal range."

He hesitated, but then asked, "Am I actually going to survive?"

She kept reading his charts. "That is the plan. There is more work to be done, but no more need for bed rest." She nodded to the nurse.

The nurse started ripping off the tape to remove the IV drip.

Tighe watched her work, wincing as the nurse removed the IV needle before placing a bandage over the wound.

Dr. Li produced a light pen and checked his pupil dilation. "You are not cancer-free, but the reagents in your bloodstream will continue their work for several weeks. The medically induced coma may have temporarily affected your memory." She regarded him. "Can you tell me where you are?"

He looked around. "On a large yacht."

"Do you recall its name?"

"The . . . *Nezur*?

"The *Nezha*. Close. And how did you get here?"

He thought back through the fog of weeks. "I remember being questioned by police. The FBI, I think."

"But do you recall coming aboard the *Nezha*?"

He concentrated. "Vaguely."

She patted his knee. "That's better than yesterday. We will continue our morning checkups. In the meantime, if certain fragrances cause you pain or any parts of you feel alien, do not be alarmed. These are common side effects of genetic editing and likely temporary. I am available at all hours if you have concerns."

"*Likely* temporary?"

She pulled back his blankets. "Try to regain your strength, Mr. Tighe. Eat more. The onboard chefs are excellent."

Though he wore a set of absurdly luxurious blue silk pajamas, Tighe felt suddenly exposed, and now that his health was improving, he felt once more the weight of obligation to his lost colleagues.

How long had he been here? What exactly had been done to him? But before he could vocalize these questions, the doctor and the nurse were already gone.

Tighe sat at a table in the sunlight. His cabin was well above the waterline and included a large window. Beyond was endless ocean. He stared into the distance for a long time, and at some point heard a knock on his cabin door. He turned. "Come in."

Jin Han entered.

Tighe smiled. "There he is."

Jin returned the smile. "I would have come earlier, but you were in quarantine. Dr. Li tells me you can now have visitors. That you should start moving around."

Tighe examined the bruise-free skin of his arms. "It's amazing." He looked up. "In fact, I don't really know what they did to me."

"They edited out your cancer—an experimental treatment. One that is only available to a select clientele."

"I keep forgetting you grew up rich. How do they 'edit out' cancer?"

"They prepare a custom CRISPR protein coded to your tumor's DNA sequence, insert it into an adenovirus, then let it spread throughout your body to destroy the tumors."

The explanation was lost on Tighe's still foggy mind. "I'll take your word for it. I don't know how I can repay you, Han."

"Continue to get better. We have work to do."

Tighe opened and closed his hands, testing his grip. "I do feel better. Better than I have for a long time." He took a deep breath, then paused. "If only we had had this treatment on the *Konstantin*. We could have saved Nicole."

Jin nodded grimly.

"If we ever get back into space, we need to take this tech and someone to operate it up with us."

"Unfortunately, getting *into* space continues to be the problem. We have been banned from launch, and, as you know, we have no resources in space even if we reach orbit."

Tighe's heart sank. "So the robot tugs are still missing."

"Yes, and there is no word from Washington, Beijing, or Moscow—or Macy and Burkette, for that matter. Any one of them could have stolen our tugs. We have no bargaining position and no funding. And our investors are suing Catalyst for fraud. Again."

They remained silent for several moments.

Finally Tighe looked around at the yacht. "Then who's paying for all this?"

"We are guests of an old friend of mine." Jin stood. "Are you able to walk?"

Tighe sat up. "Yes. I've been pacing a little."

Jin extended his hand. "Dr. Li says you need exercise, and there is someone who will be very happy to see you."

As they exited the cabin, the lavishly paneled and marble-inlaid corridor beyond was new to Tighe. Walking slowly down the hall with Jin, he began to get some sense of the scale of the yacht. As they passed a bank of tinted windows, an unbroken blue ocean lay beyond. They were cruising at an impressive pace.

"Where are we?"

"The Andaman Sea. We crossed the Pacific from Hawaii."

"Jesus, how big is this yacht?"

"A hundred and sixty meters."

"And your friend *owns* this?"

"It was a gift from his father. More a rebuke, really—one that keeps him away from the paparazzi."

They soon emerged into an enormous and luxurious salon that ran the full width of the yacht's beam—easily 20 meters and much bigger than any apartment Tighe ever had. It was decorated with custom sofas, chairs, woodwork, carpets, crystal light fixtures, and ringed by tall windows.

As pleasant as the surroundings were, Tighe was most happy to see Priya Chindarkar curled up on a sofa in a T-shirt and sweatpants, reading a book entitled *Principles of Linear Induction*. He spoke softly. "Some light reading?"

She glanced up, then smiled broadly. "Look at you!" She set the book aside and bounded across the enormous room—halting just before reaching him. "How is your immune system?"

"As impossible as it sounds, they say I'm okay. I'm still having trouble believing it myself."

She moved in and hugged him. Kissing him on the cheek. "I'm still mad at you, J.T." She looked at him. "Why didn't you trust us to help you? You could have died, you idiot." She hugged him close again.

Afterward, he looked her in the eye. "Priya, I'm sorry. I was worried my illness would mess things up. I'm not completely cancer-free, though. So promise me my health won't disrupt our plans."

"What plans? We're in limbo. I've been here the past two weeks." She gestured to the book. "Reading up on mass-drivers because I don't know what else to do."

Tighe suddenly noticed his reflection in a mirror behind the bar. He had a full head of hair. "How long have I been here?"

Jin answered. "A month and a half."

"We wasted a month and a half because of me?"

"Not because of you. Because we have nowhere to go."

Chindarkar said, "China, the US, Russia—they have all banned us from space."

"So Han said."

"And one of them stole our robot tugs."

Jin said, "No telling which one."

"To be fair, it could also have been Macy or Burkette. Or some other billionaire."

Chindarkar motioned toward the sofa opposite. They joined her. "I would have come earlier, but the Intelligence Bureau in India detained me for questioning."

Tighe thought for a moment and turned to Jin. "Didn't Chinese agents try to kidnap you? Am I remembering that right?"

He nodded.

"Are we safe here?"

"It's *why* we came here. My friend has his own security team."

Tighe noticed a suited man walk past the window on the deck outside.

"However, I think it has become clear to the superpowers that we have no answers."

Tighe asked, "What about Lukas, Sevastian, and the others?"

Chindarkar shook her head. "We've had no word from Lukas or the rest. It's Nathan's bankruptcy all over again. Catalyst's market cap is zero without those resources."

A voice somewhere behind Tighe suddenly shouted, "HE LIVES!"

Startled, Tighe turned to see a handsome Chinese man perhaps forty years old, dressed in an electric-blue suit and white silk shirt, open at the throat. His arms held wide, one hand holding a flute of champagne, and a broad, perfect smile on his face, he strode into the salon and said with a

British accent, "Look at you, James Tighe!" He came forward. "Or, as you prefer, 'J.T.' Delivered from death's door by the peerless Dr. Li." He closed the distance to enthusiastically shake hands.

Tighe returned the shake. "Good to meet you . . . ?"

Jin gestured. "J.T., this is Cheng Zhihong, our gracious host and my—"

"Best friend since childhood." He gripped Tighe's shoulder. "And call me Bobby! Everyone calls me Bobby. Any friend of Han's is a friend of mine."

Tighe nodded. "Well, Bobby, it seems I owe you my life. I don't even know how to begin to thank you."

Cheng waved it away. "No trouble at all. Happy to do it. They can perform miracles with genetic editing. If you want your eye color changed, too, let me know." Cheng sat on the arm of the nearest sofa.

"So you and Han go way back?"

"Han and I have known each other since preparatory school, though he was more studious than I." He laughed. "For all the good it did him." Cheng poked at Jin's arm. "Always studying. No time for fun. I told him his fretting would come to nothing." He gestured at Jin's grim face. "Look how sad he is . . ." Then gestured to himself. ". . . and how happy I am." He raised his glass. "Because no one has grand expectations for me." He took another sip of champagne.

Tighe just then noticed a uniformed butler who had silently entered. Cheng motioned to him. "Bring a fresh bottle of the Krug Clos d'Ambonnay. We must toast to Mr. Tighe's miraculous recovery."

The butler nodded.

Tighe said, "I'm not entirely cured just yet. So no champagne for me."

Cheng sat up. "Ah, a shame." He looked to the butler. "Bring it for us, though. And some food." He turned to Tighe. "Are you hungry? My chefs are the best. The. Best. They can make anything, and I think we have everything. I think we have ostrich eggs, if you want. Do you like ostrich eggs? An ostrich omelet?"

Tighe shook his head. "That sounds like way too much, but thank you. Just tea is fine, Bobby."

The butler nodded and hurried away.

Cheng turned to face them. "What are we talking about?"

Chindarkar answered Tighe's concerned expression. "Bobby knows we want to get into orbit."

He raised his glass. "You crazy bastards! Han has been talking about going into space since we were kids, and now you're finally going to do it."

Tighe met Jin's gaze and suddenly realized that Cheng was unaware of the existence of the *Konstantin* expedition. Tighe confirmed this with a glance toward Chindarkar, who nodded almost imperceptibly.

Cheng, meanwhile, crossed his legs, revealing that he wore bunny slippers. "You know, I have a rapper friend, Smoov-OB—you may have heard of him. He went up to that orbiting hotel—the Hotel LEO—a few years back. We partied together here on the *Nezha*." He rummaged in his jacket and withdrew his phone. "I have photos . . ."

As the days passed, Tighe's strength continued to return, aided in part by physical therapy with Dr. Li in the *Nezha*'s ample—and largely unused—gym and also by the cuisine. The onboard chefs were indeed masterful, and each meal involved lingering over multiple courses while Cheng regaled them with stories about his drunken misadventures and past famous (and infamous) guests. He seemed particularly excited to have them on board *because* they were in trouble with the authorities.

However, the luxurious surroundings did not conceal the grim reality of their situation. They had no means to get back into space, and instead, their asteroid resources would apparently be used to amplify tension between the superpowers in a new space race.

One evening, Tighe and Chindarkar leaned against a railing on the upper deck and stared up at the full moon. It was a place they desperately needed to reach, but Tighe felt powerless as he studied its cratered surface. "How strange is it that you and I have traveled beyond the Moon?"

"It does seem like it was all just a dream."

The horn of a nearby ship sounded, and he looked back to the water. Lights near and far peppered the moonlit sea. "I'm surprised there are so many ships this far out in the ocean."

She followed his gaze. "Refugee ships. Bobby said there are more every year, overloaded freighters smuggling people. And the pirates preying on them."

It was mute testimony to what Marius Hanssen had told Tighe back in Luxembourg. Mass human migrations were underway as changing climate made the equatorial zone increasingly untenable.

"Isn't he worried, being out on this floating palace of his?"

A suited and armed security man walked past behind them wearing an earpiece radio.

Chindarkar shook her head. "It doesn't seem to faze Bobby. I think he grew up in protected bubbles like this. He gave me a tour of the bridge. The crew is tracking dozens of radar contacts at all times, and the *Nezha* can outpace almost anything." She rapped the railing with her knuckles. "It's apparently bulletproof. It even has an anti-paparazzi system that blinds cameras that try to film it."

"So he's just going to stay out here and party through the end times, is that it?"

"I don't think he's got much faith in the future. Or anything, really. I actually feel bad for him." She peered down at the blue bioluminescence of phytoplankton as the waves lapped against the *Nezha*'s hull. "I had hoped that we'd be able to do something about the future."

"You mean Joyce's master plan?"

She nodded. "We could have done so much more than rescue Isabel and Ade. We could have built the next stage of civilization. We could have given people hope."

Tighe continued to gaze down at the water and wondered if that had ever really been in their power to achieve.

Days later, Tighe, Chindarkar, and Jin watched the sky. Eventually a helicopter resolved from the humid haze and descended toward the *Nezha*'s forward helipad. The aircraft deftly touched down, and Lukas Rochat emerged from the side door in his customary suit, tie flapping in the chopper wash. A woman exited behind him—one whom Tighe did not recognize. She was dressed in a simple blouse and slacks. Her mid-length brown hair whipped about, but caused her no apparent concern.

Tighe shouted over the prop roar, "Who's that with Lukas?"

Chindarkar and Jin shrugged.

The three of them walked to the edge of the Jacuzzi deck and nodded to

Rochat and his companion as they stepped down from the helipad. Moments later, the chopper lifted off behind them, sending a brief blast of wind over them all. Then there was relative silence.

Rochat squinted against the sunshine as he surveyed the massive yacht. "If I'd known your hideout was this opulent, I wouldn't have felt so bad for you." He extended his hand to Tighe. "Glad to hear your cancer is under control, J.T. No doubt it didn't come cheap."

"I'll submit an expense report."

"Don't bother. We're officially broke." Rochat moved aft, into the air-conditioned comfort of the yacht's massive forward lounge. The others followed. Rochat gestured to his companion. "This is Dr. Erika Lisowski, the NASA program executive I told you about on our journey to Lagos."

Chindarkar was about to shake Lisowski's hand when she stopped and stared instead. "Wait . . . You were the one who worked with Nathan. From the beginning."

Lisowski said, "You might say *before* the beginning."

Jin's voice had an edge as he asked, "Did you know Nathan was sending us into deep space without enough fuel to return?"

Rochat interceded. "That's enough, Han. Erika saved you all."

Lisowski ignored Rochat, keeping her eyes on Jin. "Nathan knew better than to tell me such things. We all know he had an abusive relationship with the truth, but I didn't come here to discuss him. I came here to discuss how we're going to get you all back into space."

Jin still seemed uncertain whether to trust her.

Tighe leaned in. "Well, I for one am eager to hear your idea." He extended his hand. "Good to meet you, Erika."

She nodded. "You too, J.T."

Then Chindarkar shook Lisowski's hand.

Jin relented and gave her a perfunctory handshake.

Lisowski nodded. "Good. Now that we're all acquainted, let's find a place where we can speak in private."

Lisowski sat on the edge of the desk in Bobby Cheng's wood-paneled—and entirely disused—office. She studied the three asteroid miners sitting before her, with Rochat on a wing chair to the side. "Let me get this part out of the way: your robot tugs—the *Nicole Clarke* and the *David Morra*—were not stolen by China, the US, or Russia."

Jin ventured, "Was it Jack Macy?"

She shook her head. "No, not Macy, or Burkette, or any of the other billionaire Space Titans. In fact, your robot tugs weren't stolen at all. They were simply repositioned—by *you*. Which is to say, by Catalyst Corporation. This was a maneuver planned years in advance by Nathan Joyce and his team—and something Lukas was not aware of until a couple months ago."

The three asteroid miners turned to Rochat.

Rochat held up his hands. "I fully understand if you're angry. I—"

"*Angry?*" Jin fumed. "I was nearly kidnapped over the disappearance of those tugs."

Chindarkar shouted, "Why do you keep lying to us, Lukas? Is lying just in your nature?"

Tighe said, "He learned from the master: Joyce."

"If I may continue, please," Lisowski interjected.

They turned back to her.

"It was a necessary misdirection to give you plausible deniability—and the ability to pass a polygraph test. The US and China had you all under surveillance. If the disappearance of those robot tugs was a crushing, emotionally wrenching experience for you, then that unfortunately was the point, and your reactions and actions afterward convinced Washington and Beijing that you knew nothing about the theft. Thus, their attention has, for the moment, turned away from you, and the great powers are even now launching probes to lay eyes on those resources—because they know where they have gone."

Jin asked, "And where is that?"

"Into a Lissajous orbit around L2, on the far side of the Moon."

Tighe frowned. "But how? We loaded only just enough fuel on those tugs to put them into a lunar DRO—not a kilo more."

Lisowski regarded Tighe. "Do you really think Nathan would send out an asteroid mining expedition without preparing for the return of resources? No, he was counting on their return."

Jin considered this. "We built docking ports into all the robot tugs."

Lisowski nodded. "Yes. The telepresence robots Lunargistics used to build the *Konstantin* years ago are still in lunar orbit. The fuel and other port connections on the tugs were designed to be interoperable with them."

Chindarkar laughed. "The telepresence robots that Julian Kerner controls."

"Correct. Each bladder tank on those robot tugs has a standard connection port. The Lunargistics robots can dock and use those ports to electrolyze the water ice into hydrogen and oxygen—to refill the tug's fuel tanks. This was all designed and tested years ago. That's why it's up there."

Jin said, "So before anyone would think to look, Nathan already had the equipment in place."

Chindarkar added, "In licensed orbits . . . for equipment that appeared to be for another purpose."

Rochat finished, "Yes."

Lisowski drew two circles on a pad of paper. She labeled one "Earth," the other the "Moon." Then she created a halo-like orbit on the far side of the Moon. "Once refueled, the tugs were transitioned from a lunar DRO to an orbit around L2, and it's there—over the past months—that your phase two space station was being constructed by Julian Kerner and his team using telepresence robots."

Chindarkar let out a gasp. "Julian. That lying . . ."

Tighe felt an immense wave of relief. He exchanged stunned looks with Jin and Chindarkar—but spoke to Lisowski. "This whole time, that station from Nathan's master plan was being built for us?"

Lisowski said, "Correct—something that was only possible because you and your crewmates returned hundreds of tons of refined metal carbonyls in standardized tanks to a lunar orbit. You made it possible for Kerner's team to, in effect, 'print' your space station—using a chemical vapor deposition mill that has been in place and waiting for years."

Chindarkar asked, "But if this was the plan all along, why did we meet with the US government at all? Why mislead the superpowers?"

"Because you had to appear helpless—so they would focus on each other and not you." Lisowski was silent for several moments. "It's been clear to me for some time that the governments of the world—given their inertia and the influence of entrenched interests—cannot do what must be done to save our biosphere. No matter what they say, some among them would attempt to take control of those asteroid resources in pursuit of astropolitical advantage—something we could not let happen."

Chindarkar's eyes went wide. She turned to Rochat. "That's why you had me visit Satish Dhawan."

Jin shot a look her way. "So you *were* lying to us. You didn't visit your family."

She returned the look. "If I had told you the truth, Han, you'd have thought I was selling you out to New Delhi."

"Then what have you done?"

"I went to see friends at Vestar—it's a private space launch firm in Satish Dhawan's new commercial launch complex."

Rochat interjected. "Priya was merely doing what I asked—establishing contact."

Lisowski continued. "Please understand, Han: there are many mid-level technicians, scientists, and program managers around the world who *want* the three of you to succeed in accelerating progress in deep space. Their own governments and politicians may not approve, but we have allies in many organizations who believe, as I do, that the best chance for civilization to survive what's facing us, is for this team—*your team*—to launch to the far side of the Moon and carry out Joyce's phase two plan."

The group exchanged looks.

Jin asked, "Erika, you're saying this space station is already built?"

"It will be completed in the next few weeks—but yes. We've been calling it 'L2 Station,' but since it's being built with materials that you—and your crewmates—have provided at great personal cost, we feel you three should choose the name. When you're ready."

"So it has life support, power—?"

"It will have all the critical systems necessary—but remember, only a small portion of the station is complete and habitable. It will also not be fully equipped. There's a 5-megawatt thermal plant. All the wiring, life support systems, thermal management. All conceived of and designed years ago. It won't be luxurious, but it will be a capable base of operations—and only a week's journey from Earth."

Tighe felt new waves of relief. "This will save us *years* of work. We still have a chance to rescue Isabel and Ade."

"Yes, but more than that: this is how we rescue Earth. The way we jump-start a global cislunar economy and change the course of human history."

Tighe gave her a sideways glance. "Which *includes* rescuing Isabel and Ade."

"Yes, of course." Lisowski turned to Rochat. "First, we need to get you all back into space, and what we're contemplating is necessarily extreme. However, with you banned by every spacefaring nation, it's the only way we can think of to sneak you off the planet."

Tighe asked, "And what exactly are we contemplating?"

She paused. "That you three secretly launch out of Satish Dhawan on a Vestar commercial cargo rocket, then rendezvous in low Earth orbit with Lunargistics' old lunar cycler, *Rosette*, as it passes through the lunar antipode. Then you ride the cycler toward the Moon."

Tighe pondered this. "Okay . . . a cargo rocket." He turned to Chindarkar and Jin. "That's not much different from a human-rated rocket, right?"

Lisowski said, "It is, in a couple of important ways. For one . . . there will be no capsule. Only a cargo faring, which will fall away from the payload module." She sat on the edge of the desk again. "And secondly . . . there'll be no escape system. So failure of the rocket to reach orbit would prove fatal to you all."

Tighe, Jin, and Chindarkar looked to one another for a moment, but no discussion was necessary.

Tighe turned to Lisowski. "Okay. When do we leave?"

CHAPTER 13

Cargo

DECEMBER 24, 2038

J ames Tighe, Priya Chindarkar, and Jin Han sat astride three stubby, rubberized surfboards in the Bay of Bengal, 22 kilometers off the Indian coast. It was just before dawn, and the water was calm. The massive yacht, *Nezha*, loomed in silhouette behind them, its starboard tender dock silently closing now that they'd departed.

Tighe had undergone weeks of physical and nutritional therapy to fully recover his strength—his cancer symptoms now gone. He swirled his legs in the water, feeling neither its temperature nor moisture. All three of them wore brand-new, white MCP—or mechanical counterpressure—suits that had been custom-manufactured based on body scans taken back at Ascension Island. The suits fit so closely that the team needed to bring their weight and muscle mass back into strict tolerances to match the months-old scan.

Their suit helmets—visors fashioned from transparent aluminum—were clipped into place atop a small backpack each of them wore, which also contained a bare minimum of provisions and supplies. The rest of their equipment should have been loaded into their transport vehicle—which was located on a waiting rocket somewhere just beyond the darkened western horizon, at the Satish Dhawan Space Centre.

The only issue had been how to stealthily cross the distance between the maritime boundary of India, where they currently floated, and Sriharikota Island, the location of the space center, and then how to swiftly move kilometers inland to the commercial launch center. This was a question the inimitable Bobby Cheng had answered with:

"What kind of giga yacht carries no water toys?"

Endless hours studying 3D maps had imprinted the route into their minds. Now they were simply waiting for the sun to crest the eastern horizon behind them. All was calm.

Tighe turned to Chindarkar, decidedly futuristic in her sleek white MCP suit, with the patterns of its integral LCVG plumbing variegating its surface. He could see her bright smile in the predawn darkness and thought she never looked more beautiful than at these moments of anticipation. Her every movement said, *Let's go*. There was no hesitation. Their past romance suddenly made perfect sense.

Tighe looked beyond her to Jin, who was also focused on the horizon ahead. After a moment Jin turned to Tighe—at which point a slight grin stole across his face, too. Whatever doubts Jin had had the night before the *Konstantin's* departure all those years ago seemed gone. No trace of regret for defying his father and his government. In its place was resolve. He knew who he was now—and where he was going.

So did they all.

Tighe turned ahead and took a deep breath of the morning air.

He would miss Earth, but they could never live as they had before. They had urgent business in space. Urgent both for their friends and for everyone else. And if Tighe was perfectly honest, he was also excited to go to the Moon. Incredibly excited.

Just then a ray of sunlight caught a ripple of passing water. Then another. In a few moments, the water around and ahead of them began to shimmer with the reddish light of dawn.

Tighe leaned forward and looked toward his companions. "Shall we?"

Chindarkar's smile grew. She extended her hands to both Jin and Tighe and they clasped gloves. "Gentlemen, no matter what happens today, I wouldn't trade places with anyone in the world."

Tighe and Jin smiled, clearly feeling the same.

With that, they let go and brought their legs up out of the water, into a kneeling position on their short, rubberized surfboards. They each gripped the trigger of a wireless remote in one hand, and their boards began to surge forward silently.

Tighe had practiced the maneuver hundreds of times over the last several weeks, and he now relished the ease with which he slowly rose from his kneeling position to a low crouch—squeezing the throttle, picking up speed—and then stood on the board as it rose up and out of the water atop a hydrofoil wing. Soon he was soaring at 40 kilometers per hour, half a meter above the water's surface, the electric motor of the Lift board barely audible as its blade sliced through the waves. He turned to see Chindarkar and Jin cruising alongside. Chindarkar laughed, held up her arms, and screamed in joy as they raced toward a distant coastline, leaving barely a wake as their boards slipped like razors through the sea.

They covered the distance to the coast in less than a half hour, and as the *Nezha*'s radar had indicated, they encountered no patrol boats. Tighe scanned the beachline, looking for launch and lightning towers in the distance to orient himself. Without his helmet's HUD, Tighe had to glance at his suit's integral wrist display to confirm his GPS position.

13°45'30"N, 80°15'18"E

They were right where they should be.

Sriharikota Island had several inlets to permit transport of rocket components—but the trio were going to slip in through a much smaller channel.

There. Tighe noticed the narrow waterway bisecting the beach. It had been dredged to accommodate small boats, and the gates at its entrance were also open.

Chindarkar gave a hand signal and took the lead as Jin and Tighe fell in behind her, single file. They cruised at speed toward the white-sand beach, and Tighe was momentarily alarmed at the sight of a security truck parked alongside the waterway's entrance. However, the uniformed guard there waved, smiling as Chindarkar waved back, racing past.

Tighe couldn't help but laugh at the impression she must have made—that they must all have made—as they swept past, like visitors from another world.

The guard shouted after them as he rushed to close the water channel's chain-link gate, "*Surakshit yaatra!*"

Moments later, coastal mangroves enveloped them, and Tighe's focus was total as he raced behind Chindarkar, maneuvering the narrow, winding channel—Jin close on his tail. They had no choice but to keep up their speed if they wanted the hydrofoils to function. Otherwise, the prop would plunge too deep and hit bottom. *Fast* was the only way to thread this needle. They ducked and dodged overhanging branches as they raced the boards down the winding waterway. However, they soon emerged from the narrows into a much wider pond with finished, sloping banks—part of a launch system water supply.

Just ahead lay Commercial Launch Complex One—and the first sight of their GSLV Mark III rocket, the sun illuminating its upper stages. The logo of India's leading commercial space firm, Vestar, ran down its side. The GSLV was about 50 meters tall and 4 meters in diameter—a thirty-year-old design transferred from the government space program and put to commercial use. Not exactly cutting edge or reusable, but nonetheless a reliable workhorse that could lift a 2,500 kilogram payload into a lunar transfer orbit.

Although the Indian government had launched several crewed capsules into low Earth orbit over the past decade, none of their private firms had launched humans. There was no Indian version of Jack Macy or George Burkette. At least not yet.

And what they were doing this morning was not officially happening. Especially in the event of a failure.

And failure . . . well, Tighe didn't want to contemplate failure.

The trio now cruised on their hydrofoil boards three abreast in the pond, scanning the grassy shoreline for their contacts. Jin pointed toward a white step van in a distant parking lot. Several people stood around it, waving to them.

The team adjusted course, and as they drew near, eased up on their throttles. The hydrofoils descended into the water, and soon they slid off into the shallows and clambered ashore.

A group of Indian men in lab coats and hard hats smiled broadly and extended their hands to pull the team in. They spoke rapidly in Hindi to Chindarkar. The trio of explorers moved through the knot of engineers and technicians, now both men and women, with one older man in a short-sleeved shirt and tie motioning for them to follow as he led the way toward the open door of the step van. Hindi or no, it wasn't hard to guess what the man was saying . . .

Hurry. Hurry!

As they reached the van's door, Chindarkar stopped suddenly and knelt down. Tighe bumped into her and looked to see that she was speaking to two children—a boy and a girl, each perhaps eight years old—who stood alongside their father, one of the engineers. The children spoke to Chindarkar with excitement in Hindi, and she smiled, leaning close as she spoke words that Tighe could not hear—eliciting broad grins from both of them. The girl then offered a pen and a rocket photo, which Chindarkar proceeded to autograph.

Tighe imagined that she seemed to them like a genuine superhero in her white space suit, arriving by hydrofoil.

The lead engineer hollered and pulled Chindarkar forward and into the van, Tighe and Jin close on her heels. Moments later the van door slid closed behind them, and they took seats along the wall in the windowless cargo space.

Jin gave Chindarkar an impatient look. "Hardly the best time to sign autographs, Dr. Chindarkar."

"They were kids. You want to inspire the next generation or not?"

"How about we inspire them by succeeding?"

The van suddenly lurched forward, slamming them against one another. Its diesel engine rattled as the team braced against the walls, and they removed their suit helmets from one another's rucksacks. With practiced precision they fitted and locked their helmets into place, checking the seals. Tighe then passed around portable life support units that were waiting for them in the van. He connected the input and output hoses to their helmets' life support systems—much simpler arrangements than the older EMUs, which required the entire suit to be pressurized. After taking a few readings, Tighe powered up his life support, and fresh air started flowing through his helmet. He was now on their private comm network.

The team then double-checked one another's equipment.

"Radio test. One. Two. Three."

Jin gave a thumbs-up. "I have you."

"Good seal." Tighe also gave thumbs-up. "Hell of a lot easier pressurizing only the helmet—and with regular air, no less."

Chindarkar finished activating her own life support. "This morning's launch wouldn't even be possible if we had to do a two-hour oxygen prebreathe."

Tighe's helmet HUD display soon appeared, and he regained normal visibility as the plenoptic cameras embedded into the helmet's exterior rendered it transparent through his integral optics.

"We are go."

Within a few minutes the van slowed, then came to a squealing stop. Almost immediately the van door slid open, and a man in a security uniform motioned urgently, speaking in Hindi.

Chindarkar turned to Jin and Tighe. "Follow him."

They grabbed their mobile life support units as the man led the way.

Tighe glanced up as they crossed a concrete pad toward an industrial elevator. Here at the base of the launch tower, the GSLV rocket loomed over them. A trio of lightning towers stood some ways off, wires strung between them. The rocket looked every year of its design age this close up—much less elegant than one of Burkette's or Macy's next-gen reusable rockets. If the Zenith and Starion capsules had been first class, they were about to go via FedEx freight.

The launch tower elevator doors opened, and the group pushed inside. After an interminable wait, the security guard repeatedly jamming the "close door" button, the doors clanked and rattled closed. The elevator ascended.

Tighe said, "I recall there being a lot more paperwork the first time around."

Soon the elevator boomed to a stop and the doors rattled open. They emerged to find themselves atop the gantry platform, with a shroud blocking the view. The only indication that they'd reached the top was the rocket's faring directly ahead of them. It was perhaps 8 meters tall and 4.5 meters across at its widest point. A hatch had been removed, lending access to the interior. Technicians in white smocks, booties, and yellow hard hats waited there, motioning for them to enter.

Chindarkar ducked through the entrance—with Tighe right behind her—and came to an immediate stop. The interior of the faring was crowded with equipment—not all of it comprehensible. Tighe looked up to see Chindarkar climbing a narrow utility ladder, and moments later she disappeared at the top, stepping off onto some sort of platform. He climbed up after her, holding his life support unit in one hand. As he reached the top of the 2-meter ladder, he let out an involuntary laugh. "You have got to be shitting me . . ."

Ahead of him was a metal platform near the top of the cargo faring, upon which three fighter jet seats had been bolted into place, arrayed equidistant from each other around a central core—all of them in a recumbent position. Chindarkar was already lying back in one of the seats, knees toward the sky, getting strapped into a harness, while two technicians assisted, hooking up her life support to the spacecraft.

"Time's wasting, J.T."

One of the technicians removed Tighe's pack, restrapping it across his belly. Tighe then moved to the nearest open seat and lay down in it with some difficulty within the confined space. "Erika wasn't kidding." He looked above at an insubstantial metal frame with a docking port atop it. "This is a convertible."

He heard Jin's surprised exhalation over the radio. "I can only imagine what the mission managers at CNSA would say if they saw this." He stepped over and past Tighe—with a tight squeeze against the faring wall—then took his seat.

Tighe started strapping himself in, and in a few moments, one of the technicians took over for him, also jacking in his life support and comms to the rocket's systems. He could suddenly hear a background of Hindi radio chatter from mission control.

Chindarkar's voice came in over the local radio. "Our orbital window is coming up soon. Let's clear these techs out ASAP."

The tight confines became a flurry of activity as the technicians finished and tested life support systems. One of the techs pointed out an auxiliary life support hose.

Tighe nodded and gave a thumbs-up. "Thanks. I see it." It was a nice sentiment, but the list of terminal scenarios in case of malfunction was extensive.

Soon the technicians gave the team the thumbs-up, and they all descended the ladder—pulling it away and exiting with it, before sealing the faring hatch behind them. Tighe couldn't help but notice how thin the aluminum was.

He glanced first right, then left, at his crewmates. "In terms of sketchy decisions we've made over the years, this one's right up there."

Chindarkar replied, "It might be obvious, but . . ." She paused. "If either of you have changed your minds, I can call Master Control to abort the—"

"No." Tighe waved her off. "Let's do this."

Jin's voice said, "It is appreciated, Priya. But we all know this is necessary."

She nodded. "The GSLV is a fairly reliable launch system—but it's a cargo rocket. That means the abort system is a self-destruct. And the payload propulsion module only has 500 meters per second of delta-v and no heat shield or parachute. So even if we slightly miss our orbit, we're as good as dead."

Tighe looked around at the lack of a capsule. "At least we'll have a nice view." He rapped on the cargo faring, which made a bell sound.

She let out a nervous laugh. "I hope this works. Because I really want to see this through. I want to build that mass-driver on the Moon, build that rescue ship, save Isabel and Ade . . . and establish humanity in the cosmos."

Jin chuckled. "I do not think that is too much to ask."

"Right?"

Tighe extended his arm, and they all clasped hands once more. "Then let's do it."

They sat for several minutes, holding gloved hands and listening to Hindi radio chatter. After what seemed entirely too long to Tighe, Chindarkar glanced both ways.

"We're in final countdown. One minute."

Tighe centered himself. He didn't believe in wishing for something to come true, but here and now, he didn't see the harm in it either.

The radio voices in Hindi continued, until finally vibrations and thunderous noise erupted below and then all around them. Tighe's chair and the entire cargo faring began to shudder—and suddenly they jolted upward, as though hurled by a catapult. The solid rocket boosters on the GSLV's first stage were brutal—Macy's and Burkette's reusable rockets gentle by comparison. The acceleration did not let up—it increased—and the all-consuming thunderous roar around Tighe made it impossible to hear his own thoughts. If he'd had fillings, he suspected they would have rattled out of his head. It was violent enough that Tighe briefly entertained the notion that the self-destruct had already been activated.

But no, the rocket's acceleration continued to build as its twin solid boosters thundered like the barely contained explosions they were, plowing straight through maximum aerodynamic pressure. There was no throttling down these boosters once they were lit. One had to simply hold on.

At about the two-minute mark there was a shudder, and the deafening roar died away.

BECO. Booster engine cutoff.

The acceleration eased, only to be replaced by a different, though less aggressive roar as the GSLV's Vikas main engines kicked in, and the g-forces returned with a vengeance.

Tighe laughed maniacally. It was turning out to be one hell of a ride.

Bobby Cheng made it a principle to never rise in the morning—much less at dawn. However, this was one show even he would rise with the sun to see. And in order to avoid a hangover, he'd kept up a slow, steady drinking pace all night long—meeting the sun on the deserted helipad of the *Nezha* near the bow, after his guests had quietly slipped away in the predawn darkness.

Cheng now stood in a purple silk robe and pajamas, holding a fifty-thousand-dollar bottle of Pernod Ricard Perrier-Jouët in one hand and a half-filled flute in the other, staring at the eastern sky, craning his neck upward as a distant rocket rode atop a pillar of smoke and buffeting fire. Thunderous booms pummeled the dome of the sky above, but he stared unblinking at the bright light, still climbing.

Cheng held up his glass and howled with joyous laughter. "Go, my friends! Go!" He smiled in wonder, watching the rocket continue to climb. "Never let them stop you!"

As the rocket ascended, disappearing into the distance, it occurred to Cheng that maybe, just maybe, he'd finally done something meaningful with his life. Just this once.

PART TWO

Orbital

CHAPTER 14

Transit

DAYS TO RYUGU DEPARTURE: 1,256

After a few minutes, the violence and noise of their ascent began to fade, and soon James Tighe felt the familiar sensation of microgravity. Then there was a brief jolt, and the second stage kicked in—bringing acceleration g-forces back with them. However, the murderous racket was gone now.

Jin's voice came in over the radio. "We have cleared most of Earth's atmosphere but are still parabolic."

Chindarkar added, "We achieve orbit at SECO."

Tighe asked, "What are we supposed to be again—a weather satellite?"

"Something like that. It'll be a while yet until we go 'off course.' They'll keep us clear of other registered objects."

The acceleration continued for several minutes more until the second-stage engine cut out.

Jin said, "And that is second-stage cutoff."

Chindarkar sighed in relief. "We're in orbit at least. One more good burn—our translunar injection just past the lunar antipode. Until that's complete, any malfunction is . . ." Her voice trailed off.

Tighe was about to say it for her when suddenly the rocket faring walls all around them silently fell away, like the petals of a flower opening, and were lost in the slipstream. "Oh my god . . ."

Below him was all the world.

The sunlit side of Earth spread out and away beneath them as they sat in the open cargo bay, astride the globe. Only a frame of metal rods capped by an international docking adapter enclosed them now—like a flimsy roll cage.

Gazing below, Tighe recalled again the joy and awe he'd felt when they'd reemerged after years in deep space to behold Earth's splendor.

"It's so beautiful!" Chindarkar cried out.

Jin shifted in his seat. "And of course, I am on the space side."

"Maybe she'll come around." Tighe leaned forward as far as his restraints would allow—which wasn't much. Looking across the arc of the world, he could see edge-on how thin the atmosphere was. It seemed miraculous that this tenuous haze had slowed them at all on their return trajectory to Earth all those months ago—much less that it contained all life known to exist in the universe.

They coasted, watching the world roll by below them for fifteen or twenty minutes, but then Tighe was slammed back as the second-stage engine kicked in again. They accelerated rapidly, occasional puffs of thruster gas adjusting their altitude and rotation.

"Here we go!"

"How long's this burn?"

Jin answered. "Eight minutes—our translunar injection."

Despite the aggressive acceleration, the craft rose only imperceptibly above the Earth, but Tighe knew from his rudimentary understanding of orbital mechanics that this burn was greatly extending their orbit on the opposite side of the planet, putting them on a course to loop around the far side of the Moon. However, to survive that journey, they would need to rendezvous with the *Rosette*, which was already heading that way and could provide shelter and life support for the rest of their journey to the L2 station.

Their propulsion module rotated slightly, eliminating Chindarkar's view.

Jin, however, laughed with joy. "Oh, yes! That is beautiful. Beautiful!" He laughed again. "It never gets old."

Chindarkar announced, "We coast for six hours eleven minutes after this burn, and then there's another short burn to bring us to our rendezvous with the Rosette." She paused. "Space weather looks good. Let's just hope we don't have any orbital debris impacts. There's a lot more junk up here than there was five years ago."

"How depressing would that be to go to all this trouble just to get taken out by a paint chip going Mach 34?"

But then they suddenly came around the night side of Earth, with its dazzling cities, and it was an all-new wonder to behold.

"Oh wow . . ."

Tighe did not sleep—though he hadn't slept much the night before either. Instead, the hours melted away as he stared at the Earth's surface rolling past in a full rotation every ninety minutes. Though he had UTC time displayed in his HUD, he instead counted every crossing of the Earth's terminator line. The cargo module was in a very slight rotation, so each of them was able to see the Earth for thirty minutes or so at a time.

Finally there was a sudden kick and the vehicle vibrated slightly as they began to accelerate once more.

"Thirty-two-second final burn." Chindarkar checked her display. "With any luck, we might make our rendezvous."

Jin added, "And survive this."

Tighe gripped the frame near him. "C'mon, baby!"

Jin pointed at a distant luminous white dot. "There!" It was ahead and above them.

Chindarkar checked her display. "That should be the *Rosette*."

Tighe realized just how tense he'd been right up until that moment as he unclenched his grip on the frame. Although distances were notoriously difficult to judge in space, he guessed they were only a few kilometers out.

The cargo capsule's thrusters popped to reorient the craft, even as the rocket motor continued to burn.

"Master Control is correcting to *Rosette*'s trajectory. We're still good."

In a minute or so, they were within a few hundred meters and just below their target, and the rocket engine cut out.

Chindarkar sighed in relief and grabbed for Jin's and Tighe's gloved hands, gripping them tightly. "We made it!" She turned to Jin. "Han, you ready to override autodock, if necessary?"

"Standing by." Jin produced a small joystick attached to a cable.

The cargo module's thrusters puffed occasionally on autopilot, bringing them upward and closer to the *Rosette*. As they approached, Tighe felt nostalgic for the bulbous white craft resolving before them. He hadn't seen it since 2033.

The *Rosette* was one of the late billionaire Raymond Halser's inflatable, pill-shaped space habitats, but bore the logo of Nathan Joyce's bankrupt company, Lunargistics, LLC. The ship was known as a lunar cycler, meaning it was on a cyclical trajectory between the Earth and the Moon, with the Moon's gravity tugging it along in a rosette pattern of orbits as it revolved around the Earth—thus the ship's name.

Since Tighe's last visit, mission control had adjusted the *Rosette*'s orbit. It now went from LEO out to the far side of the Moon in seven days, then seven days back to LEO, followed by another fourteen-day orbit, where it missed the Moon entirely, before the cycle began all over again. That meant it arced through L2 on the far side of the Moon every twenty-eight days.

As they approached, the word "Rosette" resolved on the hull in black letters, in addition to license numbers and a small Luxembourg flag. Solar panels extended from a collar at the far end of the ship, and there was a docking port visible on the near end (though Tighe knew there was another, even larger one and a small propulsion module on the far end, too). Their cargo module automaneuvered, bringing them ever closer to the docking port.

Jin's gloved hand hovered above the joystick: "Autodock is doing well."

Their capsule slowed as its docking port glided silently toward a matching port on the *Rosette*. Although they wouldn't have an air seal with this open faring, docking would at least provide a safer transfer to the ship.

In a moment, Tighe felt a silent *thump* and lurch—and the two crafts were joined.

Chindarkar laughed in relief. "That's one for the record books."

"It is also one of the safer things we'll be doing on this trip." Jin clipped a tether line to the cage frame around them and tugged to test it. "Let us get aboard." He then unclipped his seat harness.

Tighe and Chindarkar did the same, and moved hand over hand on the framework toward their life support packs, which were held in racks in the module's central core.

"I don't know about you guys, but I love this MCP suit." Tighe twisted and slipped his arms through the straps of the life support pack. "The maneuverability is outstanding."

Chindarkar cinched her straps. "Yeah, there's no comparison to an EMU. I'm not feeling the thermal load from the sunlight much either. At least not yet."

The life support hoses were still connected to their helmets, so they carefully coiled and stowed the excess hose line. Now wearing their life support packs, they moved hand over hand along the cargo vehicle frame, toward the *Rosette*'s docking port.

Jin arrived first and braced his booted feet against the frame, opening a small metal housing next to the port. He turned a rugged-looking key switch.

"Cycling airlock." A thirty-second pause and a red light appeared. "Depressurization complete." Jin repositioned and slid the *Rosette*'s hatchway lever—then pushed inward. He turned to face them.

Tighe and Chindarkar each gave a thumbs-up.

Jin moved inside the hatchway.

Chindarkar and Tighe floated in close behind.

The *Rosette*'s airlock was sizable and dimly lit by emergency LED lights. It contained two bulky xEMU space suits, tool harnesses, emergency breathing apparatuses, and video drones in racks along the curving hull.

This ship brought back potent memories for Tighe, but he shrugged them off and tried to focus. He pushed the hatch closed behind them and slid the locking handle. "Hatch secure."

"Cycling..."

Tighe saw, more than felt, air swirling around them, and before long a green light glowed atop the interior airlock hatch.

"Good pressure." Jin slid the interior hatch lever, pushed it inward, then glided inside. Moments later they all three floated into the large, open interior of the *Rosette*—which unlike their asteroid mining ship, *Konstantin*, had no compartment walls, only a carbon fiber grillwork to define individual sections. Thus, they floated at one end of a dimly lit, 20-meter-long-by-13-meter-high, rounded, cylindrical compartment, with workshops, sleeping bags, storage lockers, and equipment rooms visible all around them by emergency lights.

Tighe checked his helmet's HUD display. "Temperature two-point-five. A little chilly, but air mix and pressure are good." He depressed a latch and twisted his helmet, then pulled it off as it hissed. The cold, stale air felt unwelcoming. The *Rosette* was very different the first time he'd visited. A crew had been aboard back then, breathing life into it. Now it seemed derelict. But nothing seemed amiss. He turned to his companions floating nearby. "Home sweet home for the next seven days." His breath stabbed out plumes of water vapor in the bitter cold.

Chindarkar also took her helmet off, breathing in deeply.

Jin soon had his helmet off, too.

"Well, we're not dead. Always a good start." Suddenly the main interior lights kicked on, causing Tighe to shield his eyes. "Goddamn . . ."

A radio squawked to life, and the familiar French accent of Gabriel Lacroix came in over the channel. *"Mission control to* Rosette. *Mission control to* Rosette. *Do you copy? Over."*

Jin pulled along the ship's grillwork to a radio they all knew was located amidships. He manually keyed a handset mic. *"Rosette* to mission control. We copy you loud and clear. Glad to hear your voice, Gabriel. We are on station and en route to EM-L2. Thank the entire team for getting us here in one piece. Over."

After a brief delay Lacroix's voice came in again, cheering audible in the background. *"They will be glad to hear it. I expect your ascent was invigorating.* Rosette *has provisions and oxygen to support you en route. We are activating heating units now."*

Tighe spotted an empty plastic squeeze bulb floating nearby and took it into his gloved hand, sniffing it. "Of course they drank up all the booze before they left, and here it is Christmas Eve." He spun the container into a corner.

Due to the international character of their space crews, the Catalyst Corporation observed a holiday calendar centered strictly on celestial events—equinoxes, solstices, new years, and so on. During the *Konstantin* expedition, those holiday celebrations were psychologically important milestones that also reinforced personal bonds. Still, Tighe's memories of Christmas back in Wisconsin made him nostalgic, despite his rocky childhood.

Lacroix's radio voice echoed in the cavernous space, reading off trajectory information, while Tighe moved in microgravity toward a multidirectional meeting room, where a holographic projector was still set up. He surveyed the compartment. Years ago, this was where he and his colleagues first learned the Ryugu expedition was real—and that they'd been selected to go. Nathan Joyce had holographically projected himself here to outline the mission—beseeching them to take it on. Convincingly, as it turned out.

Tighe recalled the faces that were in this room then, many now either missing or dead. He turned to see Chindarkar come alongside, taking in the room as well.

She looked to him. "It's smaller than I remember it."

After the heaters warmed the *Rosette*'s interior, the vessel felt less like a mausoleum. Mission control also reactivated CO_2 scrubbers, oxygen generators, water lines, and a dozen other subsystems. It wasn't long before Tighe remembered just how much he disliked microgravity living. With all the fans blowing, nothing ever stayed where you put it—unless it was velcroed down, and without gravity, blood pushed toward his head and made him feel like he was doing a handstand. As always, his sinuses stopped up, making it difficult to taste food. The last team to crew the ship had used up all the hot sauce, too. Then there was the indignity of the microgravity toilet, which was akin to shitting into a vacuum cleaner hose.

Thankfully, they would only have to endure this for a week (if all went well), and the three of them used the time to read through technical documentation for their new space station.

Tighe also went on an EVA to bring in the nearly 250 kilos of equipment and supplies that had come up with them on board the cargo module. He pulled these back in through the *Rosette*'s airlock. Once inside, the trio started inventorying each package, marking them off on a digital manifest. The matériel ran the gamut from medical supplies, food, rechargeable batteries, hand tools, clothing, sleeping bags, and small electronic components. They'd been instructed to take nothing from the *Rosette* itself; it would need to remain habitable for future passengers.

Tighe examined the freeze-dried food packets among their new provisions—a consumer brand that he knew from cave expeditions and didn't much like. There were also utilitarian-looking foil packets labeled "Ready-to-use therapeutic food" that he'd once seen NGOs handing out in developing countries during a famine. "Bargain-basement stuff. I guess technically we *are* broke."

Jin looked up from a manifest. "At least we are only a few days from Earth this time. Perhaps later we can resupply."

Now that they were logged in to the *Rosette*'s network, they could use their familiar "crystal" eyeglasses that served as HUD displays for the ship's virtual user interface. Apparently in-eye retinal projection systems like he'd seen back on Earth hadn't yet made it into orbit. Tighe was glad; he didn't like augmented-reality objects appearing without warning.

After five days in flight, the *Rosette* began to pass by the Moon at a distance of roughly 40,000 kilometers. Although the *Rosette* had only two small borosilicate portholes in its hull, Chindarkar instantiated a shared virtual window in their crystals that tapped into an exterior camera. The resulting screen looked more like a big-screen TV hung on the wall at a sports bar, and it showed a portside view of the Moon in real time.

Although they were most of the way there, to Tighe the Moon still looked to be about the size of a walnut held at arm's length—much like it did back on Earth—an ashen crescent, starkly lit. Splayed beyond it, running diagonally from upper left to lower right, was the radiant splendor of the Milky Way. It had been months since Tighe had glimpsed it from deep space, and although his home galaxy had begun to seem impossibly remote and cruelly indifferent after their years adrift in the void, he once more marveled at its beauty.

After another two days they approached the L2 Lagrange point 60,000 kilometers beyond the Moon, and looking sternward they could now see the swirling blue-white marble of the Earth alongside and seemingly half the size of the Moon. They were some 450,000 kilometers from Earth.

Transitioning to a halo orbit around L2 would require significant propellant for something as large as the *Rosette*—not to mention disrupting its cycler orbit—and so mission control had sent out a small autonomous transit craft from the space station to rendezvous with the *Rosette* at apoapsis (or the farthest point in its orbit).

Mission control relayed updates as the uncrewed transit craft approached. Although its rocket engine had been salvaged from the robot tugs, its steel hull had apparently been fashioned in situ by the same chemical vapor deposition process used to build the space station—the same process, in fact, that Tighe and his crewmates used to form the lifting-body spacecraft that had brought them home from Ryugu.

Lacroix's voice crackled on the internal speaker. "*Transit-01, 20 meters off number two airlock. Stand by for docking*, Rosette."

By then the team had put their MCP suits back on, replete with helmets and life support packs—in the event anything went wrong.

Chindarkar spoke through her helmet mic. "We copy you, mission control."

In a couple of minutes there was a shudder and a *klunk* sound, followed by the *click* of retention bolts.

"*Transit-01 docked.*" A pause for several seconds. "*Seal is good. You are cleared to enter,* Rosette. *Seven-minute countdown has begun.*"

As calm as everything appeared out in space, they were still moving at thousands of kilometers per hour, and it wouldn't be long before the cycler started "falling" back toward Earth again. In order to conserve rocket fuel, they had to move fast to load up the transit craft and depart before they were out of position for a plane change to a Lissajous orbit around EM-L2.

Tighe looked up to see a green light over the *Rosette*'s aft hatch—which was square and larger than the circular airlock by which they'd entered a week before. He braced his feet and pulled the 1.5-meter door open, revealing another smaller hatch—this one on the transit spacecraft.

Jin, meanwhile, pushed floating bags of supplies and equipment toward Chindarkar, who staged them near the hatchway.

Tighe opened the transit craft's hatch and peered inside. Within was a cylindrical compartment 10 meters long and 3 in diameter. It had Spartan accommodations for perhaps half a dozen people. He moved inside and caught the bundles of supplies as Chindarkar shoved them through.

In a minute or two they had loaded the transit craft. Tighe called out, "Make sure you have everything you need off the *Rosette*. We're not coming back this way anytime soon."

After a last-minute check, they all boarded the transit craft, and Jin sealed the hatchways. Tighe and Chindarkar pushed their gear into unpainted metal storage lockers.

Then they all strapped into hard metal jump seats and Tighe radioed, "Mission control, Transit-01 ready for departure."

"*Copy that, Transit-01. Stand by for separation . . .*"

Moments later there was another *klunk* and a vigorous lurch as the transit craft drifted away from the *Rosette*. The autopilot turned them around, thrusters hissing.

"... and halo injection burn in three ... two ... one ..."

There was a throaty roar as a couple g's of acceleration pressed them into their seats. Objects rattled among their baggage.

The transit craft was performing a plane change maneuver to adjust its trajectory to a Lissajous orbit around the L2 point beyond the Moon. The fact that an object could orbit around an empty point in space under certain situations always struck Tighe as bizarre, but then, physics was never his strong suit. As an extreme cave diver, understanding how the human body metabolized gasses under differing pressures was his expertise, and thus far, that had served him well out in space.

The rocket motor soon cut off, and they were once more in free fall.

Tighe exhaled and unfastened his helmet, as did the others. He took a deep sniff. The entire place had an ozone odor. "Gotta love that new spaceship smell."

The second leg of their journey took less than twenty-four hours. During that time, they acclimated to the starkly lit, prefab character of the robot-manufactured transit craft. Tighe referred to it as the "pop can" because it really was just a metal cylinder, slightly beveled at the ends—somewhat like an up-sized version of the mule utility craft they had used on the Ryugu expedition. Except this vessel didn't have anything in the way of external robot arms, work lights, or equipment. There were no first-aid kits on the interior bulkhead either, or even labels on the valves and pipes. Neither were there any switches or even a virtual control interface—at least none that was available to them.

Instead, mission control navigated the craft. The trio of asteroid miners filled their remaining time reading technical manuals off their crystals and practicing with virtual telepresence flight trainers in microgravity. The sparse quarters meant there was only a foil emergency blanket for privacy when using the toilet. However, the flight was short, and the team had long ago ceased worrying about such niceties.

On the eighth day—New Year's Day 2039—the team once more donned their MCP suits and life support packs. Chindarkar patched into the forward camera to project a virtual window on the leading bulkhead in their HUD display. Since they were now exposed to the Sun's constant glare, no stars were visible, and so all three of them stared at a fascinating sight resolving from the void.

At first, the object looked like a gleaming metallic wheel with four stout spokes—one at each compass point, slowly rotating in the darkness. The solidity of the wheel seemed to change as it turned, with parts of it fading and then flickering back into view. As was typical in space, the image was crystal clear, yet it was impossible to perceive distance without something for scale reference. Mission control's broadcasts were their only guide.

"Ten kilometers out. Transit-01 trajectory nominal."

They appeared to be approaching on a vector perpendicular to the hub of a rotating space station. As they closed in, it became apparent that the vast majority of the wheel's ring consisted merely of exposed girders, formed in a voronoi tessellated pattern that they'd seen in Joyce's investor video. The only completed portions were short segments of the wheel's outer ring, a metaphorical north and south pole—although the two spokes connecting them with the central circular hub of the wheel were also clad in matte gray hull plating. The east-west set of spokes, meanwhile, were still unfinished metal framework.

As their transit craft glided closer, more spacecraft became visible, glittering like debris in the vicinity of the station. However, at this distance, the only one they could make out clearly was perhaps half a kilometer beyond the station. It was a spacecraft they instantly recognized and which also had a name legible even at this distance on its reflective solar shield.

It was the *David Morra*—a robotic tug that resembled a bundle of white grapes clustered behind the mirrored shield. The "grapes" were actually spherical polymer bladder tanks, each 7 meters across and capable of holding 180,000 liters. In total, its score of tanks represented 4,000 tons of water ice, ammonia, and nitrogen, but also smaller bladder tanks of iron, nickel, and cobalt carbonyls—an exotic state of metal that allowed it to exist as a gas or a liquid without being heated to molten temperatures. Transforming asteroid regolith into carbonyls had been a major focus of their mining operation at Ryugu.

To their dismay, nearly a third of the *David Morra* had been dismantled, with half a dozen of the large bladder tanks missing. The smaller metal carbonyl tanks seemed absent, too, but it was difficult to see the entire robot tug through the girder framework.

"Where is the *Nicole Clarke?*" Chindarkar glanced around the screen.

Tighe nodded to himself. That first robot tug was barely a quarter the size of the *David Morra.* "Gone. They must have consumed her." He was surprised how much the realization affected him. It had been a historic ship—the first vessel to ever send asteroid-mined resources back toward cislunar space. Toward our home world. However, there was apparently no room for sentimentality on frontiers.

Jin floated alongside, gesturing to the viewscreen. "No doubt they will consume the *David Morra* as well."

As they drew closer to the station, they were able to resolve smaller mule utility craft floating nearby, with robotic arms at their fronts, work lights, and cameras studding their surfaces. Likewise, thinner and more numerous lines were now visible radiating outward from the core of the space station—resembling the spokes of a bicycle. They could also see a large circular housing of something dish-like on the far side of the station, where a veiled, but powerful white light emanated—like seeing a stadium at night from a distance. Clearly there was a substantial construct extending from the station hub on the far side, with a cluster of satellite dishes and antennas protruding like the thorns of an exotic plant.

Jin pointed. "That's the thermal power station. It uses thin-film mirrors to focus sunlight onto a central tower. Those thin spokes must be the heat dissipation pipes." He nodded to himself. "I expect it is quite efficient."

That would explain why they didn't see the station covered with solar panels.

Mission control's voice squawked. "*Three kilometers. Commencing rotation.*"

Thrusters popped, and Tighe felt the sensation of rolling sideways as though on a rotisserie. However, the station in their virtual viewscreen immediately became immobile—locked in place. They had synchronized with the station's roll, and now it was clear they were gliding toward a wide but short rectangular opening at the hub. The aperture did not go all the way through, but ended at a sensor-and-light-studded steel back wall.

"One kilometer out . . ."

It was becoming clear just how enormous the station was. Now that he could see one of the familiar mule utility craft docked inside the hangar bay, Tighe could gauge distances, and it appeared that this station was roughly the same diameter as the *Konstantin*—about 200 meters. But even unfinished, this station was already far more substantial than the inflatable habs and three tenuous carbon fiber box trusses that formed the *Konstantin*'s radial arms and superstructure. One impact on the *Konstantin*'s twiglike arms and they would have snapped clean off—as training simulations all too frequently showed. This new space station, however, was a continuous ring of steel beams. The inner core and spokes as well. And although only about 10 percent was hull-plated, that portion gave some indication of just how formidable the station would be when it was completed. Rather than a pirouetting dancer like the *Konstanstin*, this would be an iron wheel—the plated sides of which were roughly 20 meters tall.

A smile crept across Jin's face. "Now *that* is a space station . . ."

Tighe was likewise shaking his head in amazement. "Julian has outdone himself this time."

Chindarkar watched them glide closer, decelerating now. "And it's not even finished." She keyed the radio. "Transit-01 to mission control. Someone please tell Julian that this space station is magnificent."

"Wilco, Priya."

Jin held up his thumb to judge sizes. "That hangar bay must be . . . 30 meters across. About 10 high."

They were only a hundred meters away now, and the interior of the hangar bay showed a couple more utility craft parked to the sides, with rows of LED lights illuminating their path.

Mission control said, *"Brace for arrival and docking."*

They cinched their safety harnesses as the hangar bay expanded in the viewscreen, slowly enveloping them. The transit craft was now within the station and eased to a stop, thrusters popping. A series of metallic *klunk*s followed.

"Transit-01 locked. Rotating to arrival gate . . ."

The transit craft vibrated slightly, turning as if on a railroad roundhouse, clamped in place by some mechanism. Soon it started moving on a track toward a recessed docking port that matched their forward beveled bulkhead.

Moments later, there was a mild lurch and *thud*—followed by bolts ramming home.

"We have good lock. Happy New Year, and welcome aboard, Transit-01."

CHAPTER 15

Base of Operations

J in Han was the first out of his harness, and he floated toward the forward hatch. Since no human had yet been aboard the space station, the team still wore their MCP suits and would remain suited up until they confirmed the environment was safe.

Once Jin had the transit craft's hatch opened, he slid a lever to release the station's interior hatch, and as it swung away, they saw a brightly lit room ahead, sheathed entirely in seamless matte gray steel. About 5 meters before them was a featureless wall curving around to the left and right, with a 3-meter metal cylinder protruding from it. They floated forward and Tighe felt the vertigo that sometimes occurred when his reference frame was suddenly shifted in microgravity. He glanced to the side, and it appeared they were in an LED-lit pressurized chamber that wrapped all around the central hangar at the station's hub, with electrical and HVAC conduits running down structural beams. This was apparently the station's arrival terminal.

As they reached the wall directly ahead of them, they noticed handholds at intervals—and that the protruding cylinder was, in fact, the top of a full-on elevator rising not from a wall but a curving floor.

Tighe gestured to the glowing buttons and closed doors. "Would you look at that? An honest-to-god elevator."

Once they rotated to orient with the elevator doors, the room made more sense. They were in a microgravity waiting area next to the departure and arrival gates.

Tighe moved via built-in handholds to tap the only elevator button. He then rapped his gloved fist against the metal wall, and the sound reverberated throughout the chamber. He tried to imagine Kerner's rolling CVD mill patiently extruding the entire, complex superstructure 1 millimeter at a time from an intricate 3D model. "We're gonna need to put up sound baffling in here."

There was no *ding* as the elevator arrived, but the doors opened, and inside was a circular passenger car that could fit perhaps half a dozen people. Railings ran along the wall at two levels. They all floated inside and took hold of the upper handrail as the doors closed smoothly behind them.

Tighe examined the (actual physical) touchscreen panel. There were more choices than he would have thought: *Core* (where they were), *L-grav*, and then *H4* through *H1*—though H2 and H3 were disabled. Next to each choice was a percentage value. "What's 'L-grav 16%-g'?"

Jin floated alongside. "I read about this in the tech documentation. It is not a floor, but the position in the elevator shaft equal to lunar surface gravity—in case you want to acclimate or test equipment."

"Okay. Let's start at H4, 90%-g." Tighe tapped the button.

The elevator accelerated, and they all grabbed hold as the ceiling pushed down on them.

"Legs down! Move toward the floor. We're going to be standing in a moment."

Once they were reoriented, Chindarkar looked up at the ceiling. "There should be Muzak in here."

Tighe deadpanned, "Heavy metal would be more appropriate."

The elevator silently crossed the 90-meter distance to the rotating ring. As it did so, their sensation of gravity increased, and they suddenly hung on to the handrails tightly.

"Woah! Feel that?"

Tighe noted that in the absence of any frame of visual reference, it actually felt like they were coming under the influence of real gravity. The potentially sickening sensation of spinning was absent. It was also much more refined than hanging from a cable in a tube, as they had done on the *Konstantin*.

The elevator came to a stop at H4 and the doors opened. They now felt as if they were in 90 percent Earth gravity. Although they'd only lived in microgravity for a week, they nonetheless had difficulty standing. It demonstrated just how critical gravity—or its spin-grav substitute—was to human function in deep space, and how shocking it was that no other space program had made it a priority.

"Little dizzy here . . ." Tighe grabbed Jin's shoulder.

Chindarkar held on to the railing with both hands. "Orthostatic intolerance. Don't walk until you're sure you can stand without fainting. Give it time."

They stood in place for several minutes, letting the doors close. After they were comfortable standing without assistance, Tighe opened the elevator doors once more. He gestured to Jin. "After you . . ."

"No, together." He let Chindarkar throw her arm around him, too.

Leaning on one another, they all walked sideways shakily, out into the well-lit cavernous area beyond.

Tighe looked around. "Good lord . . ."

Jin and Chindarkar both stared in amazement. They all stood on a railed landing some 15 meters above a yawning space wrapped by seamless, organically curving steel beams and steel hull. Tighe leaned toward the nearest wall and studied the fine grain—leaving no doubt it was of a purity that only chemical vapor deposition could deliver. So pure it would not even rust.

The trio eased forward to grip the railing and look down. They were near the top and center of a large pressurized compartment over 40 meters long and roughly 15 meters tall and wide, ribbed with steel beams and walls that bulged slightly at the waist, then curved gently inward again toward a laterally flat ceiling and floor—like the interior of a great steel tire. The circular central elevator shaft continued down to the "bottom" of the compartment (H1?), but the intervening floors (H2 and H3?) were—for the time being—absent, giving the team a longer sight line than would presumably be the case later. Although level from edge to edge, both the ceiling and floor of the compartment curved upward slightly at either end, continuing along the ring. The H4 elevator landing they stood upon was a disembodied platform high above the floor.

This was nothing at all like Tighe's first sight of the habs on the *Konstantin*, with their stocked kitchen, furniture, medical bay, and gym equipment. Here, there was nothing but exposed metal beams, hull plate, power cables, HVAC ducting, pipes, and LED ceiling lights. It was a big, hollow, curving ship's hold.

Tighe checked his HUD display and, satisfied with the atmosphere and pressure, nodded to them both. They all pressed a catch, twisted their helmets, and removed them with a hiss. They each took their first, deep breath of the station's air. The entire volume had the wet-slate smell of virgin steel.

Tighe nodded. "Not bad. I thought it would reek from the CVD chamber."

Chindarkar shouted, "Hey!" And a fierce echo came back several times.

"God, it's going to be like living inside a steel drum."

"For now." Jin knocked on the metal railing with the same results. He turned to them. "But we will furnish it." He pointed out predrilled holes in the hull. "There's an interior wall and floor plan already prepared. We just need to assemble it."

Tighe asked, "How are the rads in here?"

Chindarkar checked a wrist-mounted dosimeter. "Right now . . . point-two micro-rads per second." She looked up. "Not horrible. These two completed habs are double-hulled, with a 2-meter gap. I'm not sure how much water ice they have in between, but our solar radiation and galactic cosmic ray exposure will need to be decreased long-term—even if we bring up that genetic-editing tech they used on you, J.T."

"Believe me: better to avoid cancer than have to treat it." Tighe noticed spiral stairs descending along the wall. He motioned for the others to follow, and clanked down the treads, stopping a moment to hop up and down. Although noisy, the stairs did not shake.

He turned to the others. "Hell of a lot more solid than the *Konstantin*, that's for sure."

They continued down past two false landings.

"Careful. Hold on to the railing."

Soon they reached the bottom tread, which ended atop a half-meter-high outer beam that curved across the floor, merging with other beams in organic patterns. The upper surface of each beam was flattened and also had pre-drilled (or preformed) holes for affixing floor panels. Likewise, the beam cross sections had the same voronoi tessellated pattern of openings along their length, lowering their mass while maintaining strength, but also making it possible to run electrical conduit, data, HVAC, and plumbing lines through them, beneath future floor panels. Clearly the interior was meant to be built up when materials became available.

Tighe gazed up at the lights 15 meters above. "Well, this is going to be a project." The floor area was roughly 600 square meters, with the cylindrical elevator shaft running straight down through the center of the compartment.

"I can't help but think this is way more than we need to build a mass-driver on the lunar surface."

Jin nodded. "The thought had occurred to me that it would have been better to conserve more of these resources. Do you think Lukas is making our plan a priority—or Nathan's?"

"Or Lisowski's, you mean."

Chindarkar said, "Guys, I ran the numbers, and we don't have enough mass to build the rescue ship we need."

Tighe gestured around them. "Why can't we just pilot this station to rendezvous with Ryugu in 2042? The interior of this compartment alone could accommodate dozens of people."

"Not without a major propulsion system. This only has station-keeping thrusters. It's a space station, not a spacecraft."

"Then we spend the next few years converting it into one."

She stared at him. "We might exist in a vacuum out here, J.T., but at least initially, to get supplies, we're going to need something we can trade with partners on Earth—which means we need mass or energy to spare."

Tighe considered this.

Chindarkar added, "All this room will be necessary to house the people and equipment to build that mass-driver on the lunar surface. We do that, and we'll have more than enough resources to trade and to build a proper rescue ship."

Tighe sighed, then nodded. "I hope you're right."

They all surveyed the room.

Chindarkar pointed up at the lights high overhead. "Those should dim and change color as we get toward evening. We're on a twenty-four-hour cycle—like on the *Konstantin*." She pointed at the elevator landings. "Each level differs by 5 percent in perceived gravity. Down here on H1 we're at 105 percent Earth gravity." She pointed up to the elevator landing. "Ninety percent up on H4."

Tighe nodded toward twin pairs of steel toilet basins mounted on the wall in opposite corners of the compartment. "After a week in free fall, those are a welcome sight." The toilets formed part of what were clearly two separate bathroom facilities, consisting of the same number of sinks in the form of metal basins affixed to the wall, plus two pairs of showerheads. Piping and other conduit ran along the wall. A larger steel sink and drain assembly farther on was most likely for a kitchen. The purpose of other plumbing fixtures higher up were less obvious.

"Lab sink, maybe?" Chindarkar craned her neck to examine the pipe lines.

Near them was the critical life support equipment Tighe had been expecting—redundant oxygen generators and carbon dioxide scrubbers. However, he didn't see water treatment or water supply tanks. Looking up, he could see that the piping ran all the way down from the central core of the station; this was different from the *Konstantin*, which had separate water supplies in each hab.

As he walked around, Tighe's steps echoed in the cavernous metallic compartment. "When it's finished, this station is going to be huge." His voice echoed.

"What are we going to name it?" Chindarkar glanced to them both.

Tighe rested his foot on a beam. "I don't know. What do *you* guys think?"

Jin pondered the question. "Nicole's and David's robot tugs . . . they were consumed in building this."

Chindarkar replied, "But that's two names. We can't choose one over the other."

"The *Nicole Clarke* was fully consumed. A portion of the *David Morra* remains." Jin looked up. "I say we call this Clarke Station, in memory of Nicole." He thought for another moment. "And when we build the mass-driver on the lunar surface, we could name that Morra Base, in memory of David."

"I love it, Han."

Tighe nodded. "So do I."

Chindarkar embraced him. "It's beautiful. Dave was the army engineer. Nicole the ship captain. I think they'd approve."

Tighe gripped Jin's shoulder. "Outstanding." He looked up. "Clarke Station it is."

Chindarkar keyed her mic. "*Transit-01 to mission control. Be advised, we have arrived at EM-L2 and are now safely aboard . . .*" She paused. "*. . . Clarke Station. Please take note of the new name designation for official records: Clarke Station. Out.*"

After a moment, the return came. "*That's a solid copy, and wilco, Clarke Station.*"

CHAPTER 16

Ex Post Facto

You lied to us, Erika."

Erika Lisowski remained calm. "That's the worst-possible interpretation of my actions."

"You know it's true, and I promise you will pay for it with prison this time."

"I understand you're angry, but you need me—not in prison, but helping you. I am your liaison to these asteroid miners, and right now they're the most important thing going on in space. And space is where the action is."

The elder statesman stared at her. "You may think you can manipulate me, like you have these space billionaires, but I know better. This isn't an innovation—it's a *provocation*. The sudden construction of this space station from those asteroid resources has caused the Chinese and the Russians to accuse us of seizing L2. It's precipitated a political crisis."

"But you *didn't* seize L2, and what's more, you *know* you didn't."

"As if China would believe us, and as if their believing us would strengthen our hand. The Chinese are claiming ownership of that station because the resources that built it came from the *Konstantin*."

"You have a legitimate claim to those resources as well, and so the bigger question is, who *actually* controls the station? Answer: the asteroid miners do."

"It's a goddamned disaster."

"I disagree. It's a surprise, not a disaster. Let me ask: Were *you* poised to build the largest space station in history on the far side of the Moon using a well-researched design in just a few months? No? Then you should be grateful Clarke Station is now up there."

"It's not going to be called 'Clarke Station' either. That I promise you."

"It is a bastion of free enterprise at the edge of a new frontier. A frontier that until recently you were falling behind in. And like any frontier, space will require new ports—friendly ports—from which you can develop commercial and strategic capabilities. That's what this is."

He bristled. "This station is illegal and liable to be seized by our rivals and used against us."

"Not easily."

"We need to take control of it before they do."

"And then what? All this rapid progress at the Moon stops, and you've turned your advantage into an *actual* political crisis. Seize that station, and the world will oppose you—along with Russia and China."

He stared at her in unconcealed fury.

"You need to help these asteroid miners, not hinder them. Let them launch their supplies and their colleagues from Earth. A straightforward commercial launch."

"One of their team is a former cosmonaut. Then there's that taikonaut."

"So? There are Americans and Europeans, too. It's an international team that won't engender opposition from the world. In fact, it will ease tensions. This new station can become a free port."

"Not if the Chinese or the Russians seize it."

"At present, those asteroid miners have a major advantage in multi-orbit logistics in cislunar space. That new station has thousands of tons of propellant on hand in addition to construction mass—much more than anyone else at the Moon. All of it can be sent on a trajectory to intercept attackers. Any attempts to seize that station are likely to fail."

"They built that station in violation of international law."

She made a face. "What they're doing goes beyond settled law, I'll give you that. But certainly you're not going to agree with the Russians or Chinese if they say it's illegal, are you?"

He fumed.

"I think you should get the CEO of Catalyst Corporation on the phone and demand to know his intentions."

"We should freeze their bank accounts and seize their assets."

"I don't think that will have the effect you're hoping for."

"Then what exactly do you propose we do? Oh, let me guess: *nothing*—just like you advised us to do before we got into this mess."

"You're not in a mess. There's now a friendly port on a new frontier that we can establish formal relations with."

"Go to hell. It's a rogue outpost."

"And if you read our pioneer history, you will know how advantageous those can be."

He stared at her.

"Don't send troops. Send observers. Let the world know your intention to send observers. And suggest that the asteroid miners invite Russian and Chinese observers as well."

"Oh, and they'll all have a sing-along. Kumbaya-My-Lord."

"That's not the point. If you have US personnel on board, your rivals can't try to seize the station without causing an international incident."

"That cuts both ways."

"But *we* don't want to seize the station. Do you see the difference? The station is not a threat to us. We *want* freedom of navigation and free enterprise in deep space."

"And what if the Chinese outcompete us in this new free port?"

"I think you'll find that Lukas Rochat, the CEO, is going to insist that trade relations with them utilize a crypto-economic system that is antithetical to authoritarian control. He'll also insist on observance of human rights and freedom of navigation. That position will garner goodwill from the international community, but is one that authoritarian regimes will have difficulty agreeing to—isolating them and putting them on the defensive." She paused. "Or . . . they do agree to these conditions, and that becomes a major cultural victory over authoritarianism in space."

He pressed his temples. "God, you're giving me a headache." He tapped a button on his desk phone. "Andrew! Get me Lukas Rochat, head of Catalyst Corporation, on a secure line."

"*Yes, sir.*"

The older man ground his teeth.

Lisowski ventured into the silence. "Another way to look at this is that embezzlement solved the rocket equation—Nathan Joyce lied his way past it.

And if we play our cards right, humanity won't ever need to launch the vast majority of space resources up from Earth's gravity well."

The admin's voice cut in. "*I have Mr. Rochat, sir.*"

"Put him on."

Lukas Rochat's voice came in over the speakerphone. "*Mr. Secretary, it's a pleasure to hear from you.*"

"Cut the crap, Rochat. I'm here with Erika Lisowski, who I'm told you already know."

"*Yes, glad to speak with you both.*"

"I was under the impression we were negotiating a deal for those asteroid resources, and now I learn that you deliberately misled us and were responsible for the unlawful movement of those resources beyond the Moon. You now have a very serious legal problem. Don't think for a moment that we can't reach into the EU and freeze every last euro you possess and have you extradited to face criminal charges."

There was a momentary silence. "*I would agree that these are uncharted legal waters. You and the CCP were both claiming ownership of those resources, but Catalyst Corporation had not yet agreed to any settlement.*"

"What settlement? You don't have a legal leg to stand on. Catalyst is based in Luxembourg, and Luxembourg is a signatory to the Artemis Accords. You haven't been transparent in your actions. You haven't observed the Registration Convention to properly register objects in space. You flagrantly disregarded clauses on orbital deconfliction and space debris."

"*It is true that our paperwork has not yet caught up, but as for orbital deconfliction: there are only two defunct satellites registered in the EM-L2 region of space. All other—*"

"You don't have the right to be where you are. You don't own those resources, and you didn't have the right to build a space station."

"*With respect, whatever discussion we engage in with regard to Clarke Station is ex post facto. That is to say, nothing is going to change the fact that the station exists, and that certain individuals are in physical possession of it. Until that situation changes—*"

"This is exactly the sort of shit the Chinese pull, building artificial islands in the middle of the goddamned ocean."

Lisowski added, "There is a certain poetic justice to it. You must admit."

The secretary jabbed his finger at the phone. "Listen to me, Rochat, unless you immediately grant us access to this station and reveal your intentions there, we're going to view this Clarke Station of yours as a national security threat to the United States. And I'm certain China and Russia feel likewise."

"I'm sorry to hear that. We, of course, consider ourselves great friends to the United States and the other democratic nations of Earth."

The secretary looked up at Lisowski. "'The other democratic nations of Earth.' Would you listen to him?" He looked back at the speaker. "You think you're the Moon ambassador, Rochat? Is that it?"

"It is an interesting legal situation. There's been no precedent where new sovereign territory has been built in open space—at least not beyond low Earth orbit."

"You are not 'new sovereign territory.' As a Luxembourg company, anything Catalyst builds in space flies under the flag of Luxembourg, which is a signatory to both the Artemis Accords and the Outer Space Treaty." He picked up a highlighted document from his desk and read from it. "Article II of which states that 'outer space, including the Moon and other celestial bodies, is not subject to national appropriation by claim of sovereignty, by means of use or occupation, or by any other means.'" He looked up from the document. "If you have any confusion about that, we can freeze your Earthly assets until you reach the correct conclusion."

"But Mr. Secretary, you're forgetting Article IX of the OST, which covers 'due regard' for individual parties in space. Specifically, if any party's activity could cause 'potentially harmful interference with the activities of others,' then all concerned parties can enter into consultations to resolve the interference. However, this station hasn't interfered with any other party. There is no one else in that area. And to be certain that Clarke Station's activities are not interfered with, as provided for in Article IX, they're establishing a 200-meter 'safety zone.'"

"You have some balls—"

"The ISS had the same, as does the Hotel LEO."

"Those are legal stations."

"Again, I think you will find that no legal mechanism for resolving this dispute currently exists, but we are very interested in working with sovereign Earth nations to develop this area of space law—perhaps using legal

precedents from past disagreements about resources of the deep seabed, the water column, the electromagnetic frequency spectrum, or Antarctica as examples."

"You are already bound by Earth law."

"Ah, I see the confusion. Clarke Station is not actually owned by Catalyst Corporation."

"Don't you try this shell game with me. If we can hunt down terrorists, we will find your offshore—"

"It's not a shell game. Catalyst's board members voted to assign the asteroid resources to a decentralized autonomous organization called the Cislunar Commodity Exchange."

The secretary jotted down the name. "Look, it doesn't matter where your shell company is based. We'll find it, and we'll shut it down, if you refuse to—"

"That's the thing, Mr. Secretary: the CCE isn't offshore. It's off-Earth. As a DAO, it's self-owning. It asserts its own jurisdiction."

The secetary stared at the phone. "Jesus Christ, don't even tell me I'm hearing what I'm hearing. You're claiming you aren't answerable to any Earth law now? I hope to hell you live in a deep bunker, Mr. Rochat, because I promise you—"

Lisowski cut in. "I don't believe we want to sever relations with Clarke Station so early in its existence, Mr. Secretary. As provocative as this development might be."

"Provocative?" The secretary glared at her. "And you act as if this is a big surprise to you." He turned back to the phone. "You may think you're clever, Mr. Rochat, but you are playing a dangerous game."

"The CCE desires to establish diplomatic and legal legitimacy with Earth authorities through responsible stewardship of the cislunar commons. That will include, of course, becoming a signatory to the Universal Declaration of Human Rights."

"You have no standing to sign international treaties, and you have completely ignored treaties you are already subject to."

"Again, those are legal questions that 'ground truth'—or shall I say 'space truth'—will resolve. The US itself, in setting forth the Artemis Accords, stated their expectation that small groups of users focused on immediate solutions to pressing problems up on the Moon and in space would—in the absence of

broad international agreement on fundamental principles—need to experiment continually in the field, iterate, and coevolve principles and practices. Experience has shown this is the best means for building enduring and effective regulatory environments—not proclamations by distant authorities. With all due respect, of course."

The secretary tapped his fingers impatiently. "You're going to find this isn't just a legal question, Mr. Rochat. Astropolitics is going to decide this, not a court."

"Well, in that case, I think you will find that the presence of the Cislunar Commodity Exchange out at L2 will be a very useful ally to the free world."

The elder statesman glowered at the phone for several moments. "As a 'useful ally,' we're going to insist on a visit to this Clarke Station of yours."

"Again, it's not my station, Mr. Secretary. Clarke Station belongs to the CCE."

"Yes, the CCE. Of course it does. Well, we will send . . ." He glanced at Lisowski. ". . . a couple of observers to evaluate this new space station that you have nothing to do with. Will you personally guarantee the safety of our personnel?"

"I'll be happy to pass along your message to the governing body of the CCE, and I have no doubt that they'll be pleased to welcome your observers as diplomatic envoys and to guarantee their safety."

"You may think this is all going to turn out fine, Rochat, but you owe the United States government ten billion dollars. And you owe China fourteen billion. No matter what you call it or how many fancy tricks you play with legal and financial structures, let me give you a little advice: you're going to need friends, and soon."

"And I trust we will all be friends. It's a pleasure speaking with you, Mr. Secretary."

CHAPTER 17

Settling In

James Tighe, Priya Chindarkar, and Jin Han took up residence in the cavernous, echoing, empty chamber at one pole of Clarke Station—which they had dubbed South Hab, while naming its opposite North Hab. A compass-inspired nomenclature, they decided, would serve well as the ring-shaped station was built out, with the East and West Habs housing the landings for the station's other two elevator shafts (both of which were still unfinished girders). There would eventually be sixteen pressurized compartments along the station ring—three between each of the compartments that housed elevator landings for the station's four spokes. Jin suggested the middle compartments be named for intercardinal compass points; thus, Northeast Hab, Southeast Hab, etc. The other compartments would be named for tertiary compass points; thus, West-by-Northwest Hab, South-by-Southeast Hab, and so on—though likely to be expressed with initialisms like 'WNW' and 'SSE.'

Tighe thought it sounded cumbersome and preferred simple numbers, but the compass motif did have a certain nautical-historical appeal. And the naming of yet-to-be-built compartments was hardly worth worrying about; at this point their survival wasn't assured, much less completing the station.

After they'd toured the South Hab, the team returned to the docked transit vehicle and off-loaded a couple hundred kilos of gear and supplies—which was easy work in microgravity. This included all the provisions, first-aid kits, meds, sleeping bags, flight suits, auxiliary MCP suits, life support packs, a small, foldable microwave oven, tools and equipment, and hundreds of other necessities and minor conveniences, carefully packed by Lacroix's mission control team and surreptitiously loaded aboard the cargo rocket back at Satish Dhawan. They'd already inventoried and organized it on the *Rosette*, and the elevator was large enough that they were able to send it down to the South Hab in a single trip.

Not long after, they unrolled their sleeping bags on foam mats in the elevator landing near the top of the stairs, since it seemed like a good idea to be near an exit. There were also two sealed hatches at either end of the South Hab—one spinward and the other anti-spinward, but beyond the bulkheads there lay only the vacuum of space and exposed girders—at least until neighboring compartments were built out. With the station rotating once every twenty-two seconds, anyone exiting that way was likely to be hurled from the station and out into deep space.

After establishing a base camp in South Hab, Tighe and Chindarkar went to inspect the North Hab to be certain it was also fully operational and habitable, while Jin remained back in South Hab, unpacking their gear.

Hab-to-hab travel on Clarke Station was much simpler than traveling between habitats on the *Konstantin*. There were no winch lines, multiple airlocks, or transfer tunnels, just a simple elevator ride, then a brief microgravity hand-over-hand transfer in the pressurized core over to the north elevator bank, and then another brief elevator ride "down" into North Hab's spin-gravity well. For safety reasons (since they hadn't been to North Hab before), they'd both donned MCPs.

The elevators worked fine, and in just a few minutes, Tighe and Chindarkar stood on the H4 elevator landing of North Hab, overlooking an identical, echoey, empty steel-walled compartment illuminated by LED lights. After once again confirming pressure and air mixture, they removed their helmets.

Tighe took in the scene. "We could host a damned racquetball tournament in here."

"We'll need the room when more crew arrive."

"Come on. Not *this much* room."

"It's a spinning wheel, J.T. It needs to be symmetrical, or it would be imbalanced. Speaking of . . ." She examined the landing. "We should split our provisions and emergency gear between here and South Hab for the next couple of weeks—in case there's a structural failure and we need to decamp in a hurry."

"Good thinking."

After returning to South Hab, they subdivided their gear in preparation for the transfer. Now jacked in to the station's network, they had multi-gigabit-bandwith laser communications with Ascension Island mission control, using NASA's open-source DTN protocol. Jin navigated the familiar Catalyst entertainment UI and instantiated a shared virtual big-screen TV. Being close to Earth—unlike the asteroid Ryugu—they could now enjoy live television and radio, and since the sound only played in their earphones, it didn't echo maddeningly in the hard shell of the huge compartment.

Since it was New Year's Day, the news channels briefly covered festivities around the world—but soon moved on to reports of violent clashes as waves of climate refugees pressed on the borders of eastern and southern Europe. Then the continued drought in Africa and the Middle East. Then typhoons in the South Pacific.

It was 2039—one year closer to the return of the asteroid Ryugu. But also one year more of record temperatures, droughts, and storms back on Earth.

The trio heralded in the new year with reconstituted apple juice. Sitting cross-legged on the metal deck of the landing, Chindarkar held up her plastic cup for a somber toast. "To absent friends."

Tighe and Jin lifted their cups. "Hear, hear."

Given their eventful day and the uncertainties that lay ahead, they soon extinguished the virtual TV and went to sleep.

Tighe's dreams were turbulent—feeling himself fall helplessly and endlessly—and he awoke in the middle of the night with a start. Then found it difficult to get back to sleep.

The next morning, on his first use of a steel toilet down at H1, Tighe was dismayed to watch it clog up. "Oh, come on . . ."

Jin called from the elevator landing high above. "You should not have waited so long."

"Very funny." Tighe stabbed at the flush control, but the toilet just overflowed. "For chrissakes." He looked up. "Do we have something I can use as a plunger?"

It wound up taking half an hour and a consultation with mission control to clear the waste line. After which mission control sent up the day's task list, detailing the build-out of the station's interior walls, flooring, and ceiling panels on H1 level for both the North and South Habs. Although the station had water tanks, pumps, and moving weights to maintain the center of rotation as people and matériel moved between habs, the building materials were significant enough that their move had to be staggered to each hab. In preparation, Kerner's team already had the CVD mill outside the station producing light-gauge steel framing pieces by the dozen in accordance with a very precise interior design plan. Likewise, they were producing unique thin steel floor panels to cover the irregular gaps between the voronoi tessellated floor beams. The subsequent upper floors of each hab would rest upon this lighter interior framework, though there would be a plenum between floors to allow for an eventual drop ceiling, with HVAC ducting inputs and returns. To make the task manageable, every metal piece was numbered and had to go into place like a puzzle. Teleoperated mules were already transferring those pieces into a freight airlock in Clarke Station's docking bay for the team to pick up.

Tighe studied the parts manifest. "Why didn't they have the construction robots do this work, too?"

Chindarkar answered, "I'm guessing they had to pressurize the hull as soon as possible—so we could occupy the station before anyone else arrives."

Jin tested a battery-powered hand tool. "The holes are predrilled. We just screw the pieces in place. This should be fast work."

Chindarkar looked around. "It will be nice to have floors for the showers and toilets, but what about sound baffling and wall panels?"

Jin shook his head. "Only framing for now. Panels come later. When we can print textiles."

"In other words: this echo's going to be with us for a while."

The next few days, they worked together installing the numbered steel panels between floor beams on H1. Tighe found the work satisfying, and by the end of the first day they had the entire South Hab floor installed, along with silicone caulking around the shower drains and other fittings. The next day they did the same in North Hab. The following days saw them assembling thin-gauge steel framing, HVAC ducting, and LED lighting, installing it according to mission control's blueprint—which they projected in place using the augmented-reality feature of their crystal glasses.

They used this same AR capability as a guide to spray-paint large white arrows to the hull walls. These pointed in the direction of the station's spin—or "spinward." The arrows were repeated several times along the compartment's length and stood the full height of one interior floor. They'd had something similar on the *Konstantin*, and physiological research indicated that a visible reference to the direction of rotation helped crews avoid sickness from the Coriolis effect when moving about. Tighe's experience confirmed that hypothesis, and in any event it provided some visual interest.

After almost a week of hard work, they finally had an enclosed H1 floor in both the North and South Habs, each bisected by interior metal framing that laid out corridors, bathrooms, a kitchen, storage, sleeping quarters, and equipment rooms on an identical floor plan. The ceiling of steel panels was also the floor of H2, which still had no walls—and a very high ceiling above, due to the missing H3 and H4 floors. The spiral staircase and the elevator allowed them to move quickly between levels.

However, they needed furnishings to make South Hab livable, even in the short term. So mission control directed the team to twin large-format 3D printers mounted in the walls of the station's pressurized core. Beyond the wall—out in the depressurized docking bay—tanks of polymer pellets synthesized from the robot tug framework served as feedstock for the printers, which produced the components for a plastic table and folding chairs, followed by panels for plastic storage cabinets—all from 3D models in the station's blueprint library.

While the parts printed, the team located the computer core of the station, the pressure door to which was located next to the 3D printing bay. Inside, rack-mounted servers stood in rows with cooling units recirculating to radiator fins on the station exterior. The computers must have been sent up from Earth by Joyce back in the mid-2030s and kept in lunar orbit.

If Adisa was here, Tighe thought, he would already have the server room well in hand. However, since the three of them were not technical wizards, they merely noted its location in the event of an emergency—because it was also their radiation storm shelter.

After the 3D printing runs finished, the team carried the plastic components back to South Hab and worked together to assemble a long plastic table, chairs, and storage cabinets—setting them up near the elevator doors on the newly installed floor of level H2. It was like a curving loft apartment walled in steel.

As the team continued to prepare the station, mission control brought them through long task lists each day. The antennas and rotating arrays Tighe had seen mounted near the power plant on the station's axis were an entire scanning and communications suite. By contrast to the Ryugu asteroid mining expedition, mission control thought it likely that Clarke Station might have unannounced guests—being located just a week's journey from Earth—and so, with the aid of onboard radar and Joyce's constellation of lunar satellites, Clarke Station's situational awareness extended across the entirety of lunar orbit.

Soon Tighe and the others were accustomed to the radar signatures and timing of the other objects orbiting the Moon—NASA's Lunar Gateway, the Chinese-Russian Chang'e station, and a collection of lunar satellites—several of them defunct. A couple even followed a Lissajous orbit around L2 similar to their own, although tens of thousands of kilometers distant.

Also different from the *Konstantin* was that Clarke Station had security locks on all exterior and interior hatchways, designed to prevent casual intrusions—although, clearly they would not hold back determined attackers. Still, it was nice to know they could lock the doors. Cislunar space had become a more competitive domain since they'd been away.

Then there was spacecraft maintenance—a fact of spacefaring life they'd all grown accustomed to out at Ryugu. Mission control stepped them through maintaining Clarke Station's much more robust oxygen generation and CO_2-scrubbing equipment. The ionic carbon dioxide removal system was quite different from the *Konstantin*'s and capable of scrubbing much larger air volumes, which was necessary since Clarke Station would eventually house many more people, and contained a greater pressurized volume. Eventually the station would have fifteen of these units, but for now had only two.

Also, there was the mass equalization system (or MES), which was designed to maintain the station's center of rotation by equalizing the mass along the outer ring. Imbalances could happen as people and equipment moved around the station, and so a combined system of water pumps with storage tanks, and a more robust system of computer-controlled metallic weights on rails running along the exterior of the station's ring, permitted precise, ongoing adjustment dependent on how mass was distributed along the torus. At present the rail-mounted weights were inactive since only two compartments out of sixteen were finished; instead, pumps moved water between a several-thousand-liter storage tank in the core and smaller thousand-liter polymer tanks in the South and North Habs to equalize mass between them. The same system also provided water and waste removal—albeit on separate lines—for the showers, sinks, and toilets, with the solar furnace providing limitless hot water.

The entire system was managed remotely by mission control, but maintenance tasks still had to be handled by on-site crew. However, the ability to take a long hot shower at the end of the day as well as brush one's teeth and—most of all—use a normal toilet, made the effort worthwhile.

Nonetheless, plumbing problems soon began to appear. During showers, instead of draining, a pool of water would accumulate. Toilets often backed up, and while mission control worked to find the source of these problems, the team was directed to use the toilets in the North Hab whenever possible, to avoid fecal matter fouling the air of their living area.

"That's not a solution, Gabriel," Jin said to Lacroix over a video link. "And sooner or later this is going to become a health risk."

"*I realize that, Han. Rest assured, the engineers are working on the problem.*"

After more than a week at Clarke Station, the team had fallen into a familiar rhythm from their days sharing a hab on the *Konstantin*. Conditions here were, for the moment, more Spartan than the *Konstantin*, but there was loads more room in case they needed personal space—which wasn't often. Instead, they took comfort in one another's companionship. Jin in particular seemed to be much more at ease now that he was again in deep space, and Tighe noticed he had a ready smile most of the time—something he seldom saw from Jin on Earth.

Ten days into the new year they received news from mission control that a team of seven, led by Sevastian Yakovlev, would be joining them on Clarke Station, lifting off in one of Burkette's Starion rockets from Florida's Space Coast in a few weeks. Their capsule would rendezvous with the *Rosette* cycler during its next swing through low Earth orbit, arriving a week later near EM-L2. It would require still another day for the crew to reach Clarke Station from there, and while the thought of having friends on the station was uplifting, it also raised questions.

Over breakfast, Jin voiced his apprehension. "I am surprised that Yak and his team were approved to launch out of the Cape—when we were banned everywhere from launch. What do you suppose this means? What do the Americans expect from us in return?"

Tighe muttered, "In other words: What did Lukas promise them?"

"Exactly. I thought Catalyst was insolvent again. How are we paying for seven seats on a commercial launch? What is that . . . two hundred million USD?"

"I can't imagine Catalyst stock is worthless anymore. Look around you."

Chindarkar stirred rehydrated fruit into her oatmeal as she pondered the question. "Up until now, the superpowers probably suspected one another of building this station. Perhaps they want to curry favor with us. Now that we're up here."

Tighe said, "That's great, but we don't have time for political games. We have work to do. Ryugu will come round again before you know it."

"You don't seriously think Earth powers will just leave us alone, do you?"

"No, which is why we have locks on all the hatches."

"As if that's going to solve anything."

Jin frowned. "Let us hope it does not come to that."

Within the hour they received word that Lukas Rochat wanted a videoconference. So they placed a webcam on the plastic conference table at H2 and instantiated a virtual screen at the far end. Moments later Rochat appeared, sitting in some sort of secure room back on Earth.

"Good morning. It's good to see you all arrived safely. I'm calling to update you on the status of operations."

Jin asked, "How did you get Yak and his team's launch cleared with the US?"

"Before we discuss the upcoming arrival of your colleagues, you should know that the Cislunar Commodity Exchange will soon go live up there on Clarke Station."

"Commodity exchange? Lukas, we are not 'exchanging' anything. What are you talking about?"

Tighe added, "We barely have life support up here. We're living in an empty cargo hold."

Chindarkar frowned. "You'd better not be screwing around again, Lukas."

He held up his hands. *"The CCE is merely a financial construct for the moment."*

"'For the moment.' That's the part that has me worried."

"It may sound frivolous, but you will need an economic system up there that's able to resist wealth and power concentrations here on Earth, and which can also bypass Earth sanctions. We have designed such a system."

They considered this.

Jin asked, "Who is *we*?"

Tighe waved the question away. "Look, we aren't anywhere close to building a new financial system out here. Can we please discuss the incoming team?"

"Of course. I just didn't want the CCE to be a complete surprise."

"When does the new team arrive, and what did you promise the US to get them cleared for launch out of the Cape?"

"A seven-person crew, designated 'Blue Team,' will arrive at Clarke Station on January 29—about three weeks from today. And in answer to your question: we had to make two substitutions to be cleared for launch."

They threw up their hands.

"Here we go . . ."

"It was unavoidable."

Jin said, "Please tell me we still have our flight surgeon."

Chindarkar added, "And our chemist."

"Yes and yes."

Tighe asked, "Who's being substituted?"

"In exchange for approving the launch, the United States insisted that two official observers visit the station—to satisfy themselves that nothing nefarious is going on there. So I had to free up two launch seats. You lost your electrical engineer and your life support engineer."

"Oh, they're not important . . ."

Jin fumed. "You did not think to consult us first?"

"What happened to us 'resisting' Earth sanctions?"

"It was the best deal possible under the circumstances. You can't operate up there without supplies or additional crew, Han. Some compromises had to be made."

Chindarkar asked, "Who are these observers?"

"*US Space Force personnel. Unarmed.*"

Jin threw up his arms. "US military? And what if they turn out to be armed, Lukas? What then?"

"*Before you get too upset, China and Russia will both soon be sending observers as well. In fact, China claims that they* own *Clarke Station outright.*"

The team looked at one another.

Tighe said, "Is that a joke?"

Rochat shrugged. "*Unfortunately, no. The legal situation is in flux. The larger and more international the crew is up there, the stronger our position becomes.*"

Tighe stared at Rochat's image. "Why in the hell would we trust government observers up here? They tried to claim the Ryugu resources. If it was up to them, this station wouldn't even exist, and now they want to come for a 'visit,' as if everything's okay? I say screw that."

Chindarkar hesitated before saying, "J.T., we need supplies and our colleagues to have any chance to build the mass-driver, and the mass-driver is the only way we'll be able to build a rescue ship."

He turned to her. "Then why did we risk our lives sneaking off Earth if we were just going to cut a deal with government officials anyway? What was the point?"

Rochat answered instead. "*Because now that you're up there, you're in physical control of the only long-term habitat beyond the Moon—at the edge of the Earth-Moon gravity well. It's a strategic position. You can negotiate from strength, and no one has what you have at L2: propellant and mass. Now they have no choice but to take you seriously.*"

Tighe folded his arms. "They'll try to seize control, and we don't have the manpower to keep an eye on them. I say no international observers on board. It's too early. We need to focus on building a rescue ship."

Chindarkar said, "Which requires building a mass-driver on the lunar surface. And for that we need experts and supplies, J.T."

Jin pondered the situation.

Tighe looked at him. "You're awfully quiet. You were pissed off about us being railroaded back at Cape Canaveral. Do you agree with me?"

Jin thought for several moments before he said, "This is different. There will be representatives from the US, China, *and* Russia. They will provide checks and balances to one another."

Rochat looked visibly relieved. "*Han's right, J.T. You can't ignore the major nations of the world. Otherwise, they'll feel threatened, and while they can't easily take over your station, they are quite capable of sending a missile to destroy it.*"

Tighe: "Oh, come on—"

"*But not if other international observers are on board.*"

Chindarkar looked at Rochat's image. "So we'll have five of our own team members up here." She counted. "Which makes eight of us. Versus the two observers."

Tighe said, "For now, but then there's also the Chinese and Russians."

Rochat piped in. "*Who won't arrive until next month, and additional crew of ours will be coming up with them.*"

Jin considered this. "Then it would be difficult for anyone to take over the station by force—as long as these observers are unarmed."

"*They'll be thoroughly searched and screened by our security people prior to launch. And some more news: a cargo capsule is being sent directly to Clarke Station—not via the lunar cycler. It should arrive next week and will contain your Badger mining robot control systems and computer chips so Priya can begin to depose the chassis and housings to build the finished machines. The capsule will also contain solar power satellite assembly robots as well as four fully operational Talos robots. Celestial Robotics engineers will step you through setup.*"

Chindarkar snapped alert. "Celestial Robotics?"

Jin frowned. "That's Alan Goff's company. What does Goff have to do with any of this?"

Rochat hesitated.

"Spit it out, Lukas." Tighe stared.

"*Your Talos robots . . . They're produced by Celestial Robotics.*"

"What the hell!" Tighe pounded the table and stood.

Jin leaned forward. "The humanoid robots we tested on Ascension Island are manufactured by Celestial Robotics?"

Rochat reluctantly nodded.

Tighe shouted, "It was Goff who killed David! And afterward, he cut a deal with Joyce to conceal our presence out at Ryugu! What the hell is the matter with you?"

"It was a malfunctioning machine that killed David, not Alan Goff."

Chindarkar shook her head. "When were you planning on telling us this?"

"I thought you knew. You tested them."

"Well, someone conveniently left off the CR logo." Tighe paced. "Why would Julian do that to us?"

Rochat held up his hands. *"Look, I realize you're upset, but Alan Goff has come to a settlement with David's family. He is making amends to them."*

They all looked at Rochat in surprise.

"What happened out at Ryugu was a terrible accident, but Goff had no reason to harm you. You were his last hope to get those CR mining robots working again. He says he was sickened by what happened to David."

"Not sickened enough to tell the world about us."

"Because he and Joyce broke numerous laws, J.T., but his engineers never stopped monitoring you from the cameras on the Argo. *When the new owners took control and all contact with you was lost, it was Goff who told us you were alive. That's why we never gave up trying to contact you."*

Tighe felt the momentum of his rage ebb.

Chindarkar contemplated this news. "Well . . . those Talos robots *are* the best telepresence systems I've ever seen. And they beat risking our own lives down on the lunar surface. That's something Dave would have appreciated."

"And David's family now owns shares in Goff's company."

The team digested this news.

Tighe finally sat down again. "Well, then I guess for his family's sake, we'd better put them to use."

Jin and Chindarkar nodded in agreement.

Tighe looked up at Rochat. "So about these 'international observers'— how long will they be staying with us?"

"That's unknown."

"What's to stop more of them showing up without warning—twenty at a time?"

Jin nodded. "J.T. has a point. Any of the superpowers might try to take over the station by boarding us. Macy could cut a deal and send up fifty people in one of his Galleon rockets."

Rochat said, "*We have a strategy for dealing with that. We've declared a 200-meter exclusion zone around the station. Gabriel's team will be enforcing it from here.*"

They all looked at him.

"Enforcing it, how?"

"*With remotely piloted spacecraft—if necessary.*"

Chindarkar frowned. "That's a bit aggressive, isn't it?"

"*Remember, you are on a frontier. Rule of law is only theoretical out there. Our stated reason for restricting arrivals is that there's no margin for error. That we must carefully account for all resources—including oxygen. So invited guests only.*"

"These folks are 'guests,' then? Meaning we can toss them out if they over-stay their welcome?"

Rochat nodded. "*Theoretically.*"

"Just like we 'theoretically' own this station?"

He grimaced. "*As I said: we are, all of us, in uncharted legal territory.*"

CHAPTER 18

La Trocha

NOVEMBER 9, 2017

Ramón Carlos Marín moved through dense brush on a dusty, well-worn path littered with empty plastic bottles and assorted trash. Though it was just past dawn, the trail was crowded and the air hot. People of all ages weaved in and out of sight ahead of him as they marched, and he knew there were just as many people behind him. Some carried heavy burdens, and yet no one stopped to rest. Not here.

This area was patrolled by various armed groups—ELN, FARC, smugglers, traffickers, corrupt police—and although the border had been officially closed, five thousand people a day were still crossing from Venezuela to Colombia to escape the collapse of their economy. Taking *la trocha*—the shortcut.

And if life had taught Ramón anything, it was that shortcuts were usually dangerous. Especially when they were necessary.

As he walked, Ramón spied masked men with long guns lurking in the brush to either side of the path. He'd paid fourteen thousand pesos each for him and his little brother and sister to cross, but these men might be from a different group. It was impossible to know.

Turning around, Ramón laid eyes on his little brother, who had fallen slightly behind. "Luis! Stay close."

"Where is the river?"

"Ahead. Come along." The endless train of people indicated they were on the right path. He knew only that they had to cross the Táchira River to reach Colombia and the city of Cúcuta. That was their goal. That had been their goal for the past three weeks. If he'd known how difficult the journey from Caracas was going to be, Ramón wondered if he still would have attempted it.

Of course you would have. There was no other choice.

He had promised his father that he would take care of his brother and sister, and there was nothing left for them back in Caracas.

He adjusted the weight of his little sister, who rode on his back. She was light. Too light for five years old. Finding food on their journey had been difficult—but even more difficult back home.

She squirmed and asked sleepily, "Did we cross yet?"

"Not yet, *chamita*. Just be still."

It had been such a long journey. They'd managed to hitch rides on trucks as far as Mérida, but after that it was impossible to find transportation. They'd had to walk the last 150 kilometers, joining an endless procession of people— including the elderly, pregnant women, and single mothers with children. The locals called the refugees *caminantes*—the walkers. They might have once been white-collar professionals, tradesmen or, like his father and mother, academics. But now they were all wanderers, willing to risk their lives to get somewhere else—anywhere else. Slow death was all that awaited them otherwise.

As he walked, weary and famished, Ramón's mind wandered, as it always did. He recalled his last happy memories—back when he was a small boy, when times were better. He remembered his father making pancakes for him and his mother, singing in the kitchen. He remembered his mother's laugh. An image flashed of her speaking to her students—their fists upraised. His father with his reading glasses. Leaning close and saying, "*Knowledge is the one thing the collectivos can never steal from you, Ramón.*" Tapping his temple. "*Rely on your intellect. Not possessions.*" These memories were fragments of his shattered life. But what he remembered most of all about his parents was their love. He felt the gaping void in his heart where they had been.

"Ramón . . . ?"

It was Luis's voice. Ramón snapped alert. "What is it?" He glanced around.

A masked man in camouflage stood in the middle of the path, a black automatic rifle slung across his chest. Beyond the man, the other *caminantes* and *trocheros* receded in the distance. A glance behind showed that others had sensed the danger and taken a different way.

The man curled a finger toward Ramón. "Come here, boy."

Half a dozen more armed men emerged from the bushes, ahead and behind.

Gabriela started shrieking in terror.

Ramón lowered her to the ground and turned to comfort her. "Shh. Shh. Little one."

Luis pressed up against him and dropped his walking stick as the armed men surrounded them.

It occurred to Ramón that he had not stayed close enough to other adults on the path. That had apparently been a mistake. The line of walkers had diverted. Ramón and his siblings had been isolated from the herd. He felt the warm adrenaline of fear spread throughout his body.

A rifle barrel slowly moved in toward Ramón's chest, and he raised his trembling arms as Gabriela shrieked anew. The tip of the barrel shoved Ramón back and the masked man holding the gun stared with cold eyes. "Shut that bitch up."

"Gabriela. We need to be quiet." He eased her toward Luis, who immediately held his little sister close and comforted her. They cowered, face-to-face.

The man grabbed Ramón by his T-shirt, nearly lifting him off the ground. "Where are your parents?"

Ramón looked into those cold eyes. "Dead." His mother murdered in the street. His father dead only a month before from lack of access to his heart medication—after Venezuela's medical system utterly collapsed.

The man started patting Ramón's clothes. "They must have left you something."

"Please. We have almost nothing."

He shoved Ramón to the ground, and Ramón stayed down. He felt numerous hands roughly going through his pockets and clothes. Tearing at the fabric. Soon he felt his low-end smartphone yanked from his pocket, then saw his *carnet de la patria* card and other ID tossed aside as useless trash.

Gabriela and Luis both screamed as the men pried them apart and started roughly searching them as well. They tore open Luis's school backpack. Luis screamed again.

Ramón got up on one knee and turned to Luis. "It's okay! It's okay."

He felt a sharp bolt of pain as someone cracked him in the back of the head with something hard. Ramón collapsed forward, dazed.

"Stay down!" The man pulled a knife and put it to Ramón's throat. "You hear me?"

Ramón nodded. The pain in the back of his head made his eyes water.

"Where's your money?"

The hands tore at his clothes again. They pulled off his tattered sneakers. One of the men found the small wad of pesos in his left shoe. They found the other stash in his briefs as they pulled his clothing off.

"Do you know what happens to people who hide money from us?"

A kick to his side.

"I was going to give it to—"

Another series of kicks, to his ribs, stomach, and face.

Then a knife was held up to his ear as strong hands held him down.

"I should take your ear."

"I was going to give it to you."

One of the other men thumbed at his smartphone. "No password?" He looked up.

Ramón, still held down, felt blood flowing from his nose. His lips were swelling up. "No. You would only make me unlock it."

"Smart-ass boy . . ." Another kick.

The strong hands released him, and the men started moving away.

Ramón tried to catch his breath and looked to see Luis and Gabriela huddled together on the ground, sobbing, their shoes pulled off and clothes in disarray.

Luis convulsed in tears as he said, "Now we have nothing!"

Ramón retrieved his *carnet de la patria* card from the dirt and crawled toward them. "Shh, shh." He wiped Luis's tears away. "We have each other. We are safe."

Gabriela sobbed into Luis's chest. "I want Momma. I want Momma."

He stroked her hair. "Momma's in heaven, with Papa. Remember, *chamita.*"

Luis suddenly noticed his older brother was bleeding. "They hurt you."

Ramón shook his head. "Not bad. I'm fine." He looked up to see that the men were nearly out of sight down the path. "We must go now. C'mon. We're almost there. We've come too far to give up now."

As Ramón got his brother and sister up, he lifted Gabriela and held her in his arms, rushing down the path.

Luis ran behind him. "But even if we reach Colombia, what will we do now? We have nothing!"

"Just keep moving."

Up ahead he spotted the river.

"We can make it."

A Christian church group ran the aid station on the border in Cúcuta, Colombia. There, Ramón received medical attention for his injuries. His skull and face throbbed, and his ribs ached, but he felt a sense of elation as he looked at Luis and Gabriela sitting nearby sipping from juice boxes and eating cheese sandwiches. He smiled to them with swollen, cracked lips. "We made it. It's going to be okay."

The presence of the aid station was not a surprise. In fact, he had researched the church group and knew the precise location and the services they provided to migrants. The aid workers gave Ramón and his little brother and sister donated clothes and shoes and allowed Ramón to use a computer with Internet access, intended for migrants to reach out and connect with family or sponsors in Colombia or beyond. There were hundreds of migrants here at the station. Ramón could hear the sound of voices and cars honking beyond the tent walls. There was a whole city out there; in a country that was not undergoing economic collapse. There was hope here. He kept smiling, then wincing against his painful, swollen lips.

Once Ramón got his turn on a computer, he navigated to the website of a local mobile phone store just a few blocks away from the aid station—one that he knew accepted bitcoin. Back in Caracas he'd rehearsed what followed dozens of times: ordering an iPhone and filling in his personal details, navigating to payment, and copying the store's bitcoin wallet address. He then accessed a wallet he had hosted at a cryptocurrency exchange using his memorized password. There he'd stored a modest fraction of bitcoin, which he used to pay for the phone. He printed out the confirmation, and collected his brother and sister.

"Aren't you going to eat, Ramón?" His little brother pointed to an aid worker handing out sandwiches.

"Later. We must do something first." He thanked the aid workers, and then picked up Gabriela in his arms and led Luis through the bustling streets of Cúcuta's business district. He felt like he was hallucinating as they walked among Colombians going about their daily lives in a functioning society. Stores lined every street. The smell of roast chicken emanated from a nearby bistro. A glance down at his brother and sister showed their eyes widen as they pointed and whispered excitedly to each other. This was a whole new world to them and a long-ago memory for Ramón.

"Hurry now." He pulled them onward and soon reached the mobile phone store he was looking for. The manager there was deeply suspicious of his battered and bandaged face—and penniless Venezuelan migrants were everywhere—but Ramón presented the printout with the payment confirmation as well as his photo *carnet de la patria* ID card.

The manager nodded as he handed over the phone. "I can't sell you a phone plan without Colombian identification."

"Then sell me an hour of Internet access, and we can do more business today."

The man looked at Ramón and then his siblings. He finally nodded. "Thirty minutes."

With the new iPhone in hand and a Wi-Fi password, Ramón began to set up his new device. He could scarcely believe he had a new, high-quality phone, into which he immediately began installing a series of apps that he'd learned about from friends in the offshore coding and crypto community.

It wasn't long before he had access to another one of his accounts on a crypto exchange. He spotted a sticker printed with the QR code of the store's bitcoin wallet and captured it with his phone's camera. "I'll need a phone case, charger, and some other accessories." He focused on his phone screen. "And I'll send you three hundred USD worth of bitcoin for two hundred fifty USD in Colombian pesos."

The man thought for a moment. "One hundred fifty in Colombian pesos."

"Deal." Ramón sent the funds to the address, and after confirming the transfer, the man peeled off the bills from a wad in his pocket.

Not long after, Ramón left the store with Luis and Gabriela and his new gear.

Luis looked up at him quizzically. "So we have money again?"

Ramón nodded.

"How?"

He knelt down to look his little brother in the eye. "I'll teach you when you're older. I'll teach you that and a lot more." Then he noticed Gabriela staring at the window of an ice cream parlor next door. A boy and his father were leaving, eating ice cream cones.

He took her hand. "You've never had ice cream, have you, *chamita*?"

She shook her head—though he already knew the answer.

He looked to Luis and took his hand as well. "Then let's change that . . ."

JULY 2028

Ramón looked up from his laptop as Luis called out to him.

"Come out with us!" Luis waved as he and his friends carried surfboards out to catch the swells of high tide.

"I have work to do, little brother!" He laughed as Luis waved back.

"Your loss!"

How buff his brother was now. Eighteen years old and nearly a head taller than Ramón, but then Luis hadn't been malnourished through puberty. Neither of his siblings had been. Ramón had seen to that.

From the vantage point of his beach house deck, Ramón could see the entire strand. Gabriela was talking with her friends as they sunned themselves on a beach blanket. Ramón felt a grim pride and wondered if his father and mother would be proud of him. It had taken years, but he'd learned what he needed to know to build a business. To make a place for himself and his siblings in the world.

Blockchain systems had made that possible. The skills he'd first developed building mining rigs and then managing crypto funds, secure token offerings—these had changed his life. It had made it possible for him to provide security for his family, and now all he thought about was how to make this decentralized system work for the billions of other unbanked people in this world, suffering under corrupt regimes or the chaos of war or climate upheaval.

A voice called to him in English, "Hey, Ramón! There's someone I'd like you to meet."

Ramón turned to see his business partner, a young American named Bill Paxton, coming through the beachside gate, another person in tow—a fit and handsome man in his thirties. The man nodded at him as they came up the steps.

Paxton gestured toward him. "Ramón Marín, I'd like you to meet Nathan Joyce."

Ramón paused in shock. "*The* Nathan Joyce?" He stood.

"And I'm told you are *the* Ramón Marín."

Ramón laughed and extended his hand for a firm shake. "Mr. Joyce, it's a pleasure to meet you. I'm a big admirer."

"Then it's mutual." Joyce gripped his hand firmly and smiled. "I wanted to meet the guy who designed the wyvern architecture. You've earned yourself quite a reputation here in El Zonte, and I found your personal background inspiring. You've done a lot to help the community here." He looked at the nearby chairs. "I wonder if we might chat. I have a special project I think you might be interested in . . ."

CHAPTER 19

Visitors

DAYS TO RYUGU DEPARTURE: 1,220

P riya Chindarkar, Jin Han, and James Tighe floated in Clarke Station's arrival gate, alongside the docking hatches. Chindarkar was excited, but tried to appear calm as clanking and movement was audible on the far side, until finally an inner hatch swung open.

The first person through was a familiar and welcome face from Chindarkar's candidate selection training days—Dr. Elizabeth Josephson, a British former ESA flight surgeon. Josephson spotted Chindarkar and smiled wide. "Look at you!" She moved along handholds to finally embrace Chindarkar in microgravity. They rolled end over end, laughing. "Last time I saw you, you were just another ascan."

Chindarkar knew that Josephson had missed out on the *Konstantin* expedition only in the final selection—just like Sevastian Yakovlev. If not for that, she would have been the flight surgeon on the *Konstantin* expedition instead of Isabel Abarca.

Jin caught Josephson's ankle to stop them tumbling. "Liz, careful. There are still sharp edges in here."

Josephson detached from Chindarkar and hugged Jin. Then hugged Tighe as well.

"J.T., I heard about your genetic surgery. How are your cancer symptoms?"

"Gone, mostly."

"I'd love to talk more about it if you're willing."

Just then another woman wearing a blue flight suit emerged from the transit craft hatchway. Her eyes went wide at the size of the gate area.

Josephson gestured toward her. "Team, this is Monica Balter, out of the University of Sydney."

Balter's eyes turned to them. She smiled broadly, grabbed Jin's hand, and spoke with an Australian accent. "Lizzie's told me all about you. Regular legends!"

Chindarkar asked, "You're our solar satellite expert?"

"That's right." Balter gestured to the surrounding station. "I thought it would be decades before we'd see something like this. If ever. You've all been busy up here, haven't you?"

Another face appeared in the hatchway behind her—this one also familiar: Ramón Marín, the Venezuelan systems architect Lukas Rochat had introduced on the airship journey to Ascension. Marín seemed as quiet as ever, with wavy black hair and a diminutive frame. He nodded silently to the crew as he floated in, clutching a small black backpack close. Marín oriented himself to match the others in microgravity.

Josephson pointed. "This is Ramón Marín, IT specialist."

Chindarkar nodded. "Yes, we met back on Earth." She clasped Marín's hand. "You really went through orbital training fast, Ramón."

He spoke with a Spanish accent. "I have been preparing for some time, actually."

Tighe and Jin shook his hand as well. "Ramón, welcome."

Another woman followed Marín, smiling brightly as she came through. She looked vaguely Middle Eastern to Chindarkar.

Josephson pointed. "And this is our chemist, Sofia Boutros."

"Oh!" Chindarkar grasped Boutros's hand. "Wonderful. There's so much we need to synthesize. Great to meet you, Sofia."

"Likewise. Very nice to meet you all." Boutros nodded to the team. Her accent was part British and part something else.

Tighe shook hands with her, as did Jin. Then Tighe looked to the second docking hatch. Beyond it waited another transit craft. "So, do we let these international observers on board now, or what?"

Chindarkar gave him a look. "Of course, J.T. Yak's in there, too, and they've all been in microgravity for a week."

Jin stared at the hatch. "Perhaps we tell Yak to search them."

"Han, they've already been searched and scanned for weapons and electronic devices. What is Yak going to find that mission control's security team didn't?"

After a moment, Jin nodded. He interacted with virtual controls in his crystal's UI, and the second hatch unlocked with a *click*. Then he spoke into his bone mic. "Yak, the hatch is unlocked. Come aboard when you are ready."

"Fabulous!"

Clanking noises emanated behind the second docking hatch, and finally it, too, pushed in, revealing the beaming face of Sevastian Yakovlev—almost unrecognizable without his familiar beard.

He and Jin clasped in a hug and slapped each other's backs. "What happened to your whiskers?"

"Face mask seal comes before rugged good looks in space. You know this." He hugged Tighe heartily. "J.T.!"

"How was the trip up?"

"Magnificent! I am in deep space again, where I belong." He gazed around. "And this station! It is new wonder of civilization." He hugged Chindarkar and kissed her cheeks. "Priya, *kotyonok*. Good to see you safe." He looked up. "It echoes like mad in here, though. We must fix this."

Chindarkar watched as two more people emerged from Yak's transit craft. They both wore dark blue flight suits with United States Space Force insignia and rank. The first was a short-haired, fit blond woman in her late thirties or early forties. "Permission to come aboard?"

Jin nodded. "Of course."

She extended her hand. "Major Susan Cadot, Royal Canadian Air Force, on assignment with US Space Force. You must be Jin Han. It's an honor to meet you."

He shook her hand. "Good to meet you as well, Major." He pointed. "That's James Tighe, and that's Priya Chindarkar."

"So great to finally meet you all." She shook hands. "What you've accomplished is historic."

The second observer, an African American man in his thirties, emerged from the transit craft, smiling broadly as he extended his hand. "Major Charles Lawler. Great to meet you, Han. Priya. James."

He shook hands with them each in turn.

Lawler looked around at the station. "I'm still trying to wrap my head around this place. We've both been fully briefed, but . . . wow."

Jin spoke up. "You have probably all had your fill of microgravity in the past week. Let us go below and get you a sit-down meal."

Yak clapped his hands, causing an echo once more. "Spin-gravity. Excellent!"

The echoing voices continued as ten people floated near the elevator, holding excited conversations. Jin led the first group of five down, leaving Tighe, Chindarkar, and Yak waiting behind with the US observers.

Tighe gestured to the elevator doors. "It'll be a few minutes. They'll need to acclimate to spin-gravity before they exit the elevator."

The two majors nodded.

The group then floated in awkward silence.

Chindarkar finally said to the observers, "I know it may seem like we're a gang of privateers up here trying to lay claim to the Moon—but we really just want to get our crewmates at Ryugu back home safe." She gestured around them. "This station is the logistical base necessary to accomplish that."

"Understood." Lawler gestured to himself and Cadot. "And we realize you're probably not thrilled that we're up here, but for what it's worth, I'm impressed as hell at what your crewmates achieved on the *Konstantin* expedition. You should all be famous. In fact, I'm sure you will be, and I hope you get your crew back safe."

"Thank you."

The elevator doors opened—sooner than anticipated.

Tighe floated inside, motioning for them to follow.

Lawler and Cadot studied everything around them.

Cadot laughed. "An actual elevator. Like at the mall . . ."

"Not quite. Grab the handrails . . ." Chindarkar hit the H4 button.

As they descended, she watched the looks on all their faces—the slowly expanding smiles as the sensation of gravity returned, followed quickly by gripping harder onto the handrails.

Cadot and Lawler held each other up. "My god." She tried to stand, and to her credit did so almost immediately.

Then the elevator doors opened, and Lawler's and Cadot's eyes widened. Chindarkar walked out first, with Tighe helping Yak along.

"C'mon, comrade scientist. You're going to like this . . ."

Yak laughed in amazement as he emerged.

The two Space Force observers, still leaning on each other, moved forward until they finally stood on the elevator landing among the rest of the team, gazing out over the railing.

Chindarkar gestured toward the cavernous space below. "It's a bit basic for now, but it's home."

Lawler gripped the railing and slid down to his knees, staring in astonishment at the wide-open area curving gently upward to spinward. He extended his arm and seemed to observe the heft of it. "Spin-gravity beyond the Moon." He laughed uproariously, then turned a smile at Chindarkar. "It's . . . incredible. And the size of it. I . . ."

The other new arrivals were laughing, talking excitedly, and pointing at the floor 10 meters below the platform.

Cadot sat next to Lawler and stared out at the pressurized volume all around them. She gave him a look. "You can study the sat imagery and read the intel reports, but until you're actually here . . ." She paused, then nudged Lawler. "Feel that in your sinuses? I think my sense of smell is returning." She breathed deeply through her nose.

Lawler smiled. "Yeah. Yeah, I'm clearing up, too."

After a moment her expression changed. "What is that smell?"

He took a deep sniff. "I think it's . . ." He turned toward Chindarkar. "Sewage?"

After unloading a ton of equipment and supplies from the two transit crafts, the new arrivals were assigned quarters, split between the North and South Habs. Tighe, Jin, and Chindarkar decided to remain together in South Hab, adding their chemist, Sofia Boutros, and their introverted systems architect, Ramón Marín. Meanwhile, Sevastian Yakovlev, flight surgeon Elizabeth Josephson, and solar satellite expert Monica Balter joined the two Space Force observers in the North Hab. Even with only the wall partitions and ceiling installed on the first floor, there was still more than enough room for five people in each hab. However, the interior walls were still merely framing. Silvery emergency blankets clipped to the frames had to suffice for privacy in the restrooms and showers.

That is, when those facilities were working. Almost immediately upon arrival, the newcomers encountered problems with the station's plumbing. The modest additional usage seemed to tip a fragile balance. Toilets backed up and water mysteriously oozed up out of the shower drains, creating pools of cloudy, standing water. And Lawler was correct about the odor of sewage in South Hab, where the team had been living for the past month. Chindarkar smelled it almost immediately after returning from North Hab. It occurred to her that they must have simply gotten accustomed to the smell. There was so much else on their minds.

Yak, Jin, and Tighe videoconferenced with mission control to identify the source of the problem. The fact that plumbing issues were occurring in both the North and South Habs suggested a design flaw—the only question was where.

Chindarkar, meanwhile, helped get the US observers settled in. Majors Cadot and Lawler insisted on using an encrypted line to communicate with their superiors on Earth, and Ramón Marín seemed to understand what they needed. Rochat had negotiated a "no transmitter" policy for outside observers, meaning that they would not be permitted to broadcast radio signals of their own while on board, so as to avoid interference with telepresence robots; thus, their comms would need to go through the main laser line back to low Earth orbit (and from there back to mission control on Ascension Island). However, that line was to be available to them "at all times," according to the agreement Rochat had struck. If it ever went offline, alarm bells would sound back in DC.

Soon after his arrival, Marín installed surveillance cameras overlooking the common areas in both habs, ostensibly to detect emergency situations.

In anticipation of a series of incoming crews over the next few months, mission control had implemented color-coded team designations. Yak's incoming Blue Team wore the same blue flight suit everyone else wore; however, they also had an embroidered blue mission patch on their left shoulder featuring their team name in white letters.

Likewise, mission control had designated Chindarkar, Jin, and Tighe as the Gold Team, and Yak had brought up gold-ish shoulder patches for their flight suits. As Chindarkar examined her embroidered team patch she realized it did give her a certain esprit de corps—and she suspected that Dr.

Angela Bruno, Catalyst Corporation's staff psychologist back on Ascension Island, was behind the idea. Bruno was clever at subtly fostering teamwork.

The plan was for incoming teams to reside on Clarke Station for a one-year tour (assuming the station survived that long). Gold Team, however, had no end date.

Instead, they were up here until their rescue spacecraft was built and launched toward the asteroid Ryugu.

CHAPTER 20

Mission Plan

G old Team set up a meeting area and project management space near the elevator doors on level H2 of South Hab. Here they gathered plastic chairs and pushed together two tables large enough to seat all ten of the crew on board, as well as videoconferencing cameras and microphones. With the flooring for H3 and H4 not yet installed above them, they had lots of headroom.

As they worked, Tighe couldn't help but notice that Marín was absent from South Hab. The moment he'd arrived, Marín had gotten busy in the station's computer core and seemed to know his way around the utility rooms. He apparently also possessed access codes to everything. Looking at the station map in his crystal HUD display, Tighe noticed Marín's radio frequency ID tag was still located in the station's server room, where it remained.

He finally called down to mission control on a private channel to Lacroix. "Gabriel, this is J.T. Do you copy? Gabriel, this is J.T. Do you copy?"

After a few seconds, Lacroix's voice came in over his headphones. *"I copy you, J.T. Go ahead."*

"I have a question about Ramón. Lukas introduced him as our systems architect back on Earth."

"That is correct."

"He seems to have access codes to everything, and he's busy—but barely says anything to us. What is he supposed to be doing up here, exactly?"

Thankfully, with the relatively short distance to Earth, there was only a few seconds delay. *"You'll need to find out from Lukas, J.T. It's not that I won't*

*say; it's that I don't know. Mr. Marín has no permissions to the flight control
or life support systems of the station, but he is working on a special project
for Mr. Rochat that we are not privy to."*

Tighe exchanged looks with Jin, who was listening in. "Great. Thanks."

Jin said, "I expect it involves this Cislunar Commodity Exchange that
Lukas mentioned."

Tighe felt a familiar anger at their lack of control. "We'll have a conversation with Lukas then. Thanks, Gabriel. Out." Tighe pointed toward the spinward end of the hab. "Ramón is setting up what looks like a data center in one
of the partitions on H1, too. Running cable. I have no idea what the hell he's
doing."

"Lukas and his schemes . . ." Jin checked the time. "But we must get to our
own work."

Clarke Station ran on Coordinated Universal Time (or UTC) for scheduling purposes, and at eight a.m. sharp, nine out of the ten people aboard Clarke
Station (all but Marín) gathered around the two plastic tables that had been
pushed together in the "open-air" H2 meeting room in South Hab. All of
them wore crystal headsets, and an array of virtual screens floated around
them in AR, displaying images and maps of the Moon, system diagrams, and
live video feeds of people back on Earth—mission control on Ascension Island, where Julian Kerner and other experts also appeared as video insets.

A few meters removed from the table sat the two observers from US Space
Force, Majors Lawler and Cadot, where they could "observe," but were still
out of the way. Given the political and legal realities, neither Tighe, Jin, nor
Chindarkar saw much point in concealing their plans from Earth authorities.
Transparency was part of the Artemis Accords, but there was also the awareness that, as long as the team kept moving forward at a rapid pace, there was
very little anyone could do to interfere.

Jin stood at the head of the table and cleared his throat. The conversation
faded, and eager, expectant faces looked to him. He nodded to the people in
actual attendance, as well as the half dozen video insets participating via laser
comm back on Earth.

"Good morning, everyone. I hope spin-gravity allowed you a good night's
rest and a sit-down breakfast."

A slight laugh and nods swept the team.

"Our apologies for the plumbing problems here in the habs. We are working with mission control for a resolution. However, it is time now to pursue the purpose for which this station was built." Jin stepped back and slapped the steel wall of the elevator bank, where a date had been written in bold letters with a grease pencil:

06/02/2042

"This is the date by which we must have a crewed spacecraft built, ready, and capable of departing cislunar space for a rendezvous with the asteroid Ryugu on its next close encounter with Earth. But this time Ryugu comes no closer than 60 million kilometers, which means we'll need a very capable vessel—substantial radiation shielding, spin-gravity, and a delta-v in the 12-kilometer-per-second range. And we'll need it roughly three and a half years from now."

Whistles around the table.

"The purpose of Clarke Station is to serve as a base of operations from which to obtain and refine the raw materials necessary to build this rescue spacecraft. That means putting in place logistical prerequisites here in deep space and on the lunar surface . . ." He pointed at a diagram, highlighting each item in turn. ". . . a regolith refinery here on station, a solar power satellite, a large-scale rectenna on the Moon to receive its power, a regolith collection facility and a mass-driver on the Moon's equator. All of these have been technologically possible for decades, but none of them have ever been attempted. We are going to change that."

He studied the people seated around the table, lingering for a few moments on Chindarkar, Yak, and Tighe. "For some of you, this is a familiar circumstance. For those who are new, do not hesitate to ask questions from those with experience in deep space. Out here, mistakes—even simple ones—can be fatal."

Jin gestured to the walls and ceiling. "This station—this entire operation, in fact—is an experiment. For that reason, never remove your RFID bracelet, so that we may locate you in an emergency. Likewise, whenever possible, please wear your crystal headset to facilitate rapid communication during a crisis. Most of the UIs you will encounter on board will be virtual for reasons of logistics—in order not to ship tons of components up here that can otherwise be virtualized; this is why your workstations and other systems will appear only in AR. Relying on AR can, of course, be a problem during a power failure or other emergency." He pointed to an empty bracket next to the elevator button panel and several more empty brackets on nearby walls. "Emergency fire suppression, breathing apparatus, and oxygen candles will be placed in clearly marked enclosures in the coming months, as logistics permit; however, for now we have none of that. Therefore, be sure to always wear your flight suit with a breathing apparatus either on your person or close at hand."

Chindarkar added, "There's no margin for error up here—not yet. So stay alert, and keep in touch with one another at all times. Always inform teammates where you are going, even if it is just to the lavatory."

Jin nodded. "Fire will be an increasingly serious hazard as we build out these hab compartments. Sprinkler and detection systems will be installed as we go—and as the sensors become available. However, for the time being, our main fire suppression system will be to evacuate air from the hab. So if you see a fire or detect an equipment or station engineering failure, immediately notify mission control on channel nine. It is marked as 'Emergency' in your HUD display."

He surveyed the team. "I do not anticipate any serious personal disputes or harassment issues, given your rigorous psychological evaluations back on Ascension . . ." Here Jin paused to eye the Space Force observers. ". . . or at least most of you."

Cadot held up her hand. "I assure you, we will be well-behaved guests, Mr. Han."

Jin answered, "That is good to hear—except it is now *Captain* Han." He turned to the rest of the group. "My colleagues and mission control have nominated me to the position of captain of Clarke Station, and I will serve in that role until further notice. Dr. Chindarkar and Mr. Tighe will both serve as first officers. I understand that this station has applied for a license as a Luxembourg-flagged vessel, and I have applied for the newly created deep space captain's license. For the time being we will be observing international maritime law, in addition to the articles of both the Artemis Accords and the Outer Space Treaty, as and if they apply—although there will be plenty of new legal territory ahead of us. Bottom line: if I have a problem with you, I will put you on a direct, eight-day return to Earth. That's just 350 meters per second of delta-v, and I have the propellant to spare. So do not test me."

Jin turned to a list of tasks on a virtual screen. "Here is what we need to accomplish over the next few months. Many of these tasks will be moving ahead in parallel." He highlighted the first. "By the first week of May—about three months from now—we need to have completed construction of a 200-ton, 50-megawatt solar power satellite here at L2, based on a modular SPS-Alpha design, components of which are already being produced in our CVD mill. These components include metallic thin-film mirrors like those now concentrating sunlight in Clarke Station's solar furnace power plant. However, printing high-efficiency solar panels in orbit is going to require additional expertise." Jin pointed to Monica Balter. "Ms. Balter, would you care to elaborate on our solar panel production plan?"

Balter stood and smiled. "Well . . . my research has been to perfect thin-film deposition for creation of multiband photovoltaics in a vacuum." She laughed. "To say that this is the opportunity of a lifetime would be an understatement. I hardly knew this mission was possible six months ago, much less that I would be personally going. So I am quite literally over the Moon to be here."

The team groaned at the pun.

She held up her hands. "Right, before I wear out my welcome: I'll be working the next few weeks to get the solar panel production line up and running with the limited specialized resources I've brought up, as well as the asteroid-derived carbonyl metals I'm told we have on hand. To build the actual SPS-Alpha solar sat, we have preprogrammed Modular Autonomous Robot Effectors—or MARE units—specialized robots that can construct and maintain the solar sat from modular components that we'll manufacture in situ. The way these SPS-Alphas work is to use simpler, thin-film mirrors to concentrate available sunlight onto an array of solar panels. I'm hopeful I can get 25 percent efficiency in my first batch of silicon photovoltaics and closer to 40 percent in later multiband versions—however, those will require perovskites."

Chindarkar asked, "How long until you're ready to start production?"

"I intend to have my lab up and running by next week."

Jin took the lead once more. "Very good. Thanks, Monica."

She nodded and sat down.

"While Monica's work is proceeding, the rectenna to receive our solar satellite's microwave energy will be assembled by Julian Kerner's team using teleoperation from Ascension Island. They'll produce the rectenna in 25-meter-square foldable sections—a half kilometer square in total. Deployment of this to the lunar surface will be our job." Jin brought up an animation of the finished solar satellite being transported to the side of the Moon facing Earth. "Once the solar sat is completed, we will move it into position orbiting L1 and deploy the rectenna using a Starion Kangaroo lunar lander—two of which have been purchased and should arrive from Earth by late April." He paused. "And then comes the difficult part."

A nervous laugh echoed in the room.

"We will use the solar satellite, beaming energy to the rectenna, to harvest lunar regolith, melt it into bricks, and propel it to escape velocity using an electromagnetic launch system—more commonly known as a mass-driver. That material must arrive in the vicinity of this space station, where it will be collected and refined into a wide range of useful materials for use in building our rescue spacecraft."

Jin pointed at a virtual video inset floating nearby. "Robert Ecklund, a former NASA engineer, is our mass-driver architect. He joins us from orbital certification training back on Ascension Island. Dr. Ecklund, would you please brief the team on your mass-driver construction plan?"

One of the video insets highlighted, then expanded as it moved virtually to the front of the open meeting room. The live video feed displayed a buzz-cut Caucasian man in his late fifties, fairly fit and sitting in what looked to be a bare white cubicle. He sported several days' beard growth and looked like the sort of engineer who'd ride a recumbent bike to work. "*Yeah . . . sure thing, Captain Jin.*" Ecklund poked around with settings. "*Let me just set up here . . . There we go.*"

Suddenly a large, detailed 3D globe of the Moon appeared, floating before them. It began to expand, zooming in toward the lunar equator. "*Our mass-driver will involve construction of a 1.39-kilometer-long electromagnetic launch track—specifically what's known as a superconducting quenchgun—on the lunar equator, with work commencing at the end of May. That's roughly four months from now, with completion scheduled for the end of November.*"

To be clear, this will require safely transferring more payload mass to the lunar surface than has ever been attempted. Manufacture of the individual 6-meter conduction coil sections as well as integration of superconducting YBCO tape must begin as soon as possible up there at Clarke Station so it will be ready for installation as needed."

The 3D globe kept zooming in and labels appeared on various lunar craters as it did so, along with a coordinate grid and distance scale for reference. The image resolved in more detail as they zeroed in on the equator—and finally a glowing blue line over a kilometer long became visible to the west of a crater labeled "Maskelyne A." The perspective then angled to reveal the Moon's topography.

"Here is where we'll be building—at 33.1 degrees east longitude on the lunar equator, near Censorinus Crater and Cape Bruce—at the southeastern edge of the Sea of Tranquility."

Major Lawler raised his hand, but spoke at the same time. "Dr. Ecklund, you said the Sea of Tranquility. Approximately how far from the historic Apollo 11 landing site?"

Ecklund labeled the Apollo sites on the map. *"I take preservation of all the historic Moon sites very seriously, and while the Apollo 11 landing site is, in fact, the closest to our mass-driver, it's still 300 kilometers to the northwest. None of our inbound trajectories cross over it, and all the material we'll be launching into orbit will be going eastward—away from it. And Comrade Scientist Yakovlev, we will be 350 kilometers from the nearest historic Russian Luna lander site."*

Yak nodded. *"Bez muki n'et nauki."*

Lawler chuckled in response to Yak as he and Cadot took notes. "Very good. Thank you, Dr. Ecklund."

Major Cadot spoke up. "One more thing, Dr. Ecklund—"

"Bob. Please, just call me Bob."

"Okay, Bob. Global opinion surveys indicate that the public back on Earth vehemently opposes 'lights on the Moon'—I think 'no-LOM' is the term. I see that your proposed surface facility is on the near side, facing Earth."

Ecklund nodded. *"Understood. None of what we're doing will be visible from Earth, even with the largest telescope, and lights won't be necessary because it will be automated."*

The map image kept zooming in until a model of the mass-driver itself was clearly visible, traversing the slightly irregular lunar landscape atop pylons set at intervals. The view then began to rotate around it.

Ecklund narrated. *"It is intended as a cislunar bootstrapping site—and for a key reason: from this specific location on the lunar surface, objects can be consistently launched at lunar escape velocity up to where you all sit now—at EM-L2. By the time they reach the vicinity of L2, nearly all their excess velocity will have been spent, and they can be safely collected with the Catcher—a spinning cone spacecraft designed to retrieve payloads as they arrive—"*

Jin interjected, "Which is a subject for another meeting."

"Understood . . ." The site image panned to encompass the base of the launcher, with surrounding equipment and facilities. *"The launch facility itself—"*

Tighe interjected, "Morra Base."

Ecklund nodded. *"Correction: Morra Base . . ."* He highlighted structures in turn. *". . . includes a rectenna array and power lines. Here are transformers, along with lunar landing pads and berms. Robotic vehicle roads. The tele-robotic equipment garage. The regolith intake and processing machinery, the storage area for projectiles and volatiles, and the facility that loads the LEML. The idea is that surface regolith will be harvested by Badger robotic vehicles, which will dump their payloads into the intake chute here. The regolith will then be heated to extract volatiles."*

He looked up from the diagram. *"Lunar regolith in this region of the Moon contains 12 to 15 percent iron and has a density of about 1.5 grams per cubic centimeter. Machinery will form it into cylinders 40 centimeters long and 14.5 in diameter—or about 10 kilograms in mass—which will then be melted through electromagnetic induction and magnetically stirred along its axis to calibrate center of mass. The cylindrical shape facilitates mechanical handling and loading into the mass-driver."*

The map scrolled across the terrain and Ecklund highlighted a mound of regolith. *"Finally, this structure here is an optional human-rated habitat, buried to protect against radiation. I say 'optional' because this base will be built and run mostly by teleoperated robots up at Clarke Station, using relay sats now in lunar orbit."*

He looked up at his audience. *"Unlike the small lunar bases established by the US and the Chinese near the lunar south and north poles, Morra Base is going to have a sizable footprint—especially with the LEML track. Therefore, it will need to be constructed to withstand regular and fairly serious moon-quakes without deforming, and in the case of the mass-driver, must also permit remote realignment and recalibration."*

Tighe frowned. "Moonquakes?"

Balter added, "I was under the impression the Moon was not seismically active."

Ecklund replied, *"Not tectonically, no. However, due to the dry, cold nature of the Moon, asteroid and meteor impacts tend to ring it like a bell—leaving it quivering for quite some time afterward. Then there are so-called deep quakes caused by tidal forces with the Earth. And also dawn quakes that occur as the heat of sunlight expands the Moon's frigid crust after the two-week-long lunar night."*

Balter muttered, "Crikey . . ."

"But most worrisome are the 'shallow moonquakes'—caused by crust shifts as the Moon cools. Seismographs placed on the Moon by the Apollo missions measured some at 5.5 on the Richter scale, and they last a long time—typically at least ten minutes. Occasionally longer."

The team exchanged concerned looks.

Tighe asked, "And we can build this mass-driver to cope with these quakes?"

Ecklund nodded. *"Absolutely."*

Chindarkar looked up from her notes. "Bob, at only 10 kilograms per shot, how much mass do you anticipate we'll be able to launch into lunar orbit over, say, the course of a year?"

"In full operation with 50 megawatts of constant power through superconducting coils—moonquakes and meteor impacts aside—this machine can theoretically fire a 10-kilo cylinder into orbit once every two seconds. That amounts to 432 metric tons every twenty-four hours, about 13,000 tons per Earth month . . ."

The team whistled and Cadot and Lawler exchanged wide-eyed expressions.

". . . just over 100,000 tons per year, if we factor in one-third downtime for

maintenance and malfunctions." Ecklund looked resolved. *"Enough to keep you chemists and engineers busy up there."*

Chindarkar nodded appreciatively as she took notes on a virtual pad. "Excellent. Thank you."

Ecklund studied the team's faces. *"You need to understand something, folks: lunar mass-drivers like this aren't a new idea. Engineers have been proposing them to NASA for a long time. Decades—though with Type-II superconducting tape and nitrogen cooling, mine might be the most efficient and reliable. I'm only starting to grapple with the idea that you people may actually build it, but if you do, I will make* certain *it works. And if we pull this off, it's going to be more than an architectural achievement—it's going to alter the trajectory of civilization."*

CHAPTER 21

A Slender Thread

O ver the next few days, the crew of Clarke Station dug into their work. Jin Han, Priya Chindarkar, and James Tighe closely monitored the various efforts running in parallel because the failure of any one of them could sink the entire project. Passing by Monica Balter at her VR workstation in South Hab, Jin and Chindarkar stopped to watch her remotely pilot a mule spacecraft outside the station. Balter used the robotic arms on the front of the mule to gather solar power satellite components produced by Kerner's CVD mill and convey them to the supply yard, where they would later be used by SPS-Alpha assembly robots. That is, once they arrived.

Balter's telepresence skills with the mule appeared modest at best.

Standing behind her, Jin cleared his throat and asked, "Monica, did we allocate you enough building materials?"

"Oh . . ." She paused, still blinded by the VR glasses, but then nodded. "There's not much margin for error, but if I account for every kilo, we should be okay."

"Do you think we can still make the May completion date for the satellite?"

She answered, "Yes, I think it's realistic."

The master plan was a series of linked projects, and its success depended on the timely completion of each step. Without the power satellite, the mass-driver and regolith harvesting couldn't work, and without a working refinery at L2, any regolith launched by the mass-driver into orbit couldn't be transformed into useful materials—which meant they wouldn't be able to finish building out Clarke Station. That, in turn, would mean they couldn't bring up the scores of experts they'd need to construct the rescue ship—a ship they would then also not have the materials to build.

So their success would be hanging from a slender thread for the foreseeable future.

Chindarkar asked, "Does your mass estimate factor in repairs and maintenance?"

"There's a contingency factor, but these SPS-Alpha sats are rather insubstantial. Just a linked collection of hexagonal metal frames that are easy to manufacture. A few station-keeping thrusters and fuel tanks. We've got silica and all the equipment necessary to produce the solar panels and thin-film mirrors that concentrate sunlight. I just need the automated assembly robots and the microwave transmitter components—which should arrive soon."

Jin said, "Good. We are relying on your satellite to power *everything* on the lunar surface. So if you foresee any delays, let us know immediately."

She nodded. "Will do, Captain."

Meanwhile, Sofia Boutros, the chemist, had set up the beginnings of a lab against the South Hab's anti-spinward bulkhead on H2 level. There, she and several others connected an exhaust hood to a preexisting duct and constructed steel countertops and lockable cabinets. Soon she was able to produce chemical compounds critical to life aboard the station.

Boutros began by using monomer feedstock and equipment brought up from Earth to formulate synthetic fibers, which she then fed into a small textile printer that had been sent up weeks earlier to produce fabric in several shades of mauve. The rest of the team stretched this fabric over printed polymer wall panels, which they then affixed to the walls of their quarters on H1. Aside from privacy, the panels alleviated the maddening echo in the steel-walled hab—at least on the first level. They then did the same for North Hab, even putting the Space Force observers to work. For a while the smell of new fabric prevailed over the fetid water in the habs.

However, the station's plumbing issues continued to grow worse. Since Jin Han and Sevastian Yakovlev were both engineers, they worked on the problem with mission control—but this pulled them away from urgent construction work on the station's external regolith refinery. Almost immediately putting them behind schedule.

Water line clearing procedures didn't fix the plumbing and, worse, caused a new problem: now turning off sink faucets triggered "water hammer," a pounding noise that echoed throughout the hab and shook pipes. It was caused by the mass of a moving water column suddenly slamming against a closed valve. Unchecked, it could do serious damage to the pipes.

Jin and Yak stared up at the water lines running along the exterior of South Hab's elevator tube, toward the station core.

Yak shook his head. "Ancient Romans had indoor plumbing. How can we not have this on a space station?"

"This is a new environment." Jin studied where the pipes entered the compartment ceiling. "On the *Konstantin*, our water supply was local to each hab, but here the water lines are coming and going from the core—moving through different levels of micro- and spin-gravity."

"So designers messed up?"

"Possibly. Maybe it's just a blockage in the pipes, but either way, we need to fix it. Otherwise, this could get deadly serious."

Yak thought for a moment. "You refer to station stability."

"Yes. If the water levels get too imbalanced, and the mass equalization system cannot compensate, Clarke Station could start to wobble like a broken wheel. It could wreck the place, and we would not be able to easily evacuate."

Yak nodded to himself. "I will locate cause of this problem."

The next morning Jin climbed the spiral staircase into the open H2 level, and out of the corner of his eye spotted a shimmering object. He glanced up and saw a sizable water drop floating in the air 5 meters above the conference table and moving anti-spinward at several kilometers per hour. It resembled a translucent insect.

Alarmed, he followed it beyond the elevator column, heading toward Boutros's lab.

Tighe's voice called from behind him. "Where the hell is *that* coming from?"

"I do not know." Jin followed the droplet, with Tighe falling in behind him.

They soon watched it splash into a wet spot that had already formed on the compartment's back, or anti-spinward, bulkhead.

Jin looked toward the LED lights mounted in the hull far overhead. "It is coming from up there."

Tighe craned his neck alongside him. "We'd better find out from *what*. Before it gets worse."

After another hurried consultation with mission control and an examination of the South Hab ceiling, it was determined that the dripping water was condensation from human activity—breathing, bathing, and so on—and also pressure and temperature differences between levels H1 and H4. This was expected, but the equipment to catch and process the runoff was not yet on station. Until it arrived, the crew would need to regularly wipe down the anti-spinward wall in both habs.

The fact that this was a surprise to the crew did not ease Jin's mind.

The next morning Tighe stood on the lab counter, swabbing the bulkhead wall with a makeshift mop, and glanced back toward Chindarkar at the conference table. "Priya. Have you seen Ramón?"

"I'm guessing he's in one of the server rooms."

"I know we all have work to do, but everyone needs to pitch in with these hab chores, too. Ramón needs to be part of the team, not doing his own thing."

After mopping up, Tighe went through the system logs, overlaying Marín's RFID tag movements through the station since he'd come aboard a few days ago. It quickly became apparent that Marín moved only between the new server room here in South Hab and the computer core adjacent to the docking hangar. In fact, Marín either stayed up all hours, or he actually slept in the South Hab server room.

Tighe showed the logs to Chindarkar and Jin. "Lukas clearly has plans for this Cislunar Commodity Exchange of his, and his guy is executing them. We need to understand what those two are up to before it becomes our problem."

Just then Jin noticed Major Lawler exit the elevator. Lawler was uncharacteristically grim-faced and beelined for the trio at the conference table. "Don't look now, but here comes our minder."

Lawler nodded. "Captain Jin. There's a matter of some urgency we need to discuss."

"What is it, Major? We're in a meeting."

"I just received word that CSpOC is tracking a radar contact on a trajectory that will bring it to EM-L2 within five days."

Tighe frowned. "CSpOC?"

"The Combined Space Operations Center at Vandenberg. They track all objects in cislunar space."

Jin asked, "Do they know what the contact is?"

"Affirmative. It's a Chinese-crewed spacecraft. A seven-man capsule. Launched two days ago from Jiuquan. It was in LEO but did a TLI as it passed through the lunar antipode."

Tighe said, "Can you translate that into English?"

"It's now headed up here."

"Shit."

Chindarkar asked, "Do they know what's on it?"

"Negative."

"We agreed to the presence of Chinese observers, but they were supposed to arrive via our lunar cycler. For security reasons."

Lawler nodded. "They seem to have other ideas."

Jin said, "They could be traveling to their own lunar space station."

"If so, this is a highly inefficient trajectory, and their station has capacity for just four crew. Two are already in residence there."

Tighe sighed. "And this incoming craft is a seven-man capsule? Christ. What if they're armed?"

Chindarkar said, "But seven people in a small capsule for a week? That seems unlikely."

Jin said, "We need to get Lukas on the line. It is time for him to earn his keep down there on Earth . . ."

"I thought we made an agreement with the Chinese, Lukas. Their observers were scheduled to come up on the lunar cycler next month."

Gathered around the conference table was the entire Gold Team, Yak, and Majors Lawler and Cadot. An augmented-reality video screen displayed Lukas Rochat sitting in his office back on Earth.

Rochat said, *"True, but the PLA says it's unfair for an entire month to go by while two US observers are already on the station."*

"How many people are in that capsule?"

"They claim it's just two. One taikonaut and one cosmonaut, and there's no service module attached, only a propulsion module."

"A Russian? So these are *both* China's and Russia's observers?"

"If they're telling the truth—which we can't verify—and we didn't have an opportunity to scan them or their baggage for weapons. So we have no idea what they're bringing up there. The entire capsule could be packed with explosives, for all we know."

Lawler said, "That seems unlikely, given that there are US military personnel on this station."

Jin asked, "Do you know the identities of the capsule crew?"

Rochat checked a document. *"A Colonel Evgeni Voloshin . . ."*

Yak responded, "I do not know him."

"And . . . a Colonel Fei Liwei."

Tighe looked up. "Where do I know that name from?"

Jin answered. "He was one of the taikonauts who rescued us in LEO when we came back from Ryugu."

"Oh yeah. And also stole our ship."

Yak snorted. "Salvaged, he would say."

"Maybe he wants to 'salvage' Clarke Station, too." Tighe turned to Jin. "You know this prick. What's he up to?"

"He is a party man."

"Sounds fun."

Jin gave Yak the side-eye. "I meant *political* party."

Tighe spoke to Rochat. "Tell them we won't allow their capsule anywhere near this station."

"They claim Clarke Station was built in violation of international law and demand the right to board it."

"Who put them in charge? Tell them it's a free universe."

Rochat replied, *"J.T., a response like that is likely to precipitate an international incident. More importantly, they claim to have life support sufficient for only eight days. Not enough for a return to Earth."*

"Oh, that's convenient. What a load of horseshit."

Chindarkar said, "We can't take that chance."

Jin leaned in. "Lukas, you negotiated this international observer deal. Tell them they must comply with its terms."

"Our deal did not explicitly state the means by which the observers would reach the station, only that they would be permitted on the station after submitting to a thorough search for contraband."

Jin glared. "You didn't restrict outside spacecraft from docking here?"

"We did. There's a 200-meter exclusion zone. However, they haven't violated it yet."

Tighe folded his arms. "And we can't let them violate it either. Or we'll soon be up to our eyeballs in 'visitors.'"

The group sat in silent contemplation for several moments.

Chindarkar said, "I may have an idea how to resolve this . . ."

Five days later Tighe sat in a telepresence workspace on Clarke Station, his crystal glasses in VR mode as he operated a humanoid Talos robot, which was strapped into a jump seat inside a transit craft a kilometer away. The vessel glided toward a Chinese space capsule and propulsion unit that had recently arrived in their vicinity.

Tighe could hear a voice speaking in Mandarin on an agreed-upon hailing frequency. This was followed by a transmission in accented English. *"Unidentified station, this is Jiuquan-five-nine. Do you read? Repeat: unidentified station, this is Jiuquan-five-nine. Do you read?"*

Tighe spoke to no one in particular. "Give me a break. They know our station's name."

Jin's voice responded in English close by Tighe's real-life workstation. "Jiuquan-five-nine, this is Clarke Station. We copy you. Transit-02 spacecraft is now on final approach and will autodock with your forward hatch. Maintain your present position."

After a pause, the voice came back in Mandarin only.

In his VR headset, Tighe looked around the mostly empty transit spacecraft. Very little had changed inside the vessel over the last month, other than the addition of first-aid kits and emergency breathing apparatuses. Otherwise it looked as Spartan as ever. After a few minutes he heard a *klunk* sound, and then noticed his robot lurch slightly before locking bolts sounded in the transit craft's passenger compartment.

Jin's voice nearby said, *"Transit-02 docked."* A pause. *"Good seal. Stand by to be boarded, Jiuquan-five-nine."*

No reply came. Tighe did not wait, however, and he unbuckled his robot's harness, pushing away from the seat to float toward the secondary IDSS standard docking port in the side of the transit craft. This hatch was much smaller than the square hatch at the bow, but it was the only port that matched the Chinese craft.

Tighe's robot gripped a stationary handle with one hand while moving the hatch lever with the other. In a moment, he pulled the hatch inward, revealing the exterior of a second, sealed hatch. After what seemed like an eternity, there were sounds on the other side, and then the Chinese hatch pushed inward, revealing a forty-something taikonaut whom Tighe recognized. A cosmonaut, also seemingly in his forties, leaned in to look as well.

Both men stared in confusion, and Tighe suddenly remembered he was a robot and not a human—at least from their perspective. It was a testament to Alan Goff's robotic engineers that he'd forgotten. Tighe gestured to himself, and the Talos robot mimicked his movements. "Good evening, Colonels. This is a telepresence robot. I'm here to search you and your bags before you board our transit craft."

They turned to each other, speaking hurriedly in Mandarin. After a moment the taikonaut said, "We will not submit to a search. We are diplomats."

Tighe replied, "You're observers, not diplomats, and that's not the agreement. The Americans got searched and so will you."

The Russian colonel frowned. "We refuse."

"Then have a nice trip back home." Tighe grabbed the hatch and started to close it again.

The men both shouted and pushed against the hatch. "You have no right to search us."

"You're not getting on this transit craft or Clarke Station until I search you and your bags, and by the way: you owe me a spaceship, Fei."

Jin's voice spoke sharply in Mandarin next to Tighe back at the station and moments later his voice sounded on the radio in the Chinese craft. The tai-konaut, Colonel Fei, stiffened, but released the hatch.

Tighe said, "You guys coming or not?"

The men spoke briefly to each other, then nodded.

Tighe motioned. "Pass the bags first. One at a time."

The taikonaut exhaled in irritation at the indignity, then grabbed a pack and passed it through the hatchway. He spoke in English. "You will face consequences for this violation of our sovereignty."

"Listen, pal, I traveled to the far side of the Sun in a spacecraft that looked like it was built by IKEA. Does it sound like I worry about consequences?" Tighe's robot took the cloth pack and opened its zippers.

After thirty minutes of searching through their bags and then searching them personally (to their even greater indignation), Tighe declared them clean—or at least not carrying any obvious weapons. Instead, he found numerous electronic devices, all of which he sealed in a Faraday bag that Ramón Marín had given him. The complaints continued, but he assured them the devices would be returned once they were determined safe.

Only then did Tighe let the colonels board the transit craft, and as soon as they were buckled in, the vessel undocked from the capsule and started its return journey to Clarke Station.

The visitors examined the interior of the much roomier transit craft with interest, but Tighe sat inscrutable, as only a robot could be.

In a few minutes they eased into the huge station docking bay and the two colonels spoke excitedly in Mandarin with each other, clearly fascinated by the proceedings as the automated collars moved the transit craft about. When they docked, Tighe unfastened his safety harness and floated to open the hatch. "Thank you for flying Catalyst Spacelines."

Tighe and the colonels emerged into Clarke Station's gate area, and their amazement at the structure was cut short by the presence of Jin, Yak, Chindarkar, and both of the Space Force observers—all of whom floated at the entrance. The majors and the colonels exchanged courtesy salutes—the first time Tighe had seen this in microgravity and which he found amusing for some reason.

Then Colonel Fei nodded toward Jin. "Again I meet you on an unregistered spacecraft."

"Colonel Fei. Colonel Voloshin. Welcome to Clarke Station."

"Jin Han, your decision to construct this vessel was regrettable, and now you have created a potential dispute in deep space between China, the United States, and Russia." He gestured between Lawler and Cadot, Voloshin, and himself.

Jin stared hard. "Colonel Fei, regardless of your personal opinion, while you are here, do not forget that I am captain of this station." Jin gestured to Tighe's robot and to Chindarkar. "Dr. Chindarkar and Mr. Tighe are its first officers. You two are observers only and here at our discretion."

Fei glared. "This station is illegal and was built with materials stolen from—"

"If you continue in that line, I will send you back to Earth immediately."

"You would not dare. There would be grave consequences."

"Perhaps for me, but most definitely for you. We both know you have never had a black mark on your record. So perhaps you are unaware of how they work; if I send you back to Earth, all that will be remembered is that you failed your mission. Is that what you want?"

Fei remained silent.

"Very good. Then let us not have this conversation again." He motioned. "Now come below. My crew and I have work to do."

CHAPTER 22

Distraction

CLARKE STATION POPULATION: 12
DAYS TO RYUGU DEPARTURE: 1,166

Several weeks later, life aboard Clarke Station had become downright medieval, with the crew forced to circumvent the plumbing system entirely. Instead, they resorted to using chamber pots in the habs. These pots were emptied into a printed, resealable polymer drum, a wholly disagreeable process, and drained on a regular basis into the central water-treatment system at the core of the ship. This entailed wheeling the drum of sewage onto the elevator and transferring the contents in microgravity through sealed hose lines.

So completely had the plumbing system failed that daily ablutions had to be performed with bottled water carried in from the central supply tanks, using plastic basins with hand towels, otherwise the station drain lines would back up at unpredictable intervals. As inconvenient and demoralizing as these procedures were, it at least eliminated the odors and health risks that had plagued the habs up until now.

Weeks earlier, mission control had still been working with Sevastian Yakovlev on a proposed plumbing fix, but he'd injured himself when the blade of a metal cutter shattered in microgravity, piercing the ulnar artery in his left arm. One-handed, he managed to apply an ad hoc tourniquet, but had lost a good bit of blood before Dr. Josephson got to him. As a certified EMT, Tighe assisted in the North Hab med bay as she sutured Yak's artery, then sterilized the wound with a cold plasma wand—a device whose spear-shaped blue flame terrified the cosmonaut.

"Don't be such a baby, Yak! It's excited electrons, not a real flame." She waved her finger across it, even though it resembled a blowtorch. After sterilizing his wound, she sealed the gash with medical glue and placed Yak on bed rest for a week.

In response, mission control put a moratorium on all plumbing work, and that's where it stood. Tighe, meanwhile, found globules of dried blood floating in the pump room for weeks afterward.

Difficulties of life on the station were beginning to accumulate. Tighe suspected the encrypted intel reports sent back to Earth by the station's four international observers were scathing in their criticisms, and such opinions often surfaced during evening meals, which had become a forum where the American majors and the Chinese and Russian colonels debated among themselves everything from station mismanagement to the sovereignty of cis-lunar space.

However, the observers didn't know half of what was going wrong. Tighe often worked with the station's supervisory control and data acquisition (or SCADA) system, doing maintenance, and it held hundreds of fault or "MIL" codes on a dozen subsystems, from electrical to life support to thermal. And unlike the *Konstantin*'s early system failures, these faults were real. Worse still, the station was developing an imperceptible, though significant, wobble in its rotation, quite possibly related to the plumbing and water distribution problems. It was a well-kept secret for now, but wouldn't be if it got worse—in which case they'd have to spin-down the station and figure it out in microgravity, with all the attendant health risks and operational complications that would cause.

Fortunately, the *Rosette* lunar cycler swung through L2 on its monthly orbit, bringing Catalyst's Red Team, the second crew sent up by mission control. Red Team consisted of five people: Hoshiko Sato, a former electronics engineer for the Japanese space agency (JAXA), here to build superconducting coils for the mass-driver; Marco Lemetti, an Italian carbonyl chemist sent up to supervise construction of the station's regolith refinery; Nicolau Ivorra, a metallurgist (and sculptor) from Spain, here to assist both Sato and Lemetti; comms specialist Chelsie Birk, a second Australian, here to maintain communications gear; and finally Dr. Jaqueline Ohana, a former NASA flight surgeon—meaning there would now be two medical doctors on station. The new arrivals brought the crew count up to seventeen—thirteen civilians with four international observers.

Despite the primitive conditions, morale was still high among the Blue and Red Teams; glitches notwithstanding, they were serving on the most advanced space station ever built and executing an ambitious plan at the edge of Earth's gravity well.

Sato had her work cut out for her; Robert Ecklund's mass-driver design called for thousands of superconducting coils to be manufactured to exacting tolerances, then wrapped in yttrium barium copper oxide (YBCO) high-temp superconducting tape, a supply of which had been shipped up on the cycler. According to the schedule, Sato and her team had only ten months to complete the work.

Meanwhile, Birk, the comm specialist, sought out the reclusive Ramón Marín and thereafter the two of them were usually seen reviewing schematics or working on communications equipment. Except one time when Tighe encountered Birk moving alone through South Hab holding some sort of electronic device that warbled and whooped at intervals.

Like all the crew, Birk was physically fit—in fact, exceptionally so—and attractive, though aloof in her demeanor. Despite her standoffishness, Tighe needed to understand what she was up to. So he pointed to the device. "What is that, Chelsie?"

She glanced up and spoke with a more pronounced Aussie accent than Balter. "This is my cobber. Detects wireless transmitters. Microphones. Cameras. Things like that."

"So a bug detector."

"You might say that." Then she reached into her pocket and placed in Tighe's hand several dime-sized devices with follicle-like wires extending from them. "Good thing, too. Turns out Clarke Station has a bit of a pest problem."

Tighe examined the items. "These are listening devices?"

"Cameras. Stealthy. They upload their video in bursts in the wee hours. Usually."

The devices were unmarked. "Where did you find these?"

"Outside the data center. Lavatory. Conference table."

"Can you figure out who placed them?"

"Unlikely. I could buy these things by the dozen over the Internet. We'll just need to be more careful searching new arrivals in the future."

Tighe felt angry—mostly at the international observers. But then, he didn't know which ones or if they were even the culprits. "Do Captain Jin and Priya Chindarkar know about this?"

"Not yet. Perhaps you could tell them." Birk took the devices back. "In the meantime, I'll hold on to these. Ramón will wanna have a peek."

Tighe nodded. "I'll make sure they know."

"Beauty, thanks. Now, if it's no bother, I've got heaps to do." With that she continued scanning.

Tighe watched her go and realized they should have been doing this months ago. There might even be several people planting the devices. What could they do even if they identified the culprits—send them back to Earth? Maybe it was better to just improve security procedures and have Birk keep scanning for anything that got through.

Despite such serious issues, Tighe, Jin, and Chindarkar were often pulled away from mission-critical elements like the refinery or lunar base components. Instead they found themselves doing urgent but basic tasks: installing fire/safety sensors and emergency breathing apparatus stations in the habs. This equipment, too, had come up on the cycler, and was critical to the safety of the entire crew. Nobody else had time and Yak was still recuperating.

One day, while Chindarkar and Tighe installed smoke and CO_2 detectors, Yak approached them, his forearm still wrapped in bandages, and displayed a news item from Earth, passing a virtual screen on their shared augmented-reality layer. "Look at this . . ."

Tighe glanced at what looked to be a blurry, distant black-and-white photo of Clarke Station displayed on some website; the headline above it blared "Top Secret Space Station Beyond the Moon!" "I'll be damned. So word's out."

Chindarkar started reading through the article. "They even know the name." Then she looked up with disappointment. "But they say it's named after Arthur C. Clarke. Not Nicole."

"We can correct that, but the news going public is going to turn up the heat on us, for sure."

Yak raised an eyebrow. "Do not be so certain. Just because something is said does not mean is known."

"What are you, Yoda now?"

"Misinformation." He gestured. "This story has been up for half a day, and picked up by many conspiracy sites. Yet no major news outlet repeats it."

Chindarkar looked up from reading. "But the photo . . ."

"Is like photo of Bigfoot. Or Loch Ness Monster. Yes?"

Tighe squinted. "It is a bit blurry."

"Many people online are calling this fake news." He gestured toward a couple of the international observers, disagreeing over something at a distant table. "The psyops campaign to discredit us is already quite effective. Regardless of who is behind it."

"So you're saying this news doesn't matter."

"I am saying, in order to keep secret, someone may have released actual image and claim it is real—but only on conspiracy news sites."

Chindarkar said, "Ah. Like Joyce did with the *Konstantin*."

"Precisely. It inoculates story from *being able* to be known."

Chindarkar thought about it. "So even if video footage later leaks of this place, the story will have already have been debunked—and so it gets ignored a bit longer."

"*Da.*"

Tighe shrugged. "Man, Earth is a messed-up place, but at least it means we won't have the media coming at us. We've got enough to worry about already."

In mid-March, Jin and Tighe were on a rare in-person EVA, tethered just outside the station hangar bay as they replaced a defective autodocking transponder. The EVA was necessary, as all of the Talos and other telepresence robots were busy on refinery or other construction work.

Here on the shaded side of the station, the view of the Moon, distant Earth, the stars, and the Milky Way galaxy was stunning—though it also rotated as the station turned. This close to the station core, spin-gravity was negligible, but motion sickness from the moving scenery could be a risk. Fortunately Tighe and Jin had plenty of experience with that from their years on the *Konstantin*.

Examining the station's seamless metal hull above the hangar bay, Tighe couldn't help but admire the name "Clarke Station" in meter-high gray letters. Below this, the word "Luxembourg" was centered in a smaller font, along with its flag. Kerner's team had also taken to painting rows of flags along the top of the docking bay to represent the nationalities of everyone aboard, and there were now American, Chinese, Russian, Indian, Canadian, Australian, Japanese, Italian, Spanish, Egyptian, Venezuelan, and British flags as well. Clarke Station was becoming a burgeoning international outpost in deep space.

Looking over his shoulder, Tighe saw the chandelier-shaped framework of the partially built solar power satellite sparkling in the sunlight. It was being erected near the supply yard and was about 125 meters high by 75 meters in diameter at its widest point. Inchworm-like robots moved about its hexagonal latticework. Electron-beam welding tools flashed occasionally and teleoperated mules came and went carrying materials.

Chindarkar's voice suddenly came in over their personal, encrypted channel. "*I thought you both should know that at this moment the* Amy Tsukada's *rocket engines should be firing out at Ryugu.*"

Tighe replied, "*That's right. That was today, wasn't it?*"

She was referring to the third robot tug they had prepared out at Ryugu. It was bigger than both of the first two tugs combined—and those had supplied the resources with which they'd built all of Clarke Station and were now using to build the solar power satellite and the mass-driver sections. The *Amy Tsukada* had to wait for a low-energy transfer window to open prior to launching back toward cislunar space. This multiyear trajectory was not viable for crewed flight—and thus, not an option for Abarca and Adisa.

Jin sighed. "*Let us hope all its engines ignite—and that nothing has happened since we built it. We could really use those extra resources.*"

"We'll need to send out an interceptor to retrieve it when it arrives. It'll be going into a lunar DRO tens of thousands of kilometers from here."

Chindarkar asked, "*What if it doesn't show up in 2041? What do we do then?*"

Tighe frowned. "*What do you mean, 'What do we do'? It doesn't change anything. We go to Ryugu.*"

Jin turned toward Tighe. "*Yes. We three are prepared to take risks,*" *however . . ."* He gestured to the space station. *". . . there are other people involved now. What if someone dies helping us do this? At what point are we being unethical in trying to save two people?"*

Tighe looked at him in surprise. *"I don't think it's a valid question. Most of these people are up here for their own reasons—just like we all were. And they'll be here long after we're gone. No matter what we do."*

They regarded one another for several moments in silence.

Finally Tighe said, *"Let's just focus on our own mission."*

CHAPTER 23

Realm of Possibility

CLARKE STATION POPULATION: 17
DAYS TO RYUGU DEPARTURE: 1,148

B y early April the station's crew had fallen into a steady work rhythm, and despite the absence of proper plumbing, had managed to foster a convivial social environment. They started to bond amid their shared hardship, the remoteness, and the enforced communications restrictions with Earth—as well as the ever-present danger. In the evenings, laughter was common as the crew decompressed, either watching TV and movies or talking about home.

Dinners in South Hab were now often attended by the four international observers, whom the rest of the crew still viewed with suspicion. Nonetheless, the observers were here to observe and thus eager to be present for conversations regarding the status of projects with the Gold Team. That put nearly a dozen people around the conference tables, which in the evening performed as one long dining table. The food was lackluster—rehydrated family-style meals and side dishes that, despite their various recipes, had a similar mushy consistency. Yet, the camaraderie and common purpose of those around the table made up for much.

It was at one of these dinners that chemist Sofia Boutros described the unfolding water crisis in the Nile watershed back on Earth—and the resulting regional conflict. This elicited from around the table a litany of other climate-change-related calamities back home, from wildfires, to floods, to famines, to mass extinctions.

The Russian observer, Colonel Voloshin, usually content to just listen, chimed in by saying, "Nations which have contributed least to carbon emissions are suffering worst effects." He looked first to Lawler and then to Colonel Fei. "Perhaps the biggest polluters should pay reparations."

Dr. Ohana looked down the table toward him. "It's my understanding that Russia has actually *benefitted* from warmer climate."

Yak replied instead. "Not overall. Soil in Siberia is poor. Wildfires and loss of permafrost also disruptive."

Lawler added, "You guys sell plenty of fossil fuels, too, Colonel."

The electrical engineer, Hoshiko Sato, said, "Complete decarbonization is the only way to solve climate change."

Most of the group groaned in response.

She looked around the table. "That might sound unrealistic, but there's no other choice if we want to save civilization."

Chindarkar said, "We've been saying the same thing for fifty years now, Hoshiko. It's barely moved the needle."

"We've brought carbon emissions down considerably since 2020."

Boutros said, "You mean we slowed their *growth*."

Ohana said, "We should be planting more trees."

Monica Balter countered, "Trees require water and arable land. Climate change is causing deserts to spread, pitting food versus trees. Plus, whatever carbon a tree captures gets released when it dies—which could happen all at once in a wildfire."

Chindarkar looked down the table at her. "Nathan Joyce claimed we could use solar satellites to power direct carbon capture. Could that really be done at the scale necessary to reduce global CO_2 levels?"

Colonel Voloshin let out a laugh. "That's not even in the realm of possibility. It wouldn't even make a dent."

Monica Balter said, "I respectfully disagree, Colonel." She looked to Boutros. "And Sofia, I understand we must do everything possible down on Earth to reduce carbon emissions: solar panels, wind turbines, geothermal—all of it. But that won't remove what's already in the atmosphere."

Voloshin shook his head. "We must adapt."

Lawler couldn't resist. "Easy for Russia to say."

Balter spoke to Voloshin. "Back in 1850, atmospheric carbon was at two hundred eighty parts per million. Now it's at four hundred fifty-seven parts per million. We put over a trillion tons of CO_2 into Earth's atmosphere over that time. Humans caused the problem, and humans can solve it."

The colonel was unfazed. "Yes. All of humanity worked hard to cause this, and it still required almost two centuries to accomplish. It is naïve to think a few machines will correct it."

"Half of that excess carbon was emitted in the last forty years, and direct air carbon capture powered by solar satellites can actually work at a global scale. I can show you the numbers, if you like."

He scoffed. "Even billionaire Jack Macy says that solar power satellites are idiotic—that very little energy beamed from space reaches the terrestrial power grid due to transmission and conversion losses."

Balter nodded. "The number is 9 percent."

The crew around the table murmured.

He spread his hands. "I rest my case."

"But 9 percent of what? Jack Macy neglects to mention that a solar panel up in orbit is seven times more productive than one on the Earth's surface. The fact that he runs a rooftop solar company might have something to do with that."

Boutros asked, "A sevenfold difference just from being in space?"

Balter turned to her. "The best you can hope for on the Earth's equator at high noon is 1,000 watts of energy per square meter—and that's without factoring in nighttime, cloudy days, seasons, latitude. But a power sat in geosynchronous orbit would almost always be in 1,368 watts of sunlight per square meter. So you get a whole lot more energy from a solar panel in space even after transmission inefficiencies are factored in. Plus, a power sat won't be affected by unfolding chaos planetside."

Voloshin shrugged. "What if it is cloudy above your rectenna? You would not be able to beam down energy."

"Not true. We use microwaves in the 2.45-gigahertz range. The atmosphere is largely invisible at that frequency. We can beam the energy down regardless of weather—and directly to where it's needed. No need for long-distance power lines."

"But to what purpose? It could not be done on a scale sufficient to impact Earth."

"Again, I could show you the numbers."

Chindarkar said, "I'd like to see them, Monica. Please."

Balter put down her fork and after searching through virtual UIs for a moment, put up a shared augmented-reality screen that appeared to float over the end of the table on the station's common layer. It displayed an array of numbers and labels. "Sorry for the spreadsheet."

Colonel Fei said, "We are quite interested in seeing it, Ms. Balter."

She looked to the faces around the table. "There are four reasons I got involved in space-based solar power . . ." She pealed them off on her fingers. ". . . electrification, desalination, food generation, and decarbonization. First: electricity. We all know the environmental, economic, and political havoc back on Earth from climate change. Blackouts make that chaos worse, but a 2-gigawatt solar power satellite in geosynchronous orbit could instantly transmit large amounts of energy anywhere it's needed in the hemisphere below it. Even several locations at once. All that's needed is a rectenna on the ground, and those are cheap and easy to construct."

Chindarkar nodded. "We saw one on Ascension Island."

Jin added, "J.T. and I are building sections of the lunar rectenna. It is fairly simple."

"Right. For example, space-based energy could be beamed to coastal desalination plants in regions suffering long-term drought—providing fresh water. It can also be used to remove CO_2 directly from seawater, through what's known as single step carbon sequestration and storage, converting the CO_2 into solid limestone and magnesite—essentially seashells. This would enable the oceans themselves to absorb more atmospheric CO_2. Or we could power direct air capture plants that pull CO_2 straight out of the atmosphere."

Voloshin interjected. "Again, a few satellites will not impact Earth's atmospheric concentrations, and where would you sequester all this CO_2?"

"Just a few satellites wouldn't impact climate, no—but there's definitely a use for the CO_2—in creating food. Droughts in equatorial zones are causing famine, but hydrogenotrophic bacteria can be used to make protein from electricity, hydrogen, and CO_2. The hydrogen can be electrolyzed from seawater and CO_2 from the air. All that's needed is clean energy." She glanced to Chindarkar. "NASA first experimented with this in the 1960s as a means for making food here in deep space."

"Really? Even back then."

"The bioreactor for it is like a small-batch brewery. You feed in what natural plants get from soil: phosphorus, sulfur, calcium, iron, potassium—all of which, incidentally, can be extracted from lunar regolith. But I digress . . ."

Colonel Fei's eyebrows raised. "That is indeed interesting."

"The bioreactor runs for a while, then the liquid is drained and the solids dried to a powder that contains 65 percent protein, 20 to 25 percent carbohydrates, and 5 percent fatty acids. This can be made into a natural food similar to soy or algae. So with energy, CO_2, and seawater, we could provide life-saving nutrition just about anywhere on the planet via solar power satellites."

Voloshin was unimpressed. "Yet it would still not resolve climate change."

"At scale it could. Do the math . . ." Balter brought up her spreadsheet. "We're emitting 40 billion tons of CO_2 per year, 9 billion tons of which can't be sequestered by the natural carbon cycle and which results in an annual increase of roughly two parts per million atmospheric CO_2—even after decades of conservation efforts."

She tapped a few screens and a virtual image of an industrial structure covered in fan housings appeared. "A direct air capture facility like this one could pull a million tons of CO_2 out of the atmosphere each year at a cost of one hundred dollars a ton. All of the components are off-the-shelf and have existed for decades. Nothing fancy. But it needs 1.5 megawatts of constant clean energy to power it—and that's where solar power satellites come in."

Voloshin said, "But who would pay? Governments? Do not count on this."

Chindarkar asked, "Monica, seriously: How many carbon capture plants would it take to make a difference in the atmosphere of the entire Earth?"

Jin added, "And how many solar power satellites to power them?"

Balter brought her spreadsheet back up. "Merely to cancel out Earth's excess annual emissions—9 billion tons of CO_2—we'd need nine thousand 1-megaton DAC plants worldwide, each requiring 150 to 300 acres."

The group groaned.

Tighe said, "That's a lot of hardware and a lot of real estate, Monica."

"It doesn't have to be on land. Just 2.7 million acres total—smaller than Connecticut. And that would be spread across the entire globe. More importantly, doing that *stops* the advance of climate change. If we reduce emissions, then it would actually help reverse climate change."

Chindarkar studied the numbers. "Powered by how many solar satellites?"

Balter highlighted the number. "It would take 1.6 terawatts of electricity—or 818 2-gigawatt SPS-Alphas. Each about 7,400 tons. But again: that *halts* the advance of climate change."

The group groaned again.

"Eight hundred eighteen satellites?" Jin shook his head. "That would take decades to build."

"Not with automation and sufficient materials here on orbit. You've seen the SPS-Alpha I'm building—it's made of simple, modular components."

"Yours is one-fortieth the size of these 7,400-ton monsters."

"But it's the same design. We just need the resources up here in space, and we could scale it rapidly with automation."

Voloshin picked up his fork. "As I said: it is a technological fantasy."

Chindarkar ignored him. "Monica, what would it require to not just halt climate change—but reverse it?"

Balter clicked through to another screen. "To return Earth to a safe level—say, three hundred fifty parts per million CO_2—you'd need to pull three-quarters of a trillion tons out of the atmosphere." She made a few changes to her model. "So with forty thousand DAC plants, powered by thirty-six hundred 2-gigawatt satellites in geosynchronous orbit, you could accomplish that in eighteen years."

Fei asked, "At what cost?"

"Roughly seventy-two trillion dollars."

Again groans and an impressed whistle.

Voloshin shook his head. "I told you."

Balter added, "That's four trillion a year, over eighteen years. Spread across the entire population of Earth."

This was met with a different reaction.

Jin said, "That is actually less than I thought."

"And bear in mind the fossil fuel industry has been supported by half a trillion dollars in direct government subsidies worldwide every year for ages. Whereas this four trillion is for just a limited time and would permanently *solve* climate change, and we'd see significant climate benefits within a decade as CO_2 levels came down. And once it was accomplished, all that clean energy could be put toward other productive uses, either on Earth or in space."

She studied the faces around her. "But to accomplish it, we'd need tens of millions of tons of mass in orbit. Launching all that mass up from Earth would never work because all those rockets would damage the atmosphere, too. However, with your lunar mass-driver—and the ones that follow it—we could make this work. This is why I'm here."

Those around the table pondered this. For the moment, even Voloshin was silent.

Boutros asked, "Is it not risky to tinker with the Earth's atmosphere?"

"That's what we're doing now, Sofia. This would just reverse what we've done and return Earth to the conditions we evolved in."

Chindarkar pointed to the virtual spreadsheet. "Does that seventy-two trillion dollars include the cost of the solar power satellites?"

"Yes. And doing nothing will cost us far more. Best estimates are that by the year 2100, continued climate change will reduce global GDP by 20 percent—which is about two thousand trillion dollars. Not to mention the cost of possibly losing civilization.

"But if, as your CEO Mr. Rochat says, we intend to prove the SPS concept at scale here in lunar orbit, well . . . then you will make this commercially feasible. In other words, you can make this future happen. Everyone else has talked it to death. The bean counters and decision makers back on Earth clearly won't do it, no matter how critical it is. And this needs to be started as soon as possible—before the situation on Earth gets truly untenable."

After dinner, Tighe and Chindarkar took their turn washing dishes, a chore that evoked nostalgia from their time crewing on the *Konstantin*.

As she dried a dish, Chindarkar glanced at Tighe. "Did you see the news about that huge wind farm off the coast of Japan? Destroyed by a typhoon."

Tighe shook his head. "I'm too busy to keep up with Earth news."

"But what's happening down there matters up here."

He gave her a look. "I know that. I'm just focused, Priya. Ryugu will swing by before you know it, and we have a lot to do."

"Of course, but we should give some thought to what Monica said tonight. We're in a position to help."

He washed a bowl. "Not yet we aren't, and we still need to rescue Isabel and Ade."

"It doesn't have to be either-or. We can do both, I think."

He looked to her. "Fine. When we have the resources to build the rescue ship and have actually built it. But what Monica described is a ways off. We're still hanging by a thread up here, and the superpowers are still trying to figure out a way to shut us down or take control."

"This is a way to prevent that—by doing something that can help the entire world."

He handed her another plate. "Not everyone on Earth is reasonable or wants our help. We need to concentrate on building the mass-driver, not on getting caught up in Earth politics, Priya."

"We can't help but get caught up in it. That's why there are observers on this station." She paused. "And Isabel and Ade can't be our excuse for ignoring the fate of billions of people."

He returned to scrubbing dishes.

She observed him. "We have to at least consider the possibility that Isabel and Ade may already be dead."

He lowered his hands and glared at her. "Don't even say that to me."

"I'm not saying they *are* gone, and I'm not saying that we won't go try to rescue them. What I'm saying is that we can't *only* do that. I don't think Isabel and Ade would want us to focus solely on them. In fact, you know they wouldn't."

"We said we would come back for them. That's why this station is here."

"We will, but you also need to start following events on Earth. James, it's bad. Things are unraveling more each year. Millions of people are dying. Climate catastrophe seems inevitable to whole populations. Billions of people down there are in need of some hope. Maybe we can give them that."

He turned toward her and spoke in a whisper. "Can this really not wait two or three years? We have an immovable deadline—and practically . . ." He leaned closer, whispering more softly. ". . . *no* idea what we're doing. Right now we need to focus on one thing and one thing only: building that mass-driver."

She studied his face. "Why are you being so absolute about this?"

"Because we don't have any margin for error."

"Remember that Ade has brothers and sisters in Lagos. It was to protect them from his oga that he joined the Ryugu expedition in the first place. He saved both our lives, and he would want us to do something to save their future. If it came to it, I think he would willingly sacrifice his own life for that."

Tighe stepped away from the basin for a moment, took a deep breath, then turned to face her again. "That's not the choice. We will build the mass-driver, rescue Isabel and Ade, and then help save the world. In that order."

"What good would it do to rescue Isabel and Ade, only to bring them back to a doomed world—when we could have acted early enough to save it?"

"Priya . . ."

"Just promise me we will factor that into our priorities if we get the mass-driver working."

Tighe stared. "You mean *when*. Not if."

CHAPTER 24

Green Team

CLARKE STATION POPULATION: 24
DAYS TO RYUGU DEPARTURE: 1,136

By the third week of April little had changed with the interior of Clarke Station. However, with the help of the Blue and Red Teams and Kerner's telepresence construction team back on Ascension Island, big changes were underway outside the station. The solar power satellite was nearing completion next to the supply yard. Likewise, the refinery, located on the central axis between the station and the thermal power plant, was now half finished. Prefabricated components of the lunar base were also accumulating in the supply yard less than a kilometer from Clarke Station, ready for transport to the Moon's surface.

And it was at this point that the *Rosette* cycler delivered a fourth crew to the vicinity of L2, where they were picked up by twin telepiloted transit craft sent out by Clarke Station, and a day later the Green Team arrived.

Captain Jin Han and Sevastian Yakovlev met the new arrivals at the docking bay, but Priya Chindarkar opted instead to watch via surveillance camera in South Hab as the group floated through the docking hatches.

Green Team consisted of seven people—including yet another pair of international observers foisted on them as part of Rochat's deal with Earth authorities: the first of these was Lieutenant Colonel Hardik Katri of India's ISRO, and the second was Maximilian Huber, a German astronaut with the European Space Agency, here as a representative for the EU.

The other five members of the Green Team were Ascension Island grads and included Lynne Holstad, an agronomist in her fifties from Iowa State

University whose passage was being paid through a NASA research grant. There was Braam de Jong, a Dutch roboticist and astropreneur with a company called Life-Bot—some sort of automated space rescue robot. He was apparently going to earn his transport to Clarke by helping to prepare coils for the mass-driver before his own work could begin. Then there was Milena Jakubec, a former ESA life support specialist from the Czech Republic, and also Wu Meiling, a Taiwanese microchip designer—another astropreneur and founder of a company called Bootstrap; she was here to research silicon wafer production in microgravity using in situ resources. And finally, there was Robert Ecklund, the retired NASA physicist and designer of the mass-driver that they'd be building on the lunar surface. Chindarkar had spoken to Ecklund several times in video meetings. At fifty-eight, he was the oldest of the crew, but he looked well acclimated to microgravity after a week in transit, and was all smiles as he laughed and hugged Jin and then Yak in the gate compartment.

The Catalyst board had unanimously agreed that Ecklund's participation in telepresence construction on the lunar surface would be invaluable—something he couldn't do from back on Earth, given the lag time for effective surface operations. So here he was, clearly thrilled to be in space.

Some minutes later, after dividing up the Green Team between North and South Habs to equalize mass distribution, exclamations of wonder and amazement could be heard as the new arrivals stepped out on the South Hab elevator landing at H4. The Blue and Red Teams had gathered below to watch the spectacle, remembering well their own amazement on first sight of the station's interior.

Tighe stood alongside Chindarkar and they both looked up with some amusement as first Holstad and Wu, then De Jong and Ecklund, looked out over the H4 railing at the cavernous compartment and crew assembled below. Jin came up behind them (presumably Yak was off escorting the others to North Hab).

Ecklund shouted, "Hello, Clarke Station!" And it echoed through the compartment.

The Red and Blue Teams shouted greetings and waved. It was a festive atmosphere.

At that point, Ecklund uncoiled what looked to be a tether line linked to his belt and clipped the carabiner on one end to the metal railing. He looked up. "According to my calculations, this should be perfectly safe . . ."

At which point Ecklund climbed the railing.

Jin called out, "Bob!" And raced toward him.

Before Jin could intervene—and to the horror of everyone—Ecklund launched himself off the elevator landing and into empty air above the gathered crew 10 meters below. People screamed and fled from the impact.

However, even though Ecklund fell "downward" initially, the fact that they were in a spinning space station was brought back to them all as his downward motion slowed about halfway to the floor, and then transitioned to a sideways glide, anti-spinward—toward the back wall. This occurred gradually at first but began to pick up speed before he pulled the tether taut in his hand. "At this distance from the station's core, we are spinning at roughly 70 miles per hour . . ."

Ecklund floated as he fed the taut line through his hands, gently correcting his course, and he began to ease downward once more. Loosening and tightening the tether modulated his downward speed. Until finally he alighted onto the steel deck with both feet—perfectly fine. He smiled broadly and held up his hands. "Ladies and gentlemen—physics!"

The relieved crew roared in laughter and applauded. This was interrupted by a shout from above.

"Bob!"

Everyone looked up to see Jin—captain of Clarke Station—as upset as Chindarkar had ever seen him.

"We did not fly you up here just to have you kill yourself performing a stupid stunt."

Ecklund gestured to the tether still in his hand. "There was no danger, Captain."

"You will follow all safety restrictions while you are on this station, and I forbid anyone else here from doing what they have just seen. Is that understood?"

The assembled crew nodded and said in unison, "Yes, Captain."

Ecklund released the tether and faced Tighe and Chindarkar. "I thought it was a good demonstration of centripetal motion."

Tighe extended his hand, a slight smile slipping. "Bob. Quite an entrance."

"J.T. Great to finally meet you in person." He gripped his hand. "Priya, you too." He shook her hand vigorously. "I'm not really in trouble, am I?"

"Don't worry about Han. He's just touchy because the slightest mistake out here can be fatal—and because we're all counting on you."

"Ah. Right. Well, I'm happy to dig right in once I get a meal and a hot shower. Eight days in microgravity was enough for me."

Chindarkar held up a pausing finger. "Bad news there, Bob. The plumbing doesn't work. There's no toilets. No showers. No sinks. It's all basins and bottled water." She spread her hands. "Welcome to Clarke Station."

He looked at her and Tighe. "Seriously?"

Just then the elevator door opened, and Jin arrived on H2, helping De Jong along, while Holstad and Wu assisted each other. Jin gave Ecklund an annoyed look as one of the other crew members took charge of De Jong, who was still struggling to get acclimated to a-grav.

Ecklund turned. "I just heard about the plumbing situation, Captain. How long has that been going on?"

"Since we first arrived. Mission control is working on it."

"Well, that's unacceptable. It has to be fixed. It's a health issue."

Tighe said, "We have chamber pots. Just pray the spin-grav doesn't give out."

"Mission control might be working on it, but they're down there. We're up here. Let me look into it."

"Yak already has."

Jin seemed annoyed once more. "Bob, we brought you up here to manage construction of the mass-driver." He pointed at Sato's assembly operation not far off, where half-finished superconducting coils were laying on tables. "We have a tight schedule and cannot lose time with you pursuing a plumbing problem that mission control is already handling."

"Handling poorly, from the sound of it. It's been months?" Ecklund held up his hands as Jin was about to respond. "Captain, lack of proper plumbing has got to be a productivity killer. How much time do you waste emptying and moving chamber pots around? Filling and moving water barrels?"

Chindarkar looked to Jin. "He's got a point, Han."

Ecklund gestured to the pipes running up the elevator column. "Look, give me a day or two. If I can't find the problem, I'll grab a bucket, but if I do and this space station can have hot and cold running water—well, that's going to be a big productivity and morale boost. Agreed?"

After a moment Jin nodded. "You have three days, Bob. Then you concentrate on the mass-driver coils. Exclusively."

It wound up taking Ecklund two days to find the source of the plumbing problems. The fixes just three more, making him something of an instant hero on board. The entire crew celebrated by taking long hot showers.

The solution wasn't as complicated as mission control believed because what Ecklund discovered in crawling around the conduits of Clarke Station was that mission control had been referencing a newer version of the water system blueprint than the one Kerner's CVD robots had actually built in deep space. In fact, the newer version had been developed specifically to avoid the problems they'd been experiencing—problems caused by the inclusion of automatic water level controllers in the initial design; devices that assumed constant gravity and thus behaved unpredictably in the varying spin-grav throughout the system. However, in the chaos of Nathan Joyce's death and the subsequent corporate bankruptcies, the corrected plans had never been conveyed to Kerner's team. And no one had thought to ask.

Ecklund's replacement of the controllers with programmable pumps he drew from spare-parts inventory resolved the issues.

After having her first hot shower in months—as well as access to a working toilet—Chindarkar sat in the South Hab crew lounge on H1 and relished the comforts of civilization. She also caught up on news from Earth in her crystal. Most of it was depressing—conflicts, economic chaos, drought, wildfires, mudslides, and storms. It was tempting to just watch a sitcom instead, but she had to keep up with planetside events.

The crew lounges in both the North and South Habs consisted of a few inflatable sitting chairs and plastic tables printed and assembled by those off duty. By the time Chindarkar settled in to relax, it was late, and the only other person present was Holstad, the recently arrived agronomist, who sat on the far end of the lounge. She, too, had apparently just taken a shower and was sipping tea meditatively. Chindarkar didn't want to disturb her, so she sank down into her own chair to remain unseen.

Footsteps sounded in the corridor leading past the lounge.

From across the room, Holstad spoke. "Mr. Ecklund." The footsteps stopped. "Thanks for the running water."

"Bob. Call me Bob." There was a pause. "You're looking better. Spin-grav seems to agree with you."

"It does. My vestibular otoliths are much happier here than they were on the cycler."

"Your vestibular whats?"

"The small stones in our inner ear—vestibular otoliths. They're balanced within a fluid; when we move our head, gravity makes them move. It's how humans perceive motion."

"Ah. Well, since your otoliths are happy, may I ask you a question?"

"Of course."

His footsteps entered the lounge, and Chindarkar heard him sit.

"What's an agronomist doing up here? It seems a bit premature, if you don't mind my saying. We're nowhere close to growing crops in space."

She laughed slightly. "I'm as surprised as you. I certainly never thought I'd be going into space."

"Me neither. Strange where life brings us. Isn't it? This is a dream come true for me."

"My younger self would never have considered doing this. Too dangerous."

"What changed?"

"The world. Me." Silence for a moment. "In answer to your question: I have samples of a radiotrophic fungi—*Cladosporium sphaerospermum*—that I have to figure out how to grow within Clarke Station's double hull."

"Radiotrophic—meaning it feeds on radiation?"

"Yes. It's a species that thrived around Chernobyl and attenuates ionizing radiation better than hydrogen—and without the mass of water ice. I'm to test its effectiveness as radiation shielding. And to cultivate it."

"Huh. Interesting. Do you know yet where you'll be setting up?"

"No. I don't think they have room for my lab yet. Longer term, I'm up here to attempt to grow crop plants from in situ nutrients—particularly off-world phosphorus."

"Phosphorus, like in fertilizer."

"It's more than fertilizer. Phosphorus is integral to life. It's used to create cell membranes and all DNA. Without phosphorus, life as we know it can't exist."

"And it's present on the Moon, I believe."

"Yes, and potassium. Those, along with nitrogen—which I understand we also have—will give us the ability to sustain living things here in deep space. Meaning we could expand life into the cosmos."

"Well, that's quite a mission you have. I'm just here to build a piece of equipment."

Momentary silence. "You're here to build the mass-driver on the Moon."

"That's right."

"How does one train to do that?"

"I spent thirty years designing systems for NASA, and to be honest, in all that time, not one of my designs was ever built." A pause. "You have kids?"

Silence, which Chindarkar assumed was a shake of the head.

Ecklund continued. "I have a daughter. She's a lawyer in Houston. But I'm long-ago divorced and at a point in my life where I look back on my body of work and . . . It's like it never happened. Then out of the blue these crazy astropreneurs contact me, and now I have the chance—for once—to see something I designed become real. Something that might make a positive impact on the world."

As he said this, Chindarkar looked up at an augmented-reality window on the station's common layer. It displayed a live view of the Moon, with a *smaller* Earth visible in the distance, sourced from one of Clarke Station's exterior cameras. Chindarkar imagined Ecklund's mass-driver on the Moon's surface.

After a few moments, Holstad said, "Back in the '20s I ran a research lab at Iowa State, where I simulated growing crops under the conditions of present-day Earth. It revealed that current CO_2 and temperature levels would devastate crop yields. That we would have to figure out new ways to feed billions of people. And to preserve our biome."

"So you're here to establish greenhouses? Aquaponics?"

"Sure, aquaponics can grow plants, but we're going to need *soil* if we want to preserve Earth's entire biosphere. And learning to build soil of the complexity found on Earth—from scratch, using deep space resources—will be critical. If we can do that, we can re-create Earth's biosphere anywhere." A nervous laugh escaped her. "But to be honest, I hardly know where to begin. I can't help thinking someone made a mistake choosing me for this."

There was a pregnant silence. Then Ecklund said, "I took a pottery class once." Another pause. "I know . . . *retirement*, right? But the teacher divided the class up into two groups. The first group, he said, would be graded on producing a single pot—which they were to make as perfect as possible. The second group—my group—would be graded only on the *number* of pots we produced; quality didn't matter."

"Sounds like your group got shortchanged."

"Ah. You might think so. But you know what happened? Our group wound up making the best pots. We just kept working and gaining experience until eventually spinning a pot became second nature to us—while the other group mostly theorized and planned."

"Hm."

"That's what I thought, too. Down there on Earth, our research is just theory. But up here, it's time to put theory into practice."

They both sat in silence for quite some time afterward. Chindarkar was content to sit with them.

CHAPTER 25

Surface Operations

James Tighe gazed at a large virtual screen alongside most of the population of Clarke Station in the South Hab's videoconference area. No one wanted to miss the big event.

On-screen, their 185-ton chandelier-shaped solar power satellite was finally being moved from the supply yard to its intended location at EM-L1 on the opposite side of the Moon—the side facing Earth. The massive satellite's dozens of hexagonal facets glittered in the sunlight, which was, after all, their purpose. The event was being monitored by a second transit spacecraft at a distance of several hundred kilometers with the aid of powerful optics. A propulsion module mounted to breakaway scaffolding had nudged the massive satellite fourteen days ago onto a trajectory that would bring it around the Moon's equator and toward the EM-L1 point. Clarke Station's location at the edge of the Moon's gravity well meant the maneuver had required only 140 meters per second of delta-v, which was helpful, given the mass of the thing. The logic of using Lagrange points was becoming clearer every day to Tighe.

As a morale-boosting exercise, naming the satellite had been put to a vote, and due to its delicate array of Sun-facing mirrors, the station's inhabitants had voted for the name "Daisy" (although "Satty McSatFace" also received a couple votes). Nonetheless, the crew was on edge because Tighe and his colleagues did not have the tonnage in resources to rebuild Daisy if anything went awry. Thus, a lot was riding on today—powering the entire lunar surface mission, for starters. Gabriel Lacroix's mission control had so far skillfully piloted the behemoth from back on Ascension Island, and there was an extra rocket engine on board as a margin of safety. This, however, proved unnecessary, and the propulsion module fired on cue, performing a precise burn to place Daisy in a similar Lissajous orbit as Clarke Station, but around L1.

Tighe held his breath as he watched the maneuver. Tense silence filled the room.

Then mission control's voice came in over Tighe's headphones via the laser comm link. "*We have MECO. Good burn. Daisy is on station.*"

The entire team applauded and hooted, with a few whistles thrown in.

Chindarkar hugged an exhausted and relieved-looking Monica Balter. "Well done!"

Tighe shook her hand. "Good work, Monica."

"Thanks." She pointed to the screen. "Now let's power her up."

Tighe and Jin also shook hands. "Days like today are going to age me prematurely. I swear." Tighe noticed the Chinese, Russian, American, Indian, and EU observers recording the moment on their handhelds. He and his colleagues had received acquiescence from Artemis Accord signatories to place Daisy in its L1 orbit—however, no other countries had formally accepted it. Tighe wondered what could be done if someone sent a kamikaze satellite smashing into Daisy. Probably nothing—for now—although, as Balter pointed out, the design was light and modular enough that it would probably remain operational. Like someone firing a bullet through tissue paper.

Yak stared up at the screen. "Not yet time for champagne. Even if we had champagne—which we do not."

Tighe nodded. "Pity. I know a guy back on Earth who has the best champagne."

Jin called out, "Everyone! Listen up. If you are on a Kangaroo lander team, please attend your briefings." He checked the time. "We are T-minus seventy-one hours from lunar lander touchdown at point Morra."

Everyone clapped once more, then started clearing out. For now the show was over.

Tighe joined Jin, Chindarkar, Yak, and the rest of the lunar lander team back at the meeting room—which was just a table in the middle of the floor on H2.

Jin glanced up at a virtual screen that showed two blips marked "SK-Alpha" and "SK-Bravo," both of them lunar landers just now departing from the vicinity of Clarke Station. "There they go . . ."

Chindarkar stared at the dots. "Well, let's hope they work as advertised. Burkette sure didn't give us a discount."

The Kangaroo lander was designed by billionaire George Burkette's company, Starion, and was viewed as a reliable, small commercial lunar lander. Rochat had negotiated a license with Burkette that allowed Catalyst to fabricate the main chassis components—frame, fuel tanks, landing struts, and thrusters—up at Clarke Station, utilizing Kerner's CVD mill. The more sophisticated avionics and proprietary components had been shipped up with the Green Team weeks ago. Yak and Chindarkar formed the project team that installed and configured the final Starion components under the guidance of Burkette's engineers, and both spacecraft had passed flight trials.

Ecklund joined Jin, Chindarkar, and Yak at the lunar lander team's table, while the international observers watched nearby.

Jin deliberately turned his back on them and said, "Bob, step us through the next seventy hours. We cannot risk any misunderstandings."

"Sure." Ecklund instantiated a virtual slide listing a timeline. He aimed a virtual laser pointer. "SK-Alpha and SK-Bravo have already docked with their transit propulsion modules and have performed a 650-meters-per-second retro burn that three days from now will bring them into low lunar orbit. Once in LLO, and assuming mission control gives us the green light, SK-Alpha will undock from its TPM and descend for an autonomous landing on the lunar equator at Morra Base. That'll burn through 1.9 kilometers per second of delta-v, or just short of half its fuel."

"What's our safety margin?"

"Roughly 6 percent."

"Cutting it close, isn't it?"

"Apollo 11 cut it closer." He turned back to the screen. "SK-Bravo, meanwhile, will remain in lunar orbit." He brought up an image of lunar terrain. "This is a live image of the site for Morra Base. Barring accidents or some surprise . . ." He pointed. ". . . this is precisely where SK-Alpha will land. It will arrive half an hour after lunar dawn. That gives us three hundred thirty-five hours of sunlight to power the Kangaroo lander's solar panels—and thus our telepresence robots—in order to establish a regolith head before lunar nightfall."

Tighe raised an eyebrow. "A regolith head?"

"It's not beach—so it's not a 'beachhead.'" Ecklund brought up several slides in rapid succession. "LRO data shows the thermal environment at Morra Base ranges from 244 degrees Fahrenheit during the lunar day down to negative 298 degrees Fahrenheit at night. That's a temperature swing of 542 degrees. So there's going to be serious expansion and contraction on any joints and seals not shielded from the sun. We'll need power beaming down from Daisy before that first nightfall to keep our robots warm and functioning—or they will die. That means setting up the rectenna, power lines, and the initial base structure is critical."

Jin took notes. "We must receive power from Daisy ASAP after landing."

"Correct." He cycled through another series of slides, stopping at a flight schedule. "Once we clear that hurdle, the serious construction can begin—through lunar day and lunar night. My logistics plan calls for a total of thirty-nine Kangaroo flights over a hundred and eighty days to supply matériel, each flight a six-day round trip, not including loading and unloading—unless we can augment our fleet of Kangaroos between now and then, in which case we can increase the tempo of deliveries. In total we're sending down 170 tons of payload, 4.5 tons at a time."

Jin contemplated something, then said, "We could have done this in just a couple landings of Macy's Galleon rocket."

"True . . . unless it crashed—in which case it would wipe out the base and all our resources at once. Besides, we don't have all our mass-driver and other components ready yet."

Jin nodded in acknowledgment of this.

"Right, then," Ecklund continued. "My timeline also does not include the maintenance that will need to be done on the landers—which is unknown, since no one has ever delivered so much tonnage to the lunar surface. Manufacture of mass-driver pylons and track sections up here at the station will need to keep up with shipments to the surface, or we fall behind. We'll also need production of sulfur concrete in situ. If all goes to plan, we should be done in six months or so—that is, by November of this year. It's an aggressive schedule, but necessary given the dearth of resources you'll have left by then.

I'd rather have the mass-driver launching resources up from the Moon sooner than later."

Chindarkar was running numbers. "We'll be okay if the *Amy Tsukada* tug arrives at the end of 2041."

Jin shook his head. "We cannot count on that."

Tighe looked at the ceiling high overhead. "Maybe we shouldn't have blown all our steel on this place."

"We wouldn't have been able to stay up here this long if we hadn't."

Ecklund added, "Or been able to invite helpful guests like myself, J.T."

Jin examined the flight schedule. "So we can't land the second Kangaroo until we build a landing pad."

"That's right. The rocket motor of an incoming lander will spray tons of regolith at supersonic speeds in every direction. In that vacuum it'll send the debris flying hundreds of kilometers. At close range it'll be like opening fire with a shotgun."

Chindarkar said, "So we build berms."

"NASA advisory is 2 kilometers distance from a lander for safety, but we're going to use the first robots we set down to build up berms and sintered landing pad tiles to limit ejecta for follow-on landers." He checked the time. "The ops center will be running in shifts continuously during that first lunar day. All three hundred thirty-five hours of it."

"Okay." Jin took a deep breath. "Yak, J.T., I want you two controlling the first Talos robots on the surface. So be ready for the landing—watch your sleep schedules. We'll need to use every hour if we hope to have Morra Base established before the first lunar night."

There were just four of Alan Goff's Talos robots on Clarke Station, and there was no telling if Goff would be willing to send up more. Two would be going down to the Moon in the first flight. Both of these were clad in jumpsuits and bubble helmets to protect them from lunar regolith.

Tighe sat in a plastic chair in the makeshift ops center, his crystal glasses in VR mode and his eyes seemingly 64,000 kilometers away, soaking up the scenery with 8K ultra high-definition vision as the lunar surface rolled silently past beneath him.

He couldn't help but feel excitement. From the distant Talos robot's perspective, he was standing in a rack atop the *SK-Alpha* lander's payload deck. The Kangaroo landers vaguely resembled the old Apollo landers—but were larger. They consisted of an octagonal metal frame with four landing legs, forming a broad base. Set low within the framework were exposed spherical fuel tanks and piping, and projecting from the bottom, a single large rocket nozzle. The rocket engine burned hydrolox, sacrificing the reliability (and toxicity) of hypergolic fuels like hydrazine for something Clarke Station had in abundance: water ice. With that, they could produce the liquid hydrogen and liquid oxygen needed to power hundreds of lander missions. So operations with the Kangaroo landers could continue from Clarke Station for some time.

Atop the lander's frame was a level open payload deck about 6 meters in diameter and about the same height from the ground, with four automated davits to lower equipment to the Moon's surface once landed. Tighe knew the deck behind his robot was packed with equipment. Nearly a full 4,500-kilogram payload.

Mission control's voice came in over the comm link. *"Ten kilometers altitude. Two hundred twenty kilometers up range. Commencing retrograde burn..."*

Tighe's image jittered as the lander's rocket motor fired silently. Below, the lunar scenery began to slow its roll perceptibly. It was hard to gauge distances out here, since there was no scale reference. Looking down, he would have sworn they were just a few hundred meters—instead of 10 kilometers—above the lunar surface.

He heard Yak's voice behind him. "I cannot make out Apollo 11 landing site at this distance. Pity."

Yak's Talos robot was on the far side of the lander, likewise locked in place. The *SK-Alpha* lander was really shuddering now, and Tighe's HUD display indicated the Talos was enduring 3 g's of deceleration. Tighe smiled with anticipation. He wasn't exactly landing on the Moon—not in person, at least—but it seemed pretty damned close to that experience. And life on board Clarke Station had been getting monotonous. "Best video game ever, guys."

Mission control: *"Five kilometers altitude. Fifty-six kilometers up range."*

The lander started angling its motor partly downward now, slowing its orbit as well as its descent.

Tighe noticed AR labels pop up above lunar terrain features. Ahead and below was a curving, ashen hill that resembled a dog curled up, with its back facing him. "There's Cape Bruce. We should drop in just east of the ridgeline."

Yak's voice just behind him (at Clarke Station): "I see it. Beautiful desolation."

There was an immensity to the lunar landscape that had been lacking out at Ryugu. The asteroid had been like an islet in an immense void, but with the broad lunar horizon, this was like a continent moving past beneath them—though slowing now.

"Ride's smoothing out."

The lander's motor angled even farther downward, arresting their fall as they continued their descent. The vacuum made the gray-on-gray landscape so crystal clear that it looked for all the world like Tighe could simply step off the lander and plant his robotic feet on the ground.

Mission control: *"Two kilometers altitude. Eleven kilometers up range."*

Yak said, "J.T., look to bearing 233."

Tighe noted his artificial compass heading (since the Moon had no magnetic field, the coordinates were supplied by Marín's satellite network) and turned his head. There, just above the lunar horizon, floated the swirling blue, green, and white marble of Earth, set in a jet-black sky devoid of stars due to the glare of sunlight. "There we all are. Well, almost all of us."

Now the lander was gliding slowly over and past the ridge of Cape Bruce. Beyond it lay a flat, slightly crater-pocked plain of darker gray "maria"— powdered basalts. The region leading up to it for hundreds of kilometers was similarly flat and pocked by craters. However, Tighe knew why this location in particular had been selected: for the L2-friendly launch trajectory as well as the mix of resources to be found in this region's regolith.

Looking down to study the terrain, Tighe could hardly believe anything useful or life-giving could be found in this primordial gray desert. But then, Amy Tsukada had taught them all otherwise out at Ryugu, with her seemingly miraculous chemistry lab. The landscape was starkly beautiful in the way that deserts or barren wilderness back on Earth seemed to Tighe. Its remoteness and timelessness made the vista strangely moving.

The lander descended almost vertically now.

Mission control: *"Five hundred meters altitude. One kilometer up range. Site Morra is clear. Engine nominal. We are 'go' for landing."*

Tighe craned his robot neck downward to watch the lunar surface approach. Seemingly ever-increasing detail resolved until finally rivulets of dust first swirled, then silently blasted away from the rocket wash as contact was made with the surface. There was a slight bounce as the lander made a two-point touchdown.

The motor immediately and silently cut off, a cloud of fine particles rolling away from the craft.

Mission control: *"MECO. SK-Alpha has soft touchdown at Morra Base."*

Tighe heard applause and cheers around him, though his eyes beheld a silent world. He turned his robotic head to scan the lunar terrain. A cloud of ashen dust was still billowing away from the landing site, but the ridgeline of Cape Bruce loomed to the north, just ahead of him—perhaps 500 meters tall. "This is really something. You guys are spectating, I hope."

Chindarkar's voice nearby said, "We have both your and Yak's feed up on the big screen."

He keyed the comm link. "Mission control, Talos-1 is operational."

Yak's voice behind him said, "Mission control, Talos-2 is operational."

"Talos 1 and 2 stand by. Deploying davits . . ."

Suddenly Tighe saw his view change as the davit arms swung "him" out over the edge, and the winch lines lowered his robot toward the lunar surface. He gazed down between his robotic feet, clad in jumper booties. "Like I said: best video game ever . . ."

Jin's voice nearby said, "You have no extra lives. So be careful."

Fortunately the Talos unit handled all walking and balance, and as his robot alighted onto the lunar surface, it automatically stood and stepped over and past a small rock. The only thing Tighe had to manage was which direction he wanted to move. The robot would take the steps necessary to get him there. Arms, head, and upper body—that was all his to manage.

Tighe turned around to look back at the lander. It was still steaming slightly from below, and some scoring had occurred on the cladding during the landing. Ricocheting stones, perhaps. "SK-Alpha appears undamaged. No visible leaks. Hey, Yak, where are you?"

"I will come to you."

In a moment Tighe noticed a humanoid robot labeled "Talos-2" in AR walking up wearing a white jumpsuit, with its head in a plastic bubble.

Yak chuckled. "I am thinking this is bad 1950s sci-fi movie."

Tighe laughed along with the surrounding audience. He looked out at the eastern horizon and pointed. "That's our run line."

"I can do better . . ." Yak's robot made a few gestures and suddenly an entire, translucent projection of a lunar base appeared before them in augmented reality. "Behold, future Morra Base."

Tighe stared down the length of a construct that resembled a pipeline, with support structures at intervals. It ran over a kilometer, straight toward the eastern horizon (which on the Moon was just 2.5 kilometers away), and he could see that it would have a straight shot at the black sky. Scanning back to its origin, he saw that the mass-driver emerged from a slightly raised spectral building with corrugated walls—the "Launch House." It contacted the ground in only a few spots, where electrostatic and seismic insulator pylons were sunk in. Close at hand were spectral liquid nitrogen tanks, piping, electrical conduit, and a transformer yard with cabling that ran hundreds of meters to the west, toward a distant rectenna that was half a kilometer square and draped over the landscape like a luminous blanket.

This being in situ augmented reality, Tighe could gaze "through" the Launch House to the cableway, which passed through an open "mass yard," optimistically piled high with 10-kilogram cylinders of regolith stacked like artillery shells. The yard was traversed overhead by the cableway, which led to the "rod" processing facility and intake chute. A virtual hillock of regolith was piled up on its far side so that mining robots could roll up and dump their cargo into the chute. A cluster of nearby volatile tanks bordered the structure. Beyond this lay the robot garage and charging shed, the comm link tower, and—still farther on—a landing pad circled by virtual berms.

More berms bisected the site, as did roads, and finally there was another virtual hillock under which a human habitat was planned to be inflated, then transformed into a sulfur concrete shell, ready to be equipped, supplied, and sustained, should actual humans ever need to visit the base.

Tighe studied the ambitious mirage. "Should be a piece of cake."

Yak's robot stepped up to him and clenched a fist, silently slapping it into its breastplate. "I pledge my robot life to make it so."

"Oh no, captain's orders: you need to be cautious with your titanium carcass. We'll need it." Tighe tapped his real-world foot twice. It was the command he'd set that would cause his robot to crouch. It obeyed. Now crouched, he then leaned forward and reached with his gloved robotic hand into the incredibly fine lunar regolith—several times finer, he knew, than talcum powder. The built-in pressure pads in the robot's fingers passed the sensation on to his haptic gloves and thus to his actual fingers. In his crystal he watched the fine particles drain through gloved digits, falling slowly in the one-sixth gravity.

He looked up to Yak's robot. "Looks like good soil." Tighe stood and slapped the moondust off his robotic hands.

Yak turned. "Then let us get started . . ."

Over the next hour Tighe and Yak supervised the unloading of twin 200-kilo, six-wheeled Badger mining robots from the *SK-Alpha*'s payload deck. Once they were set on the lunar surface and powered up, Chindarkar took the telepresence helm of one, while Jin took control of the other. Tighe and Yak then opened a utility panel on the lander and unrolled a cable with a wireless charging transmitter at one end, set on folding legs. This, they placed nearby and powered up, to bathe their robots in energy as they worked.

Tighe checked his HUD display. "Mission control, we are now charging off lander power." That meant the robots wouldn't drop dead in the next twenty minutes or so.

This done, they then started assembling a framework atop and connecting both the wheeled mining robots—forming a single, larger payload deck. Yak and Tighe had practiced the task dozens of times in VR, but it turned out to go more smoothly than the simulation—which was a first.

They then connected data lines between the mining robots, slaving one to the other.

"All right, Priya. You're now piloting Badger-1-plus-2."

"Copy that. Board's all green. Ready for cargo."

Tighe's and Yak's robots then used the lander's davits to lower a 400-kilo folded rectenna netting down onto its back. Even in one-sixth gravity it was a significant mass. The wheels of the two machines depressed visibly into the regolith.

Tighe kneeled his robot down to check the ground clearance. "We might be able to fit a clean handkerchief under there. Priya, no joke: you need to find the flattest possible path to the rectenna site."

She answered close by in the real world. "Understood. Let's do this."

Tighe's robot grabbed a large coil of power cable from a compartment on the lander and threw it over his metal shoulder. He then followed Yak, who was hauling the wireless charging unit, as the two of them trudged in the ruts left behind by the loaded-down Badgers.

It was slow going. Several times the wheeled robots bogged down, and Yak's and Tighe's Talos robots had to push them forward.

Chindarkar said, "Only a half kilometer to go."

"Oh, *only* half a kilometer . . ."

It wound up taking them nearly two hours to get the machines out to the rectenna deployment site.

Tighe's robot then pulled a sledgehammer and a bundle of hollow steel poles from atop one of the Badgers. He and Yak pounded the poles into the ground one by one, bracing their feet between the heavy robot wheels to hold themselves down in the low gravity.

"This regolith: it's lighter than talcum powder for a few inches—and then it's like concrete."

With great effort, they drove in several poles. Then Tighe's and Yak's robots secured the edge of the rectenna array to the posts.

Yak said, "Okay, Priya . . . ease forward. Slowly . . ."

As the conjoined Badgers moved forward, integrated legs expanded beneath the rectenna at intervals, like the legs on a hospital gurney, suspending the coppery netting a meter above the lunar surface as it unfurled.

"Excellent. Keep going . . ."

Tighe and Yak and Priya worked for hours, and by T-plus twenty-two hours after touchdown, they had managed to get all five rectennas on the *SK-Alpha* lander deployed and linked to power cables. Even so, it represented only 5 percent of Morra Base's planned 50-megawatt power reception grid, but at least now they were ready to receive power from Daisy, 61,000 kilometers overhead—which was actually visible as a lone star at L1, alongside the Earth in the black sky.

Tighe and Yak tested the microwave-beam reception for the rectenna. After a few tense minutes, the assembled team at Clarke Station cheered and applauded as the current indicator registered microwave energy.

Jin smiled as he said, "Morra Base to mission control. Daisy is sending power accurately from L1 to our target signal. We register 2.2 megawatts at a conversion efficiency of . . . 89 percent. Over."

Lacroix's voice came in over the comm link. *"Excellent work. We confirm 2.2 megawatts."*

Keeping their eye on the Sun, they didn't celebrate long, however. Within the next twelve hours they had placed and leveled a platform onto the ground near the lander, then lowered and bolted a transformer onto it. Soon after, they completed the hook-ups, and an entire array of connectors became available to them.

Tighe plugged the wireless charger into the new power source and confirmed its wattage. They now had reliable power to start establishing the base in earnest. He looked up at Yak's robot. "Let's separate those Badgers and get the heavy tools hooked up. It's time to start surveying and leveling ground."

CHAPTER 26

Nightfall

t took seventy-two hours, teleoperating in around-the-clock shifts from Clarke Station, to grade a 5-meter-wide roadway a kilometer long through the lunar regolith, headed northward, toward the slopes of Cape Bruce. There, the ridgeline encircled them on three sides, where it would help to contain incoming and outgoing rocket blast. Using the projected AR plan as a guide, they bulldozed 10-meter-high berms of regolith between the proposed landing pad and future site of Morra Base to the south, including an angled opening for the access road.

It wound up taking another 120 hours to bulldoze and grade the berms. Two Talos robots then covered the inward slopes in white combustion-synthesis sheeting, which they melted into a durable shell-like surface with blowtorches.

Simultaneously, a portable sintering machine was melting lunar dust into puzzle-shaped bricks, according to a precise design prepared by Robert Ecklund. When the berms were finished, all equipment was transferred from the *SK-Alpha* landing site to the new berm-enclosed launchpad.

Chindarkar radioed, "Morra Base to mission control. We have secured all matériel within Pad-One perimeter. *SK-Alpha* can lift off when ready."

"*Copy that, Morra Base. Please stand by . . . Lifting off in three, two . . .*"

Jin's Talos robot gazed up into the black sky. Suddenly—and without a sound—the Kangaroo lander they'd ridden in on appeared beyond the berm wall and rocketed upward, its engine issuing a blinding white light. "Wow, that is fast without cargo."

It took a while for the rock and debris from *SK-Alpha*'s launch to settle down. Jin was surprised just how much, how far, and how fast the rocket-blast debris traveled. However, none of their equipment took damage behind the new berms, and they soon got back to work.

Glancing up again, Jin could see the Sun now leaning toward the west in the black sky. This increased the urgency of their work, as the Talos robots laid down the sintered regolith bricks into a hardened landing surface, rather like building a patio.

By T-plus 242 hours, with less than a hundred hours until sunset, they'd installed all the pad tiles and run electrical lines to landing pad sensors, along with infrared lights. For the first time on the Moon, Jin's robot stood on a built surface—a round, dark gray tiled patio, 20 meters in diameter, hemmed in by fused berm walls. He and Tighe, as Talos robots, stood next to each other, surveying their work.

Tighe clapped Jin's robot on the back. "As much as I'd like to crack open a beer..."

"Yes, you are right. We need *SK-Bravo* down here immediately."

Within an hour the crew had shifted all their equipment to a location a kilometer south and somewhat eastward, closer to the rectenna array. There, they began work leveling a quarter-acre-sized plot.

As they worked, Jin looked up at one point to see a light approaching in the black sky, angling in toward them and slowing as it did so.

Tighe's robot pointed. "There's *SK-Bravo*."

They both watched the craft's silent descent, and Jin was impressed with how deftly it maneuvered toward their new landing pad. Within a minute of their first spotting it, the *SK-Bravo* lander was illuminating the slopes of Cape Bruce on its final descent. And then it touched down, its blinding light snuffing out with very little dust.

Tighe turned to him. "Pad worked pretty well."

The voice of mission control said, "SK-Bravo *MECO. Soft touchdown on Pad-One.*"

Jin heard real applause in the ops room around him on Clarke Station. Both robots hopped a Badger vehicle piloted by Chindarkar and headed out to the landing pad along the base road. There, they were met by two more Talos robots, descending off *SK-Bravo* on davits. The machines were piloted by Robert Ecklund and Hoshiko Sato.

Jin noticed Ecklund's robot staring around in amazement at being, for the first time, virtually on the surface of the Moon. "Bob, are you ready?"

"This is incredible!"

Jin said, "You will get used to it."

Ecklund laughed. "I don't think so. I've been watching you guys for days, but to finally be here . . . Well, in robot form, at least. It's a dream come true."

Tighe's robot pointed at the Sun. "And if we're not ready when sundown comes, it'll be a nightmare."

"Right." Ecklund clapped his robot hands and helped unload equipment, tools, and construction materials. Fortunately the SK-Bravo lander also contained two more Badger robots, along with their heavy tool attachments, and also a lightweight wheeled crane developed by NASA called an LSMS that they could use to lift and precisely place objects up to 3,000 kilograms in mass.

Now that construction of the mass-driver's supporting elements was beginning, Ecklund would be project lead on the lunar surface—meaning the rest of the crew would be following his instructions. He directed them to bring all the materials to the construction site at the end of the kilometer-long road.

Over the next forty-eight hours, the crew of now eight robots drove a dozen post holes into the lunar regolith, using Badger pile-driving attachments to create footings for what would become part of the "Brick House," the regolith-processing facility where cylinders of hardened regolith would be produced. Ecklund referenced virtual plans projected in augmented reality to confirm placement.

Watching the pile drivers work, Jin said, "Would not augers be faster for these holes?"

Ecklund's Talos robot shook its head. "Not on the Moon. Lunar regolith is too dry and dense. The auger bit would fuse due to the lack of moisture."

Jin and the crew then followed Ecklund's instructions to electrically insulate, seismically isolate, and laser-level the tops of the posts before constructing and electron-welding a metal frame 20 meters square onto them, then flooring it with cobalt steel panels, lowered into place with the LSMS crane.

With all the robots working round-the-clock, both Morra Base and the teleoperations center on Clarke Station bustled with activity.

By T-plus 328 hours since initial touchdown, they had a sturdy, level steel floor raised a meter above the regolith, accessed by an electrically insulated ramp. Their equipment—chargers, tools, batteries, and more—were all stacked onto it, and cables running from the rectenna array brought ample power to the transformer, which was now mounted onto the edge of the platform.

Jin's robot looked to the west, where the Sun stood just above the horizon. It had been thirteen Earth days since they first arrived.

Tighe said, "Well, folks, night is almost on us. Let's see if these robots can survive the deep freeze."

Chindarkar's voice asked, "How long until sunset?"

Jin answered, "Seven hours."

Ecklund said, "There'll be no afterglow in the sky like on Earth. When lunar night comes, it will fall like a guillotine. Talos units should get their long johns on now."

"Long johns" were a heated garment that, while heavier and drawing more power, theoretically allowed the Talos robots to continue work in the bitter cold of the lunar night. But they had never actually been used on the Moon before, being prototypes from Goff's Celestial Robotics.

At five hours before lunar sunset, the *SK-Bravo* lander blasted off. From a kilometer away, it was quite a sight.

Ecklund's robot craned its metal neck. "Wow! Would you look at that. I'd take a picture, but I guess we're always recording with these eyes."

Hours later, the stark shadows had lengthened across the Sea of Tranquility. Eastward, beyond Cape Bruce, was already jet-black.

Ecklund's robot was examining the flooring. "Be sure to use thermal vision to check all these panels and supports. The heating elements need to be working. We don't want any of them to shatter in a dawn tremor. It is going to get very, very cold."

Soon, odd things began to happen around them. The ground seemed to become fuzzy. Here and there in the distance an occasional light flashed—silent electrical arcs. It appeared as though particles of fine regolith were floating up to a meter off the ground.

Tighe observed, "I've seen this—on Ryugu. Particle levitation."

Ecklund answered him. "Yes. The solar wind causes a charge differential between the sunlit and dark sides of the Moon. The terminator line is a zone of electrical instability. Everyone stay on the platform until it passes."

"The arcs don't look that big. Almost like the fireflies we had back home."

"They may not look like much, but that's only because we're in a vacuum. Lightning bolts are only visible on Earth because they move through air—creating white-hot plasma. Here, they're just hitting occasional particles, but they could be anywhere from 200 to 2,000 kilovolts. And right now the Moon is passing through the edge of Earth's magnetic field, so we're in its plasma wake."

Chindarkar asked, "Will this happen each lunar sunset?"

"Most likely, and at dawn. It won't always be this strong. But once we have piping and seals, this can get dangerous. During temperature swings, things contract and expand, loosen, and if electricity arcs near a leaking oxidizer, it could cause a violent explosion. We need to carefully monitor for leaks."

This put them all on edge. However, in an hour or so the terminator line had passed, and the regolith settled once more. A brilliant field of stars were arrayed above them now that the Sun had set, although the ever-present Earth cast enough light to work by.

Ecklund's robot gazed heavenward. "It's just so amazing to be here. Or to sort of be here."

Jin switched his Talos to thermal vision and noticed the heat coursing through his robot's jumper. Glancing at the ambient temperature readout, he saw that it was now negative 297 degrees Fahrenheit. "Look."

"Now *that's* cold." Tighe picked up a thin piece of framing steel left over from building the Brick House deck. He held it above one of the Badger bulldozer blades, then brought it down sharply.

The framing steel shattered like glass, pieces flying everywhere.

"J.T.!"

Tighe examined the nub of steel left in his gloved hand and turned to Jin. "Wisconsin winters have nothing on this place."

CHAPTER 27

Price of Admission

CLARKE STATION POPULATION: 23
DAYS TO RYUGU DEPARTURE: 1,085

The body of Milena Jakubec lay on an examination table in the South Hab medical bay. She was still wearing her flight suit, her eyes were closed and her face was serene though her lips were a shade of dark blue. Both of the station's flight surgeons stood next to the body in grim contemplation. Priya Chindarkar stood across from them, with Jin Han and James Tighe standing at the foot of the table.

Jin asked, "How did it happen?"

Dr. Elizabeth Josephson turned to him. "Acute hypoxia."

Tighe added, "I retrieved her body from the central pump room. She was floating in elevated levels of nitrogen. It must have pooled around her in microgravity while she was working, and she probably suffocated without realizing it was happening."

"She was our life support *specialist*. Why wasn't she using a breathing apparatus? Or oxygen sensors? And why was she alone?"

"A mistake—perhaps brought on by exhaustion."

Jin's jaw clenched and unclenched. "There are procedures to prevent this."

Tighe nodded.

"How long has she been dead?"

Dr. Ohana answered. "Rigor mortis had set in by the time she was recovered. So at least an hour or two."

"J.T., you found her?"

"No. Chelsie Birk did. When Milena didn't respond to chat, Chelsie went to investigate her RFID location."

"That was reckless. It could have cost us our comms specialist as well." Jin scanned the group. "From now on, if anyone goes missing or goes silent, we activate a general alert, and I want to be notified immediately." He rubbed his tired eyes. "This was my fault."

"You can't be everywhere. There were procedures."

"What good is that to her family?" Jin stared at the body for several moments. "I gather the entire crew knows by now. And the international observers."

Ohana and Josephson nodded.

Tighe said, "They all know how dangerous it is out here. These systems and procedures are all new. There's going to be some hard lessons learned."

Jin sighed. "We are out here to try and save two people, and already one other person is dead."

Dr. Josephson spoke to Jin. "That brings up a good point: Jackie and I need to establish a station morgue. You three need to give us a location—preferably somewhere naturally cold and dark. We were thinking one of the unused docking bay airlocks."

Tighe said, "Hm. Just don't accidentally send the new arrivals through it."

The others stared at Tighe.

"That wasn't a joke."

Jin turned back to Josephson. "Do it, Liz. But prep Milena's remains for the journey back to Earth. The supply cycler swings by in less than a week. We will need to keep her frozen en route, and arrange with mission control to contact her next of kin."

Chindarkar added, "We should inform Lukas. There will most likely be liability exposure. A death certificate. Earth authorities to deal with." She paused. "What about the rest of the crew? I think we should have a memorial service. Have us say a few words."

Jin pondered this. "Yes. You are right. This woman is dead because of us. Because of our decision to be here."

Tighe said, "It was Milena's decision, too."

Chindarkar gave him a look. "No one is saying it wasn't, but we did cause this place to be built in order to rescue *our* friends. Others will be doing that math, even if you don't."

"I don't think that's the only calculation that matters."

Jin held up his hand. "We leave that for another day. Right now we should mourn her loss and make certain it does not happen again. James, please use your expertise on air mixtures to review our safety procedures in utility spaces."

Tighe nodded. "I'll see to it."

He turned to Josephson and Ohana. "Please take care of Milena's remains, and we will prepare a service."

The memorial for Jakubec was subdued and involved the South Hab crew lining up in front of crew quarters as the flight surgeons rolled the wrapped body past on a gurney. They halted at the elevator lobby while Jin spoke a few words about the fragility of life and the importance of what they were doing out here.

"The best way to honor Milena's sacrifice is to succeed in establishing a permanent human presence in deep space."

And with that, Milena Jakubec's remains were sent to the cold and darkness of an airlock to await the transit craft that would bear her to the lunar cycler—and from there to home.

Tighe's third dawn as a telepresence robot on the Moon saw the sun rise as a piercing white light that crested the lunar hills to the east. Unlike soothing Earthly sunrises, dawn on the Moon was the arrival of a nuclear furnace. The transition between dangerous cold and searing heat was not gradual.

A significant amount of construction work was still underway at Morra Base, although none of the buildings were complete. Tighe's Talos robot glanced from the flat roof of the Brick House southeast, past the cableway to Jin's and Yak's Talos robots, which moved about the metal frame of the Launch House. That structure was slowly taking shape at the margins of its L-shaped floor plan, and bolted to the decking were pieces of complex machinery that Ecklund had worked with Nicolau Ivorra and Hoshiko Sato to manufacture up on Clarke Station. Tighe did not comprehend—and fortunately did not *have to* comprehend—most of it. Ecklund did, and his Talos robot maneuvered in and around the equipment in the semidarkness. Then he looked up. "Guys, be careful. The sun's almost up."

Tighe turned to face the lunar dawn and now noticed telltale particle levitation fuzzing the horizon. Portions of the haze zapped and arced against pipes, cables, and foundations or set outlines of equipment glowing like St. Elmo's Fire.

Within the hour, the ground began to tremble, and soon the structures of Morra Base bucked and shimmied on their supports.

"Moonquake! Watch for gas leaks." Ecklund's robot clung to machinery.

"Bob, let the Talos software handle standing." Tighe demonstrated as his robot's legs automatically compensated for the shaking deck.

"Oh. Right." Ecklund's robot released its hold on a thick pipe, and his stance immediately stabilized.

In the distance, rocks tumbled down the slopes of Cape Bruce, leaving dust trails in their wake. The nearby plain undulated gently.

Ecklund's robot looked around. "I think we're going to be okay."

"Is your kilometer-long mass-driver really going to be able to deal with this on a regular basis?"

"It'll flex, and we'll recalibrate it remotely."

Tighe knew it wasn't going to be that simple. There were always complications. If deep space had taught him anything, it was that.

The moonquake lasted nearly eight minutes and only stubbornly trailed off. By then the sun cast stark shadows over the mare.

Up on Clarke Station, Tighe removed his crystal glasses and rubbed his eyes. He was "back," and the disorienting sensation of working in VR took a while to shake off. He'd been focused on Moon operations for so long he barely kept up with what was happening in real life around him. Looking across South Hab, he could see half a dozen of his colleagues, their crystal headsets opaque, moving their hands to manipulate unseen objects on the far side of the Moon. It was like a video-gaming club.

How he'd wound up here—how any of them had wound up here—seemed as surreal as their telepresence work, but the pace of lunar operations did not allow much time for reflection. So after a brief bio break, Tighe got back to work.

Several days later, Tighe, Yak, Jin, and Ecklund maneuvered their Talos robots around the under-construction Launch House, positioning an LSMS crane. Suspended from the crane was a 6-meter-long section of the mass-driver barrel. One meter in diameter, it was the first of 232 sections. For several months, Sato, Braam De Jong, and Wu Meiling had been building these intricate components up on Clarke Station, and Kangaroo landers had been delivering them at regular intervals, with the team stockpiling the sections in the "brickyard" next to the Launch House.

The interior of each mass-driver section was lined with conduction coils and electronic switching gear spaced at exact intervals and massed over 300 kilos—though in the Moon's gravity it "weighed" only a sixth of that. Still, the team used the crane to raise it to the 8-meter height at which the mass-driver barrel left the Launch House wall. This height ensured that with pylons the mass-driver could run level across the slightly uneven lunar plain.

Tighe and Yak adjusted the crane manually on its wheels, shifting the suspended barrel section at Ecklund's instructions, while his robot stood atop nearby machinery.

This first piece of the mass-driver's 1.39-kilometer-long barrel had to be installed before completing the wall of the Launch House from which it would protrude—and which would contain the mass-driver's electrical, control, and loading mechanisms. Computers would direct immense electrical energies, activating a series of thousands of conduction coils in a precise sequence to accelerate the payload mass down the pipe within an eddy current—all in slightly over a second, at 235 g's.

Before any of that could happen, they still needed to add nitrogen cooling and electrical conduits along the entire length and build dozens of flexible, remotely adjustable trusses to support the hundreds of barrel sections that would traverse the landscape. In other words, there were still months of work ahead.

And due to a dozen complications, both major and minor, they were already two weeks behind schedule. Not much in the scheme of things, but Tighe knew that the mass-driver was just the first in a series of obstacles to overcome in building the rescue ship, and so his stress increased with every delay, no matter how small. The asteroid Ryugu would not wait.

By comparison, Ecklund seemed to be coming more alive every day as he worked. This was clearly the realization of a dream for him, and his enthusiasm and drive never seemed to falter, even when he was exhausted.

Still, Tighe couldn't help but wonder what they'd do if Ecklund was wrong. If this machine didn't work. No one had ever built a mass-driver this size—on the Moon or anywhere else—and in fact, there was no way to truly test it in the gravity and atmosphere of Earth. So Catalyst Corporation—or the CCE or whatever Lukas Rochat was calling them these days—had gone "all in" on Ecklund's idea. Tighe just hoped smarter minds than him knew what they were doing.

Ecklund's robot waved his arm. "Okay, bring it back . . . Straighten it out. We need the lugs in line." Ecklund's robot motioned. "Toward me. Slowly. That's it! Hold it there." His robot then used a battery-powered tool to silently affix dozens of thick bolts. Afterward, he walked across the coil section, examining the support truss, which was anchored at four points in the lunar soil 8 meters below. "Looks good!" He took a sight line toward the horizon with a laser. "Now just a couple hundred more to go."

Tighe spotted a bright light in the sky behind Ecklund's Talos.

"Kangaroo lander incoming." Jin pointed and paused a moment, apparently to check manifest records. "Flight 29. Coil and pylon sections."

Ecklund glanced up briefly. "Excellent! Once we get the hang of these, we'll be able to keep up an operational tempo." He patted the coil barrel. "We're getting there, folks."

Tighe had seen a couple dozen landers arrive and depart from Morra Base over the months, yet they still impressed him. He and the others stopped to watch it arcing downward and slow its descent atop a dagger of white-hot flame.

But then something went very wrong. The flame beneath it guttered and went out as the lander's thrusters puffed madly.

"Oh no . . ." Ecklund's robot put its hands onto its metal head. "No, no, no!"

The craft veered suddenly toward them from a height of several hundred meters.

"Heads up!"

"Goddamnit!"

They scattered.

Mission control's voice cut in. "SK-Bravo *self-destruct activated.*"

And yet the craft did not self-destruct, but instead spun crazily end over end before it noiselessly impacted the lunar surface at several hundred kilometers per hour. Tighe stopped to watch as the silent fireball expanded, debris hurtling out in every direction at supersonic speeds.

"J.T.!" Yak's robot grabbed his arm, pulling him to the ground as shards of metal and pieces of rock tumbled past them, piercing the corrugated wall of the Brick House and setting the cableway wires dancing when a support tower got hit. It was all eerily silent.

Jin called out, "I am offline! Something struck me."

Ecklund groaned as his robot took cover behind the Launch House foundation. "No! We're already behind schedule."

In a few moments it was over—except for the flames, which billowed lazily for several moments in the low gravity before rapidly extinguishing as they consumed whatever oxidizer was available. Smoke and dust remained for a while afterward.

The regolith-covered robots stood up and approached the fallen "corpse" of Jin's damaged Talos. Its jumper was torn open with the chest smashed by a catastrophic impact—but whatever hit it had apparently ricocheted away.

Yak's robot knelt to pick up Jin's Talos in the low gravity, like a fallen comrade. "We may be able to repair this."

Using thermal optics, Tighe surveyed damage to the base. "The Brick House was hit, too. And the volatile extraction pipes. And the west wall. Also a cableway support."

Ecklund was still shaking his robotic head in disbelief. "Damn it to hell . . ."

Yak said, "We will need to closely inspect entire site."

Ecklund's robot paced. "And we lost one of the landers—that'll halve our transport capacity. Not to mention the loss of the payload this one was carrying." He turned to Yak's robot. "How many coil sections did *SK-Bravo* have on board?"

"Four."

"Oh my god. Those will take weeks to rebuild—even if we have the extra components." Several slow deep breaths were audible, mimicked by Ecklund's Talos robot on the lunar surface. It pressed its hands together as if in meditation. "Center yourself, Robert. Release what you cannot control . . ." After a moment, Ecklund's robot seemed calmer. Then it clapped its hands. "Right. We should see if there's anything we can salvage. C'mon . . ."

Yak gently placed Jin's broken Talos on the ground, then followed Ecklund.

Tighe watched them go—taking a moment to consider that construction of their rescue ship had just slipped further behind—even as the arrival of Ryugu came inexorably closer. As relentless a deadline as they'd ever faced.

He sighed and followed them toward the wreckage.

CHAPTER 28

Declaration

JUNE 16, 2039

Lukas Rochat took the podium at the head of the largest conference room in Catalyst Corporation's offices. His audience was a standing-room-only crowd of government ministers, intelligence agents, scientists, and diplomats—nearly a hundred people in all—present for this invite-only event and all of whom wore a lanyard with their photo and name, indicating they'd been vetted and positively identified by Catalyst's staff.

He nodded to the group. "Good morning. Let me begin by saying this is a briefing, not a press conference. Since the existence of Clarke Station on the far side of the Moon has not yet been officially acknowledged by any UN member nation, everything I discuss here today is off the record and will most likely be classified by your respective governments. I'm not certain how much longer that will be the case; however, Catalyst Corporation is, for the moment, maintaining this secrecy as a gesture of goodwill and to allow Earth governments time to prepare their public response. Please note that Catalyst does not acknowledge any legal requirement to maintain such secrecy."

There was some murmuring in the crowd. Representatives from many nations were present—including those with observers already on board Clarke Station (the US, Canada, Russia, China, India, and Germany), but also attendees from France, the UK, Brazil, Japan, Australia, New Zealand, South Korea, Norway, as well as representatives from Space Titan companies: Starion, Zephyr, and Celestial Robotics, among others. Rochat noticed administrators and executives from major space agencies—including Erika Lisowski of NASA—standing along the back wall.

"My purpose here today is to inform government and corporate stakeholders of recent developments concerning the Cislunar Commodity Exchange headquartered on Clarke Station at EM-L2."

More murmuring.

One man said, "That is not a lawful organization."

"If I may continue . . ."

Another man shouted, "Mr. Rochat, can you comment on the recent death on Clarke Station and discuss the circumstances—?"

"Please hold your questions until I finish the briefing. Thank you." He glanced down at his notes, although in truth he did so for effect. He had today's agenda committed to memory.

He looked out at the expectant, though mostly unfriendly faces. "As the first fully off-world decentralized autonomous organization—or DAO—the Cislunar Commodity Exchange—hereafter the 'CCE'—is asserting sovereignty over its operations in deep space and is establishing a blockchain ledger and legal framework for its market participants. The CCE blockchain as well as its transaction and settlement network will be maintained entirely off-world and, thus, not regulated by Earth institutions."

Now discussions really broke out in the crowd.

Rochat spoke over them. "The details of the CCE's legal framework will be made available to you in writing at the conclusion of this briefing. A basic tenet of that framework will be a commitment to abide by the Universal Declaration of Human Rights—as well as the Artemis Accords and international maritime law, herein referenced as starting points for further legal precedents in deep space."

He paused to let it sink in. "As a blockchain-based organization, the CCE will maintain indelible records of asset ownership off-world via non-fungible tokens and will conduct all financial transactions in its native cryptocurrency, the lūna coin. The number of lūna coins will be set by DAO governance token holders and backed by intrinsically valuable off-world commodities, energy, products, and services contained within the CCE marketplace. This issuance design is intended to produce relative stability vis-à-vis Earth markets, with creation of lūna coins naturally throttled by the time-to-market of newly available resources and energy, which allows for predictable and sustainable growth.

"Governance of the CCE itself will also be managed by DAO token holders—the majority of whom currently reside on Clarke Station. However, as the CCE's capitalization and transaction volume increases, so, too, will governance tokens, and the governance stakeholder population."

There was a steady background discussion now, but Rochat raised his voice over it to continue. "All business transacted within the framework of the CCE will be denominated in lūnas, and the volume of trade as well as the derivatives and futures market at the CCE will be dictated by the resources available there. Quite simply, the CCE has the most robust commercial facilities and capabilities in deep space, and thus, it will be an ideal location for space market participants. Likewise, as a DAO, the CCE is a transparent, equitable, and international marketplace with clear rules ensured by the blockchain protocol itself—cryptographically—and not tied to the political goals of any sovereign Earth nation state."

He scanned the room. "A founding principle of the CCE is that the entire population of Earth should benefit from space industry, not merely a few billionaires and powerful nations. We believe that the participation of the world's people in developing cislunar industry will engender the trust and goodwill necessary for humanity to think and act globally and thus to reach the next stage of civilization's development.

"To facilitate this, a key function of the CCE blockchain will be smart contracts built into the protocol that provide the opportunity for anyone on Earth to directly earn lūna coins, or a fraction thereof, with a modest local investment in renewable energy and off-the-shelf equipment, utilizing our CarbonExchange smart contract, which rewards removal of atmospheric CO_2—based on a reverse bonding curve, relative to three hundred fifty parts per million—and which pays in lūna coins for each ton of CO_2 sequestered using solar, wind, or other green energy and delivered to a CCE signatory. Payment is also modulated to some degree by location, so as to encourage geographically distributed carbon sequestration."

The attendees scribbled notes, although several now raised their hands.

Rochat continued. "Importantly, lūna coins *cannot* be purchased. They must instead be earned either through CCE smart contracts or by having a business listed on the CCE, and subsequently attracting native lūna investment in deep space. No amount in fiat currency will obtain entrance to the

CCE marketplace. This compartmentalization between the Earth and the deep space economy is entirely deliberate and meant to prevent monopolization of the cislunar frontier by a few powerful, Earth-based financial interests or sovereign powers and to instead foster a broad-based, global prosperity for cislunar industry.

"Governance tokens, by contrast, can only be earned through long-term, reliable performance within the CCE's smart contract ecosystem. That is to say, those who consistently support the network and its functions earn the right to participate in its governance."

He looked out at the attendees. "I will now address any questions you may have."

Dozens of people put up their hands, with one of them calling out, "Is Catalyst Corporation in charge of this Cislunar Commodity Exchange—and as CEO of Catalyst, are you in effect 'king' there?"

There was a smattering of laughter.

Rochat shook his head. "No. I am not a king. Catalyst Corporation is a Luxembourg-based company with a subsidiary listed on the CCE; however, Catalyst does not run the CCE. Nor does anyone. As I said, it is a DAO." He pointed. "Next question."

A woman asked, "Why would anyone spend real money to remove CO_2 from the atmosphere, only to receive these worthless lūna coins of yours in payment?"

"Lūna coins are the only currency accepted at the CCE and they are backed by intrinsically valuable commodities, energy, value-added products, or services—or an investment stake in CCE-listed companies. And since the CCE is the largest single marketplace in deep space, we are confident the lūna coin will have inherent value—particularly if economic systems here on Earth fall into recession or worse. And once completed, Clarke Station will make it possible for astropreneurs to have access to long-term habitation as well as in situ resources and energy in deep space, creating myriad, unknowable benefits. Space startups could innovate entire new industries and markets we can't yet foresee. The idea is to have the broadest number of human beings possible invested and participating in space commerce. We want everyone here on Earth to gain a direct benefit from space."

A man called out, "What happens if someone shuts down your off-world data centers?"

Rochat nodded. "Again, we anticipate Earth nations will have a vested interest in the success of the CCE, especially as it helps them address climate change through CO_2 removal and also provides opportunities for stable investment to their citizens. That said, our network is designed for resilience and is beyond direct control by Earth authorities."

"But not beyond missiles."

"I believe I've answered your question."

Another man asked, "Will this CCE of yours tax off-world income?"

"At the moment we operate under a policy of 'zero-g, zero tax'; however, the blockchain itself will be maintained by transaction fees set by the market—as is the case with cryptocurrencies here on Earth. Of course, DAO token holders could vote to change this in the future."

Another attendee asked, "Mr. Rochat, I'm given to understand the CCE has licensed or purchased spacecraft and robotic equipment from George Burkette's company, Starion, as well as Alan Goff's Celestial Robotics, and also mining interest Cahill Heavy Industries. Last time I checked, they're owned by billionaires. Are these companies investors in this CCE?"

"There are no 'investors' per se in the CCE. There are DAO token holders, but these tokens are earned by creating and maintaining the network. As for Burkette, Goff, and Cahill: prototype equipment was provided free or at cost to the CCE-listed Catalyst Corporation in order to prove the equipment's capabilities in the field—though, I anticipate Catalyst will secure a leasing or purchase agreement with these Earth companies at some point. But they are not investors."

"And one of the Kangaroo landers recently crashed?"

Rochat replied, "Yes. However, Starion has another lander available, and we hope to have it sent up in a few weeks—once we can find space on a rocket."

A government minister said, "What's to stop Space Titans like Jack Macy outcompeting you in space—driving you out of business?"

There was another smattering of laughter.

Rochat grimaced. "I appreciate your concern. However, the significant lead enjoyed by the CCE in deep space, we believe, will make Macy's plans—Mars colonization in particular—moot. I hardly need to point out to the individuals in this room why progress with crewed deep space missions has not been a priority. Governments and investors have had to grapple with the 'Long Emergency' of climate change, and a mission to Mars does not assist that effort. It's our hope that CCE's CarbonExchange smart contract will incentivize sequestration of atmospheric CO_2 and help to alleviate that emergency—as well as usher in an era of global prosperity."

Rochat gazed out at his audience of still mostly skeptical faces before slipping his notes into his jacket pocket. "Thank you for your time today."

He then turned and left as the room erupted with more shouted questions.

CHAPTER 29

LOC/LOM

CLARKE STATION POPULATION: 23
DAYS TO RYUGU DEPARTURE: 998

J ames Tighe and Priya Chindarkar operated Talos robots close to each other on the lunar surface, electron-welding the metal framework for one of the mass-driver pylons. Their optics tinted automatically as the welder flared. Tighe then inspected his weld, and satisfied, looked up.

They were almost a hundred meters downrange from Morra Base now, slightly ahead of the mass-driver barrel, which was, week after week, being extended atop a growing number of pylons. As Tighe went to retrieve another metal brace from a pile close at hand, he looked up to regard the Earth. It hung in the black sky where it always was.

In the past several months he'd learned that the Earth appeared opposite in phase on the lunar surface from how the Moon would appear on Earth; thus, when the Moon was full on Earth, a "new Earth" was visible in the lunar sky, with the Earth's surface in complete shadow. At the moment, a "full Earth" loomed overhead, its entire swirling hemisphere illuminated.

The inviting deep blue of its oceans were a welcome relief from the unrelenting grays and blacks of the lunar surface. However, dark gray was also spreading lately across Earth's northern latitudes, where it was high summer.

Chindarkar's robot joined Tighe in gazing up at the Earth.

A vast shroud of wildfire smoke, visible even from a quarter-million miles away, spread over the boreal forests of Russia and Canada—an annual disaster that had come to be known as the "crown of fire." Millions of acres of forest back on Earth were ablaze.

Chindarkar's robot turned to him, and he turned to regard her robot as well. Nothing needed to be said. The urgency was obvious. It was urgent that they finish the mass-driver. It was urgent that they build a rescue craft. It was urgent for nations of Earth to take action on climate change. Everything was urgent. It was numbing.

Suddenly Jin's voice spoke close at hand, in real life. "J.T. Priya. Log off and come with me. This is an emergency."

Shit. Tighe switched off the VR mode on his crystal and turned to see Jin. Priya was standing up just behind him.

She asked, "What is it, Han?"

He motioned. "Just follow me. Please."

He brought them downstairs to H1 and then toward the far end of South Hab, where he entered a code for the data center—Ramón's domain—and pushed through the security door. Tighe and Chindarkar followed him inside.

Sevastian Yakovlev and Ramón Marín were already waiting in the chilly space. There was barely room for them all to stand amid the racks of servers.

Tighe looked around. "Why are we meeting in here?"

"To avoid eavesdroppers." Jin stood at the head of the aisle. "There has been an incident with Transit-02. We've lost all contact."

Tighe knew only that both of Clarke Station's transit crafts had been sent out uncrewed and remotely piloted to rendezvous with the lunar cycler in order to bring back Yellow Team. It would be the first new crew to arrive in almost five months. "Can you get a visual from Transit-01?"

Jin nodded grimly.

Chindarkar asked, "What's happened?"

Jin manipulated an unseen UI and brought up a virtual video image on their private AR layer. The image showed a spacecraft tumbling erratically—fast enough to blur with motion. It looked like every nightmare about space travel come true.

"What the hell . . . ?"

Yak said, "Mission control examined telemetry log. Forward port thruster misfired and did not stop until propellant tank was empty. This put spacecraft into couple-hundred RPM spin."

"Jesus."

Chindarkar studied the image. "We have to help them."

"They are still 5,000 kilometers away."

Jin shook his head. "Gabriel tells us the crew is experiencing 15 to 20 g's, and the irregular spin means they are being tumbled around inside. No one could survive that."

"You're not just going to leave them out there?"

"Their trajectory is bringing them away from us. And there is nothing we can do—their comm antennas have sheared off. We cannot approach it in that spin. It will destroy any craft that comes in contact with it. Mission control says the crew tumbling inside will eventually dampen the spin, but that may take days or weeks. They have declared the crew and the spacecraft lost."

They all stood in silence for several moments, contemplating the horrifying implications.

Tighe studied the image. "Transit-01 is still en route to Clarke Station?"

Yak answered, "Yes. ETA is six hours."

"Does that crew know about this?"

"Yes. They are badly shaken."

Chindarkar was still processing the news. "How many did we lose on Transit-02?"

Jin said, "Four. Berkovich, roboticist. Sventler, life support specialist."

"Another life support specialist? It's like that position is cursed."

"Miller, biologist. And Sartre, geologist."

Chindarkar winced. "I remember her from Ascension."

"Lukas will deal with Earth authorities, and next of kin will be notified." Jin checked the time. "Let us hope Transit-01 arrives safely. Word will get out when they do, and we need to be ready for that—and to receive them."

They all nodded in agreement.

Hours later, Transit-01 docked safely at Clarke Station, and the three survivors of Yellow Team came aboard. The least affected was a Canadian systems analyst named Grant Mason—who to Tighe's surprise seemed to know Chelsie Birk. Birk hugged Mason in condolence for his team's loss. The other two arrivals, a Pakistani-British metallurgist named Fatima Patel, and an Indian chemical engineer named Anaisha Chaudri were deeply distraught at the loss of their teammates.

While mission control investigated the cause of the Transit-02 malfunction, Transit-01, their sole remaining transit spacecraft, was restricted from carrying a human crew. This meant no one was leaving or arriving at Clarke Station until the investigation was completed.

Jin declared, "If necessary, we will use a Talos robot to retrieve supplies and provisions from the cycler. Hopefully mission control's review finishes soon and the cause is found. In the meantime, Kerner's team will need to produce a replacement transit spacecraft."

As the weeks went by, all teams continued their telepresence work on Clarke Station's refinery as well as mass-driver systems down at Morra Base. Kerner's team deposed the hull and hatches of a replacement for the lost transit spacecraft, along with its propulsion module. These components cut into the limited stock of electronics and replacement parts on board, to become "Transit-03." And all of it consumed crew hours that could have been used to work on the mass-driver.

The out-of-control Transit-02 spacecraft, meanwhile, continued on its wide lunar orbit, marked as a navigational hazard on charts and as a grave for its crew. The horror of it startled Tighe anew each time he thought of it. They would need to retrieve that crew one day.

A replacement for the crashed Kangaroo lander, meanwhile, arrived a few weeks later from Burkette's company—along with enough advanced components to produce two additional landers in situ. These were sent up by rocket directly from Earth, and the new lander, dubbed *SK-Charlie*, combined with the replacement transit spacecraft, soon allowed lunar surface operations to resume.

Tighe found himself swimming with a full rebreather mask and aquaflash lights deep within a cave. He heard an alert sounding and glanced at his dive computer. It showed he was at a depth of nearly 200 meters—but was breathing nitrox instead of heliox-14. He tried to adjust the mix but couldn't concentrate. He struggled for breath and then looked upward to see a decompression station hanging by a rope line on the cliff wall. The alarm continued to sound in his earpiece. He strove to reach the gas bottles dangling from the rope above, when a familiar voice came in over his radio.

Richard Oberhaus, his longtime dive mentor, spoke to him calmly. "James, help me."

Tighe looked down to see Oberhaus just below him, above a yawning darkness, his calm expression visible in a full face mask. His voice was not distorted by helium, but came through in its rich baritone. Oberhaus's gloved hand reached for Tighe.

"I need your help."

But Tighe did not help him. Instead, he pushed off of Oberhaus, propelling himself upward even as he pushed his mentor down, into the blackness below them.

"James! Help me!"

Tighe continued to push off Oberhaus, striving for a light now above him.

And then Tighe woke up gasping for air. Covered in sweat.

He wept for a few moments before looking around at his cramped quarters—and finally realized where he was. An alarm was sounding somewhere still. And then he noticed it was coming from his crystal headset on the nightstand. He put the glasses on and immediately saw the emergency alert.

Tighe spoke into the channel. "What's going on? What's wrong?"

Jin's voice came back almost immediately. "*J.T., come to the data center. Now!*"

Tighe raced down the H1 corridor toward the closed data center door at the far end, but then Chelsie Birk and the new arrival, Grant Mason, suddenly came out from an open cabin door, blocking his way. In a scene as surreal as the nightmare he'd just left, both of them held printed steel knives that looked like they'd been meticulously sharpened. The blades gleamed in the soft LED light.

Tighe slowed. "What the hell . . . ?"

Birk lowered her knife and motioned for Mason to do the same. "Mr. Tighe. Don't be alarmed. We're station security. The others are waiting for you in the data center." She moved to unlock the door and made way for him. "If you please."

Tighe hesitated, and then moved past. "Security? Since when do we have security?"

Birk said, "Since I got on board." She gestured to Mason. "Grant is my partner."

Mason nodded. "Hey."

Tighe pushed through the data center door and was relieved to see Jin,

Chindarkar, and Yak. Ramón Marín lurked in the background as well. "What in the hell is going on? Why are Chelsie and Grant carrying knives?"

Jin said, "We are in lockdown. The *Rosette* has just been hijacked. It was swinging through low Earth orbit and scheduled to take on supplies, but two unidentified spacecraft showed up instead. They docked with the *Rosette* in LEO and a dozen armed people boarded her."

A virtual screen appeared, showing live video from inside the *Rosette*. Intruders in unmarked flight suits and tinted helmets, long guns slung, moved about the craft. They were transferring gear into the cycler, clearly preparing for a journey.

"You have got to be shitting me." Tighe looked to each of them in turn and realized they were deadly serious.

Yak said, "They will be at L2 within a week. And they can use their capsules to reach Clarke Station from there."

Jin spoke over the comm link. "Lukas, do we know who is behind this?"

Lukas Rochat's voice responded, *"No. Right now Russia, the US, and China are all accusing one another and claiming no knowledge."*

Chindarkar muttered, "Little green men . . ."

"We might be able to figure out where the spacecraft launched from later, but right now we can't trust anyone."

Chindarkar asked, "Should we be guarding the international observers on board?"

Jin said, "Chelsie woke them all, announced the situation, and gave them instructions to guard one another. The thinking is that they cannot all be responsible."

The normally shy Marín spoke up. "Taiwo tells me that our space assets are under sustained cyberattack at the moment. The Transit-02 malfunction was apparently a successful proof of concept."

Chindarkar turned on him. "You're saying the Transit-02 crew was murdered?"

"I'm saying this is an orchestrated campaign against us."

Lukas answered, *"Taiwo's people found the exploit and are working to patch our flight control systems. A postmortem showed that a flaw was exploited to fire the thruster that caused the fatal spin. Fortunately they've patched the* Rosette. *We were in the middle of implementing fixes else-*

where when this hijacking occurred. Whoever is behind this believes they can cripple our spacecraft and then take Clarke Station by force while we are helpless."

Tighe watched the intruders moving around the *Rosette*. They were busy pulling panels and going through wiring. "We need to stop that cycler."

"Agreed." Jin looked to Chindarkar and Yak. "But do we all agree on that— even if it means losing the *Rosette*?"

After exchanging searching looks, they all nodded.

Jin then spoke over the comm link. "Clarke Station to mission control. Gabriel, do you read?"

"We copy you, Han."

"Do we still have control of the *Rosette*?"

"Affirmative. The hijackers knocked down our laser transceiver, but we still have a backup radio antenna. I don't know for how long."

"And they still have their own reentry capsules docked, correct?"

"Affirmative."

"Then I want you to de-orbit the *Rosette*. Empty the tanks on a retro burn, and bring it down into Earth's atmosphere while it's still at periapsis."

Chindarkar said, "Can't we just send it into an altered orbit? If we destroy the *Rosette*, we'll have no means of resupply."

Yak shook his head. "They are clearly relying on *Rosette* to house their strike team. We must deny them this shelter, or they might refuel in orbit and resend it."

"We have no choice, Priya." Tighe gestured to the screen. "Getting rid of it could buy us time to complete our work up here."

She contemplated this and then nodded once more.

Jin said, "Do you copy my last, Gabriel? De-orbit the *Rosette* immediately."

There was a pause before Lacroix's voice came back. *"Wilco, Han. Reorienting* Rosette *and commencing retro burn . . . now."*

They all watched the video as the occupants of the *Rosette* were suddenly flung about in microgravity, sliding sideways as the craft rotated to position its engines for a retro burn. Shortly thereafter, they were all slammed toward the stern, ripping apart the interior partition grills as they "fell" toward the soft, inflated hull.

Lacroix's voice confirmed, "Rosette *in retro burn. Throttle at 100 percent.*" A pause. "*It will be parabolic in approximately . . . four minutes.*"

Yak was already bringing up a projection of the *Rosette*'s orbital trajectory. He gestured to an ellipse that was shrinking back away from the Moon, going down, down, down. "They will now not reach Moon. We are safe from them."

"For now," Tighe added.

Chindarkar pointed at the video feed. The hijackers were already moving toward the exit hatches—returning to their boarding craft. "Looks like they did the math, too."

In a few minutes the invaders had all exited the *Rosette*, but by then the cycler was already doomed to Earth reentry.

Jin leaned back against the computer racks and rubbed his face. "Priya is right; we now have no method of resupply."

Tighe said, "Yes, but we have some provisions, and they didn't render us helpless." He looked around. "So Taiwo—the oga from Lagos—his gang rooted out this cyberattack on us?"

Yak answered, "*Da*, but also . . ." He thumbed toward Marín. "Ramón helped to implement security fixes."

Marín looked uncertainly at the Gold Team members. "It's critical that Earth powers not gain control of this station or our space assets. I only did what was necessary to prevent that."

Tighe felt a measure of shame about his suspicions toward Marín. He extended his hand. "Good job, Ramón."

The others shook Marín's hand and patted him on the shoulder as well.

Chindarkar took another look at the video inset, which still showed the *Rosette* in full retro burn. She looked wistful. "There goes a bit of history."

Tighe nodded. "It isn't going to do any damage coming down, is it?"

Jin watched the screen. "It's one of Halser's old inflatables. Lightweight. It should burn up on reentry."

Tighe leaned against the computer rack next to Jin. "Well, I guess we're all up here for the duration, then."

CHAPTER 30

LEML-Mark-I

T hree and a half months after the de-orbiting of the *Rosette*, the crew of Clarke Station was running low on provisions, but given the fate of Transit-02 and the cycler, they had not permitted any resupply craft to draw near. The plan was to power through and finish the mass-driver first.

Not everyone was waiting, though. Word was that billionaire Jack Macy was now building, at his own cost, a Galleon rocket to replace the *Rosette* lunar cycler—and without cooperation from either Catalyst Corporation or the CCE. He clearly hoped to be in a position to capitalize on travel to and from the Moon if the mass-driver succeeded, making the CCE reliant on his service.

But as James Tighe had once said, *It's a free universe.*

The key to preserving their security was enforcing the 200-meter exclusion zone around Clarke Station, and maintaining control of their remotely piloted spacecraft was critical to this. Therefore, the loss of the newest Kangaroo lander, *SK-Charlie*, in a crash south of Morra Base mere weeks after the *Rosette* hijacking set everyone on edge. However, the cause was quickly traced not to sabotage but to a fuel pump failure, and the fact that an invasion of "little green men" had not been reattempted seemed to indicate that Taiwo's and Marín's cyber defenses were, for the moment, holding.

Still, a replacement *SK-Delta* lander with redesigned fuel pumps had had to be constructed in addition to their many other tasks.

The months of grueling telepresence work that followed had driven the team at Clarke Station to the brink of exhaustion. Priya Chindarkar was heartily sick of looking at virtual imagery—despite their being rendered in fully volumetric light fields with the latest technology. It was beginning to wear her down. Visions of the Moon's surface lingered in her dreams, and she occasionally had waking hallucinations that she was bouncing across its surface, having actually *become* a Talos robot.

And by now their machines were breaking down. Two of the four Talos robots were inoperable and two of the four Badgers had burnt-out electric motors, with no replacements on the surface or on station. Several of the other robots were missing noncritical parts or had suffered damage. Clarke Station itself was beginning to smell rather ripe, with Monica Balter and the Russian observer, Colonel Evgeni Voloshin, suffering some sort of chronic illness.

Holstad's hull experiment with *Cladosporium sphaerospermum* radiotrophic fungi was ruled out as a source—and in fact, Holstad's fungi colony within the double hull had reduced ambient radiation inside the habs by nearly half. The specialized fungi were thriving in deep space and were a highly successful experiment by all accounts.

Instead, the source of the contamination was traced to bacteria in the air handling system—microbiota shed by the human occupants, primarily staphylococci and enterobacteria, which had been accumulating in the ducts. Cleaning them out soon resolved Balter's and Voloshin's symptoms.

Meanwhile, the chemists had been busy with the engineers and mission control completing and testing an upsized copy of the asteroid mining ship *Konstantin*'s in-space regolith refinery—replete with kilometers of piping. The new refinery was located beyond Clarke Station's docking bay, forward of the thermal power plant on the station's nonrotating axis.

Eventually, system by system, the mass-driver and the supporting structures at Morra Base began to come together. Badger robots were now autonomously harvesting regolith with rolling bucket drums and unloading them into a chute in the side of the Brick House. The harvested lunar regolith was compressed into cylinders and near-instantly melted by an induction coil furnace—any volatiles captured and stored. Over the last several weeks, they'd created a stockpile of hundreds of regolith cylinders in the brickyard.

In normal operation, the cylinders would be tipped into the magazine of the mass-driver; however, the mass-driver itself had not yet fired.

Today, that was about to change.

Weary from days of double shifts, Chindarkar brought her Talos robot to a stop nearly a kilometer and a half away from the Launch House. She then turned to gaze down the length of Ecklund's newly completed mass-driver. It resembled a meter-thick pipeline, shielded from the sunlight by a curving metallic sheath, as it traversed a series of moonquake-absorbing scissor trusses of various heights. These smoothed out the gentle undulation of the lunar maria. Running to either side of the mass-driver barrel were liquid nitrogen pipes and conduits containing power and switching equipment that would trigger the thousands of induction coils within the barrel in a precise sequence—theoretically accelerating a regolith core down the 1.39-kilometer barrel in just over a second, where, molten hot from the energy of acceleration, it would leave the muzzle at 2.53 kilometers a second—on a trajectory into orbit and up to EM-L2.

Ecklund's Talos robot—the only other functioning unit available—came up alongside Chindarkar's. Nearby, in the ops room, she heard Ecklund sigh. "I can't believe it. It's been so many years since I designed this. Such a long, difficult journey to reach this moment."

The team had spent the past two days running diagnostics, testing power systems, and making last-minute calibrations. However, the seemingly endless punch list had finally come to an end.

"After all these months, that is one beautiful sight." Chindarkar's robot pulled from its tool bag a small polymer sphere, which began to steam the moment it was exposed to sunlight. "Bob, we had a tradition out at Ryugu, whenever we launched ships . . ." She carefully extended the smoking sphere to Ecklund's robot.

"What the hell is that? It looks like a bomb."

"It's a bulb of liquid nitrogen. A bottle of champagne isn't practical out here. So, we typically christened new equipment with these."

Ecklund carefully accepted the sphere. "Okay . . ." He looked toward one of the sulfur concrete footings at the base of a nearby pylon. Raising the bulb, he said, "I hereby christen this humankind's first lunar mass-driver, the LEML-Mark-I." At which point he hurled the sphere at the footing, where it exploded with a dramatic and steaming splash. "Ha! That *is* a pretty good stand-in for champagne."

Crew members around Chindarkar in the ops room on Clarke Station applauded. Voices called out, "Speech! Speech!"

Ecklund's robot turned to study the lunar desolation all around him. "Well, I'm a man of few words . . ."

A woman's voice: "Liar!"

More laughter.

"Okay, then. I just want to say that I know how incredibly challenging it's been for us all to be out here so long, away from families and friends." He paused. "And then there are those who perished in this effort and who will never see their loved ones again. We should dedicate this day to them." He looked up. "I'm so grateful—to you, Priya, James, Han, Sevastian. To Julian and Gabriel. To everyone on this team." He turned searchingly. "And to you, Lynne. This machine is the realization of my life's work, and I know you will do great things with the potential it brings. I am so very grateful. For all of this."

Everyone applauded.

Chindarkar's robot gripped Ecklund's robot and turned him downrange, where they both stared at the black sky and the stark silhouette of lunar terrain to the east. "What do you say we fire this cannon?"

More cheers and applause sounded in the ops room.

Ecklund's robot nodded. "It's about that time." He started poking at virtual, unseen interfaces. "Shot one loaded. Power good. Coil lights green. We are ready to fire, mission control."

"All lights are green here, too, Bob. You are cleared to fire."

He took a deep breath. "And . . . three, two, one . . . fire!"

Jin's voice near Tighe said, "Activating power sequence . . ."

At first Chindarkar thought it was exhaustion catching up with her, but the shocked gasps from the invisible audience around her in the ops center confirmed that something unexpected had occurred. Chindarkar's VR display was suddenly a whirling storm of electrical snow.

She switched her crystal glasses into normal AR mode and looked around at the horrified crowd staring at a virtual big screen nearby. Chindarkar noticed that Ecklund was still staring into his VR glasses—like a zombie. Up on the big screen she saw a view from one of the Badger robots that Yak had piloted up onto the slope of Cape Bruce for a good vantage of the world's first lunar mass-driver shot.

But instead of a clear view, there was a column of lunar dust obscuring the last hundred meters or so of mass-driver barrel. A couple of the pylon supports were torn apart, with white plumes of liquid nitrogen spilling out across the land.

A voice called out, "Cut the nitrogen feed!"

"Powering down the LEML."

Chindarkar looked back toward Ecklund and could see Lynne Holstad near him now. Holstad removed Ecklund's opaque crystal headset, and he covered his face with his hands, shaking his head.

Holstad hugged him. "Bob, you'll fix it. You'll make it work."

Mission control began an immediate investigation. Meanwhile, it was determined that most of Morra Base was still operational; however, footage from surveillance cameras on both the Launch House and the Brick House confirmed that the mass-driver suffered catastrophic damage at its far end.

Worse still, both the remaining operational Talos robots had gone offline in the malfunction; their recorded footage and temperature log indicated they were probably in the spill stream of liquid nitrogen that poured out of the mass-driver's severed piping. After most of it had evaporated away, both the robots were spotted from Cape Bruce under the twisted wreckage. Neither responded to commands. They were both "dead."

Chindarkar and the rest of the team sat in the same ops center where they'd worked for months, now gathered like a grief support group.

Jin finally began the proceeding. "This is not the first setback we have faced. It is not good, but we need to figure out what happened, come up with a fix, and try again."

Yak said, "We have no Talos robots. We have only two Badgers on surface, and with these we cannot fix mass-driver."

Jin nodded. "Then we need to fix some Talos robots."

Tighe countered, "We can't—not without at least one working Talos on the lunar surface. Even then, we might not have the parts. They'll need to be brought back here."

Chindarkar turned toward him. "Or we get Alan Goff to send us more."

Jin said, "That means negotiations with Celestial Robotics and also scheduling a rocket with either Burkette or Macy, and prepping the payload for launch."

Yak added, "It would take months."

Tighe said, "Time we don't have."

Chindarkar replied, "We have almost two and a half years until Ryugu's return."

"And we *had* four years when we started. Where are we now?"

She gestured around them. "We're on the biggest space station ever built, J.T., at the edge of Earth's gravity well, with a 50-megawatt solar power satellite, and a nearly finished mass-driver on the lunar surface."

"You mean a 90 *percent unfinished* space station, and have you looked at the supply yard lately? We're running out of building materials, Priya. I'd be amazed if we have 20 tons of metal left, and unless we can finish this station, you can forget building a rescue ship in time to save Isabel and Ade. We need dozens more experts up here." Tighe pointed at a live virtual image of Earth and the Moon projected onto the hab wall. "Not to mention the fact that there are powers down there itching to take all of this away from us."

Yak said, "And we still must finalize rescue ship design and then actually build it."

Tighe turned back to Chindarkar. "That two and a half years will pass before you know it. We can't afford to sit on our hands for months waiting for Goff."

Jin asked, "Then what do you suggest?"

"We go down there ourselves, retrieve the robots, and then fix them. Hell, I'll go."

Jin held up a hand. "Hang on. We should find out what happened first. Mission control is still going through the footage and event logs—trying to determine why the mass-driver failed."

Ecklund was shaking his head. "I've been going through the logs, too. Everything was nominal . . . until it wasn't." He shrugged. "I don't have an answer from up here."

Jin said, "We'll need to start rebuilding coils. And some pylons. And piping."

Tighe shook his head. "Like I said: we are running low on raw materials. We're going to need to recycle what we've got down there. Steel especially." He looked around the South Hab. "And we've got a lot of systems running on yellow up here as it is."

Jin pondered this. "We may have to consider reducing head count on the station for safety reasons."

Yak countered. "How? Lunar cycler is gone."

"We could conceivably repurpose the transit craft for Earth return—if necessary."

Tighe shot a look at him. "We're already a month behind schedule. A lower head count and loss of the transit craft would make the remaining work even harder to complete in time."

Chindarkar said, "It's fine if the four of us want to take risks, J.T., but we shouldn't decide that for everyone else."

Jin said, "Let us see what mission control finds, and we will—"

Ecklund interjected. "I don't think they're going to find anything."

Everyone looked toward Ecklund.

He threw up his hands. "I designed all those sensors. I designed that system. I've been going through it, and I just don't see what went wrong."

Jin said, "That is why you should not be the one looking for the cause. You are too close to this, Bob."

"I need to see the LEML. I need to put the pieces together."

"We don't have robots capable of even reaching the damaged section right now."

Tighe replied, "Then let's go get them." He turned to Chindarkar. "Priya, if I bring you Talos robots, can you fix them?"

Chindarkar considered their various damage states and after a moment she nodded. "Probably. At least one of them, if I cannibalize parts—but going down to the lunar surface in person is a major risk."

"We can't wait. Ryugu certainly won't."

Ecklund took a deep breath. "And I need to go down and examine the site."

Jin was already shaking his head. "We can't risk losing you, Bob."

Ecklund pointed at the screen. "My work is done if I can't fix this. The system is built. I need to find out where it's going wrong, and I can't do that from here."

Jin turned to Chindarkar. "How long for you to fix at least one of the Talos robots?"

"I don't know. It might be fast. It might take weeks. Or not at all. It depends on how badly damaged they are."

Yak said, "Add to that three days travel down to lunar surface. Then three up. Then three down again once they are fixed."

Tighe said, "We don't have the time. Maybe we just fix the damn LEML ourselves."

Jin turned to Tighe. "We go down. We retrieve the robots. That's it."

Ecklund said, "And I go to inspect the site." He held up his hands as Jin made to object. "I went through Ascension training and orbital certification. I know how to use an EMU. We have two suits on board. We need to solve this problem, Han. And I'm telling you, mission control isn't going to find the problem from back on Earth because there's no problem in the logs. But I know I can find the problem in person. You saw what I did with Clarke Station's plumbing system."

Jin stared at Ecklund for several moments.

Ecklund said, "I don't especially want to go to the Moon in person, but it's where the mass-driver is. Let me fix it."

Jin pondered this a moment more until finally nodding. "You will inspect it to find the fault—no more. And to make certain of that, I will go with you."

Tighe said, "While I collect the Talos robots."

Chindarkar felt shock at the idea of the three of them going down all at once. "One person was bad enough—but three?"

Jin said, "We never send anyone alone. You know that. And Bob has no real experience—no offense, Bob. So he doesn't count." He looked to her, grim-faced. "Priya, you are in charge. If anything happens to us . . ." He didn't complete the sentence. Instead he turned to Tighe and Ecklund. "It is three days down and three days back. Pack only what you need."

Less than twenty-four hours later, Chindarkar walked with Jin, Tighe, and Ecklund through the South Hab. All three men carried a pack along with extra provisions. Tighe and Jin also wore their MCP suits and carried their helmets.

Ecklund looked toward Holstad's modest lab just a short distance from the elevator. "Hang on a moment, guys."

Tighe and Jin stopped. Chindarkar stood with them. It was common knowledge on board that Ecklund and Holstad were together now. Their late-in-life romance was considered charming by many—Chindarkar included.

Ecklund walked over to Holstad's tiny lab, where indigo-colored LED lights illuminated flats of seedlings, growing in narrow rows within aquaponic rigs, all wired with sensors. The space was fragrant with living plants, and the rest of the crew often visited there to breathe it in as well as to see organic, living things.

Even though it was barely five in the morning on board, Holstad was in her lab, her back facing Ecklund as he approached. She said, "Do you really need to go down there?"

"I believe I do, yes."

"You're not exactly young, Bob."

"Well . . ." He stepped into her field of view. "Lots of people my age lead full and active lives."

"This isn't a joke. We're talking about a space walk. In a 200-kilo EMU suit."

"It's one-sixth gravity down there—it'll be less strenuous than my standing here."

She just looked at him.

"I am certified. I've done the simulations."

"J.T. and Han do this for a living. They're veteran space explorers. They can do this without your—"

Ecklund took her hand. "Your confidence in me means everything."

"I do have confidence in you, but we should give the techs back on Earth time to sort through the data first."

"There's no time."

"Who says?" She looked past him toward Tighe, Jin, and Chindarkar. "Because they're in a rush to build something? To rescue their friends? Don't you count, too?"

He gestured to where some of the steel partition walls had been disassembled. "I see we're cannibalizing steel for other purposes now." He looked back at her. "Lynne, this station is running low on resources. Everyone here put their faith in me. Now it's time to prove that it wasn't misplaced."

"We can bring up more robots on a resupply flight."

"But there's no telling when that will be—and you know what the stakes are. Everything you're working on here . . ." He gestured to the nursery. ". . . This all depends on rapid expansion of capabilities here in space. If we fail at this, how long until someone tries again? How many years? Do we even have that time back down on Earth?"

She gripped his hand. "We have a few months, certainly. You don't have to go down there yourself. In person."

"This is everything I have been working toward my entire life. Like you, I need to see it through."

She pressed her forehead gently to his.

He lifted up her chin. "And I'm going to be smart about it."

She searched for words—then kissed him. Afterward she pressed her cheek to his, holding his hand tighter. "I know why we're both up here. Just be careful."

He held her close. "I will be." He stepped back to regard her. "See you in a week?"

She nodded. "Deal."

CHAPTER 31

Skin in the Game

J ames Tighe, Jin Han, and Robert Ecklund floated in the pressurized compartment of Clarke Station's docking bay. Tighe watched as Jin opened dual hatches to reveal the interior of Transit-03, the vehicle built to replace the one that had taken the lives of most of Yellow Team.

For their journey, mission control had docked a propulsion and service module to Transit-03's stern—to provide life support as well as the 1.3 kilometers per second of delta-v required to bring them to low lunar orbit and back again.

Likewise, a Kangaroo lunar lander had been docked via its upper hatch to the smaller, circular escape hatch in the side of the transit craft. Instead of the usual stuffed payload deck, the Kangaroo lander had what looked like a large metal propane tank bolted to its cargo area. This was the module for crewed lunar landings, and it had a couple of borosilicate windows in its hull. They would enter it through a hatch in the top—but only once they'd arrived in LLO. An exterior ladder ran from the crew module on the lander to the folded landing legs, and a heavy-duty space suit was bolted to the outside of the crew module—designed to be entered through an interior hatch in the back, just like the EVA suits they'd used at Ryugu (although this one was white instead of burnt orange in color). There was a second EMU back at Clarke Station, but the team didn't think the added weight on the lander (a few hundred kilos) was worth it; after all, EMUs had reliably served Tighe and Jin for years. Plus, they needed one on board Clarke Station in case of emergency.

All three of them soon floated inside Transit-03, and Jin closed the hatches.

Tighe examined the interior. "Home sweet home for the next few days."

It had been filled out with supplies sent up from Earth; first-aid kits, tools, emergency provisions, and emergency breathing apparatuses. The solar weather forecast indicated low risk of a coronal mass ejection (or CME), and he hoped that prediction was accurate because their "pop can" wouldn't shield them from much radiation.

Jin radioed mission control after they strapped in. "Transit-03 to mission control. We are 'go' for departure."

"Copy that, Transit-03. Prepare for undocking and initial maneuver."

There was a thud of detaching bolts, and then clamps moved the spacecraft away from the dock—finally rotating it to face the blackness of space beyond. And then the thrusters hissed, easing them out into that darkness.

As they slowly drifted away, they all three watched on virtual screens as Clarke Station came into view behind them. The incomplete skeleton of the station's girders underscored just how urgent their mission was. Tighe could see that almost the entirety of the *David Morra* tug had been consumed, and the *Nicole Clarke* was long gone. Just about everything they had brought back from Ryugu. There were bladder tanks of water ice, ammonia, nitrogen, and some cobalt, but little else remained.

From the expression on Jin's face, he appeared to be thinking the same thing. "Let us find the fault with the mass-driver, and bring back those robots."

Then Transit-03's rocket motor kicked in, pressing them back into their harnesses.

Over the next seventy-two hours, the transit craft orbited down toward and around the Moon, the Earth occasionally blocked from sight. Tighe tried to forget that this was the only human-rated module for the lander. If this one was damaged or failed, there was no easy way back to Clarke Station.

There was a human habitation at Morra Base—they'd built it from an inflatable polymer bag wired with heating elements to create a nickel CVD shell—which they had afterward buried beneath a mound of regolith, with a single airlock entrance. Though unfurnished (except for an oxygen generator, CO_2 scrubber, and heating unit), the surface habitat would be their redoubt in case of emergency, providing a place to await rescue—theoretically from Earth—if the lander failed them or was damaged.

The days in transit passed with Ecklund absorbed in reading through his own technical specifications for the mass-driver. Mission control's experts back on Earth hadn't discovered any obvious malfunction during the intervening days, only confirming the necessity of their journey.

Tighe and Jin spent the time checking their MCP suits, breathing apparatuses, and other equipment. On the lunar surface, they would be wearing jumpers, much like the Talos robots, which they would remove before going inside a hab or spacecraft (to keep the dangerously fine lunar regolith outside).

After a day or so, Tighe interrupted Ecklund's reading. "Bob, make sure to spend some time reviewing the EMU operation and emergency procedures. You don't want to be guessing in an emergency. Han and I know that system inside and out, if you have any questions."

Ecklund nodded and was soon reviewing boot-up procedures for the suit.

As the time passed, the lunar surface edged closer. At their target LLO altitude of 110 kilometers, they'd be orbiting the Moon every 120 minutes or so, and as that drew near, Tighe turned to Ecklund. "Start your prebreathe. Mark it: two hours."

Ecklund put on an oxygen mask and opened the valve on a portable tank. Because he was using the older EMU suit—which was not form-fitted like the MCPs—the interior of his suit had to be pressurized at less than one atmosphere with pure oxygen. That meant he'd have to let the nitrogen filter out of his blood before suiting up.

Mission control soon notified them it was time to decamp to the Kangaroo lander.

Before they did so, Tighe and Jin pulled on their MCP suits.

Then they all entered the lander and looked back longingly at the interior of the transit craft. It may have been small, but their new craft was even smaller. The Kangaroo's crew module shook as they moved about while securing the hatch.

Jin notified mission control that they'd strapped in, and with very little fanfare, the lander detached and eased away from Transit-03, heading toward the day side of the Moon ahead and below them.

Ecklund shifted anxiously in his harness as the lander's thrusters pulsed occasionally.

Jin said, "Touchdown at Morra Base estimated in T-minus eleven minutes."

Tighe added, "We've been landing these things for months, Bob."

Ecklund took a breath. "Except for those two that crashed."

"Well . . . this one is brand-new."

Glancing out the small windows, they could see the lunar surface rolling past more closely and quickly now. Tighe recalled this exact view months ago, when he'd first come here as a robot. However, today, he and the others had skin in the game.

Remain focused. Do the job and get back safe.

As the minutes ticked by, Ecklund seemed to tense up.

Jin finally looked at him. "Robert. Anxiety is optional. If we crash, no amount of worrying will save you. And if we do not crash, then worrying was not necessary."

Ecklund pondered this, and then seemed to unclench to some degree.

Mission control radioed, "SK-Delta, *prepare for retro burn in three . . . two . . .*"

The lander's fuel pump spun up, and its rocket motor fired—lurching the team against their harnesses.

"Here we go. Three minutes to touchdown."

As the rocket engine continued to fire, the passing lunar terrain slowed, and the lander angled vertically, beginning to descend toward a landscape that Tighe recognized quite well. There was the ridgeline of Cape Bruce. And beyond it Morra Base.

He was surprised by how extensive what they'd built appeared from this altitude. There was the square rectenna grid. The several buildings. The brickyard. And, of course, the mass-driver—the end of which appeared ruinous with debris scattered and twisted supports spiking upward.

Ecklund seemed to have forgotten his nervousness as he beheld his creation with his own eyes. "There she is . . ."

The lander's rocket was really ripping now, and the entire compartment vibrated. Their vertical descent continued to slow as the landscape rose up to meet them. In a few moments the berm walls around the landing pad edged up past their windows, and they felt a firm but soft touchdown, followed by the landing gear relaxing slightly lower. Then the motor cut off.

Mission control said, "*MECO. SK-Delta lander, soft touchdown. Welcome to Morra Base, gentlemen.*"

Tighe and Jin grabbed Ecklund by the shoulders and laughed. They were the first human beings at the site.

"This one should go up on the wall."

Ecklund held up his hand. "Hey, you feel that? Real gravity. Not much gravity, but it's real gravity for a change."

Jin checked a display. "Okay, it is morning. We have most of a lunar day. So suit up, Bob, and let us get on the ground."

After Ecklund had entered, sealed, and powered up his EMU suit, Tighe depressurized the crew compartment, then opened the lander's crew hatch. In a few moments he and Jin stood on the edge of the lander's payload platform—some 8 meters above the tiled landing pad. At this height they were able to see over the surrounding berms to the base buildings a kilometer away. They looked dark and abandoned—particularly with the shattered mass-driver in the distance.

"It's strange that I feel like I've already been here a thousand times."

They both climbed down the ladder and stepped onto the blackened launchpad tiles.

Tighe couldn't help but test out his MCP suit's flexibility. He felt so much more fully "here" on the Moon. "These suits really are incredible. I'm not going back to EMUs, if I can help it."

Ecklund's voice came in over the radio. *"Wonderful for you. Now, would you help the obsolete member of the party, please?"*

"Oh, sorry . . ." They headed over to the far side of the lander, and using the vessel's virtual UI, they extended davits, upon which Ecklund's suit hung. "Okay, check your wire line."

"Secure."

"Good. Now undock."

After a moment Ecklund said, *"Undocked."*

Tighe then lowered the winch lines, and they looked up as Ecklund, suspended like a marionette, gently descended onto the pad tiles beside them. In a moment he stood—though unsteadily.

Jin and Tighe grabbed him. "In this gravity that suit is still 30 kilos. Careful."

They then stood and all of them took in the surroundings.

Ecklund had activated the plenoptic camera array on his suit, and now from Tighe's perspective the opaque shell helmet was replaced with an AR projection as if Ecklund wore no helmet at all. Tighe could clearly see Ecklund's face as he stared out in wonder at the moonscape. "I'm standing on the freakin' Moon." He laughed.

"Yes, we are." It was finally sinking in to Tighe as well. He'd looked up at the Moon in the night sky all his life, and now here he was standing on it. "Dave would have liked this."

Jin nodded. "Yes. Especially Dave." He then motioned forward. "So let us get his base operational."

There was only one working Badger robot left, a scored and battered thing, and the Clarke Station ops center brought it out to meet them. However, instead of riding it, they unloaded their gear from the lander and piled it on a cargo rack as though it were a pack mule. Then the three humans started "walking" along the nearby road, with the Badger following close behind.

Tighe struggled to walk gracefully in the low gravity. "This is the drawback of having the Talos do my walking for me all this time." He stumbled, then got up. "It's harder than it looks."

Jin grunted. "I have seen Apollo films of this. Here . . ." He tried to skip along, but nearly fell.

Ecklund, much bulkier in his suit, tried it with more luck.

"There you go." Tighe imitated the hop and skip and soon they were all three moving briskly along the road on the way toward the base.

Their first order of business was to make sure the human habitation was actually habitable—since no human had ever been inside. They'd pressurized it with nitrogen, liquid tanks of which had been shipped down to cool the mass-driver. Then they added a life support unit that electrolyzed a supply of water into hydrogen and oxygen—pumping the oxygen into the habitat.

The hab was located a hundred meters or so away from the Brick House, and as they approached the barrow-like mound, it didn't look particularly hospitable. The airlock was on the far side, pointing away from other structures in case one of them exploded for any number of reasons (which Ecklund seemed happy to list). Next to the manual airlock pressure door was a docking bay for two EMU suits, and Tighe helped Ecklund back into the clips of the nearest.

"Don't exit your suit till we give the all-clear."

Ecklund gave a thumbs-up.

Jin then cycled the airlock. Once through the second door, they both activated their suits' helmet lights to illuminate a grim, bunker-like space resembling an overturned steel bowl. There were vents for life support and a heating unit, which someone at mission control had remotely activated.

Tighe took atmospheric readings. "The air is . . . well, it's okay. Temperature's not supercomfortable, but, hey." Tighe popped the seal on his helmet and took a deep breath. "It'll work."

Jin did the same. They then opened Ecklund's suit hatch, helping him out into the 10-meter-diameter circular room.

"Damn, it's cold in here! I'm getting back into my suit. Tell me when it's warmed up—and you've got the supplies off the Badger."

It took a good fifteen minutes to bring all the gear in through the airlock (including a cassette toilet), and by then Moon Hab had warmed considerably. Since they didn't have any furniture, they spread out sleeping bags and sat on those.

"Morra Base to mission control. We have occupied the Moon Hab and are secure. Will advise when we are ready to move."

"Copy that, Morra Base."

Ecklund brought up a shared virtual AR layer and started tossing images of the shattered and pre-shattered mass-driver. "So whatever failure occurred was on coil segment 212. It's difficult to tell from these images which section that is—since they're all jumbled on the surface and without power. If we can isolate the problem, we just need to rebuild three truss sections." He paused, examining the image. "The concrete footings don't look damaged." He looked up. "Let's eat something, rest up, then head out to survey the wreckage."

"Sounds good." Tighe meanwhile was tearing into an energy bar. He stopped a moment and said, "Here, Bob . . . catch." He held up a piece.

Ecklund got his meaning and moved to catch it with his mouth as Tighe tossed it. In the low moon gravity it was easier. "Ha! Got it."

Jin smiled and moved back a bit. "All right . . . try now."

Tighe tossed a piece and they cheered as Jin nabbed it in midair.

———

Eight hours later they rode atop the remaining Badger piloted by Priya Chindarkar as it navigated the service road alongside the intact length of the mass-driver. Ecklund was looking up at his 8-meter-tall masterpiece. "She's beautiful! Isn't she?"

Jin said dryly, "It will be beautiful when it works."

Chindarkar's voice said, *"I'm going to stop here. There's debris in the road ahead."*

They all slid off the Badger as it came to a stop. The scene before them was much clearer now that they were here—something their surveillance cams, the remaining Badger, and the overflying satellites had been unable to resolve.

It was apparent that the projectile had torn through the bottom of the last standing coil segment before ripping down the remaining hundred meters of the structure. Splayed out past the wreckage were unspooled glittering ribbons of Type-II superconducting tape, which had been wound into the coils. This YBCO tape was a "high-temp" superconductor, meaning that when chilled to negative 185 degrees Celsius with liquid nitrogen, it conducted electricity without resistance—which was how Ecklund's mass-driver could operate without creating massive amounts of heat and thus allowed it to keep firing repeatedly without melting. This tape was, therefore, crucial to the mass-driver.

As was liquid nitrogen, which they had large quantities of in lunar orbit—690 tons—because of the expedition to the asteroid Ryugu. It gave Tighe pause to consider all that the Ryugu expedition had made possible. They certainly had enough nitrogen to replace the amount spilled across the lunar surface during the catastrophic first shot.

Ecklund hopped and skipped across the debris field in lunar gravity, gazing upward and shining his light at the jagged tear in the bottom of the coil barrel. "The projectile went off-center, but we had no switching failure. That shouldn't have been possible."

Tighe bounded past Ecklund, evading debris, and came to a stop overlooking the fallen remains of two Talos robots. He shined his light as he knelt close to them—then looked over his shoulder. "I found your body, Bob. Cause of death: liquid nitrogen bath." He spoke through the comm link. "Priya, you seeing this?"

"Yeah, we're watching your feed, J.T."

He lifted the upper body of the other Talos robot, and it looked largely intact.

"Bring them back, and I'll see if I can fix them. Worst case, we should be able to take parts from the other two that wore out."

Ecklund pointed up at the last coil barrel before the collapsed section. "I need to get up there. I want to take a look at the exact coil where the projectile went astray." He turned to Tighe and Jin. "Let's get the crane."

A half hour later they used the Badger to haul the wheeled LSMS crane up to the jagged end of the mass-driver. Ecklund clipped his EMU suit to the boom arm, and then Tighe and Jin raised him up toward the coil. It didn't look safe, but Tighe realized he was assessing it with Earthling eyes. In one-sixth gravity, the crane was well within its safety margin.

Ecklund's thick gloved hands soon held on to the end of the coil segment, and he shined his helmet lights into the opening. "Oh yeah . . . are you guys seeing this up there?"

Yak's voice answered, *"Yes, Bob, we are recording."*

"Okay . . ." He reached into the barrel. After a few moments, he stopped short. "Hold on . . ." He reached into it even farther.

"Careful, Bob. That metal could be sharp."

"I thought this suit could stop a micrometeor. At least that's what they told us in—" He pulled a cone-shaped metal object out of the opening and studied it. "What the . . . ?"

"What is it?"

Ecklund spoke to the sky. "Clarke Station, are you seeing this?"

Yak's voice replied, *"Yes, Bob. What is that?"*

"That's a great damned question." He looked into the opening again. "If I had to guess, I'd says it's a thruster nozzle—made of some composite material. It was wedged between two coils."

Jin called up to him. "Could we have left it behind during construction?"

"We're not using composites." Ecklund pivoted around and was pointing his arm straight through the gash in the bottom of the barrel, sighting down its angle. "Take a bearing on that. Whatever this belonged to should be some-where downrange. Due east."

"You mean whatever's left of it."

"That's going to be a big area, Bob. Would we even recognize it?"

"If it isn't part of my mass-driver, I'll recognize it. Get me down."

Three abreast, they proceeded through the fallen mass-driver sections, with Ecklund carefully inspecting each piece of wreckage. At first, familiar metal debris glinted in the regolith—much of it preceded by bounding trails. But the debris field quickly trailed off, and they were left to scan the lunar surface, trying to parse false positives from among the shadows of small de-files and craters.

However, roughly 200 meters away, Jin shined a light on a spherical metal housing that had been halved into a battered mass, with circuits and piping ex-posed. "Look at this . . ." As he picked it up, he noticed an intact thruster nozzle on the far side—with five more holes, one in the center of each compass point.

Chindarkar's voice came in. *"Careful, Han."*

Ecklund was already alongside him, shining a light. "Let me see that." He took the wreckage from Jin and examined it closely. The nozzle in his hand matched the one on the device. "Six exhaust ports."

Tighe came up to look over his shoulder.

Chindarkar said, *"Six degrees of movement. It's a drone spacecraft."*

Ecklund looked up, his face both anguished and relieved. "This must have wedged itself into the barrel—look at these rods. It's smashed to oblivion, but I think someone designed this specifically to disrupt the mass-driver firing sequence." He looked up at the sky. "Someone designed this . . . and sent it all the way out here."

Jin scanned the landscape. "Whoever sent that thing could send more."

Tighe said, "Hell, maybe they already have."

Ecklund, newly emboldened, gestured with the damaged drone. "What it means is that there's nothing wrong with my mass-driver design." He gripped Jin's shoulder and laughed.

Jin looked at the drone. "We should return to Clarke Station with the Talos robots—and this drone wreckage."

"To do what? We already know what we need to do." Ecklund hopped around in the regolith. "I'm on to them now. We're gonna need some countermeasures." He turned to Tighe and held up the smashed device. "Look at how small this is. They didn't send explosives—because that would have been an obvious attack. No, this was designed to make us think *we* failed."

Jin stepped into his line of sight. "We need to head back to Clarke Station."

"I don't think this thing could have come far. It would have had barely any fuel. That means it must have been launched from something else." He looked around. "Something close by."

Tighe added, "Or something that flew close by."

Chindarkar said, *"Clarke Station radar should have detected anything orbiting in the vicinity."*

Ecklund scanned the horizon. "This little thing wouldn't have the delta-v to decelerate from orbital velocity. Priya?"

"Yes, Bob."

"Can you have mission control search through satellite imagery around the base? See if they can spot anything suspicious out on our perimeter."

"Like what?"

"A vehicle. Or tracks that aren't ours. Maybe evidence of a spacecraft touchdown."

"Sure. We'll get mission control on it."

After an examination of the fallen coil sections, Ecklund confirmed that many of them were intact. In fact, many of them were still bolted together. The 8-meter fall in one-sixth gravity onto soft lunar dust had hardly affected them.

Back at the Moon Hab, Ecklund was ebullient. Jin refused to allow the small drone inside, in case it had been powered by a toxic hypergolic fuel like hydrazine, but Ecklund was busy examining close-up photos of it with his crystal. "What we're doing here is important enough that someone went to great lengths to make us fail." He chuckled to himself.

Jin scowled. "Why is that amusing?"

"It's not amusing—it's affirming. What we're doing here *matters*." He smiled as he flipped through photos. "If only they'd focused this much effort innovating themselves, rather than on trying to stop us."

Tighe asked, "Who do you think did it?"

Ecklund looked up. "Doesn't matter. What's important is that we get building again—before they can react."

Jin was preparing a rehydrated meal for them—of indistinct ingredients. "We should return to Clarke Station with the Talos robots, get them fixed, and send them back down to rebuild."

Ecklund checked his HUD display. "That could take weeks. Or months. And will only give whoever did this time to send something else. No. Let's effect repairs and develop countermeasures. We can't wait."

Jin shook his head. "It's too dangerous."

Tighe said, "Compared to what?"

"Han, we have only three trusses to reassemble and a dozen coil sections to put back in place," Ecklund told him. "Plus, some piping and calibration. We can do that in a few days, or we wind up waiting weeks—or even months, if Priya needs parts from Earth."

Tighe looked to Jin. "He's got a point."

Ecklund continued. "I'm telling you, we're in a strong position right now, but only if we act. They can't stop us. We're here. They're not. All they can do right now is send tiny machines like this. We've got mass and human presence on our side. Let's use that."

Chindarkar's voice came in over the comm link. *"Morra Base, I think we found a suspect."*

A series of virtual satellite images appeared in Tighe's crystal. They showed a circular blast pattern—without a crater—that was familiar to Tighe from the initial landing at Morra Base. The pattern was north of Cape Bruce, several kilometers away in the Sea of Tranquility. What looked like rover tracks led away from it and ended in a gully near their base.

Ecklund nodded to himself. "We'll need a surveillance platform on top of Cape Bruce. Why didn't that occur to us before?"

"Possibly because we're a quarter-million miles from anywhere."

That night Ecklund slept soundly while Tighe stared up at the domed steel ceiling. Someone was trying to prevent them from deploying a mass-driver on the Moon. Whoever it was would rather thwart progress in space than see someone else succeed. These same people were probably behind the hijacking of the *Rosette* cycler. And the cyberattacks.

Or maybe there was more than one group.

The more Tighe thought about it, the more determined he was to defeat them.

After sleeping six hours, they rode the Badger out to the location that mission control marked as the terminus of the vehicle tracks and came upon a small four-wheeled rover. It was generic, with a rack clearly designed to hold the drone they had found. No obvious markings to indicate who sent it and no solar panels to keep it charged. It was a short-term, single-use system.

After making sure it was inert, they brought it and the four inoperative Talos robots, along with two of the three broken Badger robots, and secured them in and around the crew compartment on the Kangaroo lander.

Ecklund was more enthusiastic than ever. "I'm telling you: we can make quick repairs to the mass-driver and then head back. We've got plenty of daylight left." He gestured with arms held wide. "Getting here was the risky part."

Jin finally nodded. "Fine, but if we encounter difficulties, we leave."

Excited, Ecklund gripped Jin's shoulder, and they all made their way back to Morra Base.

As they used the lone working Badger and the LSMS crane to collect and examine the fallen coil sections, Ecklund kept up a steady monologue. "That's all they could send. They don't have anything like our capabilities out here. It might not even be a whole government doing this; maybe just a rogue element."

He hummed to himself as he worked, occasionally glancing up at his surroundings. "We're on the damned Moon! How about that? They said I would never get this built." He held up his thick EMU arms to gesture at the mass-driver. "Well, here it is, you bastards. And I'm telling you, it's going to work!"

Tighe glanced at Jin in amusement and said, "Less talking, more building, Bob."

And so work continued.

After double-checking the coil sections and collecting loose YBCO tape, Ecklund began reassembling the damaged coils. Tighe and Jin, meanwhile, started to rebuild the twisted truss sections—and here, too, some of the truss supports were undamaged. The rest were easy to repair from the strips of steel remaining on-site, using the tools in the robot garage.

But as tens of hours passed and the pylons at the far end of the mass-driver began to rise once again, the effort seemed to instill in Ecklund ever more enthusiasm. He worked like one possessed. His chatter filled their team channel while they worked. "They can't operate a little toy like that at night. If we get this work finished before lunar sunset, we can run flat out for two weeks. The LEML will run even better in the nighttime cold."

Ecklund finished repairing the last of the coils and began walking along sorting through the mass-driver wreckage, searching farther away for salvageable metal pieces for Jin and Tighe—who were cutting off bent portions of the pylons with plasma torches, and forming new girders from base inventory. The torch work was dangerous now that they were here in person, and so Tighe and Jin focused on their movements.

Ecklund's grunting exertions came in occasionally as he spoke over the radio. "*By the time they get another drone back here . . .*" Heavy breathing. "*. . . we need to have serious mass to work with up at L2.*" More panting as he hopped around in the distance searching through debris. "*Then it'll be too late for them to stop us.*"

Jin said, "Bob, watch your air mix."

He laughed. "*I'm telling you, they are not going to win.*" Ecklund peered into a fallen coil section. "*Look at this! These coils are still in good shape.*"

After a while, Tighe tuned Ecklund out—so attentive was he on the multithousand-degree plasma torch and the risk of falling metal girders. Hour by hour, he and Jin began to reerect the last two pylons that would hold the barrel of the mass-driver.

But then at some point Tighe noticed Ecklund's radio chatter amid panting over the comm line. His comments had become strange.

"*We manage the project, or the project manages us. They are all . . . Where is she?*" A pause. "*What the hell is this? Oh god . . .*"

Jin looked up. "*Bob, what is it?*"

Ecklund ignored Jin's question and was hopping around in chaotic fashion. His breathing started to max out his mic. "*What is . . . What is going on?*"

Tighe looked to Jin—then at Ecklund in the distance.

Yak's voice came in over the comm link. "*Bob, try to slow your breathing and get your heart rate—*"

"*There's something wrong with my air!*" Ecklund thrashed around, stabbing his glove at a virtual interface.

Tighe cut off the power to his torch and spoke to Jin. "*High CO_2—it can cause panic and confusion.*" He called out to Ecklund, who was 50 meters away. "*Bob! Don't worry. You're going to be fine.*"

Ecklund was still thrashing around in the heavy EMU. "*Oh god!*"

Tighe dropped his torch and started hopping across the dust toward him. "*Bob! Slow your breathing. Remember the Ascension training.*"

They both hopped toward Ecklund now—and watched as he fell forward into the regolith, shouting, "*Oh god! Oh god!*"

"*Stop talking, Bob. Close your eyes and breathe slowly, deeply.*"

There was no response other than a slight gurgling sound.

"*Bob, stay still.*" Tighe reached Ecklund and rolled him faceup. Regolith coated the surface of the suit, but the AR helmet projection still showed Ecklund's face clearly; he was unconscious, the right half of his face twitching. "*Shit. Priya, bring the Badger over here!*"

Jin kneeled close by as well. "*His CO_2 levels are at 4.2 percent.*"

"*Not good, but nowhere near fatal.*"

Chindarkar's voice came in over the comm link. "*Bob's pulse is erratic, J.T.*"

"*Damnit . . .*"

The Badger soon arrived, and he and Jin lifted Ecklund on top of it and rode it back toward Moon Hab.

"*Once we take him out of this suit, how the hell do we get him back into it?*"

Jin appeared to be checking Ecklund's vitals from his crystal. "*We can't go back to the Moon Hab. We need to launch immediately to Clarke Station.*"

"*We'll have an even harder time trying to treat him in that small lander. And there's the g-forces on takeoff.*"

"*J.T., he needs medical attention that we cannot give him here.*" Jin called over the comm link, "*Priya, drive this Badger to the launchpad. Get Liz or Jackie monitoring Bob's vitals. We are going to need a treatment plan.*"

"*I'm on it.*"

Tighe nodded to Jin and spoke into his comm link. "*Morra Base to mission control, we need an emergency dust-off. We are headed to the launchpad now.*"

"*We copy you, Morra Base. Powering up SK-Delta. Advise when you are on board and ready for launch.*"

The Badger raced along the base road. On reaching the launchpad, Jin lowered the davit winch lines while Tighe monitored Ecklund's vitals. *"He's still breathing, but he's foaming at the mouth."*

Jin secured the lines to carabiners on Ecklund's EMU. They then activated the winches, and raced to climb the lander's ladder. "Priya, bring the Badger clear of the pad."

"Wilco." The wheeled robot raced off back toward base.

Once up top, Tighe and Jin pulled Ecklund's suit toward the EMU dock in the side of the crew compartment. They secured the EMU, then entered the crew module and pressurized the compartment. Only then could they open the EMU's rear hatch and pull Ecklund out of the suit.

Jin looked to Tighe. "You are the EMT."

"Lay him down." Tighe checked Ecklund's pulse and his breathing. "Shit . . ." He commenced chest compressions. "Morra Base to Clarke Station. We've lost pulse and are administering CPR. Please advise."

"J.T., this is Liz. I'm looking at his vitals. Keep up CPR. You've got limited options down there if this is an embolic stroke."

"Do we blast off or do we try to stabilize him first?"

There was a pause. Then, *"Getting him into microgravity could make things worse—or it might ease the stress."*

"I'm looking at him. He is not going to get better down here, and we don't have TPA or anything else."

Jin said, "Mission control, we need to blast off. Now."

After a moment, Dr. Josephson said, *"Gabriel, I'm going to defer to crew on the scene. There's no good choice. I think delay could be just as bad as getting him into orbit now."*

Mission control replied, "SK-Delta, *prepare for immediate liftoff.*"

"Copy that."

"Brace." Tighe grabbed onto Jin and Ecklund—and suddenly they were pressed hard into the floor as the lander rumbled and shook. After several moments the g-forces lessened slightly.

As soon as they were able, they recommenced CPR—even as the acceleration continued.

"If we can get him to the transit craft, there's a better med kit. We might be able to stabilize him." Tighe spoke to the lander itself, "C'mon, baby. Get us up there."

"Then it is still three days to Clarke Station."

Tighe gave him a look that showed he was well aware of how bad the situation was.

After a couple minutes the rocket motor cut off.

"*MECO*, SK-Delta. *One hour twenty to rendezvous with Transit-03.*"

Jin replied, "Copy that, mission control. Thank you."

By the time *SK-Delta* docked at the transit craft, Ecklund appeared to have stabilized—or at least he was breathing on his own.

During the interminable three-day transit back to L2, Ecklund seemed to drift in and out of consciousness. Once, he even seemed to be somewhat aware. They kept him hydrated with an IV drip, but they had to use gentle pressure on the bag in microgravity. By the time Transit-03 arrived in Clarke Station's hangar bay, Tighe and Jin had been awake for several days.

As soon as the hatch opened, flight surgeons Josephson and Ohana floated in with a body board and strapped Ecklund down. Several more hands helped them rush Ecklund to the elevator, and soon they were gone—leaving Jin and Tighe behind, exhausted.

Yak leaned into the hatchway, extending his hand.

Tighe started gathering up trash instead. "Let's get this lander refueled."

Jin turned toward him. "Why?"

"Because if we head back to the Moon now . . ." He checked his crystal. ". . . we'll still have ninety-five hours to complete the mass-driver repairs before lunar sunset."

"We are not going anywhere. Neither of us is rested."

"I'll sleep on the way."

Yak interjected. "I can go with him, Han."

Jin shook his head. "No. We already have one person down."

"So what?!" The shout echoed in the compartment. Tighe stared at Jin. "You saw what they tried to do. Until we succeed, whoever it is will *never* stop, and we might not get another chance—to rescue Isabel and Ade or anything else. Now is the time. If the sun sets down there, we lose two weeks—and then we may *all* lose. Permanently."

Yak touched Jin's shoulder. "We can unload Talos robots and Badgers. Refuel and resupply, then head back down."

Jin stared back at Tighe. "You are acting out of anger."

"Yeah, I *am* angry. I have good reason to be. You know what we promised, Han. This needs to be done, and I intend to do it."

"I am captain of this station."

"I know you are. So go help them, but you are not talking me out of this."

Jin was about to speak when Yak again gripped his shoulder.

"He is right, Han. You need to be here. We need to be there."

After a moment, Jin just moved away, toward the elevator.

But by then Tighe had resumed clearing out trash from the lander.

Tighe slept for much of the journey back to the lunar surface, with Yak handling all the comms and meal prep. *SK-Delta* touched down without incident, and they began work on the mass-driver repairs immediately thereafter. If Yak was excited about his first steps on the Moon, he kept it to himself.

A glance at the horizon showed that the Sun was most of the way across the black sky, with the "new Earth" entirely in shadow, matching Tighe's grim mood.

And so they worked, finishing the last of the pylons, then unbolting the fallen coil sections from one another and using the LSMS crane to lift them individually into place atop pylon supports.

This wasn't the first time Tighe and his crewmates had taken methamphetamines to keep working through an emergency situation, and Yak had talked Josephson into providing a small supply—which Yak rationed out to avoid overdose. And through it all, they continued to work, barely resting in the Moon Hab except to recharge their air, eat, and defecate.

Once they'd placed the last of the mass-driver coil sections atop the new pylons, they positioned a camera to remotely detect obstructions in the mass-driver barrel. But they still needed to replace the liquid nitrogen pipes and power conduits. The power conduits were largely undamaged, but the nitrogen lines had to be repaired or remade in the robot machine shop, using the last of the metal available.

Glancing at the sun looming just above the gray, lifeless horizon, Tighe spoke before Yak could say anything. "I know, we're not going to finish in time."

"I was going to say, we should pull on outer suits—night will be cold here."

Tighe turned to Yak and could see the determination in his eyes. He nodded. "You're right."

They then pulled extreme-cold sheaths over their MCP suits, in preparation for the 500-degree temperature drop that was about to occur—something no human had yet directly experienced on the Moon. There was no guarantee that these suits would keep them safe, but they'd be dead soon without them.

And so they continued to work, gathering nitrogen pipe sections.

Yak put aside his electron welder. "Do you know of 'cold welding'?"

"I know to not place bare metals of the same type together out here."

"Yes, is why our bolts are nickel, not iron. Metals have natural attraction—is why metals conduct electricity; their electrons and atomic nuclei fuse into matrix naturally."

"There's no time for a science lesson, Yak."

"Here in vacuum we might not need to weld—we could just press pipes together, and they will bond." He looked up. "Only reason metals do not do this on Earth is because of air—it creates layer of oxides on metal's surface." He then slid a cobalt file across the ends of two pipes, before lining them up and carefully pressing them together.

Tighe looked closely, and they seemed to stick—as if they were magnets. He kneeled close and tried to separate them. They would not budge. He looked up and laughed.

"Much quicker this way." Yak slapped him on the chest.

Tighe tossed aside his electron welder, and they got busy.

As the sun started to dip below the horizon, deathly cold shadows crept ever closer to them across the landscape. Familiar electrical discharges flashed ominously, and lunar dust levitated above the ground all around them. Unlike their months of telepresence work, they were both now physically present on the lunar surface for the arrival of night, with all the risks that entailed.

But fortunately, they were also now working high atop the rebuilt mass-driver barrel, 8 meters above the ground, and the terminator line passed without incident. Instead, as darkness enveloped them, Tighe and Yak simply kicked on their helmet lights and continued working.

Yak warned, "Careful not to shatter metal as cold increases . . ."

Still their work continued, until finally they pressed the last two coolant pipes together.

Exhausted, Yak turned to Tighe, who had been holding the pipe. "We should power her up."

Tighe spoke into his comm link. "Mission control. Power up the LEML, load all cooling lines, and commence diagnostic check."

Too weary to celebrate, they barely managed to traverse the length of the mass-driver, heading toward the Launch House roof, their LED lights cutting through the darkness as they went. Above them the Earth cast only a pale light, with a brilliant field of stars beyond.

Once on the Launch House roof, they both turned and stood in an exhausted daze, staring down the finished, kilometer-long mass-driver barrel. It ran to a vanishing point toward the starlit horizon.

But voices spoke over the comm link. Mission control. Clarke Station. In the end, all Tighe really heard was . . .

"All systems go."

And then he felt the structure beneath him tremble, then a sudden jolt— followed by a white-hot light arcing away and over the horizon, eventually to be lost among the stars.

Cheers and shouts of joy came in over the comm link, but Tighe and Yak were too weary to do anything but lean on each other and hug.

Amid all the celebration, Tighe learned that at some point over the past few days the year 2040 had arrived. This reminder of the relentless celestial clock that would soon bring back Ryugu was not particularly welcome news.

To ensure the mass-driver's operation, Tighe and Yak wound up remaining in the Moon Hab for the entire two-week-long lunar night, sheltering against the bitter cold and radiation within the steel-lined regolith mound. Their dreary stay was punctuated with increasing frequency by a rhythmic thump—the mass-driver launching cores into the sky.

Far from being an annoyance, Tighe began to think of it like a heartbeat, getting stronger with each passing day as the techs slowly increased its tempo. He would listen to it as he lay in his sleeping bag during lights-out and nod off to sleep. Its increasingly reliable beat comforted him.

When lunar dawn rose by the third week of January, Tighe and Yak launched back into low lunar orbit on the *SK-Delta* lander and within a few hours docked with Transit-03, which in turn did a burn to head them back toward L2 and Clarke Station. The flight was uneventful, and three days later they docked once more in Clarke Station's central bay.

What became clear to Tighe during the return voyage was that his cancer symptoms had returned.

CHAPTER 32

Monument

F or days, Lynne Holstad was at Robert Ecklund's bedside in South Hab medical bay. Priya Chindarkar made herself available to provide whatever Holstad needed, and although every effort was made to allow them their privacy, there were limits, given the recently cannibalized wall partitions.

The confusion on Ecklund's face had been the hardest part. Chindarkar wished he could understand what was happening, and thankfully, he finally seemed to. He had had a stroke due to the extreme distress he'd experienced while in heightened CO_2 levels. Holstad eventually got him to realize that he was back on Clarke Station.

The right half of Ecklund's body was paralyzed, and he had lost the ability to speak. Holstad soothed him and spoke to him, and then one day, when he was doing particularly badly, she placed crystal glasses over his eyes. He struggled for a moment, but she said, "Bob, please. I want you to see."

Chindarkar stood nearby and could observe the augmented-reality layer he was viewing—a large virtual screen floating at the end of his bed. It displayed a live video feed from Morra Base—from the ridgeline of Cape Bruce, looking down on the now completed mass-driver.

Ecklund suddenly went stock-still in realization of what he was seeing. His eyes momentarily focused on her.

"Watch, Bob. Watch."

As she, too, watched, voices on the comm link stepped through diagnostics and finally the words came across . . .

"Activating coil sequence in three . . . two . . ."

And suddenly a white-hot slug of regolith shot out of the end of the barrel, arcing out over the horizon and up into the black sky.

"Good trajectory! We have a good trajectory on shot two-three-nine. Preparing shot two-four-zero . . . Fire."

Another white-hot slug silently zipped over the horizon.

And another. And another.

Ecklund tried to smile, even as his eyes welled with tears.

She leaned down and kissed him on the forehead, holding his face close. "It's been working. Just like you said it would."

He shuddered and gripped her hand weakly. Unable to speak, but clearly wanting to.

She spoke softly to him, but Chindarkar could not help but hear. "So many things will now be possible, Robert." She squeezed his hand and there was both joy and sadness in his eyes.

Chindarkar sensed his struggle for breath and felt herself welling up, too.

Holstad said, "Thank you for this gift."

Ecklund died two days later.

Holstad spoke with his daughter back on Earth, to let her know that her father had passed—and also what he had achieved. Officials at NASA were "unable to confirm or deny" Holstad's story to his family; however, when his daughter consented to cremation of Ecklund's remains off-world, it seemed obvious that someone at NASA or in the government had had the decency to tell Ecklund's family the truth, even if off the record.

The entire crew attended the funeral service in South Hab, and there were tears on many faces as they watched a mule spacecraft position Ecklund's remains into the focal point of the solar furnace that powered Clarke Station itself. Wrapped in silvery material, his body burned with a blinding light. Chindarkar thought it a fitting tribute for a space pioneer to be consumed by the Sun.

Chindarkar, Jin Han, James Tighe (looking gaunt from traditional chemotherapy), and Sevastian Yakovlev stood nearby as Holstad took the floor before the gathered mourners, her lab's seedlings the only "floral" arrangement available. Holstad had looked away when Tighe and Han offered their condolences, which was not surprising; Chindarkar had been present for their first conversation on Tighe's return, when Holstad had looked him in the eye and said, "Robert was a beautiful human being, and now he is *dead* because you could not wait—not even a month—to continue your reckless adventure. There are nine billion people back on Earth facing the ravages of climate change, but all you want to do is rescue *your two friends*—who are probably already dead. You selfish bastard!"

Tighe had remained silent, and she had not said a word to either him or Jin since.

But none of that was discussed today. Today was a day of remembrance.

Holstad surveyed the crew—all of whom could truly begin their work because of the resources now coming up from the lunar surface. She let slip a smile and said, "I remember . . ." She paused to contain her emotions. "I remember when Bob first arrived on Clarke Station, and . . ." She pointed up to the H4 elevator landing above them. ". . . swung down like Tarzan to prove some point about physics."

The mourners laughed and clapped.

"Or at least that's what he claimed he was doing. He always put everything he had into his work. And now his work will bring life to countless others, far into the future." She held up a small slip of paper. "I have gone over the chemical analysis of the lunar regolith." She paused and again struggled to speak through her grief. "There is phosphorus contained within the cores we've processed—a third of a percent by mass."

Once more the mourners applauded.

She turned to the AR screen displaying the immolation of Ecklund's mortal remains. "And to this supply, with his family's blessing, I will add Robert's phosphorus as well. To go on and become future life. I think that he would approve."

CHAPTER 33

A Going Concern

CLARKE STATION POPULATION: 25

DAYS TO RYUGU DEPARTURE: 802

RESOURCES LAUNCHED TO L2: 16,300 TONS

n March of 2040, billionaire Space Titan Jack Macy launched one of his massive Galleon reusable rockets—a ship named *Let's Be Friends*—on a 3:1 resonance with the Moon, more or less precisely the same lunar cycler orbit the *Rosette* once occupied.

This meant—for good or ill—that Clarke Station was no longer isolated.

Jin Han was relieved to have a connection to Earth once more—to obtain much-needed parts, provisions, and crew. Nonetheless, concerns over Clarke Station security still kept him awake at night.

Galleon rockets were enormous Earth launch systems, 9 meters in diameter and 120 meters tall, not including their even bigger reusable booster. They could (theoretically) fit up to a hundred passengers, but had so far ferried only a few people back and forth to NASA's lunar gateway and, on one memorable descent, to the lunar south pole. Galleon rockets were mostly used for uncrewed cargo shipments, and for this they were ideal—able to lift nearly a hundred tons into LEO. However, their lack of an escape system, combined with a retro-rocket-style landing, was as problematic for passengers returning to Earth as Kangaroo landers were on the Moon. Failure of one of its three surface engines on landing could spell doom for everyone on board.

However, since a lunar cycler never had to land, Galleons were well-suited to this purpose, and they had lots of interior space. Now that the *Rosette* was gone and a lunar mass-driver was producing a wealth of resources in deep space, Macy apparently saw his chance to take over cislunar transport and jumped on it. That meant *Let's Be Friends* was swinging by L2 every twenty-eight days.

Since Catalyst and the CCE had no control over the vessel, in addition to providing transportation to Clarke Station personnel (for a price), Macy's company was also selling seats to rich space tourists who wanted to take a lap around the Moon. So far these "guests" were few, and none of them had tried to board the transit craft during the exchange of Clarke Station crew at L2, but the image of armed "little green men" swarming by the dozen aboard a Galleon rocket headed toward Clarke Station was a constant concern. The only thing that protected Clarke Station was the sheer mass-on-orbit and propellant now available to the CCE—and that stockpile was growing every day.

The success of the mass-driver at Morra Base had changed everything with regard to Earth relations. Nations of the world were eager for discussions with Lukas Rochat, and the entire crew of Clarke Station was scrambling to make use of the new resources. Fresh teams were cycling in now.

Most of Sevastian Yakovlev's Blue Team—the very first group to join Tighe, Chindarkar, and Jin up on Clarke Station—rotated back to Earth after their yearlong tour; this included the departure of trusted flight surgeon Elizabeth Josephson, chemist Sofia Boutros, solar sat expert Monica Balter, as well as both of the US Space Force observers. However, Yak and Ramón Marín stayed on and transitioned to Gold Team—meaning they, too, were now here for the duration.

Replacing Blue was Purple Team, a crew of seven, including a flight surgeon, chemists, and replacement international observers from the US and Australia.

Then in late March, Red Team also rotated back to Earth, their year up, causing the departure of still more familiar and trusted faces. The Chinese and Russian observers also departed in their own capsule.

In came Orange Team, which included new Chinese and Russian observers, another flight surgeon, biologists, astropreneurs, still more chemists, and new Clarke Station security operators.

Not long after the arrival of the new crew members, Jin floated in the gate compartment of Clarke Station, staring through a window of transparent aluminum that looked out onto a cathedral of piping, valves, and pressure vessels clustered along the non-spinning axis of the station. Next to him were the newly arrived international observers and the station's carbonyl chemist, an American named Priscilla Voorhees.

Voorhees pointed. "This microgravity refinery is an expanded version of the design first proven by the *Konstantin* expedition to Ryugu."

The Chinese observer said, "I notice the hull of Clarke Station remains mostly unfinished."

Jin fielded the question. "We will be restarting construction soon, now that we have resources, and expect to have the hull ring completed before year end."

The Russian observer gestured to the refinery. "My understanding is that moondust contains much oxygen. Is this not lost when the regolith cores become molten during their acceleration through the mass-driver?"

Voorhees took over again. "Lunar regolith does contain oxygen, but it's tightly bound into oxides in minerals like ilmenite, volcanic glass, basalt, olivine, pyroxene—and not released when the rock is melted. Instead, we liberate this oxygen during the refining process, which begins by pulverizing the arriving cores—"

An EU observer interjected. "Pardon . . . The regolith that comes up from Morra Base—what is its composition?"

"Here . . ." Voorhees clicked through virtual UIs. "This is the average composition of the Morra Base regolith processed thus far . . ." She projected an augmented-reality table onto the commons layer:

Silicon dioxide (silica)	42.2%
Titanium dioxide	7.8%
Aluminum oxide	13.6%
Chromium oxide	0.3%
Iron oxide	15.3%
Manganese oxide	0.2%
Magnesium oxide	7.8%
Calcium oxide (quicklime)	11.9%
Sodium oxide	0.47%
Potassium oxide	0.16%

Phosphorus trioxide	0.05%
Sulfur	0.12%
Total mass	99.9%

"Notice the oxides. That's the oxygen we liberate. Of course, these compounds also have industrial uses on their own—for example, calcium oxide (or quicklime) is useful in wastewater treatment, glassmaking, and more. However, we put the regolith through molten oxide electrolysis, the FFC Cambridge method, gaseous carbonyl extraction, and other processes, leaving us with these pure elements . . ."

Another virtual screen appeared:

Oxygen	44.46%
Silicon	19.73%
Iron	11.89%
Aluminum	7.20%
Calcium	8.50%
Magnesium	4.70%
Titanium	2.46%
Sodium	0.35%
Chromium	0.17%
Manganese	0.15%
Potassium	0.14%
Sulfur	0.12%
Phosphorus	0.03%
Total regolith mass	99.90%

"As you can see, the cores we've been receiving are nearly 45 percent oxygen by mass, but also rich in silicon, iron, and aluminum. Given the 16,000 tons of regolith processed so far, we've been able to refine nearly 2,000 tons of pure iron. Twelve hundred tons of aluminum. Four hundred tons of titanium. Seventy-two hundred tons of oxygen. The availability of ample solar energy out here for the refining process is key."

Jin knew the tonnage was orders of magnitude greater than what was coming up from the US and Chinese operations in Shackleton or Peary Craters—and the mass-driver was just getting started.

The Russian observer squinted at the image. "I cannot help but notice the total is not quite 100 percent. What of the other tenth percent?"

"Yes. The regolith contains trace amounts of other elements—a wide mix from meteor impacts, the solar wind, and so on, occurring at just a few parts per million."

"I would be curious to see these."

"Of course . . ." Voorhees clicked around virtual UIs until she produced another AR table. "Here's a list. Note their industrial uses . . ."

Rare Earth Metals		
Cerium (Ce)	0.0068%	oxidizer
Neodymium (Nd)	0.0066%	magnets, lasers
Dysprosium (Dy)	0.0031%	magnets, lasers
Lanthanum (La)	0.0026%	specialty glass, optics, electrodes
Gadolinium (Gd)	0.0025%	magnets, specialty optics, computer memory
Samarium (Sm)	0.0021%	magnets, lasers, neutron capture
Ytterbium (Yb)	0.0018%	infrared lasers, chemical reducer
Erbium (Er)	0.0016%	lasers, steel alloyed with vanadium
Terbium (Tb)	0.0005%	lasers and fluorescent lamps
Holmium (Ho)	0.0005%	lasers
Lutetium (Lu)	0.0003%	specialty glass, radiology equipment
Europium (Eu)	0.0002%	colored phosphors, lasers, mercury-vapor lamps

Other Elements		
Chlorine (Cl)	0.00193%	medicines, computers, cell phones, refrigerants, solar panels
Barium (Ba)	0.02280%	magnet production, welding, fluorescent lamps
Tantalum (Ta)	0.00010%	capacitors, heat-resistant materials, prosthetics
Copper (Cu)	0.00051%	wiring, plumbing, motor parts
Selenium (Se)	0.00007%	fertilizers, glass production, solar cells, photoconductors
Scandium (Sc)	0.00760%	aluminum alloy, stadium lights, fertilizer
Hafnium (Hf)	0.00215%	microelectronics, high-temp shielding

Gallium (Ga)	0.00029%	smartphones, LEDs, solar panels, semiconductors
Cobalt (Co)	0.00290%	batteries, alloys
Zinc (Zn)	0.00029%	medical, DNA synthesis, batteries
Rubidium (Rb)	0.00057%	superthin batteries, ion propellent, plant growth, catalyst
Cesium (Cs)	0.00002%	atomic clocks, smartphones, infrared optics, lasers
Strontium (Sr)	0.01640%	Medicine, displays, alloys

Voorhees continued. "There are also some trace radioactive elements . . ."

Fissile Material	
Thorium	0.0002%
Uranium	0.0001%

The Russian observer took a snapshot of this last table. "How much uranium would you say you have gathered thus far, Ms. Voorhees?"

"I expect it's in the neighborhood of perhaps . . . ten kilos. Though, of course, there is no enrichment being done."

"I see. Thank you." The Russian observer turned to Jin. "This tour has been most illuminating."

By now, the existence of Clarke Station was everywhere in the news media back on Earth. The space station beyond the Moon went from being a fringe theory and classified intelligence to a cause célèbre seemingly overnight. Outlets worldwide ran articles, photo spreads, and video segments.

And almost none of them agreed with one another.

Priya Chindarkar forwarded Jin a cover story from Chinese state media. Its headline read: "China Makes Bold Leap in Space." Below it was a clear photo of Clarke Station, except that the international flags had been edited out, leaving only the CCP flag on its hull. The words "Clarke Station" had been replaced with Hanzi characters for Nónglì gōngdiàn—or lunar palace. The station was, it claimed, built from in situ resources mined in deep space by taikonauts.

The article was clearly aimed at a domestic Chinese audience and lionized Jin as the station's captain, claiming he led the top secret construction project. It also claimed he'd renounced his corrupt billionaire father and that Jin had "refused his inheritance." That he was "bravely charting the way" for China in space and also detailed how he led an all-Chinese crew back in 2033 to mine a distant asteroid.

The more Jin searched, the more he found. There were video clips from the *Konstantin* mission as well, with all the other crew members replaced by deepfakes of taikonauts. It occurred to Jin that the propaganda department might have all the onboard video from the *Konstantin*—obtained from Joyce's creditors.

And then Jin found deepfake interviews with his own doppelgänger on state media, where he praised the Party's vision and leadership in space. Jin was being celebrated as a great hero back in China—captain of *Nónglì gōngdiàn*, a project being carried out by the CCP to save the world.

Much of the other international coverage of Clarke Station, though sensationalized, at least got the basic facts right: that a group of international commercial space pioneers were out beyond the Moon and had built a space station there and a mass-driver on the lunar surface. Where it got hazy was who initially financed the project and under whose authorization it was all built, with each major nation claiming a decisive role—along with some minor ones like Luxembourg (which, to be fair, actually did play a role early on).

Yak shook his head as he read through the media blitz. "They say success has many fathers—while failure is an orphan."

Shortly thereafter all their inboxes filled with interview requests forwarded by Lukas Rochat.

There was no denying, however, that the existence of Clarke Station going public back on Earth stirred tremendous enthusiasm among the crew. They were all making history now and the excitement was palpable.

Entire profiles were written on Chindarkar, Tighe, Yakovlev, and Jin. Yet, the *Konstantin* spacecraft and the Ryugu expedition appeared to have been lost or forgotten by the Western media—dark territory without a mention.

Jin, Tighe, Yak, and Chindarkar sat at the conference table in South Hab, mulling over the implications of these developments.

Now that Clarke Station was no longer isolated from Earth, experts and CRISPR gene-editing tech had finally arrived via Macy's Galleon cycler. Tighe was once more undergoing the specialized treatment, and he already looked much improved, sitting with them as usual. He looked up from reading an article. "It seems like the powers that be want Joyce's secrets to die with him."

Yak turned to Jin. "You are apparently great hero, Captain Jin." He chuckled.

Jin rolled his eyes. "I had nothing to do with that propaganda."

Chindarkar was reading through major websites in India—every one of which had a photo of her with her ISRO badge on its main page. She shook her head in disbelief. "It's so strange that I'm famous now. I wonder what my family will think of this."

Tighe sighed. "This is going to be a huge distraction to our work." He glanced around at other crew members talking excitedly. "One we can't afford. We were just beginning to make headway, and now the attention of the whole damn world is going to come down on us like a ton of bricks. I say we refuse all media interviews and just keep working."

"What about Jin? Shouldn't he deny those deepfake interviews?"

"Why? Nobody is going to convince anyone of anything down there. You do remember how Earth is, right? Let's just stay focused on the challenges out here. At least they're real."

Yak was reading. "Hm. Lukas held another press conference on Cislunar Commodity Exchange. He is promoting lūna cryptocurrency—and carbon sequestration smart contracts." He looked up. "CCE will apparently pay in lūna for each ton of CO_2 pulled from Earth's atmosphere."

Tighe scowled. "Pay? With what? Jesus Christ . . . Lukas is probably the one who orchestrated this media blitz."

Chindarkar looked at him. "So even after all he's done for us, you still don't trust Lukas?"

Yak added, "Lukas helped make Clarke Station possible. He did get us here."

Tighe shook his head. "I don't think he did that to help us. He and Erika Lisowski have their own priorities."

Chindarkar looked dismayed. "That doesn't mean they can't be trusted."

Jin stood. "Whether we trust them or not does not change our mission. We have work to do, and this media attention will soon blow over—when the world gets bored of us."

Jin's prediction proved incorrect, when a week later Dr. Fatima Patel, British geologist, former ESA scientist, and one of the three surviving members of Yellow Team on board Clarke Station, announced that she was pregnant. That she had, in fact, conceived the first human life in space.

CHAPTER 34

Conception

CLARKE STATION POPULATION: 34
DAYS TO RYUGU DEPARTURE: 788
RESOURCES LAUNCHED TO L2: 25,500 TONS

The Earth media frenzy over Fatima Patel's pregnancy and the identity of the father—Nicolau Ivorra, a handsome Spanish metallurgist and sculptor who had returned to Earth with Red Team the month before—reached a fever pitch in the coming weeks. Fanning the flames was the charismatic Ivorra, father of the "star child," who had been doing interviews all over, expounding on the profound implications of human life expanding into space. The pregnancy was main-page news worldwide, with millions upon millions of opinions bouncing around social media, for or against human development of space.

De-growth activists protested what they called the "plunder of the Moon" by billionaires and claimed that humanity would only despoil it like they had Earth—declaring that the only viable path for humans was to relinquish aspirations in space, reduce our population, and live in harmony with the planet we have.

Yak scoffed at this idea. "Who decides who gets to live and who does not in this 'de-growth' fantasy? History suggests such things are decided at gunpoint."

Tighe suggested, "If these de-growth people want to reduce population, they should volunteer to be first."

"Such people seldom do."

However, the majority back on Earth praised the recent rapid progress in space, given the continuing droughts, floods, migrations, pandemics, and resource depletion from ongoing—and accelerating—climate change. It was a welcome contrast to the usual news, which had been almost uniformly bad.

Thus, endless articles were written about Patel's background, education, political leanings. About the future prospects for child-rearing in space. The challenges. The implications for society.

By comparison, scant attention was paid to the death on station of a recently arrived member of Orange Team, an American engineer who was electrocuted in an accident while working on expansions to the station's thermal power generation plant. Instead, his body was placed in the station's ad hoc morgue in preparation for return to Earth (at the request of his family), and standard operating procedures were updated to avoid a recurrence.

Given that few crew members were well acquainted with the new arrival, his memorial service was lightly attended. Selective empathy seemed a side effect of the danger all around them, with the rite of passage being months of shared sacrifice.

Thus, attention quickly turned to more positive news—that, for example, funds were being raised back on Earth to lift healthy whole food to the far side of the Moon so Patel would not have to subsist on rehydrated processed meals for the term of her pregnancy.

Likewise, since the secret of Clarke Station was now out, the crew was growing impatient with having their comms back to Earth filtered and censored by mission control. They wanted direct two-way links back to Earth and to the Internet.

Tighe was against the idea. "We already have enough distractions with crew members reading and discussing the news about themselves. We don't want them spending all their time posting on social media and taking interviews. Nothing will get done up here."

Turning to Jin and Chindarkar, he said, "We should return Fatima to Earth. She and Ivorra could go on tour. Let the media frenzy continue down there."

Chindarkar said, "She's seven weeks pregnant, J.T. The g-forces of reentry would be too dangerous."

Jin nodded. "Priya's right."

"We're not seriously contemplating having Fatima come full-term and deliver a child on this space station, are we?"

Jin said, "What choice do we have?"

Tighe gestured to their unfinished, Spartan surroundings. "This is a frontier outpost, not a day care center. It's filled with dangers even to full-grown adults. One was killed not three days ago."

"Presumably infants won't be wiring power junctions."

Tighe leaned forward, speaking softly. "I think it's the temptation of becoming a historic figure—of wanting to conceive and deliver the first baby in space."

Jin raised an eyebrow. "You think she did this intentionally?"

Chindarkar said, "Birth control isn't perfect."

Tighe shrugged. "That won't lessen the effect of galactic cosmic rays during the gestation period."

Yak hmphed. "Radiation is like death—best not to be exposed to too much at a young age."

Tighe: "Exactly. I mean, Priya, how am I the bad guy for not wanting a baby in the middle of all this? This station is meant for explorers. Babies must wait until true settlements are built in space."

Chindarkar said, "Fatima's pregnancy is a positive message for the world. People are hopeful about what it represents. That actually helps support what we're doing up here, J.T." She pointed. "In fact, her conception should go up on the wall."

"The flight surgeons are monitoring every minute of the pregnancy like it's some kind of experiment."

"Pregnancies are always monitored. That doesn't make this an experiment."

Yak looked to her. "Isn't it?"

"Well, it's too late to send her back to Earth."

"We should make sure it doesn't happen again here on station."

Yak looked alarmed. "Surely you are not suggesting celibacy?"

"No, but maybe the male recruits should have vasectomies."

"J.T.! That doesn't sound like any frontier I've ever heard of."

He threw up his hands. "I don't know. It's just that this is a huge distraction to our purpose here, and while we might have resources coming in now, we've still got a huge number of obstacles to overcome if we're going to make a 2042 rendezvous with Ryugu." He then walked off.

———

A day later, Jin announced that Clarke Station would be "spun-down" for the first time in over a year so that telepresence robots could affix two of Julian Kerner's robotic chemical vapor deposition mills at opposite poles of the station—onto the naked girders of East and West Habs. The spin-down would last just a few hours, but attaching the CVD mills would make possible the long-awaited completion of the station hull.

Kerner's CVD mills were like large-format printers, except that their frames had been made to match the cross section of Clarke Station. They would be sealed around the girders and begin a process by which pure iron would depose into a slowly accumulating film of precisely formed hull plating, seamlessly encasing the station ring. As the metal deposed in the reaction chamber, the computer-controlled mill would slowly, imperceptibly advance, rolling along the newly finished hull, printing the station as it went.

More important, since the two CVD mills were symmetrical in mass, once they were clamped in place and started, Clarke Station could again be spun-up, and artificial gravity returned even as the construction continued.

CHAPTER 35

A Modest Proposal

CLARKE STATION POPULATION: 37
DAYS TO RYUGU DEPARTURE: 735
RESOURCES LAUNCHED TO L2: 35,000 TONS

James Tighe sat at a desk in his cramped quarters in South Hab, watching a virtual TV with Priya Chindarkar.

On-screen, Tighe's brother-in-law, Ted Vinter, was being interviewed on a major American cable news show. An inset photo of Tighe on a caving expedition appeared alongside the man.

Vinter, as always, spoke authoritatively. "*We always knew Jim was destined to do great things. Not everyone could see it, but I had a sense he was a visionary. I was the first person to invest in his ideas.*"

Chindarkar sighed in exasperation. "Is he for real?" She turned to Tighe. "He thought you went to *prison*, not to Ryugu. He didn't invest in you—he loaned you money. Your family is really something, James."

Just then, Jin Han and Sevastian Yakovlev walked past, Yak motioning. "Come! It is time for you to see."

"See what?"

"Come."

Tighe dismissed the virtual TV window, and he and Chindarkar followed.

Yak led them to the elevator, where they rode to the station's core. The four of them floated around the central gate compartment as he brought them not to the familiar North elevator, but to the West elevator—which ever since their arrival back in 2039 had been blocked off by steel panels, stir-welded to an airtight seal.

But now they could see elevator doors and a physical call button.

Yak beamed. "It is time!" He tapped the button.

After a moment an elevator arrived—with a *ding*. Everyone "oohed." Then the West elevator doors opened.

Chindarkar said, "I can't believe this is finally happening."

Yak gestured for them all to get inside.

They floated into the elevator car. Tighe breathed in the odor of newly installed polymer fabric panels. Yak tapped the H4 button. The doors closed, and the elevator descended smoothly into the station's spin-gravity well. In less than thirty seconds, the sensation of gravity returned, and they stood once more on the deck.

Yak boomed, "Welcome to our new home!"

The doors opened to reveal a wide steel-paneled floor, curving upward and away from them, with overhead LED lighting, bundles of wires, and mounting holes at intervals. There were no partition walls to break up the floor plan. It was all wide open.

They exited the elevator and moved out into the long upward-curving, echoey room.

Tighe shouted, "Hey!"

"*Hey… Hey… Hey… Hey*" returned.

Chindarkar turned around to see the room extending behind them, since the elevator column pierced the center of the floor. "It's nice to have so much room!"

"Six hundred square meters. Forty long. Fifteen wide. Each floor."

She sniffed the air. "And it doesn't smell funky like South Hab—after a year of plumbing and HVAC problems."

Jin asked, "East Hab has life support, too?"

"Yes—although East elevator is not yet operational."

Tighe peered down a nearby spiral staircase. "The floors below are decked?"

"Let us go." Yak motioned once more toward the elevator. They followed him inside.

Chindarkar looked to him quizzically, her hand near the buttons. "Where to?"

Yak said, "We are going to H2."

She tapped the button.

Jin asked, "What is on H2?"

"You will see."

The elevator descended for a moment, stopped, and the doors opened. As Yak led them out into the floor, they found themselves in what appeared to be a corporate lobby, replete with carpet and decorative paneling. The letters "CCE" as a stylized logo were stenciled on one wall, along with smaller letters spelling out "Cislunar Commodity Exchange."

Tighe just stared. "You have got to be kidding."

Yak spread his arms outward. "Official headquarters."

"So this is what Ramón has been working on?"

"Along with Lukas's designers back on Earth, yes. Is meant to project image of solidity."

"Well, hell . . . for a spaceship it sure does. But I thought we were going to get some personal space."

Yak gave him a look. "This entire hab is for us, J.T. For CCE, for Catalyst. For us to plan rescue mission. In privacy."

The others exchanged looks.

Tighe said, "Okay, now we're talking."

Yak walked toward twin doors, opening them to reveal a conference room containing a dozen cushioned chairs, arranged around a boardroom table. "For private discussions. With so much interest in our activities back on Earth, it will be useful to not be in South Hab."

Tighe and the others entered. Through their crystals they could see a wide virtual window in the conference room wall that looked out on a live exterior camera view of the Moon, Earth, and the bustling supply yard. "Very, very nice . . ." He sat down in a cushioned chair. "I could get used to this."

Chindarkar and Jin did the same.

"Who made the chairs?"

"Chemists are making polyurethane foams now. Chem lab will expand in South Hab once other compartments are complete."

Tighe looked up in alarm. "So we're going to finish all the compartments?" He turned to Jin. "We could be using these resources to build the rescue ship."

Chindarkar said, "J.T., we need more room to house the experts we'll need."

Yak sat down. "She is right, and metal resources are no longer our constraint. We have 4,000 tons of steel. Twenty-five hundred tons of aluminum. A thousand tons of titanium. These amounts will increase, and we have two years of time to design and build this ship. This will allow us to do much—you will see."

Chindarkar added, "We'll need scores more experts up here for the construction. This isn't a last-ditch lifeboat we're building this time. This vessel has to support us there and back, along with Isabel and Ade—and they might need medical attention."

Yak interacted with virtual UIs. "And this is task I have been working on with Lunargistics and Julian Kerner's team."

Tighe leaned forward eagerly. "You have a ship design?"

"*Da, tochno.*" He looked up, paused for dramatic effect—and then gestured to instantiate an AR model of an enormously impressive spacecraft. It rotated slowly above the middle of the boardroom table.

Tighe stared at it. "Wow."

Where the *Konstantin* had composite box trusses and small inflatable habs, this vessel had a sturdy superstructure of gleaming metal, with sets of elongated fuel tanks, and a sizable, cylindrical habitat up near the bow, along with docking ports, communication masts, and half a dozen rocket engines at the stern.

"It has spin-gravity, of course . . ." With a gesture from Yak, the habitat expanded with beams unfolding between segments. "A solid habitation ring so that it can be occupied even while under acceleration." He pointed. "Titanium superstructure. Lighter. Stronger. Dry mass of 463 tons. Drop tanks for multistage propulsion. Fully fueled with hydrolox, is 3,300 tons. One hundred twenty-eight meters in length."

It was a shockingly impressive vessel. Tighe couldn't help but smile as he beheld it.

Jin turned to Chindarkar. Then to Tighe. Then said, "Thirty-three hundred tons—that's more than 2,000 tons of propellant."

Yak nodded. "It will require much energy to make the 60-million-kilometer crossing to Ryugu in reasonable time. However, with drop tanks, this design has delta-v of 13.6 kilometers per second—enough to accomplish a sixty-day trajectory to Ryugu in June 2042. It also has substantial radiation protection."

Tighe looked with surprise at Chindarkar and Jin, who were considerably less enthusiastic than he was. "I think it looks amazing, Yak. My biggest concern is whether we can build it in time."

"That's not my main concern," Jin said.

Yak held up his hand. "I know what you are going to say."

"You're an astronautical engineer, Sevastian. You should know that we—"

"This design can bring back everyone alive. What purpose is there to rescue someone, only to cause them to perish with you on return journey?"

Chindarkar looked up from doing the math. "You'd need just about every liter of water we've got to fuel this thing. In fact, we'd have to split some of our ammonia to scrounge up all the hydrogen necessary."

Tighe said, "But we have the propellant."

Jin turned to him. "We have plenty of oxygen, yes. But not hydrogen. And we will have even less two years from now."

Yak said, "*Amy Tsukada* tug will have water."

"For the last time: we cannot count on the arrival of the *Amy Tsukada*."

Tighe said, "What about the mass-driver?"

Chindarkar said, "We get lots of oxygen from the regolith, J.T., but almost no hydrogen. In fact, the volatile tanks down at Morra Base are not even full yet."

Jin added, "We have about 7 tons of volatiles stored there. That's out of 35,000 tons of regolith processed." He gestured to the hologram. "How much work has been done on this?"

Yak expanded the graphic, showing its interior. "Conceptual and preliminary design work only."

Tighe held up his hand. "Hang on." He turned to Chindarkar and Jin. "Are you telling me you want to rule out this design because it uses up most of our hydrogen? The entire purpose of what we're doing up here is to launch a rescue ship."

Jin said, "It is not the entire purpose. Remember Lukas's observation on the airship. If we expend all our resources on the rescue mission, what would the purpose have been for Nicole's and David's and Amy's sacrifice? Do you really want to burn through all the water and ammonia they gave their lives to harvest, just to go back to Ryugu?"

"That's not the situation. There's a lot more water and ammonia out at Ryugu."

"We cannot count on anyone gathering and refining asteroid regolith out there. We do not know what happened after the North Koreans arrived, J.T. Isabel and Ade might already be dead."

The room suddenly got quiet.

Jin sighed. "That is not what I meant to say. You know that I believe in this rescue mission. I am simply saying that we must not destroy all that they worked for in the process."

There was silence for several moments more.

Tighe finally said, "If we need hydrogen, then let's just go buy a metric fuckton down on Earth and have it launched up here."

Jin sighed again. "J.T., even Macy's Galleon rockets consume 95 percent of their mass in fuel just climbing out of Earth's atmosphere. To fill up a single Galleon rocket with hydrogen in LEO would require dozens and dozens of launches. And who knows how many months. Maybe years."

"So? We have the money, don't we?"

Chindarkar said, "It would also damage the atmosphere. Macy uses methalox—that's hundreds of tons of carbon in the atmosphere with each launch. And we would be spending lūna lavishly down on Earth. Giving it directly to Jack Macy, of all people."

"You mean that cryptocurrency Lukas made up? Fine! Who gives a damn?"

"J.T., have you even gone through the training for the CCE block-chain yet?"

"No! I haven't had the time. I've been operating Talos and Badger robots to keep the mass-driver up and running."

"You think we haven't all been working?"

Yak looked to Jin. "I will revisit this design—scale it down."

Tighe shouted, "Scale it down? Then why the hell did we do all this? We have the resources to build this huge space station, but no resources to build a proper rescue ship."

Chindarkar said, "This space station did not consume most of our propellant. We're not trying to launch Clarke Station halfway across the inner solar system to catch a flying rock, J.T."

Jin held up his hands. "Everyone, please. I know tempers are running high, but let us remain civil."

Chindarkar took a deep breath. "We must not transfer a large percentage of lūna to a single entity on Earth, or they will gain major influence over the course of the cislunar economy. And thus, the CCE."

Tighe held his head. "Now you sound like Lukas."

Chindarkar thought for a moment before saying, "What if we sent an uncrewed vessel out to Ryugu in 2042?"

Yak frowned at her. "Uncrewed?"

"Yes. That would reduce the ship's mass. We could provide—"

Jin shook his head. "Priya, we have no assurance that Isabel and Ade could make their way to the ship or even detect its arrival. What if they are incapacitated?"

"True."

Tighe leaned back in disgust. "Do you even want us to go on this rescue mission?"

"Don't you dare say that to me. I'm trying to make sure this rescue actually happens. Do you think those international observers in North Hab are up here to root for us? We will have to be very careful in our dealings with them, because mark my words, they still have designs on our entire operation. The situation on Earth has gotten worse, not better. In the wrong hands, what's in our supply yard could ensure domination of cislunar space. And using up our propellant supply would make us sitting ducks."

They all sat in silence for several moments.

Tighe looked to Chindarkar. "Look . . . I'm sorry I said that. It was out of line, and I didn't mean it."

She nodded. "You're upset. I understand. I am, too."

Jin said, "Let us reconvene later." He looked to Yak.

Yak gestured and the model of the impressive spacecraft winked out. "Pity. I guess I will go back to drawing board."

Several days later, news came that Fatima Patel's pregnancy had ended in a miscarriage. Aside from being personally devastating to the mother, it was a serious blow to the crew. After the months of hardship and constant work, things had been looking up—and now this sad news. Humankind's first "star child" was no more.

Back on Earth the media turned instantly from Clarke Station boosterism to unfounded suspicions of forced abortion and essays on the irresponsibility of conceiving children in deep space—an accusation not without merit, given the frontier conditions on board.

Earth-first activists, meanwhile, had a field day, splashing fake blood onto the lobby doors of Catalyst Corporation's offices in Luxembourg. It was as though the public resented the optimism they'd been given, now that it was revealed to be so fragile.

But as with all news from Earth, the public's attention soon turned elsewhere, and a devastating drought, followed by waves of economic and climate refugees on the borders of Europe and the US, chased the death of the first space child out of the headlines.

Tighe shared his relief with no one. Aside from the media circus the first human birth in space would have caused, he had sat awake at night wondering about the embryo developing in spin-gravity and being exposed to galactic cosmic rays several times higher than on Earth, even behind the protection of Holstad's radiation-eating fungus. It didn't seem fair to do such experiments with an innocent. The crew, after all, had chosen to be here. The fetus had not.

Within a month, Fatima Patel returned to Earth on the *Let's Be Friends* lunar cycler, and from then on new crew on Ascension Island were required to go through counseling with Dr. Bruno to screen for wannabe "star mothers" and "star fathers."

This safeguard was better than nothing. But not by much.

CHAPTER 36

Biosphere

Clarke Station compartment NNE (which stood for "North by Northeast")—commonly known as "Ag Lab"—had not been finished long, and yet it was clearly Lynne Holstad's domain. Or at least it had become the domain of the half dozen biologists and botanists whom she directed. Nominally part of an Iowa State University project funded by the US Department of Agriculture, the Ag Lab was more accurately a collection of research projects and astropreneurial endeavors that crossed many different disciplines, organizations, and nations, and it was increasingly coming to be known as "the Biosphere"—a project that Holstad had spearheaded and helped to shape. Its goal was the preservation and recreation of the basic building blocks of Earth's various biomes beyond our home world, to make life flourish in space. And the scientists involved in this effort had an almost spiritual zeal in its pursuit.

As admirable as she found this goal, Priya Chindarkar had to admit that she could just as easily have supported it out of sheer selfishness—because walking through Ag Lab's rows of seedlings, flowering plants, and grow chambers filled her with joy. Unlike the other compartments in Clarke Station, this place was bursting with life. Not all of it was as natural as home; there was the indigo lighting and vertical farm flats, where researchers in lab coats monitored various species of plants in different stages of growth, watching as robotic systems cared for them with reproducible precision. But there were still sections filled with greenery where Chindarkar could brush her hand across leaves and feel herself part of a greater whole.

But the most popular place on Clarke Station was the Terrarium—a two-story-high chamber being cultivated as a rain forest oasis, or what the team called "syntropy" agriculture, using filtered sunlight beamed in via fiber optics. In a masterstroke of station-wide relations, Holstad had created a refuge here where those on board could feel human again in deep space. One could "vacation" there among the living things, pruning branches and reconnecting with Earth life. The Terrarium would no doubt help to ensure Ag Lab's continued funding.

And it was here in the Terrarium that Holstad chose to hold today's event, briefly halting her team's research to honor a request from Chindarkar. It had become clear that Holstad—like Jin, Tighe, Chindarkar, Yak, and Marín—was here for the duration. Here until her purpose was achieved. And there was no telling when that would be. Until then, a return to Earth would have to wait. In fact, Green Team had returned to Earth three months ago—without Holstad. For this reason, Chindarkar had invited her to join Gold Team, the permanent team.

It was with great joy that Chindarkar received word that Holstad had accepted. There were no real benefits to speak of. It was an informal, made-up thing, these teams. But the sense of belonging, the feeling of common purpose, seemed to matter to everyone, and Chindarkar wanted to share that bond with Holstad.

A couple dozen people had gathered in the nascent Terrarium for an informal "ceremony." Chindarkar stood at the center of the room amid polite applause. Jin, Tighe, Yak, and Marín stood to her right. Holstad and her senior assistants stood on the left. After a few very brief words of appreciation for Holstad's contributions to life on the station—and on Earth—she presented the professor with an embroidered arm patch denoting her as a member of Gold Team.

The gathering clapped and whistled, the surrounding plants muffling the echoes.

Holstad nodded and took the floor, gazing down briefly at the embroidered patch in her hand. After the applause died down, she said, "Thank you,

Priya, for allowing me to join with you all. I feel honored." She did not, however, acknowledge either Tighe or Jin. Instead, Holstad looked out at her audience, a collection of the international observers on board the station, as well as astropreneurs and fellow scientists.

She gestured to the surrounding Ag Lab. "What you see around you is the result of thousands upon thousands of years of human experience. Knowledge and wisdom passed down to us from all our ancestors. And while the crisis back on Earth may be human-made, the story of life *is* the story of crises. Of facing them. Adapting and surviving. There have always been blights and pestilences that challenged our forebears. It now falls to us to use the knowledge they bequeathed us, to find a path to flourishing." She gazed at the lush plants. "Here we have begun the process of learning how to build from scratch the biosphere from which we evolved—to build, beyond Earth, environments consisting of hundreds of thousands of interacting species—bacteria, fungi, invertebrates, plants, mammals, fish, birds, and more. This will be the key to safeguarding Earth's legacy, of which humanity is just one small part. We are its stewards, but we cannot save ourselves alone. We must preserve it all and convey it into the cosmos."

Chindarkar felt herself overcome with emotion at the love that this woman had for all living things. For what she had accomplished despite her personal pain.

Applause filled the Terrarium.

After the ceremony, the other Gold Team members rode an elevator back to West Hab. The group was uncharacteristically silent—especially given their recent debates.

Chindarkar finally said, "Lynne would like to request the Northeast compartment as well, once it's complete. So that they can have one large, contiguous facility."

Jin looked up from some reverie. "She wants two whole compartments for the Ag Lab?"

Tighe spoke without looking up. "I say give it to her."

The others looked to him in surprise.

"Can you think of a better use for it?" Tighe exited the moment the doors opened.

CHAPTER 37

Topping Out

CLARKE STATION POPULATION: 85
DAYS TO RYUGU DEPARTURE: 606
RESOURCES LAUNCHED TO L2: 66,400 TONS

James Tighe tried to recall what it felt like the first time he'd come aboard Clarke Station, not quite two years earlier. It seemed impossible that it could have been that long already. Back then the station was just a sinuous torus of steel beams with only two compartments out of sixteen finished, and yet those compartments had seemed cavernous compared to what Tighe, Priya Chindarkar, Jin Han, and their crewmates had endured on the *Konstantin*.

Now the entire circumference of Clarke Station was fully enclosed by pressurized double-hull plating, with racked layers of radiotrophic fungi between the inner and outer hull as radiation shielding. Each of its sixteen compartments consisted of four stories, 600 square meters in size—38,000 square meters of pressurized area in total. Building out the living quarters would require more time, but the mere existence of that much room was an unimaginable extravagance over what he remembered from those early days, and all of it was possible for one reason only: none of it had to be lifted up from Earth. Instead, the core steel that formed this station came from resources harvested and refined at the asteroid Ryugu, while the hull plating that enclosed the remaining compartments and aluminum that partitioned its inner spaces had been shot up from Morra Base. In total, over 15,000 tons of metal had been used in its construction.

That feat had been remotely directed from Earth by a man whose transit craft was just now arriving in Clarke Station's hangar bay. A man who had, in fact, built the transit craft itself. As well as the *Konstantin*.

Jin, Chindarkar, and Sevastian Yakovlev floated alongside Tighe at the microgravity arrival gate, as did several other station crew.

Soon the gateway hatch opened and pushed inward. After a moment, several wide-eyed new crew members floated through—part of the thirty-strong Red-2 Team that had ridden billionaire Jack Macy's lunar cycler up from low Earth orbit. Half a dozen transit craft had been sent out to rendezvous with this Galleon rocket as it swept through L2 a few thousand kilometers from Clarke Station, before the cycler fell back toward Earth again.

A member of the station's orientation team greeted the new arrivals as they came in, while Tighe and the others watched the hatchway closely.

Before long, their indispensable construction foreman, Julian Kerner, glided gracefully through the opening.

Chindarkar shouted, "Julian!"

Kerner looked up and smiled, pulling away from the coordinator as Tighe and the others hugged him.

"How was the flight?"

He gave an unimpressed look. "Zephyr's build quality is shoddy. Too lightweight for my tastes." Kerner studied the walls around him. "But *this* . . . This was built to last. And it's good to finally see it with my own eyes."

Chindarkar smiled. "We couldn't celebrate its completion without you here."

Jin nodded. "Yes. Without you and your team, none of this would have been possible." He paused. "Now, can you help us build a rescue ship?"

Kerner shrugged. "Of course. Unlicensed spacecraft are my specialty."

A few days later, Tighe emerged from the South Hab elevator into the midst of a party. As he moved out into the crowd, someone shoved a cup of spiked punch into his hand, while others patted him on the back, or took selfies with him.

The "topping out" celebration might have seemed completely normal at first glance, with several dozen guests engaged in raucous conversation in a carpeted room framed by fabric wall panels—except that the floor, walls, and ceiling curved slightly upward, and people on the far side of the room appeared modestly tilted, relative to Tighe. It made for a surreal backdrop, but only if you weren't used to it. Drinking helped.

Due to the cost of hauling liquor up from the bottom of Earth's gravity well, "imported" drinks were hideously expensive; the going rate was twenty thousand USD for a shot of single malt, with only two bottles on board. However, some of the station's chemists had furthered the frontiers of space science by utilizing Holstad's starchy test crops to create a moderately passable vodka they dubbed *In-shit-too*, as an homage to both its origin and the slurring speech it induced.

For reasons of practicality and safety, not everyone aboard was present for the celebration, but it was still an impressive crowd. Ever since the founders of Clarke Station had moved in to West Hab, the crew seldom got a chance to see the now "famous deep space explorers." So pretty much anyone who could wrangle an invite was here.

At some point, Jin, as captain of Clarke Station, held up his cup of punch and spoke loudly. "Everyone. Please, I would like to say a few words, if I may." In the silence that followed he beheld the crowd. "We all know what was required to complete this space station. There are those who cannot join us tonight, although they deserve a place of honor. Nicole Clarke, after whom this station is named. David Morra, after whom Morra Base is named. Amy Tsukada, after whom the refinery and the spacecraft that will arrive next year are named. And of course, Robert Ecklund, for whom the world's first lunar mass-driver is named—and the many others who sacrificed their lives to make this space station a reality. Their names are all commemorated on that wall." He pointed at a series of engraved titanium plaques.

Tighe turned toward them. Fourteen in all. *So far.* As civilized as this environment seemed, those names were mute testimony that this was still a frontier. Clarke Station and everyone on it enjoyed a fragile existence at the very edge of the possible. Death was one mistake or malfunction away, and they seldom got a chance to forget it. Tighe's cancer might have been in remission—perhaps even cured—due to gene-editing treatments, but he never took that to mean he'd survive long. There were no guarantees in deep space.

Jin raised his cup once more. "Today, let us honor their memory and their sacrifice. We owe our future to them all."

The gathering replied, "Hear, hear."

Afterward Tighe felt a profound melancholy and moved about the room with feigned purpose, more as a means to avoid conversation than to get anywhere.

There were over a dozen astropreneurs on the station now, each of them building out their sub-compartment to suit their business needs. The vagaries of commercial real estate were alien to Tighe, and the core team had turned issues of escalations and triple-net leases over to Rochat's new space law division. Apparently Rochat's leases included a requirement that the CCE retain a small percentage in each tenant's startup. It seemed extreme, but then again, landlords back on Earth didn't have to provide every essential of life in the midst of an endless sucking void. Plus, the funds would go back into the CCE, powering the blockchain and its smart contracts—whatever all that meant.

The population of Clarke Station was international and diverse—decided more by their skills and goals than their origin. English seemed to be their common tongue, and Tighe caught snippets of conversation as he moved among them.

"The de-growth crowd back on Earth doesn't seem to realize that others will expand to fill whatever space they give up."

"... transfers possible to Venus, and an atmosphere thick enough to aerobrake. You could scoop CO_2 and nitrogen from the atmosphere and ship it back here to ..."

"Earth trojan asteroids like 2020 XL5 and 2010 TK7 represent hundreds of millions of tons of resources—and they're right here in cislunar space. And now they can be cost-effectively accessed ..."

"I'm telling you, telepresence adventures on the Moon could be *huge*. Tourists on the cycler would have low latency ..."

Gazing out at this second wave of astropreneurs, Tighe increasingly felt like an old prospector who had helped launch a gold rush—but who no longer really belonged in the town that grew around it.

There were advantages to this prodigious growth, however. A commercial-grade kitchen was being installed in North Hab—which would finally be able to prepare proper food. Lynne Holstad's Ag Lab was cultivating even more plants, and the new Synbio Lab was synthesizing everything from cultured meat to coffee in bioreactors—even cultured wood (which somehow involved growing wood without the need to grow a whole tree). The entire "biofacturing" craze seemed like black magic to Tighe. Still, it was nice to be able to taste a real steak. Or real enough. He'd eaten enough freeze-dried food on the *Konstantin* expedition to last him a lifetime.

As Tighe walked through the party, people nodded to him. Now that Clarke Station was finished, more would be arriving soon—astropreneurs eager to make use of a location in deep space with access to thousands of tons of elemental resources and energy, but also with spin-gravity and life support. Incoming companies included startups developing chargeable atomic batteries, ZBLAN fiber optics, metallic hydrogen research, even rubber made from dandelions. Spacecraft manufacturing, satellite servicing and support, chemical synthesis, robotics, data centers, debris cleanup, solar satellite manufacturing—the list went on. There was an atmosphere of excitement here that went beyond the location.

He passed by Ramón Marín, who was conversing with the representative of a low Earth orbit crypto-mining concern. Diplomatic and trade relations between the LEO-crypto and deep-space-crypto communities were apparently expanding, but that entire industry was still a mystery to Tighe.

A Black man in his early thirties approached Tighe, trepidation evident as he extended his hand. He wore the green jumpsuit that identified him as a commercial tenant. "Mr. Tighe. Jimiyu Onyango of Proteonics, Nairobi, Kenya. I wanted to thank you for selecting our firm for tenancy on Clarke Station. This has been such an incredible experience."

Tighe shook his hand. "Don't thank me. It's Gabriel or Lukas back on Earth who choose."

"Of course." Onyango tapped his head. "You are no doubt busy on many weighty matters, but I want you to know that it is an honor to meet a historic figure such as yourself."

Tighe laughed. "Well, I assure you, I don't feel historic. Old, maybe. What does Proteonics do, Mr. Onyango?"

"Please, call me Jimi. We are utilizing the microgravity at the station's core to research protein crystallization for new drug discovery—specifically new classes of monoclonal antibodies. The combination of spin-gravity and microgravity research facilities in one location is transformational to our work. I hope you'll come by and take a look."

"It sounds like it would all go completely over my head."

Onyango laughed. "I would be happy to explain it."

Tighe spotted Chindarkar nearby, speaking with several of the international observers—eliciting laughter as she chatted them up. She always had that knack. Her diplomacy was probably helping with Earth relations—though it was hard to tell. Some days it seemed like her efforts were just pulling them into Earth's dysfunction.

Onyango noticed Tighe's distractedness. "Well, once more, Mr. Tighe, it is a pleasure to meet you."

"Likewise, Jimi."

Onyango stepped away with a nod.

Chindarkar excused herself from the knot of international observers, and approached Tighe. "Making small talk with the tenants. That's good."

"The idea that we have *tenants* out here is pretty strange, but I get it: we'll need some of these people if we want to build the rescue ship on time."

She extended her arms, and they hugged, kissing each other on the cheek. "Congratulations. To all of us. That we're here at all is a miracle."

He nodded. "I'll feel better when we have our ship design resolved. We only have a couple years left."

She held up her cup. "Is this half empty or half full, Mr. Tighe?"

"It's entirely full, if you include the air."

"Ha! Good answer."

The international observer from Brazil came up to her and extended his hand as the station band started up. "May I have this dance?"

She laughed. "See you, J.T."

The two of them migrated to the dance floor as the station band played a cover version of "The Air That I Breathe" by the Hollies. Dancing to live music—that was another first in space. *"Put that on the wall!"* Isabel Abarca would have said.

Tighe took another sip of punch. He now had a good buzz going.

A few couples were slow dancing—which was the *only* dancing advisable on a spin-gravity ship of this radius.

The band was composed of researchers and scientists who had built their electronic instruments in situ.

The song ended and an emcee took to the mic. "The Ka-band, ladies and gentlemen!"

The crowd applauded.

Tighe waited a respectable period of time before passing by Jin and Yak and indicating with his thumb that he was headed out. He took the elevator up to the core and crossed over to the West elevator bank. His face and RFID tag unlocked the elevator car, and within a minute he entered the lobby of the CCE. He found himself unwinding as if arriving at his own apartment—which, in a way, the CCE was. Four stories and 2,400 square meters of space in space. Both Yak and Chindarkar had been actively engaged in the build-out, and there were now partition walls, carpeted corridors, and a main reception desk (not yet staffed).

As Tighe entered the lobby he studied the new metal sculpture on a pedestal that occupied the center of the circular room. It was an orrery fashioned by a previous crew member, metallurgist Nicolau Ivorra—father of the first child conceived in deep space. It had Ivorra's signature brutalist style, replete with scorch marks. However, instead of the entire solar system, this orrery consisted of the Earth, Moon, and Clarke Station. It was, Tighe had to admit, crudely beautiful.

Cushioned seating was arrayed around it, presumably for the day when supplicants would arrive here for meetings. Thankfully, now there was just the four of them and a few CCE staff—probably Marín's security people. And also Kerner, come to think of it. Tighe, Chindarkar, Jin, and Yak had private quarters in each corner of H3. Tighe entered his own suite—a space 7.5 meters by 10 meters, subdivided between a living area, tiny kitchen, bedroom, and bathroom.

It was modern and sterile—reminding him of the corporate apartment Catalyst Corporation had leased for him in Luxembourg City. And yet, he felt more rooted here than he ever had down on Earth. Strange, since this apartment was rotating while simultaneously hurtling around a Lagrange point on the far side of the Moon.

There was a sectional sofa, basic nylon carpet, a brushed metal and glass coffee table (glass was a new addition to the station's industrial repertoire), and armchairs. Nothing was high quality, but they were lavish considering the location. That he had a bedroom with a queen-sized foam mattress, plus a private bathroom with shower—that was once almost impossible to imagine in deep space. In fact, it *would* have been impossible if they'd had to drag it all up from Earth. In situ resource utilization really had changed everything.

Tighe settled onto a chair in his small living room and instantiated a virtual orrery for the inner solar system that highlighted the current location of the asteroid Ryugu in relation to Earth. Right now, it was almost on the opposite side of the Sun—320 million kilometers away.

Suddenly it seemed obvious to him that Isabel and Ade were both dead.

He decided he'd had too much to drink—Tighe didn't have alcohol all that often these days. So he dismissed the orrery and headed to his bedroom. As he undressed, he glanced at a framed photo on his nightstand that he'd recently reprinted using what little paper there was on board. Tighe lifted the frame and studied the image of his father as a handsome young man. Eternally standing at a trailhead, heavy pack on his back, turned slightly toward the camera. Gone to the wilderness and never seen again. Tighe was now a decade older than his father would ever be.

He wondered if recovering the man's bleached bones would mean anything to him—like Abarca discovering her father's frozen body near the summit of K2 had meant to her.

Tighe realized it wouldn't. His father had disappeared when Tighe was small, and he'd barely known him. This photo had once evoked such longing, but now it seemed to belong to someone else. He slid the frame onto the nightstand and finished undressing. Then he paused.

Lately he'd been vexed by a recurring dream—a dream involving someone who *had* been like a father to him. He felt a sudden, intense guilt.

A man you killed.

He froze. It was an idea that was beginning to take hold of him: that he didn't deserve to be here. The memory was too painful to recall, and yet it was waiting for him each night. Lately getting worse.

He had to face this, and he did have a way to access the real event.

Tighe laid back, donned his crystal headset once more, and searched his private folders for a recording he hadn't seen in eight years—since before he'd attended Ascension Island training. It wasn't hard to find. Tighe knew right where it was. After a moment he clicked on an inscrutable file name, and a virtual screen filled his view.

The video's perspective was from his own helmet-cam, deep in an underwater cave, moments after an earthquake had destroyed his team's supply of decompression gas.

Tighe felt his heart move into his throat as he beheld—for the first time in years—the face of Richard Oberhaus, his fifty-something mentor. Oberhaus was checking his dive computer, and his full face mask permitted him to speak over their radio link as he said with his slight German accent, *"Without that deco station, there's not enough gas for the two of us, James."*

Tighe's voice responded, *"We can make it work."*

Oberhaus looked up, calm as always, his voice was no longer tinny with helium. It was his normal baritone. *"Yes, we can make it work. But not for both of us. One of us is not going to make it back this time."*

To survive at 90 meters depth, it was necessary to add helium into their gas mixture, but watching the video now, Tighe knew that Oberhaus had already made his decision. In shutting off his helium, he had already killed himself—and done so in order for Tighe to hear what he was saying, to hear his mentor's voice.

Tighe, still unaware, said, *"You go, Richard. I'll stay."* His helmet-cam looked down as he began to unsling air bottles.

A gloved hand on his wrist. *"We must be rational about this, James."*

Tighe tried to press an air bottle into Oberhaus's hand.

Oberhaus pushed it away. *"I have lived twenty-two years longer than you. My children are grown. You have so much of life ahead of you."*

Tighe's helmet-cam shook vigorously, side to side. His voice, still squeaking from helium: *"You said it yourself: you have a wife and children."*

"And you should have a chance for the same."

"I refuse to go."

Oberhaus was unslinging all his oxygen and nitrox canisters. *"There is no gas to spare discussing this. Leave now and you may have enough to survive decompression. You are in better physical shape than me, James. You've always been better able to withstand nitrogen narcosis than I. Between the two of us, you stand the better chance of making it."*

Tighe's helmet-cam remained focused on Oberhaus's face.

"I will not remain conscious for much longer. Go."

In the present, Tighe was once more gripped by grief. Staring into the face of the man who'd been a father to him. Those calm eyes, reassuring him once more.

"We do not have the luxury of a long good-bye. Say good-bye to me, James."

Tighe heard his own voice squeak, *"Good-bye."* His gloved hands accepted the gas canisters. He then embraced Oberhaus.

Oberhaus's voice, weaker now. *"Go!"*

Tighe grabbed the controls of a diver propulsion vehicle and accelerated away, upward.

After a few moments, Tighe's helmet-cam turned back to see Oberhaus's aquaflash lights illuminating him. Oberhaus nodded as he receded into the gloom, and then the lights went out. Oberhaus had extinguished them purposely—so that Tighe could not look back.

Lying in the present, as grief coursed through him, Tighe decided that, rather than feel guilt, he would instead justify Oberhaus's sacrifice. He would make it matter.

CHAPTER 38

Proliferation

The board of Catalyst Corporation convened around a new table with a surface of sintered and polished lunar regolith. James Tighe, Priya Chindarkar, Jin Han, and Sevastian Yakovlev were physically present, while an augmented-reality projection of Lukas Rochat in Luxembourg City was beamed in from Earth on a few-second delay.

They all stared at a virtual spacecraft floating above the table, while Yak addressed them. "I took to heart issues raised regarding previous design, and this new concept requires greatly reduced mass, while still satisfying all mission requirements."

Chindarkar said, "It certainly looks more reasonably sized."

"*Da*. It uses one-third the fuel of first design."

"Outstanding. I'm impressed you were able to reduce it that much."

Jin asked, "Lunargistics worked with you on this design?"

"No. Julian and I worked with new company out of Czech Republic. A firm called Star Power. They have designed spacecraft for both ESA and private European aerospace firms." He rotated the model. "No such spacecraft has combined these features before. However, we will obtain experts necessary to—"

"*Do you have a cost estimate?*" Rochat interrupted, possibly due to transmission delay.

Tighe cast an annoyed look in his direction. "Relax. He'll get to the cost."

Yak turned back to the model. "Spacecraft has overall length of 128 meters, and carries 712 tons of fuel." He highlighted each section of the model in turn. "Propulsion, two in-line fuel tanks, star-truss module, which contains avionics and life support module. Mounted around this star-truss are four 100-ton drop tanks. Solar and communications array, docking ports, and finally, tensegrity structure containing spin-gravity crew habitats." He animated the model so that the habitat ring expanded origami-like from a solid ring not much wider than the four external drop tanks into four trapezoidal wedges linked to the ship's axis by unfolding trusses, which locked into place to complete the ring. Connecting each of the four habs were narrow telescoping tunnels. Yak retracted the habs and repeated the expansion and contraction several times.

Chindarkar smiled. "That's elegant. Much better than the *Konstantin*."

Jin pointed. "Those connecting tunnels between the habs, they're pressurized?"

"*Da*. You can move from hab to hab while spun-up." He looked up from the model. "However, radius of rotation is only 80 meters. Nonetheless, we expect a crew well-conditioned to life aboard Clarke Station will be able to cope with Coriolis effects sufficiently for two-month mission."

Jin asked, "And propulsion?"

Yak paused a moment before expanding the model and zooming into four rocket engines arrayed as nodules around the stern of the craft. A label appeared near the edge of the model. "Craft is designated NTR-01, meaning nuclear thermal propulsion."

Jin frowned. "Nuclear?"

Yak held up his hand. "USSF has Conestoga-class spacecraft. Russia and China have—"

Rochat said, *"We've already received expressions of concern regarding our stockpile of uranium from the board of governors of the International Atomic Energy Agency. That's thirty-five nations."*

Tighe said, "Can we please hear what the design is first?"

Rochat relented.

Yak continued, zooming into a cutaway view of a single engine. "NTR-01 is powered by four 3-ton, 500-megawatt, trash-can-sized nuclear propulsion engines, each containing roughly 50 kilograms of uranium—"

"Fifty kilos each!"

Tighe said, "This is going to be a long goddamned meeting if you keep interrupting."

Jin turned to Tighe. "How many kilos of uranium do we currently have?"

Yak answered. "Eighty-two. However, we will have more than sufficient supply a year and a half from now."

"You do not seriously intend to enrich that uranium."

Yak breathed in. "We will use standard HALEU fuel—high-assay low-enriched uranium."

Chindarkar frowned. "And what is that?"

"Enriched to between 5 percent and 19.75 percent. Which is below weapons grade."

Rochat asked, *"And what percent does your engine require?"*

Yak winced. "Nineteen point seven five percent."

"And you propose to start building centrifuges and enriching uranium—on Clarke Station?"

Yak looked to Rochat. "You make it sound nefarious."

"Even if we got approval, there would need to be UN inspectors monitoring the enrichment—and that's if we got approval, which I doubt we will."

Tighe turned to Rochat's spectral image. "No one said we're *asking approval* for anything."

Chindarkar said, "J.T.—"

Yak held up his hands. "May I please complete presentation? At least then we will know what we are arguing about."

The room grew quiet.

"Spasibo." He turned back to the model, highlighting the reactor core. "Engine has 'cercer,' or zirconium-carbide-fueled, beryllium-moderated reactor core. Of this, only beryllium would need to be sourced from Earth. We can obtain or synthesize all other materials from lunar regolith." He looked up. "Each engine would have specific impulse greater than 950 seconds—over double efficiency of any chemical rocket. Delta-v of roughly 15 kilometers per second."

Jin nodded. "Wow."

Chindarkar whistled.

"Body of this engine would be made of tantalum-hafnium carbide ceramic, with melting point of 7,208 degrees Fahrenheit and working temperature of 6,020 degrees Fahrenheit. It can be manufactured in situ, since we have refined sufficient hafnium and tantalum from lunar regolith."

The model animated as the nuclear reactor lighted.

"Propellant would leave rocket nozzle at 10 kilometers per second at this temperature." He gestured and additional piping appeared outside the engine. He looked up again. "But with addition of O_2 afterburners, we can increase thrust by 62 percent—although this would lower fuel efficiency, reducing specific impulse to 700."

Jin stared at the model, clearly impressed.

"Is drag racer, yes?" Yak pointed at a fuel tank. "Hydrogen is ideal propellant, but ammonia is ideal fuel—of which we still have 600 tons, plus 720 more tons if *Amy Tsukada* tug arrives on schedule."

Jin said, "How many times do I have to say—?"

Tighe said, "Fine. Then we pay to have the ammonia we need launched up to us from Earth."

"Which would cost a fortune and require cooperation from Earth authorities."

Chindarkar asked Yak, "If hydrogen is the best propellant, why do you want ammonia for the fuel?"

"Saves us difficulty and mass of maintaining liquid hydrogen—ammonia consists of three atoms hydrogen, one of nitrogen. We extract hydrogen on demand via electrochemical cell with proton-conducting membrane integrated with nickel calcium amide catalyst. Ammonia splits into nitrogen and hydrogen efficiently at a temp of just hundreds of degrees—easily done near reactor." Yak then turned to his audience. "Other questions?"

Rochat said, *"Yes. Are you insane?"*

"Any sensible questions?"

Rochat continued. *"You're planning on enriching uranium—the very thing the Russians, Americans, and Chinese have already expressed grave concern over."*

Tighe said, "Because they want the uranium for themselves. We're not doing anything wrong. We're trying to rescue our friends, not build weapons. We should just do this."

"Concealing uranium enrichment is a *really* bad idea." Chindarkar hesitated for a moment, then said, "J.T., we've only just recently commenced stable relations with the international observers. As hard as it may be to accept, enriching uranium is potentially going to bring a strong international call for us to be put under external control. And if that succeeds, how would we even launch a rescue mission?"

Jin clenched his jaw, then turned to Tighe. "Priya is right that the world is not going to just sit by while we become a nuclear power. This will require delicate negotiations. And inspections."

Rochat added, *"Things are going very well up there lately. Don't forget how important the CCE is to the future of civilization. People down here on Earth are pulling CO_2 from the air in order to earn lūna to invest in the off-world economy. That will make a huge difference against climate change. But we've all seen what happens here on Earth to nations that start enriching uranium in pursuit of nuclear weapons. They—"*

Tighe shouted, "We're not pursuing nuclear weapons!"

Chindarkar held up her hands. "The world won't know that. We need to engage with the international community first to be sure they do know what we're up to."

Rochat said, *"Even if they allow it, there will need to be IAEA inspections."*

Tighe said, "And how long will it take to organize that? Are the necessary people even launch certified?" He gestured toward the model. "We should start planning to construct this ship. We've only got a year and a half until Ryugu arrives."

Jin said, "There is still time. I think we should table this until we determine how it will be received by the international community."

Tighe shook his head. "We can't wait."

"J.T.—"

"At the very least we should commence building the body of the ship. If not the reactors, then the superstructure, plumbing, and crew quarters."

"Which will be an enormous waste if we don't obtain international approval."

Tighe stared. "Then I suggest we make certain to get that approval." He pointed at the model. "Because this is the ship we need to reach Ryugu."

Yak piped in. "I agree with J.T. We should commence construction of spacecraft superstructure—otherwise, we may run out of time."

"But we hold off on building the engines and enriching the uranium?" Chindarkar ventured.

Tighe sighed.

Jin said, "If we obtain the necessary approvals, only then do we proceed with uranium enrichment."

Tighe looked around the table. "But in the meantime we commence construction of the spacecraft superstructure. Correct?"

The rest of the board nodded.

Rochat said, "*Very well, I move that we commence construction of the non-nuclear portions of the NTR-01, but hold off on the reactors and the fuel until I can sound out Earth authorities on the issue of uranium enrichment in deep space.*"

Tighe objected, "Don't put it like that. Context is important. Tell them we just want reactor fuel. We're not making weapons."

"*Votes in favor?*"

Everyone present raised their hands.

"*Then the motion passes unanimously.*"

As Tighe and Yak walked to the elevator, Tighe said, "I have renewed appreciation for what Joyce—scumbag though he was—managed to accomplish back on Earth."

Yak nodded. "I often think this."

Tighe looked behind them to determine they were alone before leaning close and saying, sotto voce, "Out of curiosity, Yak—what's involved in enriching uranium?"

Yak glanced around as well, and seeing no one, nonetheless leaned closer still. He spoke softly. "First: avoiding detection. Much easier out here."

"And the enrichment—could that be done in situ?"

"*Da.*" He paused. "Process involves leaching uranium in sulfuric acid—which we have—to create uranium oxide liquid. Uranium is then pulled out of solution using ammonia—which we also have. This creates a 'yellowcake' powder—almost entirely U-238 isotope. But we must isolate the 0.7 percent that is U-235—which is what we need for reactor."

Tighe tried to read Yak's expression. "And we can do all that?"

Yak nodded. "By transforming yellowcake into gas with fluorine, of which we have small supply on board for refrigeration. Resulting uranium hexafluo-ride gas is put into specialized centrifuge, where differing mass of isotopes separates them after repeated cycles."

"Could we build this centrifuge?"

"*Centrifuges*—and yes, we could. When finished, enriched U-238 is then transformed from gas back into solid by adding calcium—which we have in abundance. Calcium reacts with fluoride to create a salt and leaves behind only U-235 oxide, which is then heated and extruded into U-235 fuel pellets. Our end product."

"How long would all this take?"

"Once equipment is set up . . . some months."

They regarded each other.

Tighe finally whispered, "Like Joyce always said, Yak: better to ask forgive-ness than permission."

CHAPTER 39

Monster

CLARKE STATION POPULATION: 137
DAYS TO RYUGU DEPARTURE: 493
RESOURCES LAUNCHED TO L2: 102,300 TONS

James Tighe and Sevastian Yakovlev sat in an open workspace in the sparsely furnished Catalyst Corporation offices in West Hab, listening to a Czech nuclear propulsion engineer named Oleg Gusev speak over a virtual videoconference line back to Earth—the screen projected into their crystal headsets.

Tighe spotted Jin Han approaching at a fast walk, Kerner with him.

Yak interrupted Gusev. "Oleg. Terribly sorry. We must go. We will call you soon." He cut the conference line as Gusev tried to say something in response. Yak dismissed the screens just as Jin leaned into the room.

"Follow me to the ops center. This is an emergency." He headed down the hall.

Tighe and Yak jumped up and followed him.

Tighe asked, "What's up?"

Jin instantiated a shared virtual screen as they walked. It showed a shadowed image of the Sun. "Space Weather Prediction Center reports a monstrous coronal mass ejection, and it's headed directly at the Moon. They estimate it will reach us in fifteen to eighteen hours."

"How bad are we talking?"

"Big—an S5 solar storm. Much bigger than the flare we experienced out at Ryugu. An explosive outburst of solar wind plasma—a billion tons of charged particles going up to a few thousand kilometers per second. Powerful magnetic fields. We'll know just how big when the bow shock of the storm passes the Deep Space Climate Observatory at SE-L1. Depending on how much energy is behind those particles, at that point we'll have anywhere from fifteen minutes to an hour until it hits us."

Just then they entered the ops center, a control room of desks arranged in a circle, facing out toward a swarm of virtual screens. Half a dozen CCE and Catalyst staff manned the workstations.

Yak said, "What do you need from us?"

"Yak, go help Priya. She is working with mission control and the telepresence teams to reposition supply yard mass. We can't move a hundred thousand tons between us and the Sun, but whatever we can deploy as a shield before it hits will help."

"That will degrade the thermal power plant."

Jin nodded. "I know, but every system on this station needs to be powered down before that storm hits. We'll be running on emergency power only—and even then, as little as possible."

Tighe recalled the solar flare that hit the asteroid Ryugu after Amy Tsukada's funeral. If it had caught them in the open, they would all have been dead. Fortunately Ryugu shielded them. However, Clarke Station had no such protection and was in almost constant view of the Sun—handy for creating energy with a thermal power plant, but not so great at moments like these.

Jin was checking virtual screens. "We'll concentrate most of the supply yard mass directly in front of Clarke Station's core—shielding the power plant and the refinery as well. That'll leave the spin-gravity ring lightly shielded. So I'll order everyone on station into the core."

Tighe said, "But we've got well over a hundred people on board. How many do you think we can fit in the core compartment?"

Yak answered, "They will fit. It does not matter if it is tight."

Just then Professor Lynne Holstad entered the ops center and spoke matter-of-factly. "Captain, you wished to see me?"

Jin looked glad to see her. "Yes, Lynne. What's the status of your radiotrophic fungi project?"

"I can have one of my assistants get you—"

"I need best estimates. Now. How much protection does it give us?"

She paused. "We have . . . ten screens of approximately 1.7 millimeters within the double hull. It blocks probably 90 percent of incoming radiation—although, GCRs are—"

"Good! That is good."

Yak said, "Your fungi are about to get all-they-can-eat buffet."

She looked at him quizzically.

Jin said, "A major radiation storm is predicted to hit us by day's end. I'll be making an announcement, but get your people ready. We can expect a trail of energized protons in this storm's wake; complete communications disruption—no telepresence with our mules and other spacecraft. No comms with Earth. With a storm of this magnitude, we'll need to shut down just about every computer system—except the most critical and most shielded. Otherwise there will be bit flips, latchups, burnouts."

"I need to move as many plants as possible to shelter."

Yak said, "There is 10,000-liter 'on-demand' water tank near base of elevator columns—where piping runs into station ring. You could shelter plants behind this."

"All right. We'll get busy . . ." She left the ops center in a hurry.

Yak turned to Jin. "Solar panels facing the storm will take damage. We must make sure all solar panels on spacecraft and satellites are turned away from Sun before CME hits. Daisy most specially."

Jin nodded. "Priya, did you hear that?"

Her voice came in over a comm link. "*Yes. Daisy is mostly mirrors, but we're turning all solar panels away from the Sun—or at least we're trying.*"

Jin was cycling through virtual screens. "Julian, how long will it take to spin the station down?"

"Thirty-seven minutes once thrusters are activated."

Tighe looked up in surprise. "You're putting us into microgravity?"

"Yes. If a computer malfunction occurs in the mass equalization system during the storm, the station could wobble out of control. So we're spinning down."

Tighe looked around. "How can I help?"

"Batten down Morra Base. After that, walk the ring and make sure everything in the habs is ready for microgravity." Jin noticed an incoming call. "Here is Space Force." He opened the video line and made the screen visible to everyone in the ops center.

Their current US Space Force observer, Major Erol Vasquez, appeared in a virtual video window. He was clean-cut with a Texan accent. *"Captain Jin, CSpOC just beamed these up to me."* An image came in to Jin's inbox and he tossed it up among the other virtual screens. It showed a blue-hued silhouette of the Sun, with fiery tentacles reaching out from it. *"Coronagraph imagery. This CME is a monster."*

Yak sucked in a breath as he examined the coronagraph. "Aurora borealis will be lovely in Svalbard tonight."

Jin studied the image also. "How many rads could we be facing, Major?"

"They estimate anyone caught in open space could get a dose of radiation equivalent to three hundred thousand chest X-rays—and forty-five thousand is enough to kill. This might be the biggest storm since the Carrington Event back in 1859. Certainly bigger than the CME in 1956. The difference is, we now have thousands and thousands of satellites and billions of low-voltage precision devices running society down there on Earth." He looked up from the images. *"And if it's bad down there, it's going to be living hell up here, without the protection of atmosphere and the Earth's magnetic field."*

Jin frowned. "The other lunar stations will be in great danger."

Vasquez nodded. *"I copy that. The Shackleton bases should be fine—they have regolith shielding. But Lunar Gateway has two ESA crew on board at the moment. The Chinese station has four crew on board. They won't be able to get down to Peary Crater in time. So they're going to attempt evacuation in a capsule—try to put the Moon between them and the Sun. The timing'll be tricky, though."* He looked up. *"In other words: both of those teams might be in trouble."*

Jin said, "And they cannot reach us in time?"

"It would take days."

Jin turned to Yak. "Reach out to Roscosmos. Let them know we might be able to render aid, if they need it. I'll reach out to CNSA." He turned to Vasquez. "Same with ESA and NASA personnel."

Vasquez nodded. *"So what's the plan here on Clarke?"*

Over the next several hours, Tighe and the others scrambled to secure Morra Base and Clarke Station. Jin made an announcement over the emergency PA system instructing crew to take refuge in the station core, after which tensions ran high. Not long after, Tighe moved through the station's outer compartments in his flight suit, checking for anything that could become dangerous in microgravity, when he noticed several researchers and astropreneurs making tearful calls to loved ones back home. Others comforted panicked colleagues. Word of the chest X-ray dose estimate had gotten out.

Chindarkar's voice soon came in over the PA system—sounding more soothing than Jin's. "*A major solar storm is anticipated to arrive in approximately four hours. Station spin-down will commence in five minutes and continue for thirty-seven minutes. Please secure your work and living area in preparation for microgravity, unplug all electronics, and don your protective flight suit—though it does not need to be pressurized at this time. If you need assistance, please notify Clarke Station staff.*"

The thought of sudden microgravity among a crowd of people had Tighe concerned. Undoubtedly one or more of them would vomit, and in the confines of the core compartment, packed with over a hundred crew, that could start a very unpleasant chain reaction.

A few minutes later, Clarke Station rumbled and the floor quivered slightly under Tighe's feet. Voices in nearby cabins expressed alarm. Tighe called to them. "It's just the spin-down! We're okay. Free fall in thirty minutes!"

Ramón Marín passed by carrying a rack computer while simultaneously tapping at virtual screens.

"Hey, Ramón . . ." Tighe tugged his arm to stop him. "Get your flight suit on."

"Yes, I will. Once I get the satellite constellation secured."

"Put the flight suit on first."

Marín nodded and hurried off. "I will."

Tighe called after him. "And get to the core!"

Alarms whooped for several moments before another PA system announcement began. "*Please move to the station core. This is an emergency. Move to the station core immediately.*"

As the sensation of gravity slowly decreased, Tighe was eventually floating through the station corridors. Few people remained in the ring, and those he saw were hurrying toward the elevators in something like a panic. He monitored their departure. The sounds of *booms* and *clangs* throughout Clarke

Station's hull didn't help calm nerves—but were most likely just equipment on the exterior of the station being stowed or removed by robotic craft.

Outside, Tighe knew, polymer bladder tanks from the supply yard were being gathered into a shield, clustered between the station's core and the Sun. Not only had those resources made building a rescue ship possible, but they might now save all their lives. Tighe had difficulty imagining a solar storm that could penetrate tens of thousands of tons of mass.

And although Clarke Station had stopped spinning, its solar thermal station was still functioning—though at diminished capacity as more and more of its mirrors were shaded from the sunlight. Emergency battery backup had only recently been installed, and those batteries were estimated to only last an hour or so, and even then with only critical systems online.

Another set of alarms whooped.

Then Jin's voice came in over the PA system. *"Attention: this is your captain. The Deep Space Climate Observatory just detected the leading edge of the CME magnetic field. The storm has now been calculated to strike us in sixteen minutes. Clarke Station is now switching to emergency power . . ."*

The lights dimmed and small emergency lights kicked on.

"Within the next ten minutes, remove and power down your crystal headset. Power down all electronic devices. Do not panic, but proceed to the station core compartment immediately."

Chindarkar's voice came in over Tighe's comm link. *"J.T. I'm looking at a map of RFID tags. Almost everyone is in the core."*

"Who's left?"

"You and Ramón. He's still in West Hab, and he's not answering my messages."

"Damnit. I told him to get to the core. I'll swing through West Hab and grab him on the way to the elevator."

"Hurry."

Tighe pulled himself along the corridors via handles placed for microgravity use, consulting a pop-up map of the ship to locate Marín's RFID tag.

As he floated into West Hab's H1 level, he entered the computer room. Marín was there, frantically pulling servers as he braced himself against the racks in free fall.

"Ramón! Time to go. We've got less than ten minutes until this thing hits!"

"I'm staying out here on the ring."

"Bullshit!" Tighe noticed he was strapping the servers to a cart with bungee cords. "What the hell are you doing?"

"I must move these servers to safety."

"Why the hell didn't you do that hours ago?"

"Because they must not be accessible to other crew members."

"They're computers. I'm sure you have backups. Now, c'mon." Tighe could see Marín had dozens and dozens more servers to pull. "We don't have time for you to finish that. We need to get to the core."

"There's a 10,000-liter water tank next to the elevator column. I will be sheltering behind it—with these servers."

"This far from center you might not be shielded by the supply yard tanks."

Marín looked up. "I cannot bring these servers into the core—among all those people. There are intelligence agents among the observers on this station."

"Forget that—we can't even *fit* these things in the core with all those people!"

Marín kept pulling servers and lashing them down to the cart. "This is too important, J.T."

Tighe moved up to him, getting in Marín's face. "Enough of this crypto bullshit. Whatever get-rich-quick scheme Lukas has you doing for him doesn't matter. It's only money, Ramón. Now come on . . ." He moved to grab Marín's arm.

But Marín drew away. "Let go of me!"

"Just how greedy are you?"

"This has *nothing* to do with greed!" He went back to pulling servers. "You don't even know what money is."

"I know that being willing to die for it is stupid."

"You are confusing money with wealth. Money is a technology that keeps billions of people alive."

"You won't be alive if you stay here."

"*I don't matter!*" He pointed at the servers. "This matters." He looked pained. "You don't know because you have not seen what happens when money fails. My country went from the most prosperous nation in South

America to absolute destitution and societal breakdown in a single generation. People I loved died before my eyes. It was failure of money that did that. That was all it took."

Tighe could tell Marín was hurting. "I'm sorry to hear that. But we need to go."

"Without money, social order dissolves—because it is just the shared hallucination of money that allows human society to expand beyond mere tribal affiliations. That permits us to mediate transactions beyond those we know. And industrial civilization requires that. The billions of people alive now on Earth require that. In its absence, they will perish."

He looked up. "Earth money is going to fail, J.T. And when it fails, there must be something to take its place." He went back to pulling servers. "This new economic engine could preserve our civilization. Prevent a catastrophic war. It could save the Earth's biosphere. It could save all of us. The industries being financed on this station—we must prevent this candle in the darkness from being snuffed out. This could make life possible for a thousand generations to come. Can you not see that?" He struggled with emotions. "I must not fail them."

Tighe stared at Marín and realized that he wasn't the only one on board Clarke Station with a singular focus. That perhaps Marín's was more rational than his own focus.

Just then Chindarkar's voice came in over the comm link. "*J.T., what the hell is going on? You've got five minutes left! Get to the core!*"

Tighe sighed. He spoke into his mic. "Negative. Ramón and I are going to ride this out behind one of the water tanks on the ring."

"*J.T.! That's crazy. You—*"

He muted the comm and looked to Marín. "How can I help?"

Marín glanced up and, after a moment, nodded to the racks. "By pulling these servers. Thank you."

After working together frenetically, they gathered the last of the rack servers with only a couple minutes left. They then floated the overloaded cart of servers to the elevator and rode down to Hl. There, Marín powered down the elevator and unlocked the nearby pump room. They pulled the cart inside—into what would become the "shadow" of a polymer water tank several meters in diameter and barely taller than either of them.

As they floated next to the stack of servers, Tighe checked the time. "Thirty seconds to spare." He looked up. "So is it crazy to ride this out here?"

"We have 3 meters of water and 17 millimeters of radiotrophic fungi shielding us. Plus, whatever parts of the supply yard extend this far out. That is not insignificant." He extended his hand. "Thank you, J.T."

Tighe shook his hand. "Let's just hope this works."

Marín pulled a dosimeter out of his shirt pocket and took a deep breath. "We're about to find out whether Clarke Station has a future."

"Yes we are."

When the CME came, it began with erratic behavior by the emergency lighting. First the LEDs dimmed, and then they glowed and pulsed brightly.

In the shade of the water tank, Marín's dosimeter began clicking faster— but not alarmingly so. They both exchanged concerned looks, because the storm was just beginning.

Strange noises emanated from distant portions of the station—the sound of arcing electricity and sparks. The emergency lighting continued to throb and pulse. A distorted alarm could be heard somewhere.

However, without their crystals, neither of them could know what was going on beyond their little compartment. This was clearly one drawback to a virtual command and control interface. It occurred to Tighe that now that they had more mass available, it might be smart to add more physical instruments.

The radiation storm continued for several minutes, but Marín's dosimeter never rose to dangerous levels. Then its clicking began to fade slowly away, until finally returning to normal background radiation.

Moments later Jin's voice came in over the PA. "*SWPC reports the CME has passed. We are now powering up station systems. Fire-safety teams, please conduct your sweeps and submit your reports. All other personnel remain in place.*"

Marín looked at his dosimeter, closed his eyes, and mouthed silent thanks to someone.

To their great astonishment, damage from the largest CME to graze human civilization in modern times was manageable. True, the solar blast didn't score a direct hit on Earth, and so the casualties among satellites in LEO were few, and there wasn't terrible disruption to systems and services on Earth.

The region of the Moon, however, took a direct hit.

Jin turned to flight surgeon Zara Volkova. "Any injuries?"

She replied, "We have four suffering extreme anxiety, but other than that, no visible radiation sickness. Dosimeters in the core compartment were within rad limits. So the shielding plan worked."

"A hundred thousand tons of mass has its uses." Jin turned to Chindarkar, Yak, and Kerner. "And damage to the station? Equipment?"

Kerner said, "We lost a mule; it was slightly exposed to a direct blast from the CME and its systems got fried. We had voltage spikes along the supply yard latticework, but we placed wiring to direct it away from volatiles." He looked through a virtual list. "Six small electrical fires on board, but we evacuated atmosphere from the main electric vault, so nothing spread. We're inspecting the power system, but so far the damage appears to be contained. Breakers functioned as intended." He looked up. "We'll want to order replacement parts as we go through our inventory, but we should be able to restore full operation."

Jin slumped in relief. "So we survived it, and we are still operational."

The group nodded to one another in grim recognition of their close shave.

Yak interjected, "However, we have lost contact with taikonauts and cosmonauts in lunar orbit."

Vasquez added, "Crew on the Lunar Gateway blew past their career rad limits in that one event. Their dosimeters show they're in trouble. We need to get them to Clarke Station for treatment. If they only develop cataracts from this, they'll be lucky."

Jin said, "We should rescue them."

Vasquez said, "I'll go. It's what I signed up for. If you can lend me a spacecraft, that is."

Jin turned to Kerner. "Do we have any working transit craft?"

Kerner nodded.

Jin then turned to Yak. "If Roscosmos can't reestablish contact, be prepared to head out in Transit-05. Meanwhile, keep trying to raise those taikonauts and cosmonauts. Let everyone know we can provide aid."

CHAPTER 40

Legacy

CLARKE STATION POPULATION: 137

DAYS TO RYUGU DEPARTURE: 461

RESOURCES LAUNCHED TO L2: 113,500 TONS

I n the days following the great solar storm, radiation victims—some of them in critical condition—arrived at Clarke Station from spacecrafts throughout lunar orbit. Cosmonauts, taikonauts, and astronauts received emergency treatment in the only spin-gravity hospital—or indeed hospital of any kind—in deep space. Likewise, over the past year a genetic surgery wing had been formed in the East Hab med lab to treat James Tighe's cancer, and now it was put to work repairing genetic damage experienced by the spacefarers. One cosmonaut died, but the other injured survived to return to Earth.

The one consolation was that the radiation storm established beyond all doubt the resilience and utility of the CCE's communications network and Clarke Station's logistics. Over the months that followed, the US, UK, Australia, Russia, EU, Japan, and India officially recognized the legitimacy of Clarke Station's Luxembourg ship license, and the lūna was listed on several Earth exchanges—though most holders did not want to sell, preferring to invest their lūna off-world instead.

Bizarrely, in the midst of all this, the Chinese government declared that they were "gifting" Clarke Station (or as they called it: Nónglì gōngdiàn) to the entire world, and that it would be administered by the CCE as a DAO. It was a surreal bit of political theater, but it handily sidestepped the issue of the station's ownership and resolved a thorny problem. Now who was to say who owned Clarke Station?

US Space Force, EU, and Russian observers performing rescue operations out of Clarke Station following the storm later inspired the creation of an international Cislunar Search & Rescue Corps (or CSR). Jin Han and Priya Chindarkar encouraged this, and after consultations with Lukas Rochat, as well as Tighe and Sevastian Yakovlev, the CCE endowed the CSR with transit spacecraft and an entire floor in East Hab. The CSR's charter declared it an international body committed to the protection of life and property anywhere in cislunar space, staffed on a rotating basis by astronauts from several nations.

During this time of international cooperation in space following the storm, Rochat also helped to negotiate an international legal framework that gave rise to the Orbital Deconfliction Service, an international registry of trajectories within cislunar space.

And through it all, Tighe felt a twinge of remorse because he knew this period of deep space harmony couldn't last. Especially when he knew what must be done.

CHAPTER 41

The Exchange

CLARKE STATION POPULATION: 161
DAYS TO RYUGU DEPARTURE: 423
RESOURCES LAUNCHED TO L2: 126,800 TONS

James Tighe entered the well-lit CCE computer lab on the H1 level of West Hab. Inside he found Ramón Marín sitting at a well-lit workbench cluttered with circuit boards, chips, wires, and inscrutable electronic devices.

Marín looked up and smiled, speaking in accented English. "Mr. J.T. What brings you to my corner of the station?"

"Priya tells me I have to learn how the CCE blockchain works. We're financing the construction of a nuclear thermal propulsion spacecraft, and apparently I've got to do something with my 'issuance tokens,' or whatever they're called."

"Ah." Marín rose from his workbench. "Have you changed your opinion of cryptocurrencies as a Ponzi scheme?"

Tighe considered the question. "All I know is that whatever you and Lukas have cooked up has the superpowers back on Earth placated. For now. And if that buys me time and resources to build a rescue ship, I'll be grateful."

"Very good. I was wondering when I would see you." Marín was methodically putting his tools away. "You are the last of the CCE administrators to receive training."

"I've been busy. I was hoping someone else could handle this stuff."

"As an exchange stakeholder, you must perform your role directly. All legitimate power comes with responsibilities."

"Can we skip the moralizing?"

"Certainly." Marín gestured to a metal stool across from him.

Tighe sat, looking around at the lab. The countertops were crowded with what looked to be cube sats in various stages of completion. "What is all this anyway?"

"Our atomic clock factory."

Tighe prepared to step away. "Atomic? As in radiation?"

"No need to worry. The strontium will be installed outside. These are just the clock housings."

"What are they for?"

"The CCE transaction and settlement network. These clocks will be added to larger satellites that will be launched into far orbits throughout the Earth-Moon system. All of them will be linked by laser transceivers."

"Why the atomic clocks?"

"The precise timing of transactions is crucial to a well-functioning market—and also to deep space navigation. Both are invaluable to commerce. If we launch a satellite on a specific trajectory at a precise time, with an accurate onboard clock, that satellite will know precisely where it is at any moment, and that will allow us to transmit directly to it, permitting us to expand the network's capacity and survivability. Thanks to you, we have more than enough strontium for the task—a dozen tons—because we will eventually be launching and maintaining tens of thousands of these satellites."

Tighe whistled. "So many."

"Too many for an attacker to locate and destroy." Marín put his tools away. "Let us talk about cryptocurrencies. Aside from believing them a Ponzi scheme, what do you know?"

"I know that Nathan Joyce made a fortune in crypto markets when he was still in his twenties—and that he was someone who played fast and loose with the truth."

"Oh, but he was so much more than that, was he not?"

After a moment Tighe nodded. "Yes. I suppose he was. But back on Earth, if it didn't involve cave diving, I wasn't interested. So I don't really know much about crypto."

"Then know that it is based around something called 'the blockchain'—a form of public general ledger. Like the Internet itself, blockchain can be used for good or bad. But it is useful, and thus will be used. So we should learn it."

"Well, I'm here."

"I think you will find it quite illuminating." He started interacting with an unseen UI in his crystal. "I have fashioned the training program into a video game. It is easier to understand complex systems if you can play around with them and see them working in a consequence-free environment. It was, in fact, play-to-earn video games that gave me my first experience with crypto as a child in Venezuela."

Suddenly a virtual model of a robot tug, not unlike the *Amy Tsukada*, appeared, floating above the desktop between them.

"Let us define basic terms first. Our Cislunar Commodity Exchange is a blockchain-based economic system. Blockchains like the CCE can establish order in untrusted environments—like here in deep space—though I take exception with the description of blockchains as 'trustless.' More accurately, blockchains reduce the trust required of any single entity and instead distribute trust among the various participants through an economic game that incentivizes them to cooperate under transparent rules defined by the system's protocol. In practice, this means no centralized authority is required to facilitate orderly operation. Do you follow me so far?"

"Honestly? No."

"Then let us start simply. Five basic things can be traded here on the Cislunar Commodity Exchange: raw materials, processed goods, services, financial derivatives, and financial indexes. All transactions, all ownership, and all governance are managed through three distinct digital constructs. First: the lūna, which is the native currency of the CCE, and used for all value transfers and transaction costs. It is a unit of account, initially backed by the trackable resources accessible through its accounting and satellite infrastructure. Which is to say that the lūna is a unit of credit, initially backed by access to the network capacity itself, and eventually backed by everything within the CCE's accounting ecosystem.

"Second come non-fungible tokens—or NFTs—"

"Even I've heard of NFTs, and what I've heard isn't good."

Marín nodded. "Grifters back on Earth have indeed used NFTs and so-called 'shitcoins' to defraud investors; however, Wall Street and major banks have also engaged in trillions of dollars in fraud over the centuries. What's important in any economic system is transparency and oversight. What we're doing with NFTs is quite different from the digital 'collectibles' that became so notorious back in the '20s. Instead, we use the cryptographic surety of NFTs to represent ownership of physical assets or potential energy; anything of value in our economic network can be assigned an NFT, like a digital twin. Resources returned from an asteroid or lunar mining, or units of energy, or value-added products are prime candidates for NFTs because in the CCE ecosystem everything needs a digital double to function as a proxy for ownership and service access required in executing smart contracts—which I will cover momentarily.

"NFTs are also subdividable and can be used as a basis for taking investment and paying out derivatives from the use of represented assets, as well as selling outright ownership. So, the cargo containers, the spaceships, the parts on the spaceships, the satellites used to communicate and account for the location and status of all the resources in the system—in short, most things of durable value in space have a corresponding NFT. This makes it possible for everything to participate in complex layers of financialization and resource management through the lūna accounting and smart contract infrastructure."

"I thought you had this set up as a video game."

"I do. However, one must understand the basic rules of a game first, yes?"

Tighe settled in.

"Third, we have exchange stakeholder tokens—or ESTs. These represent governance authority in the ecosystem. This is why you have come to me today—to exercise some of your power, through your ESTs. ESTs are normally used to vote on all updates to the CCE protocols, on whether a company can go public on the Exchange, and on any other material issue concerning the evolution of the CCE.

"But in addition to voting privileges, members holding full EST tokens also act as credit-issuing authorities. Think of it as being like a federal reserve. An EST holder's lūna credit accounts are allowed to go into the negative to an amount based on their yearly average profit within the CCE over the previous seven years. This methodology deepens a member's stake in the ecosystem, and helps to flatten the macro-inflation cycle, creating a more stable instrument suitable for value exchange. Any negative balance for EST holders is automatically offset by fees they receive or from the proceeds of their own credit issuance."

Marín gestured to the floating spaceship, and a UI appeared showing balances of lūna and ESTs as well as a list of NFT objects, one of which was the spaceship itself. "And so, to finance a theoretical asteroid mining mission, you might invest your lūna with a startup such as this . . ." He nodded toward the model.

Tighe leaned forward. "So I just move lūna to it?"

"Yes. Do not be concerned about making errors—it is all fictitious. Just a game."

The interface looked fairly intuitive, and Tighe used his crystal to interact with the controls, moving an amount of lūna required by a fictitious mining firm, RockHound, to its account. In doing so, his own account went negative.

"Do you see that you have spent more than you possess?"

"Yeah. Like using a credit card."

"Oh, no. Think of it more like a 'reserve' tank on your account. If you had no EST tokens, you would not be able to spend into the negative. What you are doing is literally *creating* new lūna, and these will persist within the system, like any other lūna."

Now that Tighe had assigned the funds, the model animated, and the spacecraft receded to a tiny, distant asteroid with cartoonish sound effects. In a few moments a bulging robot tug returned from the asteroid. A manifest of its contents appeared.

Marín pointed. "Notice that NFTs were created by the fictitious ship captain to identify the various contents of the returned cargo. Each of these NFTs are now visible to the CCE markets for trading . . ."

Animations of mule spacecraft appeared, taking away one or more bladder tanks of the cargo. Each time they did, one of the listed NFTs in the tug's manifest disappeared, and lūna appeared in Tighe's account.

"As an investor in this mission, when the NFTs created from it are sold, the smart contract automatically pays out to you in proportion to your investment. The original NFTs are burned, with new ones created as these resources are converted into other products."

Tighe's lūna account was now well into the black once more. Higher than before.

"You have successfully brought more value into the market by returning physical resources to it."

"Hm." Illustrated this way, it actually did seem straightforward. "Does everyone get these EST tokens?"

Marín shook his head. "No. ESTs are only for those with a proven record of supporting the network and being invested long-term in its success. Founding members of the CCE—yourself and a few others who were instrumental in its creation—were given EST tokens in addition to lūna to bootstrap the network. Likewise, the durable property you possess has been assigned NFTs. Clarke Station and all the equipment within have been assigned NFTs as well.

"Now that the initial infrastructure has been put in place, an EST member like yourself can issue a loan or investment in lūna to, for example, a mining company. Or you could issue a loan or invest in an astropreneur with an innovative business idea for a space-based business, as your group has already done with several Clarke Station tenants.

"However, new entrants to the CCE network also have a clear path to EST membership over time. People or companies contributing raw resources to the ecosystem, or performing activities such as futures market making, spot financing of new infrastructure development, or lending out lūna to finance commerce, for example, could earn a full EST token—and thus lūna-issuance capability—across seven years of reliable performance— just as EST owners can *lose* tokens for unreliable performance."

Tighe considered this. "Why make the ESTs separate from the lūna coin? Why not just lūna?"

"There are a number of reasons to separate the capital layer from the governance layer, perhaps most importantly because it helps contain hostile takeover attempts and slowly integrates new stakeholders into the decision-making body of the CCE. The rule of law and trust necessary for business in frontier territory like deep space is best supported when actors cannot leave with a significant portion of their available capital, in the sense that one cannot sell governance tokens or the ability to go into a negative lūna balance as an EST member to someone else."

Marín gestured to the game, which presented new objects to interact with—satellites and factories. "Feel free to play. Become familiar with the operations of the market."

Tighe hesitated a moment and then decided to poke around the interface. Pretty soon he was interacting with cartoon factories and futures markets, buying and selling in lūna. Voting on network expansions with ESTs, creating and burning NFTs from mining and energy creation. It was an entertaining game, actually.

After playing for some time, Tighe looked to Marín, who was back at work on his atomic clocks. "So did you design this CCE blockchain?"

Marín looked up. "I had a great deal of assistance, but yes. It was a labor of love for me." He grew wistful. "It may *seem* inconsequential, but a blockchain-based DeFi system like the CCE is, to me, the key to containing the spread of authoritarianism here in space. The moment any citizen of an authoritarian regime starts using lūnas to invest in the CCE here in orbit, they are no longer bound by centralized authority. They are instead presented with limitless opportunities. The market undermines centralized control. The open protocol itself is the authority, and no self-appointed power can control or constrain it, and so individual autonomy prevails in the cosmos—and into the future."

Tighe pondered this. "I've been wondering for a while now how we managed to interact with Earth's economy. I mean . . . I understand the lūna out here in space, but how are we buying things from Earth? Launches. Provisions. Equipment. And how do you prevent billionaires like Burkette and Macy from buying up everything out here?"

"A fair question. Stated simply: they do not control the network. The CCE only issues lūna in relation to real assets and network capacity, and it also throttles incoming capital by making the lūna the only path for incoming old world investment. We do convert small quantities of lūna into Earth-based cryptocurrencies, like bitcoin or ethereum, as a reserve for foreign exchange—mostly through third-party crypto-mining concerns in low Earth orbit. Given the nature of cryptocurrencies, no Earth government is able to block these sales—it's just transmission of a line of text—and there is a ready market for lūna back on Earth.

"We then invest a portion of that reserve in Earth real estate and businesses to generate an operating fund from which to purchase needed supplies and launch services from Earth. But the vast majority of lūna must be *earned* and cannot be purchased. This is designed to ensure the broadest level of support for off-world industry by the population of Earth. Because it is very much in their interest that commerce in space expand rapidly."

Tighe asked, "Okay. How is it earned?"

"There are two ways—the first being much more difficult. The second being quite easy. First, astropreneurs, voted in by EST holders like yourself, can establish an enterprise here in cislunar space and become a signatory to the CCE bylaws, and be capitalized in lūna.

"But the much more common way to earn lūna is through the CarbonExtraction smart contract, which anyone on Earth can use. It pays fractions of lūna for each ton of net CO_2 removed from Earth's atmosphere using carbon-free energy and sold to a CCE signatory."

"Well, not everyone can do that."

"You'd be surprised. Direct air capture—or DAC—equipment is not advanced. The components can be obtained from a typical HVAC supplier. Open-source designs are freely available. The smart contract pays on a reverse bonding curve—meaning the reward for pulling CO_2 out of the atmosphere is lower the closer to our 350-parts-per-million target you get. But it's a race at the beginning to join in because the reward per ton is higher—which matches our level of urgency to reverse climate change."

"And you think people will go for this CarbonExtraction smart contract?"

"They already have." Marín brought up a slowly spinning virtual globe of the Earth, with thousands upon thousands of tiny orange dots on it. "Don't forget, climate change is disrupting economies worldwide. People are eager for opportunity in a chaotic world." He pointed. "These are the locations of CCE-registered direct air capture plants for removing atmospheric CO_2."

Tighe noticed the dots were scattered worldwide. "So they're doing this in developing countries, too?" He peered closely. "Somalia? Turkmenistan?" He looked up. "Really?"

"As I said, the machinery is not complex. And corruption is a tax—perhaps the most common tax in the world. Our lūna coin gives people the ability to earn money and safeguard it from corrupt local officials—to build wealth instead of having it stolen from them. And in the process, pull CO_2 out of the atmosphere to build a better future for their children. In fact, the CarbonEx-traction smart contract could even encourage bad actors to aid the environment out of self-interest. Eventually we hope to have hundreds of millions of people working with as much entrepreneurial zeal to *remove* CO_2 from the atmosphere as the previous generations had when putting it there in the first place.

"More importantly, once earned, this lūna can be invested or spent up here at the CCE. Thus, if someone on Earth wants to invest in the most vibrant off-world marketplace, lūna is their only means to do so—providing an added incentive to pull CO_2 out of the atmosphere."

Tighe spun the virtual globe, looking at all the nodes in the DAC network. The effort was clearly widespread. He tried to recall the numbers Monica Balter, the solar satellite expert, had shown during dinner years earlier. Would this be enough to make a difference? He recalled that her plan required giant solar power satellites in geosynchronous orbit—none of which existed yet.

Marín folded his hands. "Now, J.T., tell me about this nuclear propulsion spacecraft you wish to finance."

"We're doing it as a group. Yak was telling me it's probably going to cost something in the neighborhood of fifteen billion USD—or whatever that is in lūna."

"That should be no problem. Let me step you through the process . . ."

CHAPTER 42

Debtpocalypse

CLARKE STATION POPULATION: 161

DAYS TO RYUGU DEPARTURE: 327

RESOURCES LAUNCHED TO L2: 153,000 TONS

On July 10, 2041, stock markets on Earth began to go into free fall. The steady accumulation of climate disasters, corruption, and resource wars had spiked international debt beyond sustainable levels, and financial markets could no longer hide the fact that the world's economies were shrinking. Servicing all that debt was now clearly inconceivable. Once the first domino fell, the inevitable occurred.

And so, in mere minutes, tens of trillions of dollars in "value" evaporated—although Tighe wondered how "valuable" it all was if it could vanish like a mirage. In the US, Europe, and Asia, currencies plunged along with their stock markets. In a matter of days, millions upon millions of people were thrown out of work. However, the expanding global financial depression did nothing to relieve the droughts, wildfires, hurricanes, pandemics, war, and mass migration chaos. It was all happening at once, and modern society was ill-equipped to deal with it.

Two new regional wars began within a week.

James Tighe could not help but encounter the news. Everywhere he went on Clarke Station, crew members were watching TV or talking on the phone or having video calls with distraught family members back home. And though he felt guilty about it, his first reaction was to be concerned about the effect all this would have on the effort to build a rescue ship.

But here and there, fragments of Earth's tragedy came back to him where he tangentially had links. For example, the death of a Nobel Prize–winning economist who had predicted all this back in the 2030s stood at the top of the news worldwide for an entire day. Sankar Korrapati—or "Dr. Doom," as he'd been derisively known among Wall Street types—had died during widespread unrest in Mumbai. Beaten to death by looters in his home.

Tighe recalled the mild-mannered Korrapati, speaking in earnest to him in Nathan Joyce's study back on Baliceaux Island all those years ago. *"In the modern world, money does not represent value, Mr. Tighe. Money represents debt."*

The memory felt like it was from another life—from a time when Tighe still thought space was the domain of NASA astronauts.

Korrapati's seemingly outrageous prediction of a global economic collapse had come true, and now the media hailed him as a great visionary. And like all true visionaries, he had been roundly ignored until his vision was no longer of any use. Or at least of any threat.

Then it occurred to Tighe that Ramón Marín had been right, too, though less famously. The widespread suffering on display around the world—it was due to the failure of money. And the lifeline of the lūna currency was eagerly embraced.

As economies collapsed across the world, the map of nodes in the CCE's CarbonExtraction smart contract exploded in number. And with each day, it expanded further still. People on Earth were desperate to get involved in the lūna economy, whose stability was like a harbor in a raging storm.

The only way to (quickly) get involved in lūna back on Earth was to pull CO_2 out of Earth's atmosphere. Even flailing billionaires, leveraged to the gills, were racing to unload limited-edition Ferraris and Warhol paintings to buy direct air capture equipment.

As the Debtpocalypse continued to expand day by day, hyperinflation wracked the major fiat currencies of the world. The dollar, the yuan, the euro—they all tumbled. Earth-based cryptocurrencies were locked in frenzied trading, but planetside data centers and exchanges were quickly embroiled in the general unrest. Transactions were sluggish, resulting in panics that mirrored bank runs.

Real estate skyrocketed in price—being used solely as a hedge against hyperinflation, as opposed to any useful purpose. Homelessness exploded.

Meanwhile, for the CCE, the chief concern was that the only means of reaching Clarke Station was controlled by Jack Macy and his Galleon rockets. Macy tripled the ticket price to orbit. Then he quintupled it. The very wealthy were all too happy to pay, eager as they were to "escape Earth." That escape didn't last long, however, and after a couple of weeks riding the *Let's Be Friends* lunar cycler, they'd be back in low Earth orbit again.

Well before the market crash, Catalyst Corporation had voted to challenge Macy's monopoly on lunar cyclers and contracted with Lunargistics to design a replacement for the *Rosette*. This time, however, the company had serious mass to work with. Their design, a 5,000-ton spin-gravity vessel with an integral solar storm shelter, required very little delta-v to send back toward Earth from L2 and to adjust into lunar cycler orbit. Christened *Kepler*, it was completed at Clarke Station only a month after the economic collapse.

With the *Kepler* going into service, helmed by a Catalyst Corporation crew, Macy's monopoly on lunar transportation was broken. Galleon rockets not only lacked spin-gravity, but provided an inferior solar storm shelter. Now spacefarers—and even tourists—could travel beyond the Moon and back in spin-gravity comfort, able to eat, shower, and sleep normally within three habitats. Macy's Galleon service was crude by contrast. Likewise, Clarke Station now had control of its own transport infrastructure, and the size of incoming teams grew.

Jin Han and Priya Chindarkar, meanwhile, had worked with Lukas Rochat to reach an agreement with Artemis Accord signatories as well as Russia and China that gave legal sanction for the CCE to utilize the thorium refined from lunar regolith, to power something known as a "breeder" nuclear reactor, 2 gigawatts in size, which would be constructed at Morra Base. Thorium fuel apparently did not raise the same nuclear weapons concerns as uranium, even though this reactor would be big enough to power half a million homes back on Earth. The idea was to use it to power a newly proposed second mass-driver, the MD2, drawing 250 megawatts—five times the energy of Ecklund's machine—and launching 50-kilogram cores into orbit.

Morra Base would also need to be expanded to accommodate dozens of additional Badger harvesters, to increase regolith processing and handling, and so on. It would take months of work, and Tighe opposed the idea as yet another major distraction from building the rescue ship. It caused serious debate among the Catalyst board members.

Jin and Chindarkar maintained that this thorium nuclear reactor—and the abundance of resources it would make available in cislunar space—would build enough trust between the nations of Earth and the CCE to speed approval for enriching the uranium necessary to fuel the reactors of the NTR-01 rescue ship—whose superstructure was already well underway in the shipyard.

Approval for which had not yet been granted.

Nonetheless, Tighe eventually realized—as more and more expert crew members came aboard Clarke Station—that the additional teams would be able to handle the thorium reactor work, and since the second mass-driver was scheduled to come online four months before any departure to Ryugu, the additional resources might help secure the rescue ship's completion.

Meanwhile, the Daisy solar power satellite in orbit around EM-L1 would no longer be needed once the thorium reactor was finished. Several meetings were conducted to determine what to do with it. Certainly there were many places where 50 megawatts of power could prove useful on the Moon. NASA, the ESA, and numerous governments submitted proposals. Likewise, there were suggestions by some that they could bring Daisy into geosynchronous orbit to beam power down to a rectenna on Earth, helping to alleviate blackouts in crisis areas.

The endless meetings were not something Tighe was suited for, and he often found himself gazing out the virtual window at the shipyard, where scaffolding surrounded the metallic framework of the NTR-01, already under construction. Instead of listening to the interminable details of station management, he imagined the day the NTR-01 would be launched.

Not long after the global economic collapse on Earth began, Lukas Rochat contacted Tighe about an "urgent personal matter." Tighe warily returned Rochat's video call from his private quarters.

"What's so urgent, Lukas?"

Rochat appeared via the comm link in his office in Luxembourg City. *"I am well, thank you, J.T."*

Tighe sighed. "Sorry. Are things okay there in Luxembourg?"

"For me? Fine. Listen . . ." He tried to find words. *"I know you're estranged from your family, but I received a call from your brother-in-law . . . a Mr. Vinter of Sheboygan, Wisconsin."*

"If he wants the twenty grand or whatever I owe him, go ahead and pay it . . . again."

"It's not that. Your whole family is apparently in desperate circumstances due to the economic crash."

Tighe stared. "Tell Ted to sell his sports memorabilia."

"Your mother also contacted me. Trying to reach you."

That shocked Tighe.

"I thought you should know."

He processed this news. The last conversation Tighe had had with his mother occurred years ago—via sat phone just before his departure on the *Konstantin* expedition. The distance between him and his mother, both physical and emotional, even back then was immense. "What did she want?"

"Your family in Wisconsin is destitute. Your sister's law firm folded, and they are facing foreclosure on their homes." Rochat spread his hands. *"My research confirms they need assistance."*

Long-forgotten emotions roiled Tighe. A flash of memory of his mother when he was still a young boy, speaking to him in the darkness as they slept in a car. His mother's desperation at their homelessness after his father's disappearance. And then the security that Andrew, his stepfather, had given her. Her continued disappointment in Tighe—that he would not accept the world she had provided for them. And yet . . . she was once more without safety and security.

He realized then how deep his wound was. Her rejection of him—who he was—still stung. Tighe breathed deeply to center himself.

Security. He owed her that.

Rochat waited patiently.

"Send her money."

"Do you wish to speak with her?"

After a moment Tighe shook his head. His family no longer had any conception of who he was—if they ever did. "Just send money."

"How much?"

"I don't know . . . a few thousand lūna."

Rochat gave him a look. *"That's more than a billion US dollars. A bit much, don't you think?"*

Tighe gave him a startled look. "Jesus. I have a billion dollars?"

"You really have no concept of what's happened, do you?"

He tapped the table impatiently. "Fine. Send her whatever they need to keep their homes and to get a fresh start. Figure that out, and tell me a number."

"You'll need to transfer the lūna to them. I can't do it."

"Right. Fine. Just give me a reasonable number. And don't trust my brother-in-law to come up with one."

"Okay, I'll be in touch, J.T."

Tighe cut the line. He then spent the next half hour in his quarters, staring through a virtual window at a live image of Earth—trying to resolve Wisconsin with his naked eye.

CHAPTER 43

Overton Window

OCTOBER 10, 2041

rika Lisowski stood near a podium as tanned, bearded billionaire Sir Thomas Morten approached a microphone. He wore a white suit with a pink dress shirt, open at the throat, as his long gray hair flowed in a tropical breeze. It was a pleasant, sunny day here on Baliceaux Island. The summer heat and humidity (and hurricane season) was over in the Caribbean, but damage was still evident all around them, with most palm trees of any size either stripped of their fronds or snapped near their base, leaving only jagged stumps.

Nathan Joyce's former Great House stood behind Morten's podium, its exterior ravaged by high winds, though not destroyed. By contrast, piles of wood debris, the remains of scores of guest bungalows that had been leveled down to their concrete foundations, made for a surreal, postapocalyptic backdrop for such a festive occasion. Dozens of press and VIPs had been flown in for a lavish cocktail reception beneath newly installed grass umbrellas and awnings that shaded a tiki bar. Uniformed serving staff patrolled with hors d'oeuvres as if the destruction all around them was just a party theme.

Sir Morten cleared his throat into the microphone and smiled with brilliant white teeth. "Good afternoon. You are so very welcome at Baliceaux." He spread his arms magnanimously. "Those of you who have visited before, when it was the home of the late Nathan Joyce, may look on this destruction with dismay." He shook his head. "But I see the potential for rebirth. This is why, as others flee the Earth's climate-change-ravaged equatorial regions, I was glad to purchase Nathan's former estate." He spoke from the side of his mouth for effect. "Albeit at a very steep discount."

The gathered press and guests chuckled.

Lisowski surveyed the crowd. The press in attendance were busy hitting the bar, but the VIPs seemed to be focused on Morten's every word.

"I purchased this estate despite current weather patterns as a gesture of faith in humanity's future—faith in our ability to effect positive change. I firmly believe that not only Baliceaux's, but all of Earth's, best days still lie ahead. By expanding our industrial and energy infrastructure into cislunar space, we will relieve the unsustainable burdens we have imposed upon Mother Earth, while not abandoning the developing world to a calamity not of their making, but instead uplifting and enriching the lives of billions."

Someone near the bar called to the staff, "Can I have a lime in that?" to the tinking of glassware.

Morten continued, unaffected—his skin apparently thick as well as tanned. "As a demonstration of my commitment to this goal, I've gathered you here to announce that Vestal Aerospace's hydrogen-oxygen-powered Gyrfalcon prototype hypersonic aircraft..."

Here a holographic projection system displayed alongside Morten on the diminutive stage a long, sleek, needle-shaped aircraft with outsized air scoops in its underbelly.

"... which flew last year from London to Tokyo in a mere two hours and ten minutes, at an altitude of sixty kilometers, producing no sonic booms and with near-zero carbon emissions—will become part of a larger Vestal single-stage-to-orbit system, offering humanity unprecedented, low-cost access to space."

Here, the hologram zoomed out to show the Earth edge-on from low orbit as a hundreds-of-kilometers-long tether slowly rotated.

"Catalyst Corporation, our cislunar partners, propose to manufacture the first of a series of 500-kilometer-long, 6,000-ton rotating orbital skyhooks. Such a tether, counter-rotating in low Earth orbit, can descend into Earth's atmosphere at an altitude of 100 kilometers and a speed of 4 kilometers per second—well within the capabilities of our Gyrfalcon."

Here the hologram zoomed in to show the Gyrfalcon hypersonic aircraft meeting the rotating skyhook as it slowed briefly while the longer tether rotated beyond it in orbit. The hypersonic aircraft's payload was then lifted from its open bay doors, at which point they separated.

"Ten tons of payload to space in a fully reusable aircraft that flies with the frequency of a regular airliner—delivering per-kilogram costs to LEO at a fraction of all rocket-based launch systems and with little environmental impact. Later versions will be able to double and triple these payloads as stronger crystalline structures are developed in the microgravity research labs of Clarke Station. Single-stage-to-space with an assist from the heavens, and at very little impact to the environment." He gestured to the hologram. "Not bad for a parabolic carnival ride."

This jab at Morten's billionaire rival, George Burkette, was met by laughter and applause from the crowd—including the press.

As Morten began to take questions from the reporters, Lisowski headed through the throng and out toward the edge of the gathering. As cringey as Morten's press conference was, at least his plan was no longer entirely impossible—and that was progress.

A voice nearby said, "I suppose you must be happy about all this."

Lisowski turned to see a face she recognized. The elder statesman stood in a polo shirt and khakis, completely generic amid the gaggle of press and digerati.

She nodded to him and continued toward the tiki bar. He fell in alongside her. She picked up a glass of white wine from a tray that contained a dozen and offered one to him.

"No thanks. I like to stay sharp when I'm talking to you."

"Suit yourself." They both moved toward the edge of the gathering, while in the near distance Morten pontificated to outstretched smartphones.

The elder statesman gestured. "Look at him. These guys all act like they invented this stuff. We were designing skyhooks back in the 1980s."

"But they didn't happen. Did they?" She sipped her wine.

"No. They didn't." He turned back to her.

"Because you lacked the critical mass in orbit. That problem is now solved."

"I suppose this scheme of yours worked. My son-in-law won't shut up about increasing his 'exposure' to the lūna. Applications to engineering and math programs at US universities are spiking. My grandkid no longer wants to be a YouTuber. You made a Gordian knot out of our 'China problem,' and now the CCP will have to grapple with a decentralized commerce monster in space—which will cause them to doubt the loyalty of anyone they send up there."

She leaned her glass toward him and then took a sip.

"So we disrupted our own markets. Now what?"

She gestured to Morten. "We invest in the future—instead of fearing it."

He shook his head. "Oh, I don't think it will be that simple. Fear is a great motivator."

"So are pre-IPO stock options."

"And does this 'cislunar Renaissance' create more or less enemies for America?"

"Less. Much less. It will weaken the appeal of authoritarian ideologies, including those within our own borders."

"Hmph." He leaned against a cobblestone wall overflowing with bougainvillea. "We're helping establish great powers in space that are not beholden to us. That's going to come back to bite us."

"Only if we live in the past. This step was inevitable if we want humanity to thrive. We now have a chance to fix the climate. To not go extinct. You saw the news about that African solar sat?"

"Oh, right. Nigerians with a space death ray. Like that's a good idea."

She laughed into her wine. "It's a geosynchronous power satellite, not a death ray. It'll bring 2 gigawatts of clean energy to the African continent. If you're going to fearmonger, you'll need to be more scientifically rigorous . . . and sound less racist. What the Star of Africa project shows is that average people worldwide can now earn fractions of lūna coins by pulling CO_2 out of the air—helping to solve climate change—and then invest it off-world—in a rapidly growing economy. It's a good thing."

"Fine. I get it. Political power is shifting. Let's just make sure the US doesn't become helpless in this new cislunar economy you're creating. Your asteroid miners, for example, are poised to become the first nuclear power in deep space."

She laughed again. "You mean the Morra Base reactor? It's *thorium* powered. It can't be easily weaponized—especially with IAEA inspectors monitoring it—and breeder reactors aren't portable."

"No, but I'll tell you what *is* portable . . ." He looked around. "Three-ton uranium reactors."

Lisowski gave him a confused look.

"I'm told that, along with the thorium your miners sifted out of the moon-dust, they also refined a few hundred kilos of uranium. What's to stop them from enriching it? They're already building a nuclear thermal rocket ship up at Clarke Station. This 'NTR-01.'"

"The NTR-01 isn't a secret. They've sought approval from Earth authorities for enrichment."

"And do you think they'll receive that approval?"

She gave him a look.

"We now have an off-world organization that technically isn't 'owned' or controlled by anyone, possibly sitting on top of a strategic nuclear stockpile in lunar orbit. You don't see the danger in that, Doctor?"

Lisowski was surprised that she was surprised by his perspective. "They're just trying to rescue their lost crewmates."

"And what happens after that? You need to understand that we will not allow your asteroid miners to enrich uranium in lunar orbit. We wouldn't allow it here on Earth, and we aren't going to allow it out there." With that, he walked away, melding back into the crowd.

Lisowski pondered his words as Morten drew another laugh from the global press nearby.

CHAPTER 44

The *Amy Tsukada*

CLARKE STATION POPULATION: 110
DAYS TO RYUGU DEPARTURE: 181
RESOURCES LAUNCHED TO L2: 204,000 TONS

M ission control on Ascension Island first detected the autonomous cargo tug *Amy Tsukada* on December 1, 2041, at a distance of 100,000 kilometers from the Moon—a task made easier because the tug was on the precise trajectory where it was expected. If all went according to plan, on December 3 the monstrous 6,000-ton vessel would fire its eight engines retrograde as it reached EM-L1, decelerating enough to be captured into a lunar distant retrograde orbit.

The fact that Catalyst Corporation was not the only one who knew of the existence of this spacecraft, or its trajectory, had been a source of concern for some time. And yet, whether the robot tug would appear at all after all these years had been an even bigger worry for Priya Chindarkar. This third and largest of the Ryugu expedition resource tugs had been waiting on a timer for years a few hundred kilometers away from Ryugu, and when its low-delta-v orbital window opened on March 17, 2039, its engines were programmed to fire, imparting 551 meters per second of delta-v, and putting it on a two-plus-year trajectory back to cislunar space. That is, if nothing went wrong.

But here it was.

Chindarkar, James Tighe, Jin Han, Sevastian Yakovlev, Ramón Marín, and Julian Kerner sat in the Catalyst Corporation ops center—a collection of chairs and desks surrounded by a swarm of virtual screens, large and small— that had been set up in a closed room in West Hab. Half a dozen Catalyst technicians sat with them, monitoring radio traffic, telemetry, and radar scans.

Ascension Island mission control was on the laser comm link as well, along with Catalyst Corporation CEO Lukas Rochat in Luxembourg City.

All of them were focused on a shimmering dot emerging from deep space on the main screen. A dot that was a rich prize for any of the participants in the current astropolitical contest between the US, China, Russia, the EU, India, Brazil, and their proxies—or for that matter any of the billionaire Space Titans. Nathan Joyce's maxim had never felt more true to Chindarkar than today:

In space, possession is 99.99999 percent of the law.

The *Amy Tsukada*, 40 meters in length and 20 meters in diameter, consisted of dozens of multiton, 7-meter and 2-meter polymer bladder tanks, and one of the innumerable virtual screens hovering in the Ops Center displayed its detailed manifest:

Resource	Metric Tons
Water	3,800
Ammonia	700
Nitrogen	750
Iron	300
Nickel	280
Cobalt	180
Silica	450
Total Tonnage	6,460

The tug was, itself, fashioned from the resources it carried—with the silica and some of the iron providing the latticework to hold the bladder tanks and its rocket engines in place. Thus, it resembled an elongated bunch of grapes, but was instead a vast treasure of water ice, ammonia, nitrogen, and metals in the form of liquid carbonyls. Even by the current standards of the CCE market, this much water, ammonia, and nitrogen was worth billions—and much more to non-signatories of the CCE, who did not have access to lūna coins or the Exchange where these resources could be traded. And as of yet, these resources were just floating in space—free for the taking.

Marín got busy on his own unseen UIs. "I need to set up an incoming NFT for the futures market . . ."

Chindarkar couldn't help but wonder how many interested parties had learned of the existence of this shipment over the past two years. And then there were the *Konstantin*'s new owners, who'd had access to its onboard records. Likewise, the low-delta-v Hohmann transfer that the tug was following was hardly a secret; the tug's trajectory could be derived as the optimal course from Ryugu for a year to either side.

So Catalyst sent spacecraft of its own to secure it early.

The team's focus shifted from screen to screen. Radar showed a cluster of dots on an interception course to the tug. This was the small flotilla of spacecraft that Clarke Station had sent to retrieve the *Amy Tsukada*—a respectable portion of the spacecraft in the CCE's fleet: four propulsion tugs, three teleoperated mules with robotic manipulators, two transit craft, plus a couple of humanoid Talos robots and video drones riding along for close-up inspections and repairs, if necessary.

Tighe muttered, "We should have gone in person—to greet her."

Jin looked to him. "A fine sentiment, but one that would have angered Amy."

Chindarkar nodded. "Han's right. She wouldn't have wanted us to take unnecessary risks—especially this close to saving Isabel and Ade. Six days out and back. And what are you going to do out there that we can't do from here with telepresence?"

Yak said, "Die, most probably."

Tighe sighed impatiently and crossed his arms.

The team remained in the Ops Center for hours watching screens, and then in the wee hours of December 2, the CCE's satellite network detected a worrisome contact.

A *beep* followed by a message from mission control that roused them all.

Radar contact. No transponder.

Tighe focused on the screen. "What is that?"

Jin turned to Kerner. "How long until we intercept the *Tsukada*?"

Kerner checked a few virtual interfaces, then said, "Nineteen hours, eleven minutes." He looked up at the new dot on the radar screen. "The interloper will encounter the *Tsukada* in just under eighteen hours."

"Goddamnit."

The team did not budge from the Ops Center. Instead, they had food and coffee brought in. Tighe paced the room. Finally, early on December 3, they got their first actual visual of the *Tsukada*.

Chindarkar felt trepidation as she strained to discern its outline against the blackness of space, but as their craft closed in, the *Tsukada* came into focus—intact—and furthermore, it had already rotated to position its engines stern-ward for a retrograde burn. This was expected.

She shouted, "There she is! Look. She's beautiful."

Yak added, "A bit faded from cosmic radiation, but intact."

Jin said, "That unidentified radar contact has already closed with her. We need to locate it."

Kerner directed their flotilla of spacecraft to spread out and pass the *Tsukada* on three sides at a distance of 1 kilometer.

The entire team held their breath as the robot tug came closer and closer.

Kerner pointed. "There! Look—linked to the forward docking port."

Tighe sat alongside the others. "Can we magnify that?"

In a few moments, the techs zoomed in to reveal a modular spacecraft with box truss frames, gold-foil-wrapped fuel tanks, thrusters, antenna dishes, and solar panels. It was a fifth the length of the *Amy Tsukada*, but much less massive—like the head of a bee compared to its abdomen.

More and more screens in the Ops Center zoomed in to the unknown craft from various angles.

Chindarkar sucked in a breath. "It's a parasite ship."

Jin studied a close-up, pointing where it connected to the robot tug's docking port. "They must have had access to schematics for our tugs. This vessel has linked to her."

Rochat's voice came over the comm link. *"That's possible. Those spacecraft designs could have been stolen by any of several governments or groups over the past eight years."*

Yak said, "Easier still: our supply yard and docking standards have been filmed by international observers. Video is all over Internet."

Kerner nodded. "It's behaving like one of our own robotic craft—possibly preparing to alter the *Tsukada*'s course." He zoomed closer. "It doesn't look like a crewed vessel."

Tighe leaned in. "Ram it. Knock it off the docking port."

Jin answered, "That could damage the *Tsukada*. Or destroy it." He turned to Kerner. "Does the vessel have any identifying marks?"

"Negative."

Tighe said, "They're pirates."

Chindarkar also opened up a listing of their spacecraft. "We could come in close and try to disconnect them. I'm taking control of Talos-11. Can someone bring Mule-06 in alongside the *Tsukada*?"

Jin said, "Wait, Priya. Let's find out what we're dealing with first."

Tighe started interacting with unseen UIs as well. "If we wait, the *Tsukada* might commence her retro burn—and then we won't be able to shake that thing off. It'll be pressed down into the docking port by deceleration."

One of the zoomed-in camera insets showed side thrusters on the parasite vessel outgassing.

Kerner said, "It is altering the *Tsukada*'s course slightly."

Tighe hissed angrily as he worked unseen UIs. "To hell with this . . ."

Jin talked into the comm link. "Lukas, can you confirm that no sovereign nation claims responsibility for this craft?"

"I will make inquiries, but do not let that craft claim our robot tug as salvage."

"How do we prevent that?"

Chindarkar glanced to Kerner. "How long until the *Tsukada* does its retrograde burn?"

Yak answered instead. "Two minutes, thirty-three seconds."

"Shit!" Chindarkar sat down and put her crystal into VR mode. In a moment she was looking out from the perspective of a Talos robot standing on the running board of one of the mules a kilometer away from the *Tsukada*. It was rather breathtaking seeing it again, close-up. She was diagonally above it, but then she could also see the parasite craft affixed to its front—hooked to the docking port just beyond the tug's mirrored solar shield.

Yak said, "Retro burn in two minutes."

Jin said, "Julian, broadcast on hailing frequencies that this craft must disconnect immediately."

Suddenly Chindarkar's view lurched as the thrusters on her mule fired, turning the craft to face the *Tsukada*. "Woah! Who's controlling Mule-06?"

Tighe's voice came from nearby. "I am, Priya."

The mule started accelerating toward the robot tug.

"Good! My Talos is tethered to the running board. Bring me in alongside."

"Negative. Hop off."

"What do you mean, 'hop off'? J.T., bring me alongside. I'll try to disconnect them."

"What good would that do? As long as there's a docking collar, they'll just come back again."

She could see that the mule was angling toward the parasite craft at the front of the *Tsukada*—and was accelerating. They were barely 500 meters from it now and coming in fast. "J.T., slow down!"

"Hop off, Priya."

Jin shouted, "J.T., do not ram that spacecraft! You could destroy the *Tsukada*!"

Chindarkar watched in horror as the *Tsukada* and the parasite craft at its bow loomed in her headset. She unclipped her Talos robot's tether and pushed off from the mule's running board, activating her attached SAFER harness to slow her forward velocity, thrusters blasting. The mule zipped past her, still accelerating.

"J.T., turn aside!"

Then Chindarkar saw the mule silently slam into the parasite craft just forward of the docking collar, shearing the connectors and buckling the aluminum box truss as the two vehicles came apart—but also crushing the mule and causing its thruster tank to burst, sending it spinning away like a bottle rocket. A scintillating debris cloud expanded from the point of impact, and the parasite vessel's remaining thrusters stabbed out erratically.

Yak's voice said, "Parasite craft disconnected from *Tsukada* and drifting to port."

Jin called out, "Damn it, J.T. That was reckless!"

Chindarkar brought her Talos to a relative stop 50 meters from the *Tsukada* and watched as the parasite vessel drifted away amid debris. Its docking port had been sheared off and torn hose lines vented white gas.

The *Tsukada*'s docking port was also torn half off.

"Well, we're not docking with the *Tsukada* anytime soon."

Tighe's voice said, "And neither are they. We can fix ours."

Jin's voice asked, "Does that ship look occupied, Priya?"

Tighe answered, "It doesn't matter."

"It does indeed matter. We are obligated by law to render aid, if they are disabled."

Tighe said, "To hell with them."

Chindarkar took her crystal out of VR mode and looked at Tighe in surprise.

Jin glared.

Tighe looked defiant. "You and I *built* that tug, Han—along with Dave and Ade." He turned to Chindarkar. "We all harvested the resources in those tanks, and some of our friends *died* doing it." He pointed at the screen. "It's ours, and we *need* what's on it."

Yak nodded. "The ammonia."

"That's right—fuel for the NTR-01." He watched the parasite vessel slowly tumble away. "Look! *Now* they show up. Now that we've proven this—now that it's obvious. They try to hit us where they think we're weakest." He turned back to Jin. "Sixteen people are dead since we started building Clarke Station, and I'm not going to let these weasels undermine that sacrifice—along with everything we've accomplished."

Jin stared. "Rule of law matters. If we do not have it out here, then we have achieved nothing."

Just then the engines of the *Amy Tsukada* ignited.

Kerner called out, "We have ignition. *Tsukada*'s programmed retro burn has started."

They all turned to the screen and watched the blinding white light of its engines—only gradually altering its trajectory, so massive was the ship. But finally it began to slow, pulling away from the damaged pirate ship, which was still wallowing off to the side. The distance between the two spacecraft expanded to nearly a hundred meters.

Suddenly the pirate spacecraft disappeared in a silent blinding flash—sending pieces hurtling away in every direction as a glowing ball of plasma flared.

Kerner said, "The pirate vessel seems to have exploded." He turned. "Or perhaps self-destructed."

Tighe gestured to the screen. "See? They're willing to destroy all these resources rather than let the people who mined them have it. To deny us of the capabilities it will give us. That's the mentality we're dealing with."

Pieces of metal ricocheted off the tanks and latticework of the *Tsukada*. After a few moments, the debris wave passed, causing only minor damage.

Kerner pointed. "We may have some leaks."

Jin said, "Can we fix them?"

"Yes, we can patch it with a Talos unit."

Tighe sat down and cradled his head in his hands.

Chindarkar sat across from him. "Let's just bring Amy home."

It wasn't until the *Amy Tsukada* was moored in the Clarke Station supply yard three days later that Chindarkar spotted something strapped to the latticework frame—something that had not been there when Tighe, Jin, Abarca, and Adisa had first launched the vessel into deep space. She zoomed in on it with a surveillance camera.

The object was a faded dehydrated food pouch secured to the polymer frame by several windings of Kapton tape. Unfortunately there was no handwriting on the outside—or if there had been, it had faded under years of bombardment by solar and cosmic radiation.

Jin examined the image alongside Chindarkar. "It could have been placed there by the North Koreans. We cannot bring it aboard the station."

Chindarkar said, "But it could have been placed by Isabel or Ade. We can't open it out there. Whatever's in it might get expelled into space. We need to open it up in a contained area."

In the end, Chindarkar and Tighe teleoperated Talos robots equipped with medical kits. Tighe first secured the bag by threading a needle and tether cord through one corner, and then Chindarkar's robot used surgical scissors to cut the tape. She peered inside to see a bundle of dirty cloth. Carefully unwrapping it, she found only a single flash memory chip.

Within minutes the robots placed the resealed bag into the pass-through airlock in Clarke Station's docking bay. The entire group was waiting in the microgravity gate, and they gathered around in free fall as Tighe examined the foil bag directly. It felt cold, with the label faded. Inside, he found the bundle of dirty cloth and the flash memory chip. He held the chip up. And then the empty bag. "That's all there is. No note."

Kerner sifted through his utility bag and came up with a handheld diagnostic computer. "Give it here, please." As Tighe handed it over, Kerner inserted the chip into one of several different slots in the side of his device. He stared at a virtual screen. "It appears damaged."

The others sighed in frustration.

"It could have been the radiation storm."

"Wouldn't Ade or Isabel have known enough to protect it?"

"Not against a CME that big."

Kerner said, "Give me some time with the chip. I will see what I can do."

It wound up taking a couple of days, but Kerner finally gathered them into the CCE boardroom, where he brought up a virtual screen on which he projected a grainy still video image of a person on an EVA in one of the *Konstantin*'s burnt-orange EMU suits.

Chindarkar pointed. "Isabel!"

Abarca's face was projected onto the solid helmet of the EMU, and her outline reflected also in the mirrorlike solar shield of the *Amy Tsukada*, in front of which she floated.

The entire group shouted in joy.

Tighe pounded the table. "I *knew* they were still alive!"

However, the image looked as though someone had peppered it with buckshot. White dots and artifacts riddled the frame.

Kerner sighed. "I am afraid the audio is no better than the image." He played the video and Abarca moved in jerks and stops as the audio track screeched and popped. Kerner talked above the noise. "I tried to interpolate missing data, but this chip is badly corrupted."

They listened intently as the voice of their lost friend crackled from across hundreds of millions of kilometers and several years.

Abarca's face looked indistinct, but she appeared to be smiling—or perhaps wincing? Her voice was scratchy as though on an old recording, and her mouth moved for several moments before words could be discerned. "... *the*

Konstan . . . got to get there . . . five . . . emerge from . . . now or we won't . . . feri . . . there can't be a way to . . ."

Kerner paused it.

The others looked to him.

Tighe said, "Please tell me there's more."

"I am sorry to say, no," Kerner replied. "The chip may have been damaged during the coronal mass ejection event. The *Amy Tsukada* must have ridden through the storm."

Tighe groaned. One of the biggest plasma storms ever recorded. He wondered how bad it had been out at Ryugu. And then he wondered about the *Konstantin*'s solar panels. Were they burned out, too? He looked up. "Is there nothing you can do to reconstruct the data, Julian?"

"I have done all I can. Perhaps an expert back on Earth could do more." He held up the chip. "But you would need to send the original media."

The others looked demoralized.

Tighe then rapped the tabletop. "But they were alive. Now we *know.* This was recorded a *year* after the North Koreans arrived at Ryugu."

Jin said, "But still two and a half years ago."

"If she was alive a year after, then why not three years after?" He then pointed at the virtual window in the side of the boardroom—which looked out to the enormous spacecraft under construction in the nearby dry dock. "It doesn't matter what Earth nations say about our enriching uranium. We *need* the NTR-01. And it must be completed." He looked back at the video image. "Because Isabel and Ade are alive."

CHAPTER 45

Oberhaus

At the end of 2041, Catalyst Corporation put a second lunar cycler into service, launching the *Copernicus* from Clarke Station's shipyard. It was an identical sister ship to the 5,000-ton *Kepler*; however, since they ran on opposite ends of the same 3:1 resonant orbit, there was now cycler service twice monthly between the Moon and the Earth. This made it even easier to transfer crews to and from Clarke Station.

As 2042 arrived, Tighe sensed the relentless celestial clock bringing Ryugu ever closer. He no longer examined the virtual orrery displaying the proximity of the asteroid to Earth because he knew it would only cause him anxiety.

Instead, he watched the outline of the NTR-01 taking shape amid the scaffolding in the nearby shipyard. Many were talking about it. Videos were being shared online back on Earth. However, few people outside of government ministries knew what it really was, and that mystery was intentional.

Just four months before they were to depart for Ryugu, the 2-gigawatt thorium reactor down at Morra Base achieved "first light," easily producing 300 megawatts of a potential 2,000 megawatts. It was basically idling, and supplying power to *two* mass-drivers now: the historic Ecklund MD-01 and now the MD-02, which was capable of launching 50-kilogram cores of regolith into orbit at a rate of half a million tons a year.

There was so much power now that construction had already begun on a third mass-driver, MD-03, which would be completed sometime by year's end. Meanwhile, dozens of Badger robots were roving the terrain around Morra Base, harvesting more regolith.

As a result of all the new lunar construction, and under the auspices of the UN, Lukas Rochat, as Earthly representative for the CCE, signed a No-LOM (or "no lights on the Moon") treaty with eighty-one nations, pledging that no artificial lights would ever be visible on the surface of the Moon from Earth as a result of any CCE signatory. No one could say whether this document was legally binding, but it put Rochat on the cover of *NewSpace* magazine and seemed to calm diplomatic relations with Earth—for a time.

The recurring sticking point had been uranium enrichment. Rochat negotiated for months with diplomats from the US, Russia, and China, while Jin and Chindarkar did the same with their representatives on Clarke Station—touring them around the NTR-01 vessel under construction and explaining the situation with regard to Ryugu.

And yet, the idea of Clarke Station becoming a nuclear power, in combination with its vast and rapidly increasing logistical and financial might in space, was too much for established sovereign states to countenance.

Thus, the UN Security Council issued a resolution demanding that no uranium enrichment take place in deep space and furthermore decreed that the CCE's uranium be secured in the collective custody of the international observers on station.

It was at this point that Chindarkar, Jin, Yak, and Tighe convened an unofficial Catalyst board meeting in the CCE conference room. Since they held the majority of shares, Lukas Rochat was not in attendance, and in truth they felt this was their decision to make.

Chindarkar looked to Tighe, who stared at the tabletop, expressionless. "I want you to know, J.T., that we tried everything we could to get them to see reason."

Tighe spoke without looking at her. "I told you we shouldn't have asked for permission."

Yak nodded.

Jin said, "Then we are agreed." He turned to Chindarkar.

She nodded.

Tighe was about to speak, but Jin continued . . .

"We conduct the enrichment regardless. The fuel must be produced, and the rescue mission must proceed."

Tighe looked to them both in shock. And then to Yak. "Then you're not giving in to their demands?"

Jin turned to Tighe. "We are not a danger to anyone and have done a lot of good. We will simply have to ask forgiveness."

"Well, well . . . my old friend, the adventurer, has decided to reappear."

Jin sighed. "Regrettably, I will not be able to go with you on this journey."

Chindarkar grimaced. "Neither can I."

Tighe frowned. "Why not? We all go."

Jin shook his head. "No. Think it through. There is no reason for another several hundred kilos to come along. You'll need all the delta-v you can muster."

Chindarkar added, "And there will be hell to pay when you leave. They'll know we enriched the uranium. They'll know we violated the Security Council resolution. We need to be here to deal with the fallout, so to speak."

Jin placed a hand on the table. "If we all went on this mission, then the station would be vulnerable to takeover. However, we have some political stature back on Earth."

Chindarkar said, "We will appeal to the public of Earth, and fight like hell to keep control."

Jin looked pained. "I wish I was going with you." He looked to them in turn. "Just bring them home."

Tighe launched out of his seat and wrapped Jin in a tight embrace. "I should never have doubted you. Both." He then embraced Chindarkar.

Yak did the same, kissing them both on each cheek. "*Vy luchshiye!*"

Tighe then grew serious. "I have a personal favor to ask, though, and I hope you don't mind."

They all regarded him with fresh concern.

"I want to suggest a name for the NTR-01. I know this has been a group effort, and I won't ask for this favor again . . . but I'd like to ask that we christen the ship after my dive mentor, Richard Oberhaus. That perhaps we name it *Oberhaus.*"

Chindarkar knew the story of Tighe's mentor and nodded. "That would be beautiful, James. I think he'd have liked that."

Jin and Yak gripped his shoulder and nodded. Jin said, "*Oberhaus* it is."

Tighe looked relieved and smiled. "Thank you. I really appreciate it."

Jin asked Yak, "How long will it take to get the uranium enrichment up and running?"

Tighe and Yak exchanged guilty looks.

Chindarkar narrowed her eyes. "What was that?"

Yak turned to her. "Ah. We may have done . . . perhaps, tiny bit of enrichment already."

Jin frowned. "Are you joking?"

Yak held out his arms. "Please understand, James and I knew you would both come to correct conclusion. We merely anticipated this."

Tighe added, "You might say we had faith in you."

As the weeks passed and the construction of the *Oberhaus* neared completion, Chindarkar worked with Rochat to hire several prominent Earth PR firms, preparing a comprehensive publicity campaign recounting the *Konstantin* asteroid mining expedition—including detailed accounts of the mission and hundreds of hours of onboard video. Profiles of Nicole Clarke, David Morra, and Amy Tsukada were revealed to the world, along with their historic accomplishments, finally giving them their moment of posthumous fame.

And also, the identities of Isabel Abarca and Adedayo Adisa were revealed, as was their current predicament out at Ryugu. The best PR experts money could buy produced moving videos celebrating Abarca's and Adisa's life stories, as well as their personal courage and sacrifice in helping the *Konstantin* crew return home—and in making Clarke Station and the off-world economy possible.

Given his impoverished background, Adisa was an inspiration to young people worldwide; unlike the rest of the *Konstantin* crew, he was not a born adventurer, but became one by circumstance. However, watching a documentary about Isabel Abarca's life—her upbringing in Buenos Aires and her early climbing days—Tighe couldn't help but smile, finally understanding the woman she would later become. Her driven nature. Abarca had been handed a comfortable life, but she chose time and again to go to the very edge. No wonder they got along so well.

One scene in the documentary showed Abarca's team standing atop the summit of K2, having mounted the first successful winter climb. She wore goggles but no oxygen mask—climbing, as always, Alpine style—speaking in voice-over from an earlier interview. *"Unless we test our limits, we will never know what we're capable of."* Another scene of her speaking to a reporter. *"I will attempt any mountain. No matter the difficulty."*

Little wonder that Nathan Joyce chose her to head the *Konstantin* expedition; Abarca would never relent until she reached her personal summit. It was in her nature, and others followed in her path. Certainly that's what Tighe had done.

The entire media campaign was meant to reinforce one message: that these were exceptional people who deserved rescue. And a rescue mission was only possible with the nuclear thermal propulsion ship, *Oberhaus*, now sitting in Clarke Station's shipyard—the reason, in fact, for the existence of the shipyard, and indeed the station itself.

In short, the team made the case for lighting the *Oberhaus*'s nuclear engines not to government leaders but to the entire population of Earth, and coming from the people who had brought the lūna—and thus hope for a better future—to hundreds of millions during a time of global crisis, that case was powerful indeed.

By the time the *Oberhaus* went out on space trials to test its engines, the entire world was watching.

CHAPTER 46

Confrontation

CLARKE STATION POPULATION: 199

DAYS TO RYUGU DEPARTURE: 0

RESOURCES LAUNCHED TO L2: 317,200 TONS

I f it had been possible, no doubt there would have been thousands of reporters, paparazzi, and news drones flitting about to capture the departure of the *Oberhaus* for Ryugu. Instead, Earth media had enticed some of the crew on Clarke Station into accepting considerable sums to capture the event for home world audiences.

And yet, none of the endless think pieces and social media posts about the asteroid miners expressed fear or outrage about the nuclear engines powering the *Oberhaus*. The ship was instead widely admired as the most advanced and capable spacecraft ever built. All over the Internet, space enthusiasts and schoolchildren pored over photos of its construction in deep space. Every single module and thruster. Physics and engineering departments in universities worldwide were turning away applicants, so intent were young people on joining the growing adventure in deep space. Space was now clearly humanity's future.

James Tighe considered this as he zipped up his pack and took one last look around his quarters—a suite large enough to notice the slight upward curve in the sitting room floor.

How odd that this seemed normal to him now. He had an apartment on the far side of the Moon. What would his younger self have made of that? The weeks and months and years of effort had accumulated, and this was now his reality. And it was time to finally go. All of the seemingly insurmountable obstacles had been overcome—though precious lives had been lost in the process. It all came down to this moment.

He examined the mementos on his desk: tchotchkes made by astropreneurs seeking investment, a rock he'd picked up on the Moon, a sample of cultured wood he'd been given by the grad students in Lynne Holstad's Ag Lab, an embroidered *Konstantin* mission patch—a gift from US Space Force observers—depicting the historic spacecraft alongside Ryugu.

On the wall above his desk were blueprints, illustrations, and technical specifications for the NTR-01 *Oberhaus*. Now that they had resources in orbit, he preferred tactile documents—physical things—whenever possible. Images he could look upon and touch even without his crystal on.

Dozens of photos were tacked onto a bulletin board and hung in frames on the wall above his desk. Clarke Station crew members. Scenery of the Moon. A treasured framed photograph of the original crew of the *Konstantin*—all eight of them—arm in arm in free fall just before the *Konstantin*'s departure; autographs over their image. And newer photos: one of four Talos robots, also arm in arm in their jumpsuits and bubble helmets, taking a selfie on the surface of the Moon; a half-constructed Launch House behind them with their disposable suits customized by painted-on images of UFOs and stylized nicknames. Though they were robots, Tighe recognized who they were: Jin Han, Robert Ecklund, himself, and Sevastian Yakovlev. And he could almost imagine them smiling. The sense of camaraderie, of shared hardship and purpose, it gave his life meaning.

Next to this was a photo of Tighe standing alongside Richard Oberhaus, in a base camp in Mexico, wearing orange trog suits and caving helmets. Oberhaus's genial face as he laughed at something Tighe had evidently just said. Tighe could not recall what. This man who had willingly laid down his life for him all those years ago—and in doing so, had made all of this possible. What did Tighe owe to such a man? He realized he owed everything—and yet also nothing—for that would be how Oberhaus would have wanted it. He recalled his mentor's calm last words. *"We do not have the luxury of a long good-bye . . . Go!"*

Tighe caught a glimpse of himself in the mirror by the door, wearing his MCP suit. If only Oberhaus could see him now. What would he say? Tighe would give anything for one last conversation with him. Or with all the other dear friends who had perished.

He took a final look around his quarters, well aware that he might never return. But he also realized that was okay. Tighe was ready.

There was a knock at the door.

Tighe hesitated for a moment before he opened it to discover Priya Chindarkar standing in the hall. Their disputes in recent years over mission priorities weighed on him, and he was glad to see her before he left.

She looked sad, but also glad to see him as well. "My contacts at CSpOC tell me that no other spacecraft has been launched toward Ryugu by China, North Korea, or anyone else. The *Oberhaus* will be going out alone."

He nodded. "Good." He stepped aside to let her in.

She hesitated a moment, then entered. "It could be because of the longer distance this time—or because of all the disasters China and other nations are facing down on Earth." She paused. "That and the fact that nothing was ever heard from the North Korean mission—and they never sent robot tugs back."

"You came to remind me of that. *Today?*"

"Those are the facts."

He just stared at her.

"I know it may have seemed like I was fighting you about this mission at times, James, but I want you to know it was always my goal. All the compromises and capitulations were for a reason. So much was riding on the success of Clarke Station. And on the CCE. Not just for ourselves, but also everyone on Earth. Still, I never gave up on this rescue."

"I know. I'm beginning to realize that if it wasn't for what you and Jin did, we never would have gotten this far."

They stood there in silence for a few moments, and it occurred to him that he'd had the luxury of being so single-minded *because* of her. Yes, the *Oberhaus* was smaller and leaner than he'd have liked—but it was finished. And it was undoubtedly the most capable spacecraft ever built.

He turned to look out the virtual window in his sitting room wall. It showed a view outside Clarke Station of the burgeoning deep space industry thriving there—the sleek form of the *Oberhaus* docked a kilometer away. "It's good that you and Jin will stay—and see that this all continues." He turned back to her. "We've done all that the world has asked of us, Priya, but it's time for me to go."

"I know." She extended her arms and they embraced for several moments. "It was an honor to crew with you, James Tighe."

"And an honor to crew with you, Priya Chindarkar." He held her at arm's length, looking into her eyes. "If I don't return, Lukas has instructions to transfer all my shares to you and Han."

She looked him in the eye. "Then you'd better return, or we'll have to come looking for you."

He let a slight smile slip. "Don't go through any trouble."

With that, he picked up his bag and helmet, and they departed his suite, heading out to the lobby of the CCE. Waiting for him there in their own MCP suits were Sevastian Yakovlev, Dr. Elizabeth Josephson—who had returned to Clarke Station after two years studying genetic-editing medicine on Earth—and nuclear propulsion engineer Oleg Gusev. They all stood in front of the metal orrery sculpture and would be Tighe's crewmates for this journey. Next to them were Jin Han and Ramón Marín, both in standard-issue flight suits.

Tighe nodded to the *Oberhaus* crew. "You guys ready?"

They nodded back.

Jin looked uncharacteristically distraught. He extended his hand. "I wish I could go with you. I hope you know that."

Tighe took his hand. "Of course I do, but we can't afford the extra mass."

Jin laughed in spite of himself. "Is that all I am these days?"

"We'll be back. If Isabel and Ade are alive, we will bring them home."

"I know you will." With that, Jin embraced Tighe. "Come back safe, brother." They held the hug for a moment. Jin then hugged the other crew members as well.

Tighe clasped Marín's hand. "Ramón, thanks for building us a whole new economy out here. I'm not sure any of this would have been possible otherwise."

"You give me too much credit—but it was my pleasure. Truly."

The crew picked up their gear and moved toward the CCE HQ's double doors.

Jin, Chindarkar, and Marín remained behind, watching them leave.

Jin called after them. "There is a crowd out there. So I asked CSR officers to escort you to the transit craft. To avoid any incidents."

"You don't trust our international observers?"

"I do not want to take any unnecessary risks. The UN Security Council has not yet changed its ruling on the *Oberhaus*."

"Don't hold your breath."

Chindarkar said, "We'll be in the ops center. Catching every moment."

The crew waved their final farewells, and then moved out into the CCE elevator lobby.

There, dozens of CCE staff stood applauding and cheering as the four crew of the *Oberhaus* emerged. Phones and crystals recorded them passing by in their MCP suits, carrying gear. Several CSR officers pushed staffers back, clearing a path. "Make room! Make room, please!"

Tighe and the others nodded as they walked through the gauntlet of well-wishers and the upheld phones capturing this moment. No doubt many millions—perhaps tens or hundreds of millions—were watching back on Earth.

The *Oberhaus* crew proceeded to the elevator, where the CSR commander, a clean-cut Caucasian Brit in his early thirties—the name "Wilkins" stitched onto his silvery-gray flight suit—used a physical key to open the locked elevator doors. He then extended his hand to them. "Major Roger Wilkins, Cislunar Search and Rescue. It's an honor to meet you all. I have people securing the way ahead."

"Thank you, Major."

Wilkins entered the elevator with them and tapped the button for the station's core. The crowd shouted farewell before disappearing from view as the doors closed.

The elevator ascended as the CSR commanding officer looked to the four of them. "What you've achieved here in deep space is historic. I hope you all know that."

Tighe said, "We had lots of help."

Wilkins then put a key in the elevator's fire control panel and turned it to "Stop." The elevator came to a sudden halt. An alarm sounded.

Yak looked up in surprise. "What is this?"

Gusev frowned. "We have a departure window to catch, Major."

"Yes, about that . . ." The commander turned to face them again. "There's still no authorization from Earth regarding your uranium reactor cores. In the absence of this, I have been ordered to prevent you from launching the *Oberhaus*."

Tighe stared at him. "Is this a joke? We're not going to *proliferate* nuclear weapons. The whole world knows this. We're going to rescue our crewmates." Tighe gestured around them. "That's what this was all about! The station! The mass-drivers! Everything!"

"And I am very sure the world is grateful. But the UN Security Council forbids operation of unauthorized nuclear reactors in cislunar space."

Josephson scoffed. "This is insane . . ."

"You were supposed to escort us to the transit craft."

"Do Priya and Han know about this?"

Wilkins shook his head. "Of course not."

Yak said, "You ungrateful—"

Gusev glanced at his crystal. "Time is of the essence here."

Tighe pointed at the officer. "Unlock this elevator. *Now*."

Yak raised his hands to calm the situation. Then he turned to the officer. "What is your name again?"

"Major Roger Wilkins, barracks commander of the First Cislunar Search and Rescue Corps."

"Cislunar Search and Rescue Corps—which CCE founded in coopera-tion with nations of Earth and to which we donate habitation, life support, and logistics."

"That is correct, Comrade Scientist Yakovlev."

"Do you realize, Major Wilkins, how many millions of people back on Earth expect us to walk out of this elevator and head to our ship?"

The officer nodded. "Yes, I have some idea."

"Everyone knows why we built *Oberhaus*, and what we intend to do with it. We are danger to no one."

Josephson added, "Do you know how many people on Earth have bene-fited from the CCE? From what's been accomplished here?"

Tighe said, "We run a massive nuclear reactor at Morra Base."

Wilkins nodded. "A thorium reactor. And a stationary one. You were warned that you would not be allowed to activate a nuclear thermal propulsion rocket."

"And you seriously think we're going to create bombs?"

"It isn't just about bombs . . ." The officer sighed. "The *Oberhaus* represents a strategic capability that is unmatched in deep space. You have the most powerful and capable spacecraft by far. What if you and your ship get taken over by the North Koreans when you arrive at the *Konstantin?*"

Tighe, Yak, Josephson, and Gusev exchanged incredulous looks.

The officer took a deep breath, then drew a concealed semiautomatic pistol from his flight suit.

Tighe stared in disbelief.

Yak shook his head sadly. "Do not do this . . ."

Josephson said, "This is wrong."

At which point the officer turned the gun around and handed it, grip-first, to Tighe. "You may need this." He looked up. "To defend your ship."

Tighe stared at the gun and then at the officer in confusion.

"I have duly notified you that you will be in violation of UN Security Council Resolution 5213 if you light the *Oberhaus*'s reactors. However, I cannot in good conscience obey what I believe to be an unlawful order to physically prevent your departure." He paused. "Although, again, you lack an operating license. Something you should look into obtaining."

Tighe felt relief wash over him. "They'll crucify you, Major."

"Quite possibly, yes." He took a deep breath. "I was hoping you would be willing to testify on my behalf at the court martial." He pushed the gun into Tighe's hand. "Which you can only do if you make it back."

Tighe nodded. "Or we could write something on the way."

"That would be . . . very much appreciated."

Yak laughed uproariously. "Most fortunate . . ." With that, he folded back the flap of his rucksack and withdrew a sawed-off double-barreled shotgun that included a third rifle barrel as well—which he'd been concealing.

"Good god, man." Wilkins stared at it in shock. "What is that?"

Yak held it up. "Is TP-82. Standard issue."

"Why in the hell do you have that?"

He patted it. "In case of bear attack." Yak holstered the weapon and then extended his hands, hugging the major and kissing him on both cheeks. "*Druzhishche!*" Then he slapped the officer's back. "You are good man, Major. I think you have big future in space." Yak took the pistol from him. "We may have need of this. Thank you."

The officer passed along two clips of ammunition. "Frangible rounds. Designed not to pierce a hull." He gazed at the butt of Yak's shotgun. "Unlike your heavy artillery."

Wilkins then turned the key and pressed the elevator button for the station core.

By the time the elevator doors opened, they were all in free fall.

Wilkins glanced at his antique aviator watch. "So you're two hours, twenty-one minutes until pushback."

They each shook hands with him as they glided through the door.

A little over two hours later, Tighe and Yak donned their MCP helmets and went on a space walk outside the *Oberhaus*, moving hand over hand to the comm tower of the massive ship. As they did so, Tighe listened to radio chatter between Clarke Station and mission control, while Yak, as captain of the *Oberhaus*, issued commands to Gusev, who was strapped into one of the hab units with Dr. Josephson.

Tighe and Yak then maneuvered to grasp the service rail at the bow of the ship. It seemed like the ideal place from which to publicly bid farewell to Clarke Station—and Earth—and they knew dozens of cameras were recording this moment.

As the countdown began in his earphones, Tighe thought of how many years it had been since their journey to Ryugu on the *Konstantin*. He beheld the growing industial complex around the station, with the massive framework of a next-generation solar power satellite—the Star of Africa—under construction in the distance. He marveled at how far they'd come. Looking down at the ship beneath his feet, he knew that, unlike the *Konstantin*, the *Oberhaus* was not fragile. It was powerful and capable.

Yak's voice was in his ear now. "*Four . . . three . . . two . . . one . . . ignition.*"

The *Oberhaus*'s smaller chemical pilot engine ignited, safely easing them away from the vicinity of Clarke Station without spraying radiation in their wake, and now that they were moving, they felt a quarter g of acceleration, enabling them to "stand" on a grillwork deck that ringed the comm tower.

Checking that their tethers were secure, they then watched Clarke Station, now fully lit up and glorious with celebratory lights, passing before them.

Tighe noticed members of Cislunar Search & Rescue floating in a line in their EVA suits at the entrance to the station's hangar bay. They all saluted the *Oberhaus* as it glided by.

Tighe and Yak waved in return, and video of that moment was no doubt what the cameras were hoping to capture.

Gabriel Lacroix's voice came in over the comm link from Ascension Island. *"Farewell and following seas,* Oberhaus."

After watching Clarke Station recede into the distance, Tighe and Yak moved hand over hand to enter the *Oberhaus*'s airlock. Once inside the hab, they strapped in.

Five hundred kilometers downrange, Gusev ran through the ignition sequence for the *Oberhaus*'s four nuclear engines—and then officially violated Security Council Resolution 5213. As he throttled up the reactors, a deep hum encompassed the ship—and then Gusev kicked in the O_2 afterburners. The intensity of the hum around them increased, conveying the sensation of immense, barely contained power, followed by constant acceleration. Their initial burn lasted several hours—a feat not possible with chemical rockets—and once it was finished, they spun up the ship's twin habitats to provide artificial gravity.

By then, the *Oberhaus* was moving at well over 20 kilometers per second on a trajectory to encounter the asteroid Ryugu in thirty-two days.

CHAPTER 47

Return

AUGUST 4, 2042

J ames Tighe felt a surge of adrenaline as the familiar outline of the asteroid Ryugu loomed dead ahead and the *Oberhaus* hove to in its shadow. There in the sheltering darkness of the asteroid blinked the navigation lights of the fragile mining ship *Konstantin*. Its solar mast still glinted in sunlight as it protruded above the asteroid's horizon, harvesting power while the rest of the ship remained shielded from the Sun's radiation.

After all these years and all this struggle, there it was: the *Konstantin*.

It remained. And it appeared operational—or at least it still had power and seemed to be on station, 3 kilometers from Ryugu's surface. That meant the bang-bang control was still operational—and thus the ship's computer. The vessel's name, "Konstantin," and the Luxembourg flag, along with its hull license number, were still illuminated on the white hull of the central habitat.

What's more, in the distance, Honey Bee mining robots were still visible in terminator orbits around the asteroid, focusing sunlight onto bagged boulders—their parabolic lenses turned toward the Sun. There were also several enormous robot tugs docked amid a supply yard bulging with spherical polymer bladder tanks—the number difficult to calculate from this angle. However, the smallest of the robot tugs was nearly twice the size of the *Amy Tsukada*.

Sevastian Yakovlev whistled. "The North Koreans have been busy."

Tighe remained stone-faced. "You mean *we* were busy." He gestured to the Honey Bees. "We automated most of that years ago."

"But why have tugs not been sent back toward Moon?"

The likely answer to that question brought an uncomfortable silence. Dr. Elizabeth Josephson glided over to them in the *Oberhaus*'s Spartan cabin.

They had spun-down the ship for arrival, and all compartments were in microgravity now. She joined them in examining the virtual imagery displayed on their crystals.

Tighe pointed out another object. "There's the cairn."

Yak zoomed in to the compact silhouette of the tomb—a collection of polyamide cylinders packed with silica to create a vault. Inside, Tighe's deceased crewmates were interred. The cairn was still on its wide terminator orbit around Ryugu.

Meanwhile, the *Oberhaus* continued to glide closer to the *Konstantin*, now a mere 10 kilometers away. Their four nuclear-thermal propulsion engines had performed two postinjection burns, one the day prior—a retrograde maneuver to reduce their extreme velocity, engines firing full throttle for half an hour. Then, turning forward once more, an hour ago they had executed a comparatively modest burn to match orbits with Ryugu and were now maneuvering on thrusters for rendezvous.

In preparation for their arrival, the entire crew of the *Oberhaus*—Tighe, Yak, Josephson, and nuclear propulsion engineer Oleg Gusev—strapped into a row of seats, with Gusev navigating.

As Tighe studied live images of the *Konstantin*, he zoomed in on the upper airlock. "Only one mule docked. There were two last time I was here."

Yak said, "Their radar mast is not rotating. They may have no idea that we are here."

"The Ade I know would never let the radar go down."

Yak offered, "Perhaps they have no replacement parts."

Tighe pointed at the North Korean spacecraft docked on the far side of the airlock. It appeared half disassembled—its solar panels gone. "Looks like they've been cannibalizing their own ship."

Yak studied radar screens. "No other spacecraft moving."

Instead, the only things in motion were the *Oberhaus* and the *Konstantin*'s three habs at the end of their radial arms, navigation lights tracing out their endless rotation.

Yak continued to work the radio, hailing the *Konstantin* on numerous comm frequencies. "*Konstantin, Konstantin*, this is NTR-01 *Oberhaus*, requesting permission to come aboard. Do you copy? Over." A pause. "*Konstantin, Konstantin . . .*"

Now that they were close, Tighe tried to link to the *Konstantin*'s wireless network using every password he knew, but none of them worked. "They changed the codes."

"Or network is down."

This second possibility seemed far worse.

Tighe made a radio call of his own on the local emergency channel. "Isabel. Ade. If you are there, this is J.T. We've come to rescue you." He listened to static. "Please respond. Over."

And yet there was no answer.

Then the *Oberhaus* came to a relative stop, with a final burst of forward thrusters, 2 kilometers distant from the *Konstantin*. They all unbuckled their harnesses.

Gusev announced, "Bang-bang control activated."

Yak turned to his colleagues. "Time for some light." With that he kicked on a cluster of million candle-power LED lights on the bow of the *Oberhaus*— bathing the entire *Konstantin* in illumination. What it revealed did not comfort them.

"Good god . . ."

The pitiable state of the mining ship and its environs was now clear. Particles of debris glinted in space all around it, and bits of torn cladding and Kevlar stays that normally held the radial-arm transit tunnels in place hung off like ripped cloth as the arms swept past in their rotation.

Josephson looked mortified. "What happened?"

"Time." Tighe studied the screen. "Nathan didn't build anything to last."

Yak turned to Josephson. "Liz, you and Oleg stay here. J.T. and I will go aboard *Konstantin*." He caught her by the shoulder. "If there is problem and you do not hear from us, you and Oleg depart. Understood?"

She frowned. "No. It is not understood. We're not leaving without you both."

Yak sighed, then turned to Gusev. "Oleg, you understand my instruction, yes? *Oberhaus* is too valuable to lose."

Gusev nodded. "I understand, Captain."

Then Tighe and Yak moved through the *Oberhaus*'s compartments, into the airlock. Already in MCP suits, they silently donned and pressurized their helmets, tested each other's life support, then added tools and supplies to their utility harnesses.

Tighe radioed, "Liz, how do our camera feeds look?"

Josephson's voice replied, *"Good video from you both. Now's a good time to activate your suit intercom. Otherwise you won't be able to speak with anyone you encounter."*

"Suit intercom activated." It was at this point that Yak produced the semi-automatic pistol that the CSR officer had given him back on Clarke Station. He offered it to Tighe.

Tighe just stared at it. Then at Yak.

"Then I will carry. I have training." Yak loaded a clip, pulled the slide back, and confirmed the safety was on before holstering it. He also stowed the two spare clips. "Frangible ammo was good idea. Let us hope we do not need it."

Then they opened the hatch to enter *Oberhaus's* docked transit craft. This was one of a dozen transit craft they now had up at EM-L2. Tighe had to marvel at how far they'd come. If only Abarca and Adisa could see it. That thought suddenly darkened his mood.

To keep his mind busy, he helped Yak secure the docking hatch, then slapped its surface and called to Josephson. "Transit-08, hatch secure."

They both strapped into jump seats, and Yak announced their departure, followed by a *klunk* as the docking bolts released. Using a virtual interface, Yak piloted the spacecraft away from the *Oberhaus.* "Transit-08 . . . clear." Thrusters popped. "Cycling toward *Konstantin."*

Josephson's voice came in over the comm link. *"Copy that. Use caution, Transit-08."*

Tighe instantiated a virtual forward-looking window sourced from one of the transit craft's exterior cameras. Its thrusters popped occasionally as Yak brought them a safe distance above the rotating arms of the *Konstantin,* then slowed as they approached the four-sided upper docking collar below the solar tower and communication mast. As they glided closer, occasional pieces of debris clanged off the transit craft's steel hull.

Tighe frowned. "No one's been policing space junk. That's not a good sign."

Yak said, "But full supply yard means system is still working." He brought them within a few meters of the upper airlock, and then rotated the transit craft to align its side IDSS hatch to the *Konstantin's* docking port.

Meanwhile, looking at the virtual screen, Tighe gestured just above the vehicle dock, where four heavy EMU space suits were usually locked in place. "Look. There's only one suit. Could they be out on EVA?"

Josephson's voice said, *"There are no unidentified radar contacts, J.T."*

After a few bumps, the transit craft's docking bolts rammed home. They were docked to the *Konstantin*. After a pause Yak looked up. "Good seal. I am locking flight controls."

"I'll get the hatch." Tighe unbuckled and moved hand over hand in microgravity toward the hatch lever. "Be ready."

"Da." Yak unholstered the pistol, but held it downward as he floated nearby.

Tighe released the hatch and pulled it inward.

The exterior of the *Konstantin*'s closed airlock hatch now faced him. It had been four years since he had last seen it. He ran his gloved hand across the familiar scratches and dents. After another beat he slid the release lever and pushed the hatch inward.

"Let me go in first, J.T." Yak glided forward with the gun held low but ready, floating through the circular hatchway and into the *Konstantin*'s cylindrical upper airlock. Tighe followed close behind.

Inside, he noticed cabling and piping that would normally be bound in conduits along the hull wall, but were instead pulled out and spliced in places. Evidence of hasty repairs abounded. "Look there." Tighe pointed at punctures in the aluminum beams.

"Bullet holes." Yak scanned the compartment. "Not the only ones ..." He gestured to the hull itself, where a dozen or more patches had been spot-welded into place.

"There was a fight in here." Tighe checked the atmosphere. "Pressure's good, though."

"We continue. Yes?"

"Absolutely. But hold on." Tighe moved back to the transit craft's hatch and pulled it closed behind them. "Liz, can you lock Transit-08's hatch, please?"

There was a metallic click. "Transit-08 hatch locked."

Tighe then moved toward another hatch in the "floor" of the docking collar—a hatch that led to the axis tunnel that ran 40 meters to the Central Hab and the core of the *Konstantin*. He braced his legs on two beams with practiced ease, having opened this hatch a thousand times over the years. "Be ready."

Yak held the pistol with both hands, aiming down its sights at the hatch. "Ready."

Tighe slid the worn handle with a squeak and pulled upward, revealing the 2-meter-wide tunnel—and also startling a wild-haired, heavily bearded Korean man in a patched and bloodstained flight suit with the hood opened up who floated just beyond the opening. The man was anywhere from thirty to fifty years of age—it was impossible to tell.

Yak aimed the pistol at him. "Hands!"

The man's eyes widened, and he threw out his hands, shouting, "*Nal ssoji ma! Jebal!*"

Yak replied in Russian, "*Ne shevelis! Ponimat?*"

The man nodded. "*Ya bezoruzhen. Pozhaluysta, ne strelyayte!*"

Yak turned to Tighe. "He says he is unarmed."

"No more guns. Please!" The man's voice quavered. "Please!"

Tighe moved to the edge of the hatch. "You speak English?"

The man looked feral—like a castaway—and he began to weep. "Rescue. Please."

Tighe looked to Yak. "These MCPs are supposed to be bulletproof, right?" Tighe extended his hand and pulled the man into the upper airlock, glancing down the tunnel behind to be certain it was empty.

Tighe then patted down the weeping man and came up empty. He spun him around in free fall and looked into his wild eyes. "How many are you?"

The man hugged Tighe. "We are four. Just four." Then he gripped Tighe's MCP suit tightly and sobbed, overcome.

Yak lowered the gun.

A raspy voice suddenly spoke over an intercom speaker mounted nearby. "*Nae chingudeul-i deul-eogage haejwo.*" It was a voice that sounded somewhat familiar.

Upon hearing it, the wild-haired Korean man released Tighe and nodded. "Yes. Please follow." He smiled and motioned as he glided toward the hatch again.

Tighe and Yak instead gazed at the intercom.

The raspy voice spoke again, the breath labored. It spoke in Nigerian-accented English. "*J.T., Sevastian. Is it really possible that you are here?*"

Tighe gripped Yak's shoulder and called out, "Ade! Ade, my god! Where are you?" He spoke into the comm link. "Liz! Ade's alive!"

Yak spoke. "Ade, the North Koreans—"

"Do not worry. My Korean friends have been hoping for this day. They are overjoyed to see you."

Tighe asked, "Where are you?"

"I am in Hab 2."

Tighe noticed the Korean man down in the tunnel, smiling and motioning for him and Yak to follow. Tighe instead turned to the intercom. "Damn, Ade, it's good to hear your voice. Why were the codes to the *Konstantin* changed? Why can't we connect?"

Adisa's voice sounded weary. *"So much has happened, J.T. Just come. I need to know that you are not just a figment of my imagination. Please come."*

They followed the North Korean through the *Konstantin*, and as they did, powerful memories assailed Tighe—recalling moments of terror and of joy from his four years here. Memories of those who did not survive. There was also anguish at the *Konstantin*'s condition. The ship was clearly beginning to fail, with seals split and air-handling units rattling and leaking. Fatigue cracks showed on the carbon fiber trusses.

Josephson spoke over the comm link. *"J.T., Yak, I know you want to greet Adedayo, but keep your helmets pressurized. This crew has been out here for some time, and we do not want to expose them to our germs."*

Yak replied, "Is probably good idea anyway. Konstantin air looks iffy."

As they entered the Central Hab, another North Korean in a gray flight suit, similarly long-haired and bearded, floated toward them, waving and smiling. "Thank you! Thank you!" He shook Tighe's and Yak's gloved hands repeatedly, and then patted them on their life support packs.

Near the tunnel to Hab 2, both Koreans pressurized their own flight suits, and all four men pushed through the interior airlock. They clipped carabiners to the tunnel winch line and hung on as the cable descended into the spin-gravity well. Yak pointed out rips in the polymer tunnel wall—the black of space visible beyond. *"Konstantin* has not much time left."

Tighe studied the tunnel. "She was a good ship, though."

Minutes later they reached the tunnel's "bottom" and cycled through the Hab 2 airlock, descending the ladder into the hab itself—as Tighe had done innumerable times before. The sleeping quarters on this level were a mess—with hash marks carved into the aluminum wall next to formal portrait photos of Asian people, both young and old.

Tighe rotated the wheel on the hab's pressure door and pushed into the crew quarters, intending to move immediately to the right and the crew lounge, but as he emerged he was instead greeted by a third Korean man—this one in a green uniform. He was in his fifties, with short groomed hair, graying at the temples.

The man bowed with his fingers peaked before him and spoke in accented English. "Honored to meet you. I am Dr. Kim, flight surgeon."

Taken aback, Tighe and Yak both bowed slightly. "Dr. Kim. Where is Adedayo?"

Behind the man, Tighe could see the entire hab was a shambles. The sofa and chair fabric was ripped. There were more bullet holes in the kitchen cabinets, and laminates peeling up at the corners. However, as Tighe glanced around, the handwritten list of historic "firsts" that he and his crewmates had scrawled on the steel core wall over the years of their expedition remained. Unchanged.

A voice called from beyond one of the hab partitions. "I am here, J.T."

He and Yak pushed the partition aside and entered the medical bay. Here, too, the equipment was worn and the glass-fronted medical cabinets empty.

However, in the lone hospital bed, an emaciated Adedayo Adisa rose up on one elbow to shakily greet them. His eyes were milky white with cataracts—but he smiled unseeing. "Can it really be you?" He extended a bony hand.

Tighe and Yak stood on either side of the bed.

"Ade, what's happened?" Tighe took Adisa's hand and looked up as Dr. Kim came alongside. "What's wrong with him?"

Dr. Kim adjusted Adisa's IV feed. "His cataracts and lymphoma are a result of long-term exposure to ionizing radiation. I regret to say I could not perform cataract surgery here."

"And his lymphoma?"

The doctor shook his head grimly.

Adisa ignored tears that ran down his face as he weakly gripped Tighe's gloved hand, and then reached for Yak's as well. "You *are* real."

Yak said, "Yes, we are here, Adedayo."

Tighe knelt close and Adisa ran his hand across his helmet. "We came for you."

Adisa's face contorted in grief. "J.T., I thought I had killed you. The return trajectory—"

"It saved us. *You* saved us. And Han flew an amazing aerobraking run. You should have seen it."

Adisa wept, relief evident on his face. "They are both alive?"

"Priya and Han are fine—waiting for word of you." Tighe stroked Adisa's bald head gently with his gloved hand. "We've been trying to contact the *Konstantin* for years. What happened to the comm array?"

Adisa looked up suddenly with his clouded, blind eyes. "What of my family—my brothers and sisters? My mother?"

"They're all well. We have photos. Video. I know you can't see it now, but they're all living in a big house you bought them on Victoria Island."

"That *I* bought them?" Adisa seemed as if he were afraid to believe it.

"Yes. You'll see them all soon."

At this his face once again twisted in grief. "It is kind of you to say this, J.T., but I know I do not have long. I just—"

"No, Ade." Tighe leaned close. "Listen to me. We brought new medical tech with us. Genetic-editing equipment. It can treat cancer. So much has changed in the last eight years. I promise you, you will see your family. I promise you will see Earth again."

Adisa was shaking his head, clearly afraid to hope.

Yak spoke over the comm link. "Liz, please come aboard. Adedayo needs immediate medivac to the *Oberhaus*."

"Copy that. I'm on my way."

Tighe squeezed Adisa's hand again. "It's going to be all right." He realized how healing it was for him, too, to finally be able to say those words to someone who had been willing to die in his place. "I promise you it's going to be all right."

Yak glanced around the med bay. "Adedayo . . ." He leaned toward Adisa. "Where is Isabel?"

At the sound of her name, Adisa's grief returned. He shook his head, and could not speak for several moments. Again tears flowed down his face. "I am sorry . . . she is gone."

The news hit Tighe like a sledgehammer. He leaned forward, trying to control his breathing. Within the pressurized helmet, he knew any tears could not be swept away. In fact, he recalled Abarca's own face leaning close to his, the day he went out on EVA to euthanize Nicole Clarke.

You cannot tear up. Do you hear me?

He nodded to himself, and took slow, deliberate breaths.

Yak knelt close as well, a devastated look on his face. "When?"

Adisa spoke, but with difficulty. "August . . . 2040."

"Two years ago . . ." Tighe clenched his fists. "Shit!"

Adisa spoke softly. "I tried . . . but I could not stop her."

Tighe paused and along with Yak turned back toward Adisa. "What do you mean, 'stop her'?"

Adisa stared into an imagined distance. "She said she *had* to go."

"Go? Go where?"

Adisa turned to him, as if it were obvious. "To Mars."

Tighe and Yak exchanged stunned looks.

Yak recovered first. "Mars? How could Isabel go to Mars?"

Adisa's sharp intellect reasserted itself. "November 22, 2040, Ryugu came into conjunction with Mars. Isabel and Captain Jeong modified the *Argo* to suit their purpose and departed on a Hohmann transfer to Mars in August."

Tighe leaned in. "The captain and Isabel left . . . together? *For Mars?*"

Yak spoke over the comm line. "Oleg, check radar. Is *Argo* still orbiting Ryugu?"

After a few moments, Gusev's voice replied, *"Negative, Sevastian. The Argo is absent."*

Tighe tried to wrap his head around it. "Why would she go to Mars, Ade? We came here to save you."

Adisa was in tears once more. "She thought you all perished. We both did. I thought it was possible that someone would come for us this year, but I did not know who. Isabel . . . she wanted to go farther. And I think she awakened in Captain Jeong a spirit he did not know he possessed."

Yak said simply, "Adedayo Adisa, tell us what happened here."

Adisa collected his thoughts. "Not long after the North Koreans arrived, there was a falling-out among the crew—some, like Dr. Kim, supported Captain Jeong. Others supported political officer Gwon."

Yak narrowed his eyes. "Did they harm either of you?"

Adisa shook his head. "The captain would never have allowed that." He seemed to be recalling past events. "And as time went on, Isabel fascinated him. The others noticed—especially their political officer, Major Gwon.

"You must understand, they brought a totalitarian dictatorship way out here. One that demanded absolute obedience under pain of death. And yet . . ." Adisa took a deep breath. ". . . these are human beings—with only a faint radio link to their leaders. Within months, there were arguments between Captain Jeong and political officer Gwon. Factions formed. And Isabel . . . she began to inspire him to go on an epic journey."

Tighe felt a sudden kinship with this Captain Jeong.

Adisa looked up with his blind eyes and away from a past he'd been reliving. "I tried to dissuade her. To make her see that it was suicide. But slow death was our reality here. Isabel wanted to choose the terms of that death."

Tighe asked, "We saw bullet holes in the airlock. What happened?"

Adisa's face tensed. "Major Gwon and his followers would not let Captain Jeong and Isabel leave. They ambushed them as they were about to depart. Major Gwon was killed. Captain Jeong wounded—but he and Isabel launched the *Argo*. Others died or were injured in the fighting that followed the *Argo*'s departure." Adisa looked down. "Terrible things were done."

At this point, Dr. Kim squeezed Adisa's shoulder in support.

Yak asked, "Why did Isabel not prepare *Argo* for return to Earth instead?"

"She said she had unfinished business—something that Nathan Joyce had promised her, but she would not say what it was."

Yak looked confounded. "And she left you here, with no way home?"

Adisa glanced up. "No, of course not. I was retrofitting the Korean ship—taking out its remote controls and augmenting its systems." He paused. "But after the mutiny . . . I fell ill."

Tighe asked, "How far will their journey to Mars be?"

He turned grim. "Ninety-five million kilometers."

Yak whistled.

Adisa added, "The *Argo* had a very comprehensive navigation system, as well as capable rocket engines and a solid frame. It gave me much to work with."

"You helped her do this?"

"She was going anyway. I could not in good conscience withhold my assistance. And you know how persistent Isabel can be."

Tighe realized he did know. They all knew. That's why they were all standing there. "Goddamn it, Isabel..."

Just then Dr. Josephson arrived, looking around at the historic *Konstantin*. "Liz. Great!" Tighe turned to Adisa. "Ade, this is Dr. Elizabeth Josephson. You remember her from Ascension. She's going to bring you back to the *Oberhaus*—to our spacecraft."

Adisa nodded blindly to Josephson. "I've been meaning to ask you about it."

"Of course, Han and Priya will want to speak with you on the comm link. But get some rest. Elizabeth is going to start treating you."

He again shook his head. "I appreciate your optimism, but I believe my illness is beyond medicine."

Josephson took Adisa's hand. "You may be surprised what medical science can do these days, Mr. Adisa. Besides, we can't let historic figures like yourself succumb to treatable diseases like cancer." She began to prepare Adisa for transport.

Dr. Kim motioned to the other two Korean crewmen, who came to assist, and he then turned to Yak and Tighe. "If I may ask, Mr. Tighe, what will become of us?"

Tighe glanced at Yak, who nodded in obvious agreement, before Tighe turned back to the doctor. "You're all free now. And free to come with us, if you wish."

The doctor looked emotionally overcome for a moment.

Tighe added, "And you'll all receive pay for your work here—which should be more than enough to last a lifetime."

The doctor smiled and bowed, before relating what Tighe had said to the other two crewmen—who began rejoicing and hugging each other. And soon after began to weep in relief.

After several hours aboard the *Konstantin,* Tighe and Yak watched Transit-08 take Adisa away, headed with Josephson back toward the *Oberhaus,* a few kilometers distant. Tighe decided the *Oberhaus* looked remarkably advanced compared to the rickety frame of the *Konstantin.* They'd done a decent job over the past few years, after all.

He and Yak then climbed onto the running board of a new mule, which they'd brought with them on the *Oberhaus*. They clipped in tethers to its guide rail, like Tighe had done so many times before with Morra and Jin. He grew wistful all over again. As ramshackle as the *Konstantin* now appeared, he had an enduring fondness for her. And it was, after all, a piece of human-kind's history.

He looked back toward the tattered old ship. "We'll need to spin her down and move her to a safer orbit."

Yak nodded. "*Da*. She should be preserved for future generations."

Tighe then looked out at the collection of bulging robot tugs and addi-tional bladder tanks filled with resources in the supply yard. "Would you look at that? It's a treasure trove."

"The tugs hold 46,000 tons."

He cast a disbelieving look Yak's way. "Get out."

"Iron, nickel, cobalt, water ice, ammonia . . . you know the mix. The sup-ply yard holds 30,000 tons more. I reviewed manifest with crew."

"Wow. The futures market back at the CCE is going to go nuts over that news."

"Which reminds me . . ." Yak made some gestures at a virtual interface. "We will need to assign NFTs to these resources."

Just then the mule, piloted remotely by Gusev, was clearing the *Konstan-tin*'s radial arms and headed outward, toward the sunlight, toward a block-shaped silhouette in a terminator orbit around the asteroid Ryugu—toward the cairn that held their deceased crewmates.

In a few minutes, the mule's thrusters popped, bringing them to a slow halt, and the two of them moved from sunlight into the shadow of the cairn. The structure hadn't changed at all since Tighe had been here years ago, to inter Amy Tsukada. He and Yak activated their helmet lights and moved through the narrow opening, into the crypt's dark and frozen interior.

Tighe felt a lump in his throat as he beheld the familiar forms of Nicole Clarke, David Morra, and Amy Tsukada lying in state within their blue flight suits, arms velcroed peacefully across their chests, as if in restful sleep.

A fourth body in a white flight suit was there as well—one of the fallen Koreans who had fought alongside Adisa—but there was no trace of the other casualties.

Tighe moved close to his crewmates as Yak floated alongside.

Through her visor, Amy Tsukada's face looked perfectly preserved—as if made of porcelain. Adisa had considered whether to bring her remains back to Earth, but ultimately decided that she should be here, with her fallen crewmates, for posterity. Tighe knew that Adisa would be back again someday to visit, when he was healthy once more. Tighe's own feeling of renewed health made this seem likely.

He then looked to Nicole Clarke's sleeping form. Her eyes closed. At peace. Tighe recalled the moment those eyes closed forever. *"Do you realize how fortunate we are, J.T.?"*

And then, finally, Tighe turned to behold David Morra, arms clasped across his chest, handsome face calm, composed. Exactly as it had been when his body was found. Knowing then, as always, why he'd come all this way. Tucked under his frozen hand was a photograph of twin young Black girls, smiling as a red-haired woman embraced them both.

It took everything Tighe had to keep his composure as he removed another photo from a pouch on his harness and, after a momentary look, tucked it in alongside the one in Morra's hand. The new photo showed the same two girls, now young women, standing in front of an office building in Luxembourg, arm in arm. Joyful.

Tighe looked onto Morra's face. "You'd be so proud of them, Dave. They're shareholders now. Smart and in the best university—learning how to manage the estate you left to them. Not that *anyone* knows how to manage this, but I guess that's for the next generation to figure out."

Tighe remained for a while. After an unknown number of minutes—or perhaps hours—he left the cairn and discovered Yak floating outside, waiting for him near the mule.

It was only then that it occurred to Tighe that everything he, Chindarkar, Jin, and Yak had done over the past nine years; after all the obstacles, the insane risks taken, and the many lives lost; after all the hundreds of thousands of tons of off-world resources had been refined, exchanged, and reconstituted into the building blocks of life—humanity now, finally, had its start in the cosmos. And it had a new chance at restoring the Earth as well. Strangely, Nathan Joyce seemed to have been telling the truth—or at least his version of it—all along. Even if by accident.

Tighe finally felt the burden of his mentor Richard Oberhaus's sacrifice lift from him, and he now also sensed being freed from his responsibility to those he left behind—both in space and on Earth. For the first time in many years, Tighe finally felt free to chart his own course.

Yak still floated nearby, but was now facing out into deep space, toward the awe-inspiring Magellanic Cloud and the spray of light that was the Milky Way galaxy in the far, far distance. He spoke without turning. "So . . . do you think Isabel Abarca has become first human on Mars?"

"I don't know. Maybe."

"What do you suppose Nathan Joyce promised her?"

"Good question."

Yak said, "She took Far Star with her."

Tighe nodded. "As she should have. It belongs with her now. She's gone farther than any of us." Tighe's visor tinted as he turned toward Earth, which at the moment was lost in the Sun's glare. So instead, he turned to scan the heavens, looking for another, fainter light. Several degrees away, he found it.

Mars. His crystal indicated it was currently 310 million kilometers away— over five times the distance they had traveled out to Ryugu. He pondered its light until a remembered voice came to him: "*Nathan funds all my expeditions.*"

Abarca had told him that the first time he spoke to her—back on Ascension Island—almost a decade ago. He thought back to the recent documentary about her, where she said in an interview, "*Unless we test our limits, we will never know what we're capable of. I will attempt any mountain. No matter the difficulty.*"

After a few moments he said, "Hey, Yak."

"Yes, James."

"What's the tallest mountain on Mars?"

"Easy: is Olympus Mons." He paused, then looked at Tighe. "In fact, Olympus Mons is tallest mountain in solar system. Tallest mountain known to exist."

A smile stole across Tighe's face, and he laughed. "Yes. Of course." Tighe turned back to gaze at the glowing light of Mars. "Of course it is."

Acknowledgments

Several years ago I set out to write an epic adventure that realistically depicts humanity's journey from our dire present to a more promising, spacefaring future. *Critical Mass* is the second entry in that journey. Bringing this book to life required wide-ranging research as well as the advice of many experts who graciously donated their time and insights to help me root this story in real-world science and technology.

First, my profound thanks to the indefatigable James Logan, MD, former chief of flight medicine at NASA, for sharing his deep knowledge on the physiology of crewed spaceflight, radiation exposure, and so much more. I'm especially grateful for his valiant public efforts to counter wishful thinking concerning deep space exploration.

Thanks also to William C. "Bill" Stone, legendary cave diver and chairman of Shackleton Energy, for sharing his perspective on the risks and realities of commercial lunar mining. Likewise, I'm grateful to Jim Keravala, cofounder and CEO of Offworld, a startup specializing in semiautonomous robots for off-world mining operations, whose designs inspired the Badger robots in this story.

Sincere thanks to former NASA physicist John C. Mankins for answering my many questions regarding solar power satellite designs and also for his decades-long commitment to popularizing space-based clean energy. Thanks as well to Paul Jaffe at the US Naval Research Laboratory for discussing his trailblazing work on microwave power beaming (and congratulations on the recent success of his Photovoltaic Radio-frequency Antenna Module in low Earth orbit). Thanks to Christopher Morrison at Ultra Safe Nuclear for helping me understand the state-of-the-art in nuclear thermal rocket engines and atomic batteries. Huge thanks to my longtime friend JPL physicist Eric Burt for calculating spacecraft trajectories and energy requirements for my fictional lunar mass-driver.

Tremendous thanks to Nicholas Perrin for expanding my understanding of crypto-economics, blockchains, smart contracts, and decentralized autonomous organizations—and most especially for help with the off-world economic system of my fictional Cislunar Commodity Exchange. Thanks as well to Michael Bloxton of Nebula Compute for sharing his ideas regarding data centers in space. Thanks also to Bruce Cahan of Stanford University for drawing my attention to the pressing need for a commodities exchange in space.

I'm also grateful to Peter A. Garretson, senior fellow in Defense Studies at the American Foreign Policy Council, for insights into space defense, and to Alexander MacDonald, senior economist at NASA, for his views on sovereign versus commercial space exploration. Thanks to Dr. Michele Gaudreault, deputy chief scientist at US Space Force, and Casey DeRaad, director of NewSpace New Mexico, for inviting me to fascinating discussions on the state of the space industrial base.

Thanks as well to the many dozens of current and former NASA, ESA, and JAXA scientists and engineers whose research on a wide array of topics informed this book in ways both large and small, including especially: Michael R. Wright, Dr. Steven B. Kuznetsov, and Kurt J. Kloesel for their 2010 paper "A Lunar Electromagnetic Launch System for In-Situ Resource Utilization" and T. A. Heppenheimer's 1985 paper "Achromatic Trajectories and the Industrial-Scale Transport of Lunar Resources."

My profound thanks to the late Gerard K. O'Neill, Professor Emeritus at Princeton University and author of the 1977 book *The High Frontier*—which captured my imagination as a boy and continues to inspire me today, not only for its technical vision but also for its love of all humanity.

A huge thanks to Lunar QuickMap (a collaboration between NASA, Arizona State University, and Applied Coherent Technology) for making available detailed lunar imagery that was vital to this story. I encourage anyone interested in lunar exploration to check it out here: quickmap.lroc .asu.edu.

The following YouTube channels also proved invaluable during my research for this book: Dave Borlace's *Just Have a Think* and Brian James McManus's *Real Engineering*.

I'm grateful to Meishel Menachekanian for curating an amazing music playlist to inspire me while writing key scenes in this book.

Heartfelt thanks to my editors, Lindsey Rose and Lexy Cassola, at Dutton, for their patience in working through the several iterations of this book, and thanks also to my longtime literary agent, Rafe Sagalyn, at ICM/Sagalyn.

And no book of mine would be complete without thanks to my wife and partner in all things, Michelle Sites. Without you, Michelle, this book and so much more would not have been possible.

Appendix

Clarke Station - Habitation Ring

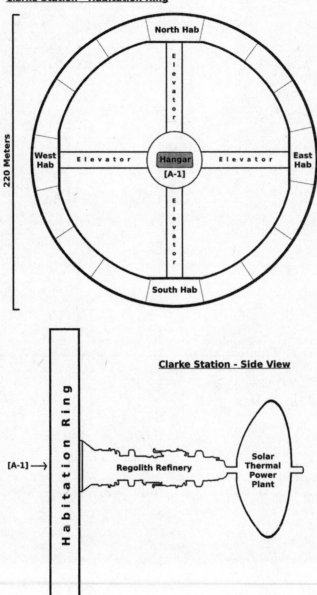

Two perspectives of a 15,000-ton, spin-gravity space station to be placed in a Lissajous orbit around the Earth-Moon L2 Lagrange point. In addition to a habitation ring with central hangar, Clarke Station includes a regolith refinery and solar thermal power plant on its non-rotating axis. *(Copyright 2022 Daniel Suarez)*

Robotic return tugs (from bottom to top): the *Nicole Clarke*, the *David Morra*, and the *Amy Tsukada*. (*Copyright 2019 Daniel Suarez. Illustration by Anthony Longman*)

Artist's rendering of SPS-ALPHA Mark III (solar power satellite by means of arbitrarily large phased array) concept, transmitting power to the lunar surface.

Note: the SPS-Alpha uses thin-film mirrors to concentrate solar energy onto a central disc of solar panels; microwave transmitters on the opposite side of this disc transmit energy to a rectenna on the Moon's surface. A 2-gigawatt SPS-Alpha would mass 7,400 tons and measure 3 kilometers in diameter. Whereas the 50-megawatt "Daisy" SPS-Alpha depicted in this story massed just 185 tons and was 125 meters across. *(Concept/image copyright 2022 John C. Mankins; reproduced with permission)*

Further Reading

You can learn more about the science, technologies, and themes explored in *Critical Mass* by visiting Daniel-Suarez.com or through the following books:

The Case for Space Solar Power by John C. Mankins (Virginia Edition Publishing)

Electrostatic Phenomena on Planetary Surfaces by Carlos I. Calle (Morgan & Claypool Publishers)

The High Frontier: Human Colonies in Space by Gerard K. O'Neill (William Morrow & Company)

The "How To" of Satellite Communications (2nd ed.) by Dr. Joseph N. Pelton (Design Publishers)

Moneyland: The Inside Story of the Crooks and Kleptocrats Who Rule the World by Oliver Bullough (St. Martin's Press)

The Overview Effect: Space Exploration and Human Evolution (4th ed.) by Frank White (Multiverse Publishing)

The Sixth Extinction: An Unnatural History by Elizabeth Kolbert (Henry Holt & Company)

Space 2069: After Apollo: Back to the Moon, to Mars . . . and Beyond by David Whitehouse (Icon Books)

Space Is Open for Business: The Industry That Can Transform Humanity by Robert C. Jacobson (Robert Jacobson)

Spacefarers: How Humans Will Settle the Moon, Mars, and Beyond by Christopher Wanjek (Harvard University Press)

The Uninhabitable Earth: Life after Warming by David Wallace-Wells (Tim Duggan Books)

The Wright Brothers by David McCullough (Simon & Schuster)

About the Author

Daniel Suarez is the author of the *New York Times* bestseller *Daemon*, *Freedom*™, *Kill Decision*, *Influx*, *Change Agent*, and *Delta-v*. A former systems consultant to Fortune 1000 companies, his high-tech and sci-fi thrillers focus on technology-driven change. He lives in Los Angeles, California.